The Sea Whisperer

By the same author

Taming Amy

The Sea Whisperer

Seth Gardner

purplefeather

First Published in 2020 by Purple Feather Publishing
The Stables, Blair Estate, Dalry, North Ayrshire, Scotland

ISBN Paperback: 978-0-9931728-7-8
E-Pub: 978-0-9931728-8-5

A CIP catalogue copy of this book can be found in the British Library.

Cover illustration by Louise Scott
Internal illustrations by Sandra D'Arcy

Published with the help of Indie Authors World

www.indieauthorsworld.com

For Sophie and Charlotte

1
The Sea Angel

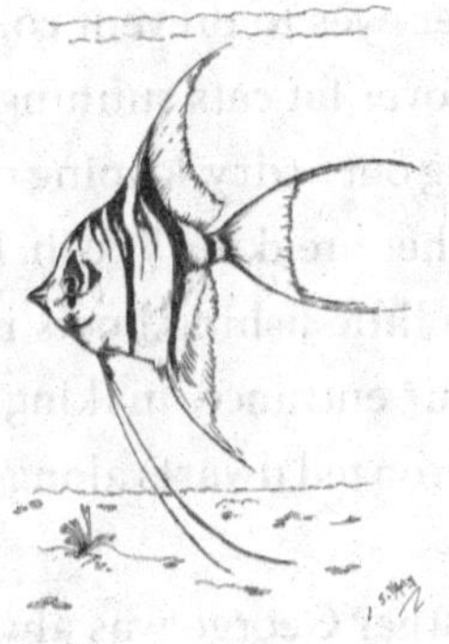

Heather responded with her usual glee as the cry went up that the fishing boats were approaching the harbour. She threw her shoes on and began her race down the steep and slippery slope that curved through the heart of the village towards the sea. Faster and faster she ran, daring herself to remain upright as she dodged past the wives, widows and daughters all hurrying to greet the boats. Heather's tall and wiry frame exuded a boundless energy that seemed to whoosh everybody out of her way. Her long thick black wavy hair whipped out around her, flung up into the air by the sea breeze, making her look twice as large as she was. She had to keep pushing it from her eyes to prevent colliding with her neighbours. Jumping over fat cats sunning on porches, swerving to avoid nets hung out to dry, leaping over lobster baskets, Heather continued her breakneck rush. Her one aim was to be first to greet the little fishing boats now edging between the narrow harbour entrance, making for the old iron moorings that lay like bronzed dwarfs along the granite harbour wall.

However fast she ran her grandfather George was always there first, pipe clenched between toothless gums, plumes of sweet-smelling smoke surrounding his grey head, arms tightly crossed, counting every ship in like a shepherd might count the sheep home. Truth was, he never had to shuffle very far. During the days, and for most of the nights that the boats were at sea, he was to be found stuck in the same position, on a wooden stool fashioned out of some part of a long-lost vessel, in the doorway of the local glue pot, the Fisherman's Arms. Rain or shine he would sit there from the moment the vessels put out to sea to the moment they returned. Now, due to his old legs he said, he would often rest there even when the boats were home and safe. Nonetheless, Heather knew that on every first evening back on shore, he would, along with her brother and the rest of the men, stagger and weave his way back up the steep climb to their houses, singing shanties to which only he knew all the words.

Heather skidded to a stop at the harbour wall. As she watched the wee flotilla arrange itself in tidy rows she steadied herself for her daredevil leap of love. Even at high tide, the drop to the deck of the boat was quite a distance.

Ever since she was knee high to a grasshopper, Heather had defied death and would leap off the harbour wall into her father's strong arms. For her doting father Robert, this was a ritual he had always encouraged. It was an act of trust and love that bonded them tighter than glue. It was lucky that he had amazing reactions and had powerful arms from his time at sea because Heather was now almost full grown.

'Hi Dad,' she yelled, 'Are you ready for me?'

'Wait a moment princess,' called her father as he steadied himself, legs shoulder-width apart, feet rooted to the slightly rolling deck, huge arms held aloft.

'Come on then my darling,' he called, and Heather threw her tall, slim teenage body off the pier. Both father and daughter loved this moment of madness. Her flight would always cause a couple of the women to scream slightly, her mother would turn away and hold her breath, and the men would all cheer as she landed safely in the arms of the huge bear of a man who was her doting father. She always hugged tight into her father's huge chest, enjoying the moment of rib cracking embrace before pulling free, her clean dress covered in fish scales with the white cotton already picking up the heady perfume of oily fish.

Heather's dad was built like a rugby player. He was tall wide and stout with a rug of dark hair and a full beard showing only a few wisps of grey. His gimlet blue eyes sparkled fiercely and twinkled with good humour. If he was cross he would thrust his chin out like the prow of his boat and frown so intensely that his big black bushy eyebrows would meet in the middle of his forehead like a huge caterpillar. This was a look that would only be used on special occasions usually when the crew had made a stupid mistake, or the pub needed emptying. Robert's natural air of authority made him the small towns natural spokesperson and the fleet's trusted leader.

Once on board Heather would scramble along the slippery deck eager to discover what surprises her father had for her. Every time *The Flying Fish* returned to port, she knew that a large steel pail would be waiting for her below deck. She called it the mystery bucket. Her father, brother and the men who manned the small vessel knew of her love for the creatures of the sea and whenever anything interesting was accidentally picked up in the nets and was still alive, it would be tossed into a large bucket of salt water so that Heather could see it. From this holding station seahorses, baby octopuses, sea porcupines, small spider crabs and other fascinating flora and fauna of the deep were transferred to an old ice cream container and carried by Heather, back up to the house. The destination: a large glass tank that nearly filled her small bedroom. It was her very own Oceanic Zoo.

Heather's Oceanic Zoo was a very grand name for a large seawater tank that had once held lobsters in a local restaurant. But, when the restaurant closed down, owing her father money, he had taken the tank as payment intending to fatten up crabs and lobsters himself. The moment the tank got home a small dark-haired girl had looked up from her picture book and shouted 'Thank you Daddy, a fish zoo for me!' Her father had sighed and looked at her mother who shrugged and smiled in the way that mothers do when they know the secret inner workings and desires of her family.

'Och, you would never have got around to stocking it Robert,' she'd said, 'just make sure that it doesn't leak on my carpet and that she can't fall into it.'

So that was that. Heather had her sea zoo, which, once she had read more grown-up books, became her very own

Oceanic Zoo. It was so big it filled up most of her bedroom. It was surrounded by gnarly pieces of driftwood and stood on the floor as no shelf would have supported it. Heather's poor father was grateful that she treasured it enough to keep it clean and well looked-after. He did however have to continually fork out hard earned cash on a seemingly never ending list of vital equipment for the Oceanic Zoo. This included pumps, filters, lights, fish food and yards of tubing that doubled up as an underwater vacuum. Plus, it was Robert's job to keep it stocked with exciting sea creatures. A never-ending role as Heather continuously returned them to the sea after she had studied them.

Heather usually kept her precious guests until they were fit and strong enough to be released back into the ocean. Some firm favourites got to stay though. On a backdrop of carefully arranged rocks were well-established winkles, whelks, barnacles, sea anemones and healthy strands of seaweed to provide cover. Her favourite long-term guests were a pair of seahorses that provided her zoo with babies every year to the astonishment of the grown-ups. A wide variety of sea creatures had made an appearance over the years. A typical snapshot of the huge aquarium would feature a few large prawns swimming up and down while razor fish emerged from the sandy bottom to get startled by a juvenile plaice flapping past hunting for tit bits. The Oceanic Zoo was an ever changing source of delight for Heather. It was her window to the amazing undersea world from which her family drew their livelihood. Almost from the time she could walk the sea had become Heather's greatest source of joy. She learned fast. By the age of ten she was able to name every specimen that the fishermen plucked from the cold waters of the Atlantic Ocean for her. Encouraged by a huge encyclopaedia of the ocean that took up most of the space on a bookshelf in her bedroom Heather turned twelve could call every weird and wonderful sea creature by their fancy Latin names as well.

'What's in the mystery bucket Dad?' Heather called out as she headed for the lower deck.

'Not sure princess, we didn't get much of anything again.'

A shadow quickly passed across the brow of Heather's father's face. His huge body seemed to slump for a moment as his wild-eyed daughter happily skipped past him. Heather's brother Michael, only just out of his teens and already as tall and wide as his father stopped lifting the ice-covered trays of fish.

'What's the matter Da'?'

His father replied softly so Heather didn't hear them.

'We shall have to invest in those new nets if it gets much worse, that's for sure. It's either getting to be a desert out there or we are looking in the wrong places.'

'But we'll have to upgrade her first Dad. The Flying Fish isn't modern enough... think of the cost, the extra strain on her.'

'Needs must Michael, needs must, she's still the best wee boat in the harbour.'

Heather was untroubled by the concerns of her father and brother. She was intent on her quest. Like a gymnast she vaulted down steep steel steps to the part of the ship where the catch was sorted, gutted and then put into boxes of ice ready for the market. Skipping past white boxes crammed with fish she made for the stern of the ship. There, in its usual place was the old steel bucket. She grabbed a small green mesh net down from a hook and plunged it into dark water with complete concentration. At first, Heather thought that there was nothing in it apart from a few large shrimps and a couple of sand eels. Then, beneath a piece of bright green seaweed, she disturbed one of the strangest wee creatures she had ever seen. Trapping it in her net she quickly transferred it into an old ice cream container full of brine. She lifted up the container and stared at it quizzically. Even Heather was stumped by what she saw. Picking up a huge box of gigantic cod, Tom the third member of the crew, gingerly stepped around the captivated teenager. He was a good humoured and hardworking second mate, small and wiry and could gut a cod as big as Heather in seconds.

'What you got there then Heather?'.

'Not sure Tom.' Heather replied with great excitement. It had been a long time since her knowledge of the deep was challenged. 'It's a weird looking specimen to be sure.'

Quickly popping a lid on her container she walked with great care, back up the steps and onto the deck of the ship. Her father lifted her and her precious cargo onto the pier and smiled as he watched his daughter hurry away, tongue peeping out between bright red lips, eyes frowning in deep concentration. She disappeared into the small but rowdy crowd, only to reappear again, halfway up the steep slope steps that led up to their house that nestled on the edge of the harbour.

Heather's mum had taken up her usual position on the harbour wall and was quietly waiting for her family to disembark. Maria pushed back her long, slightly greying, dark curls that seemed in competition with the wind to hide her face and watched as her daughter disappeared from view. Maria's face wore her usual kind and welcoming smile and a time-honoured expression of resigned acceptance. Maria was still as beautiful and as slight as her daughter and it was only a few deep laughter lines that gave away the fact that they were not sisters. Her compassion and kindness was legendary as were her amazing home-made cakes which always seem to feel the house with the delicious smell of baking. Her large and warm kitchen, the biggest in the small village, was the obvious destination for the women folk to sit, relax, share concerns, tell stories and even occasionally as, in the old days, fix nets. Maria sighed quietly to herself and turned to watch her husband climb up the steep ladder from the boat.

'We won't see her until tomorrow now Robert.'

Robert smiled warmly at his wife. As he clambered onto the pier he hugged her, his huge arms easily encircling his wife's waist. For a moment they both paused as they watched their daughter dwindle into the distance. Robert wondered how a wee girl could have grown so big so quickly. As if reading his thoughts Heather's mother turned and smiled at her man.

'You have always spoiled that child Robert, she wants for nothing.'

'Aye, well, that may be the case but it's all for free. She's got something strange in that bucket today that's for sure. It'll keep her occupied for hours. So then, Maria, are you coming for a wee dram?'

'No way, Robert, and don't you be coming home at all hours.'

'As if, as if.'

They both accepted this moment of deception with a warm and knowing smile as only those who truly love each other can. As Robert turned to head for the pub he glanced back up the harbour, but his daughter had already disappeared into the house.

Heather dashed upstairs, barely able to contain her excitement. She carefully opened the plastic container and even more carefully tipped the contents into her big tank. Then, rushing to get her inspection glass, she peered at the strange creature that seemed to float lifelessly just below the surface. The magnifier showed the most delicate and strange looking creature she had ever seen. It looked like a miniature angel with large grey eyes that stared back at her in a blank sort of way. A small, slender body ended in a tail and instead of fins two feathery wings, like fronds of seaweed, fanned out on either side.

'Oh my dear, you don't seem so well,' said Heather, 'I had better keep an eye on you. Oh you poor thing. I wonder where you came from.'

Heather had had some strange looking creatures in her tank in the past. Some had originated in oceans far away, maybe caught on the huge currents that flow between continents. Some of the weirdest and unfortunately short-lived creatures had originated from depths of the ocean. Even Heather's huge encyclopaedia couldn't find names for some of them. In spite of all Heather's best efforts these pale dragon or gargoyle-like creatures never lived for long. After she had drawn them and added them to her very own encyclopaedia Heather always solemnly carried them back to the ocean so that they could rest in peace.

Just as Heather was beginning to really worry about the health of her latest guest she got a shock. The small crea-ture suddenly burst into life and shot like lightning into a clump of seaweed in the corner of the huge tank. It was a area designed to provide protection and cover for some of the smallest creatures in her Oceanic Zoo. It's dark green fronds extended all the way to the surface of the large tank like an underwater forest.

'Wow,' she said, 'you are a fast mover. Now then, what are you? '

She lifted down her large encyclopaedia and started to pore over its pages. She was still sitting cross-legged on her bed, flipping pages when her mother came up to her room with some supper several hours later.

'What have you got today then my precious?'

'Don't know Ma. I've never seen anything like it. Perhaps it's a new species.'

'Oh I'm sure that someone somewhere would have recorded it sometime...'

Her mother, seeing her daughter's crestfallen face, added quickly,

'But then, you never know. Well then where is it?'

'It's gone behind the weed.'

'Ah, oh, erm, I see, well maybe it's just shy?'

Maria took a deep breath and smiled. She felt like someone who has tried their best to understand the passion of somebody else's hobby but failed. She made a few comments about how the tank should really be 'kept outside in the shed' and that Heather 'really should have a wardrobe like other girls' but gave up and quietly slipped out of the room. Heather had already gone back to her book. Sandwich in one hand, she was furiously flipping pages, jumping from section to section trying to locate her new specimen.

*****

Heather suddenly awoke. She had fallen asleep. Her empty plate had dropped to the floor. Somebody had covered her with a blanket and her book had somehow become her pillow. It wasn't the discomfort of her sleeping arrangement that had woken her but something far more exciting, something that made her gasp and hurry across her room.

Soft strange lights seemed to be emanating from her huge aquarium. As Heather rubbed her eyes she glanced at the tank's light switch: it was definitely off. What was it then? A mini light-show seemed to be coming from behind the seaweed. The unusual display had captured the attention of the assorted sea life that were Heather's permanent guests. Heather stared with wonder at their unusual behaviour. They were all swimming gently in a semi-circle around the dense clump of weed in the corner. Ever changing pulses of light lit up the dark fronds of the underwater forest. Heather picked up her net and cautiously approached the tank. She held her breath afraid that she would disturb the bizarre spectacle. Not a single fish noticed when Heather gently tried to part the seaweed's fronds with the handle of one of her smaller nets. Then suddenly, like the parting of the clouds revealing the sun, a miniature rainbow appeared to grow wings and glide out into the open.

The display took her breath away. The little drab creature was lit up like the softest, gentlest most brilliant disco lights she had ever seen. Colours seemed to float like ripples across the delicate surface of the creature's frond-like wings. It had transformed into a miniature sea angel. The two huge eyes now shone like two small stars. Heather and the residents of Oceanic Zoo were transfixed. As Heather gazed into the eyes of the creature, she seemed to feel different. As the colours changed so did her emotions. She felt a jumble of happy, joyful, peaceful, loving, smiley feelings ripple over her. Remembering to breathe again Heather found herself smiling with open mouthed delight and fascination. Like an everchanging firework display the stunning creature started to glow green, even brighter than midsummer fireflies.

The huge aquarium was illuminated. Heather felt as if the pulsing light filled her whole being. A cascade of colours and images of the sea flooded her head. It was as if a huge movie screen opened up inside her mind. She could hear huge waves crashing around her, she could see shoals of the most exquisite sea creatures swimming in front of her eyes. Heather span around and blinked rapidly as great whales seemed to swim overhead. The aquarium seemed to extend into her whole bedroom. Heather's mouth fell open in amazement as thousands of sea creatures sped past her, around her, under her and above her. The walls and floor of her bedroom seemed to vanish amid a plethora of colours and images.

Slowly the scene seemed to change. Gradually at first, the movement of the sea creatures sped up and then became more erratic. They swirled around Heather, buffeting her from side to side. Heather began to grow alarmed as the whole mood of the room changed. Suddenly a huge roaring wall of water rose up in front of her like a tsunami. It seemed as if a million fish and sea creatures in tightly packed shoals were hurtling towards her. Heather called out as she tried in vain to stop the vision. She could see that the sea creatures were all as terrified as she was. As they sped towards Heather she realised that they were trapped in the biggest fishing net she had ever seen. Tightly squashed together and fighting for life the deluge of terrified squirming sea life was about to crash into Heather. The terrified girl ducked and covered her face and head with her hands as the wall of roaring water crashed over her. She crouched down terrified and waited to be washed away. But nothing happened. No wall of water throwing her against the wall. No crammed net of sea life crushing her. Nothing. No sound. No Light. Terrified and still holding her breath Heather dared to open her eyes again. The room was still, silent and dark once more. Heather fell to her knees breathing as hard as if she had just run a marathon.

A flood of heavy emotions washed away Heather's earlier happiness and excitement. Feelings of sadness, despair and futility flooded her until she felt herself start to sob with salty tears. Heather found herself weeping uncontrollably overcome with the her own tsunami of intense and invasive emotions that flooded her heart and mind. It was several minutes before Heather could wipe her eyes and blink in the direction of the huge tank once more. Sniffing loudly she noticed something worrying in the corner the Oceanic Zoo. She leapt to her feet and peered into a now darkened tank as, to her dismay, the small sea angel floated lifelessly back to the surface.

Heather flicked the light switch on, grabbed her dressing gown and slippers knowing what she had to do.

'Oh don't die, don't die my love.'

She quickly filled her plastic container with seawater, and in one movement had transferred the strange creature into it. Pausing only briefly to note that the sea angel was still floating lifelessly in the water, she sped down the stairs and out into the cold night.

As quickly as her slippered feet would allow she started down the steep, cobbled road to the harbour. Every step seemed to her to be too slow. As she walked, carefully cradling her container she had to hold her tears back so that she could see where she was going. As she sped down the path towards the harbour almost collided with three familiar men staggering and singing loudly as they made their way home. She ducked into a doorway to let the male members of her family pass by before she continued on her way.

Down to the harbour, down the steps to the deep black sea and then at the edge, heedless of the waves that drenched her slippers and pyjama bottoms, she tipped the small creature into the depths where it slid silently down into the darkness.

She didn't know how long she had stood there. It felt as if she had been holding her breath for ages when suddenly she was lifted into the air. Two strong arms hoisted her up into a beery cloud of warm breath.

'Hmm, thought I saw a wee princess scurry past me a moment ago. What on earth are you doing down here sweetheart? You're all cold and wet and should be safely tucked up in your bed. Your mother will...'

Heather's father didn't finish his sentence as Heather had buried her face in his chest and started sobbing as if the world was about to end.

Later that night – after she was dried, warmed and tucked up, exhausted, in her bed– a furious exchange took place in hushed whispers downstairs.

'I don't know what she was doing, she was just...?'

'She wasn't, in danger or sleep walking was she?'

'No, don't be daft; she had her fish collection container with her. My guess is that some poor bugger had perished, and she had put him back.'

'Well, Robert, it's going too far. That blessed tank takes up most of her room. She hardly plays with the other teenagers. All she does is walk the shores and read her books – it's not normal.'

'Hush now, Maria, she's only a kid, and a bright one at that. She knows more names than I do.'

'Well I'm worried, Robert. In the morning that tank gets drained and she gets a wardrobe and that's that.'

Heather's mother turned and went to go upstairs to bed. Her husband turned off the lights and slowly followed her. He knew it was just talk, that the zoo would stay, but he shared his wife's concern. His daughter had been sobbing as if her poor wee heart would break. She hadn't stopped all the way back to the house. She only stopped because she had fallen asleep. Any father would have been worried. He would talk to her in the morning. Try to suss it out then.

2
The Selkie

The next morning delivered such a honeyed dollop of magnificent sunshine that Heather was up and out of the house before anyone knew it. She stood facing the ocean, wind in her hair, warming her face in the sun and breathing in deep draughts of sea air. She had literally danced down to the small sandy beach that lay to the south of the village. When Heather woke up that morning the memory of the night before had drifted into a kind of haze. Rather than feeling sad, she felt as if she had been given a new purpose, a new sense of wonder. She felt refreshed and renewed. Heather kicked off her bright red wellies and gulped in more of the fresh sea air. Something had happened. The sea smelt saltier, the sun felt sunnier and warmer; the crashing of the waves, the calling of the sea birds and the whisper of the wind all sounded like music while the soft sand felt like velvet beneath her toes. It was as if the whole world had somehow got brighter.

A seal's face popped up out of the water, making Heather laugh as she stared at her with soulful eyes. She laughed and danced and laughed and danced until she collapsed in a heap on the sand.

'Someone seems happy,' said a voice.

Heather looked up. She was sitting on the sand, wiggling her toes into the warm softness until her feet disappeared. The voice was not familiar to her yet it sounded kind and she expected to see a holidaymaker or a day-tripper out for a stroll. Unconcerned, she looked around.

She tried to twist her head in a full circle and collapsed giggling onto her back with the effort. There was no one there. She must have imagined it.

'Yes,' she called to the wind, 'today I am deliriously happy, and my head is full of the ocean.'

'Consider this,' said the voice again, this time making her jump slightly, 'is the ocean in you or, are you in the ocean?'

'Huh?' said Heather and this time she sat up and gave the beach her full attention.

Heather looked up and down the beach. The rock pools were still there and she could easily see every detail of the small sandy cove. She glanced towards the cliffs. They were not so high at this point so she could see the old lodge high up on one of the bluffs. Its windows sparkled in the sun but there was no one standing there. She observed the line of her own footprints reaching towards her and noted where they suddenly entered a mad dance and then disappeared into a jumble of marks where she had sat down. There were no other marks.

'OK,' she said loudly and bravely, still not losing her good humour. 'Who do I have the pleasure of speaking with?'

'My, what a polite little girl you are. Please forgive me, my name, in human terms is, I believe, Cuilein Mairi, or Selkie, but my name to my friends is Ran.'

With that introduction the seal that Heather had been watching before popped herself out of the water and ambled towards her.

'You, you are a seal?'

'Today a seal, tomorrow the ocean – all comes from her, all returns to her – but yes, my daughter, yes today I am a seal.'

'I am talking with a seal?'

'My, how observant you are, and how beautiful you are. The wind likes to play with your hair I see.'

Heather's thick black curls were being tousled by the wind, sometimes threatening to hide her eyes. She brushed her hair back so that she could focus on the seal in front of her. The animal appeared completely normal, her small black nose glistened, her soft sleek dappled brown fur was smooth and very real. As she moved with a half-gambolling, half-sliding motion she left very real seal tracks in the sand. All these signs told Heather that Ran was indeed a real live seal.

'Ah,' said Ran, 'you look for signs to tell you what is and what isn't. Signs can be deceptive you know.'

Heather stared. The seal hadn't moved her mouth. Her voice seemed to echo like music in Heather's head. She felt all giggly again.

'Can I touch you?' asked Heather suddenly.

'Of course my angel,' said Ran.

Heather reached out her hand to touch the wonderfully soft silky coat of the seal.

'Oh, your fur is so soft and warm, I always wondered how it felt.'

'Yes, it is much better on me isn't it?' smiled Ran.

Heather found herself blushing furiously. She had once touched a seal, but it was a fur that her father had been given by a fisherman, who would often catch seals saying that they ate all the fish.

'Don't be shy, my daughter. You were not to blame,' said Ran as if reading her thoughts. 'You are a child of the ocean; you seek to live in harmony. You knew the lie in your young head when you heard it.'

It was true, even though she had been very little she had called out 'Aren't there enough fish for everyone?' She remembered the laughter that had mocked her. But she also remembered that she had been allowed to sleep on the fur, in front of the fire, until she was carried up to bed. The next morning it was gone, and Heather loosely recalled her mother's cross remarks about old Mick who still caught seals when he could. She has seemed really cross and vaguely remembered her mother saying that he would bring bad luck on himself and the village. Her mother must have been at least half right. Old Mick's small boat was dragged down into a terrible whirlpool that had been created by an unusually fast-running tide one spring evening. They had never found him, and the villagers had all seemed reluctant to go to his funeral.

'I have long watched you, my daughter,' said Ran. 'I have watched as you grew and learned to love the ocean with all

your heart and with all of your tiny human might. You have
been a great reward to us. You have a thirst to know which is
driven by love, not the impulse to exploit, conquer or harvest.'

Heather sat as if in a trance.

'How come I can hear you?' she asked.

'All men can hear me, they just choose to ignore my voice,'
said Ran, gently nuzzling the girl's hand when she forgot to
keep stroking her.

The seal flipped over onto her back and allowed Heather
to gently stroke her soft belly, her flippers moving idly. If
she were a cat, Heather would have sworn she was purring.

'We sent a messenger to you and you listened. So now you
have been rewarded with your sight.'

'My sight?' asked Heather.

'My child, you will not just see the world from behind
your human veil, you will see and hear and sense the world
as it really is.'

Then the seal flipped over and sat up straight in front of
Heather. Her face seemed to grow sadder.

'Oh my young one, you have a difficult journey ahead and
I will try to guide you the best I can. The creature that you
returned to us last night has never been seen by man before.
They are the deep guardians of the ocean. They live deeper
than I can go in this body. They hear and see all. The nets
of your boats are like greedy claws, which reach deeper and
deeper, wider and wider. You were sent the angel because
only she had the power to ensure that you awoke properly.
Now listen carefully to me, my young human.'

Heather shivered slightly, as if the sun had just darted
behind a cloud for a moment making the temperature drop.

'With your gift comes a great responsibility, a great task, a
lot will be asked of you. You must not speak of our meeting

to anyone and you must never say my name to another human. They still live in fear of me. You will hear me in your dreams, and I will come when you call. For now that is enough. Enjoy your morning, your birthday, and your spring. You will hear me soon. Time is passing by quickly. The Raven is coming. He will be important in your life. Be gentle. He does not yet see as you and he has a difficult journey ahead of him.'

With a flick of her powerful body the seal suddenly seemed to whoosh forward down the few feet of sand into the water; before Heather could stand up, Ran was bobbing in the foamy waters.

'Wait, seal, erm Ran, wait, don't go,' called Heather, but the seal had disappeared beneath the foam and swell of the sea.

Heather stood still, allowing the water to gently lap her toes, a reminder that the tide would soon be coming in. She hadn't wanted the conversation to stop. All her life she had dreamt of talking with the sea animals and birds. In fact, she had often chatted away to them anyway. But to actually be spoken to! Heather tried to recall the seal's words but already they seemed to vanish, just like the wake of a boat.

'Oh please come back,' she called out to the sea.

'Who are you talking to?'

Heather jumped. The voice was hard, strong, real in a different way. It came from behind her. She spun round, her heart racing. A boy of about the same age and height as Heather was standing in front of her. He didn't seem very friendly; he had dark eyes that seemed to reflect his mood. He didn't speak with the usual strong Scottish burr but with a lilting American accent that rose at the end of the sentence. Heather was too cross to be surprised by his accent.

'Nobody,' said Heather defensively.

She felt annoyed, and cross. It must have been this boy that frightened Ran away. She felt as if her space of peace and laughter had just been invaded.

'You were talking to that seal, weren't you?'

The boy seemed to accuse her.

'No, I was not, what seal?'

Heather hated lying but something in the boy's manner made her aware of what Ran had said about telling no one. He looked as if he was playing a fine balancing act between trying to pick a fight and being really interested in what he thought he had just witnessed. He frowned, crossed his arms and gave Heather a slightly superior look.

'I saw you.'

'You didn't.'

'I was looking through my grandfather's telescope, and you were sitting down here talking to a seal.'

He turned and gestured back up the beach, up the ridge to the old lodge house.

'Are you staying in the lodge?' asked Heather.

'Yes, with my grandfather.'

The boy had a strange accent and at the mention of his grandfather he seemed to darken even more till his whole face became one big sulk.

'He has a large telescope and I saw you and a seal.'

'Oh that seal,' said Heather. 'Oh yes, she sometimes comes out of the water when I call. It's because I feed her scraps of fish and things.

'Please don't tell anybody. Some people round here still kill seals.'

To Heather's surprise, she had lied again. It may have been her strong and defiant stance, or because at that moment the wind whipped up Heather's hair and made it flap around her head as if it had a life of its own, but the boy seemed to believe her.

He gave a great sigh.

'I wish I could have stroked it,' he said. 'Can you make it come back?'

'Er, no, I can't. I erm, don't have any more fish you see and she only comes occasionally and, well, in fact, that's the first time she has ever come out of the sea and let me stroke her like that.'

'Where is your bucket then?'

'What bucket?'

'For the fish,' said the boy accusingly.

'Oh, well, I found a dead one. Look, who are you anyway and why do you think you can come down here, invade my space and talk to me like a teacher? I haven't done anything wrong and I really don't feel like talking to a sulky boy like you so could you please go away?'

'Well that's nice,' said the boy. He frowned and pulled his hoodie down over his face. As he turned away his dark eyes flashed angrily and he headed away without another word back up the beach.

Heather felt a strange knot in the pit of her stomach as the boy began to head towards the path that led back up the cliff. His shoulders were hunched and he kicked up sand and stones as he walked. He was plainly furious. Heather sighed. She hated upsetting anybody. She hated lying. She felt a pang of guilt. Maybe she had been a bit harsh. With a big sigh she picked up her red wellies and ran after him, quickly catching him up.

'Look, I'm sorry.'

The boy's shoulders hunched into his hoodie even more and he increased the length of his stride. Heather wasn't to be put off now. She caught him up again.

'What's your name? Where are you from? What's that strange accent you've got? How come I haven't seen you in school? Are you a visitor?'

The boy just ignored her, lengthened his stride even more and began to head up the beach towards the dunes and the narrow cliff path. Heather felt defeated. Well she had tried her best with the stranger. He was probably just a grockle, a tourist and he didn't seem to be very nice.

'Oh well, suit yourself!' called Heather after him.

Heather remembered that the tide was coming in. She glanced back at the boy again; he was now disappearing up the cliff and heading back towards the ridge. Heather was not going to let the incident upset her mood though. She could not believe what had happened to her over the last twenty-four hours. As she turned to head home, she pondered everything. She felt full to bursting with news but she knew that Ran had been right. If she started telling everybody what she had seen and experienced, then they would think that she was mad and probably not let her out on her own again or something. The trouble was that the secret was already so huge inside her, she felt as if she would explode.

Heather was not used to having secrets or having to lie. Even taking the long way back from the beach to the harbour didn't lessen the pressure she felt. Maybe she was going mad. Maybe she needed help. She remembered when, a long time ago, one of the fishermen's wives had gone mad. Her husband and her sons had perished at sea and she hadn't been able to cope. In those days mental health wasn't discussed in her village and you were expected to deal with things behind your closed doors and within the family. The village doctor was just for illness of the body and, even then, it was rumoured he gave the same medicines for most ailments. This poor unfortunate lady was so beside herself with grief that she had started to hear voices and she was eventually found standing on the end of the harbour wall talking to the gulls. When she was helped into the ambulance that silently wooshed her away, never to be seen again, she was shouting and screaming that the seabirds were her family come back to life. Heather shuddered at the memory. She would have to tell somebody just in case – but who could keep a secret?

'I know,' she thought. 'I will tell Grandma.'

She could keep a secret and, besides, everybody had been just a little bit scared of the small wiry, steely woman who would happily stroll into the local pub and drag out the protesting male members of her family in time for dinner and before they spent all their money.

Heather had an old large leather-bound notebook, which had been given to her by her grandmother when she was small. The huge book still smelled of libraries and only she had the key which would release its small brass lock so that she could turn the heavy, old-fashioned pages. The inside of the book had a swirling marble effect that had once been popular and, unlike the workbooks at school, the markings seemed to make Heather's writing somehow special. The book had scribblings in it from when she was smaller. Heather had turned it into a record for her Oceanic Zoo. All of the visitors and guests in the zoo had been entered, their health recorded, how they grew and what their names were. She had even drawn pictures of them all. It was in this book that Heather still spoke with her departed grandmother.

Heather missed her grandmother. For the short time that Heather had known her the two were almost inseparable:

from the moment Heather was born, according to her mother. The little toddler had listened in awe to her grandmother's stories. She would hang onto the folds of her grandmother's heavy fisherwoman's skirt and walk with her to collect seaweed, sea coal, and driftwood for the fire. It was on these long walks that the excited child was introduced to all manner of sea life. Heather's grandmother had ignited the spark of restless curiosity and passion that she had for the sea. She had known all the animals, about which she would sing softly in her songs, by their old Gaelic or Celtic names. The child had not understood the words but had never failed to be carried off to faraway places by the soft lilting melodies that seemed to bring the sea air alive and make evenings beside the fireplace magical.

Heather's grandpa always said that it was a storm that carried her grandmother away. He said that she had always seemed more alive, active and excited than usual when there was a storm. He said that she would know the ferocity and length of any storm just by breathing in the swirling air and listening to the roar of the waves on the beach. The women of the village would come to her house if the men were at sea in the boats in these terrible and frightening conditions. They would all sit quietly, drinking tea, listening to her grandmother's stories and songs and wait. It was as if they all believed that her grandmother knew the whereabouts and condition of every fishing boat miles out to sea.

When Heather's mother Maria had married Robert – a brave, clever and talented young skipper with his own fishing boat – she found, to her amusement, that her own mother doted on him like the son she never had. The grandparents shared the same stone fisherman's cottage as their newly married daughter and husband.

One story that was often told around the fire was that Heather's father had been at sea whilst still a new skipper and that his boat had been hit by a huge wave. The little boat had started to take on water and the crew had started to say their prayers, thinking that the next wave that crashed into them would carry them to the bottom of the sea.

Back on shore, Heather's grandmother had leapt up from the fire where she had been sitting quietly rocking and knitting, surrounded by other fishermen's wives and the assorted women folk of the small village. Even though the storm was raging outside, Heather's grandmother had jumped up suddenly, spilling her knitting to the floor scattering the women around her. Then she had raced to the door and flung it open, shouting out a stream of Gaelic words to the storm. All the women had leapt up, taking this to be an omen. Standing in the doorway old lady was hit square on by the storm, the wind and rain lashing her. She was soaked in an instant, yet she had clung to the doorway, refusing to budge, refusing the help of the women, and continued her strange prayer in the ancient tongue. Staring straight out to sea, straight into the storm she stayed like that all night, holding on, singing her strange song – refusing help, refusing hot tea and refusing to shut the door – until, just before dawn, the storm subsided, and she sank to the floor exhausted. The women had put her to bed but they all feared that the old woman had got too wet, too cold and had used up too much of her life force to fully recover.

When Heather's father's little boat had limped into harbour the women were already waiting. Without a thought for his boat or crew he had rushed up the steep road to his house and then up the steps to his mother-in-law's bedroom. Heather's grandfather said that he had been sitting holding her grandmother's hands while she lay there, white as a sheet, unmoving, when suddenly their son-in-law burst into the room and rushed to the bedside. He was weeping and saying, over and over, 'thank you, thank you. I saw you, you were there, thank you...'.

After a couple of minutes, the old lady's eyes had fluttered and briefly opened. She sat bolt upright, unable to speak, and held out her arms to her son-in-law. As Heather's father had wrapped her grandmother up in those same strong arms that caught Heather leaping from the harbour wall, the old lady had silently slipped away, a tear in her eye and a smile on her face. When Heather woke in the morning, the storm had gone but so had her dearest grandmother.

Heather's father would always go quiet and fiddle with a piece of net or a corner of his jumper when Heather's grandpa kept them entertained with this story in the long dark evenings. When she bothered her father to explain what he had seen, and to tell his side of the story, he would growl that he couldn't remember and then head out to the pub.

Heather had no memory of the storm, but she remembered how upset she had been when the old lady had died. It was at that time that she started to spend time walking on the beach alongside the sea. Somehow the ocean took on a new meaning to her. Heather felt as if she could sense her grandmother in the sea. It was as if her soul inhabited the winds and the animals and birds.

So sometimes, when she had something that she just had to tell her grandmother, she would write it in her book. Heather liked to imagine that, at night, her grandmother's spirit would enter her bedroom and read her messages. Whether this was true or not, she always felt better in the morning.

So, Heather quietly slipped back into her house, gave a beaming smile to her father and mother, who were just getting ready to go out to town, and scampered upstairs to share her secret with her grandmother.

'Well mother, she seems better today. She's fairly glowing.'

'Aye Robert, I hope you're right,' said Maria 'Come on, or else you'll be late. You mustn't keep the bank manager waiting.'

3
New Beginnings

The following morning Heather got up and started getting herself ready for school. The task took her longer than most teenagers as she had all sorts of chores to do.

Being a zookeeper meant that you had to accept the responsibilities that came with the job. She had to clean the filter on the water pump and use the pump extension to vacuum the fine sand, being careful not to accidentally suck up any small guests or frighten the flatfish that liked to hide beneath the sand and gravel on the bottom of the tank. She had to continually top it up and ensure that the right amount of salty water was in the tank. Then she had to carefully feed the fish and animals. Sometimes, if she had a couple of crabs as guests, this would mean that she would have to go to the fridge and cut up some of her father's smelly fishing bait and carefully feed the scuttling creatures. The seahorses always needed live brine shrimp food, which was rather expensive and had to be kept in the refrigerator. The light of the large tank always needed a careful wipe as it soon turned green with algae and Heather had to thin out the seaweed which always grew so well under her loving care and protection.

This morning, as she was thinning the seaweed, she discovered that one of her seahorses was hiding amongst it with a very swollen belly.

'Oh I say, my love,' said Heather. 'I think you are going to have babies soon aren't you, my dear?'

She carefully put the fronds back so that the tiny creature felt safe and secure. Her treasured seahorse would soon be giving birth. Heather was so excited. She had read that seahorses were becoming very scarce and she was also particularly proud of these permanent guests. When she had found them in the mystery bucket she had screamed with joy. Heather had been able to get the interest and attention of everybody in her class when the seahorses had, by special request of her teacher, a lady called Miss Boniface, paid a visit to the school in an old large ice cream container. That day everybody had been given a science project to draw and write about them. Heather had been asked to tell the class all about the wonderful strange creatures and everybody had listened spellbound as she related at length the secrets of successfully caring for one of Britain's rarest sea creatures.

Heather quickly lifted down her big encyclopaedia of the ocean to remind herself of how to care for baby seahorses. She read that it was the male seahorse who carried the babies, which made her giggle, imagining what a world it would be if the men were the ones who got pregnant. She had read a lot about seahorses and had even written a letter to a lady scientist who was an expert on them. Heather had been thrilled when she got a long letter back and lots of pictures and tips on how to keep them. She knew that the scientist would love to hear that they were expecting babies again, as it was a very unusual occurrence in captivity. The scientist had been very impressed at Heather's success as the encyclopaedia had very little to say about rearing baby seahorses other than it would be best to separate them from anything which might eat them.

Most of all Heather liked to watch for hours until, all of a sudden, making sure that no crabs were around, the seahorses would come out from behind the seaweed, holding each other's tails, to dance around the tank.

Heather scampered down the stairs to tell her mother and father the good news. She was amazed; both of them seemed to be in the very best of moods, and, when she mentioned the zoo, even her mother had some good things to say about it.

'Aye my little one, you will need to float a tank within a tank again and put in plenty of weed so that the little ones can hide and not get scared.'

'Yes,' said her father. 'I'll get you some more fresh shrimp. You will need more food now that we have more mouths to feed.'

Then her mother and father both fell about laughing.

'What is it?' said Heather, finding their good humour infectious.

She loved it when her mother and father smiled and laughed together.

'Well,' said her father. 'We have been truly blessed.'

'In more ways than one,' said her mother looking slightly mysterious and excited at the same time.

'We managed to secure the loan we needed for the new ship with the big nets and, well, your mother and I are, well you see...'

'Oh Robert shh! Come here my angel.'

Heather went to her mother and sat on her lap. What on earth had come over them?

'How would you like a little brother or sister, Heather?'

Heather's jaw hung open.

'Wow, a real little brother or sister? Wow, fantastic! Oh Mum, I'm so happy for you.'

Her mother started to sob.

'Mum, what's the matter?'

'Oh nothing, my love, I'm just so happy. You remember the doctor said that I wouldn't be able to have another child after you? Well he was amazed. Said it was nothing short of a miracle and, well, now that we have the loan for the bigger boat, your father and brother will be able to provide enough for all of us.'

Heather skipped all the way to school. She wasn't sure if she felt so fantastic because of the amazing angelfish, or the fact that she had spoken to a seal, or the fact that one of her seahorses was pregnant or because she was to get a new baby brother or sister. Still she thought, how lucky she was to have so much good fortune.

Just before she rounded the corner to the old schoolhouse she stopped and looked back at the sea. She could see the gulls heading out to catch their food for their young that live precarious lives on the cliff face. She could see the little boats moored in the harbour and the men who looked more like ants scurrying around servicing them. She could see right across the harbour and the small bay to where, far out at sea, the sun broke out from behind grey clouds. She inhaled the sea air deeply and set her dark hair free to dance in the wind. She smiled and experienced a deep happiness welling up inside her again. The ocean seemed to touch everything in her life and the life of her village and, as she stared out to the sea, it was as if she could hear it singing.

Heather stood absolutely still. She grabbed her hair to silence its dance of freedom and listened intently. The cries of the seabirds, the sound of the waves, the calls of the men below all seemed to make a beautiful song. It was as if all the sounds wove a melody that she couldn't quite recognise but which seemed sweeter than birdsong. Suddenly Heather was jolted out of her reverie.

'What ya looking at now weirdo?'

She spun round. It was the sulky teenage boy from the beach. His hands were pushed deep into the pocket of his black hoodie and his face was almost covered.

'Who are you calling weirdo?' she answered. 'You are the one who creeps up on people who are minding their own business and just feeling plain happy.'

The boy glared at her. He appeared to be enjoying his menacing appearance. His strange accent over emphasised every word he spoke.

'You fishing folk are all the same. My grandfather says that you carry on as if the world owes you a favour. He says that your days are all numbered and that pretty soon there won't be any more village here anyway, so there!'

Heather was taken aback by this outburst and felt her good mood darken. She folded her arms in front of her and stood tall. She had grown up with an older brother and wasn't scared of teenage boys.

'Well, we've been here a thousand years and my father says we'll be here a thousand years more, so why don't you go back to where you came from and take your nasty little thoughts with you!'

They both stood glaring at each other, neither willing to speak next, both unsure of what to say next. Then suddenly the wind wrapped around Heather's long black curls and completely covered her face. Heather was momentarily blinded, and her scowling appearance completely vanished from the boy's view. Heather chuckled and just let her hair dance freely in the wind for a moment or two. In the wonderful glowing sunshine of the day and with all the good news the boy's sulky manner seemed hilariously funny to her. So bright and carefree was Heather's laughter that, as she eventually tamed her hair, the boy's expression seemed to thaw. It was like watching the snow melting on the top of some far away mountain. Just like the sun peeping out from behind a cloud a slight smile crept across his face, banishing his scowl for a moment. The wind seemed to read the humour in the situation and shifted to cause Heather long black locks to rise up above her head like a small tornado. For a split second the two teenagers looked at each other wondering what to do, then, suddenly they both laughed out loud. The wind celebrated with them, making Heather's hair whip up into the sky again. Just as the boy's smile began to give way to a shy and embarrassed grin, Heather caught a breath and gave the surprised boy a playful push.

'Quick,' she said, 'we'll be late – race you!'

Heather started to run the last few yards towards the school door. The boy leapt after her, laughing. In a few strides he had caught up with Heather and they both nearly crashed into Heather's teacher, Miss Boniface, just as she was about to shut the front door of the school.

'Oh, Heather, I see you have met our new student. Come on in the pair of you. You were almost late on your first day young man.'

She said this with mock severity but the boy didn't get the teacher's hidden good humour and his face returned to its dark scowl again.

Once all the children and teenagers were settled Miss Boniface asked for quiet and began to introduce the new boy to the rest of the class, who were all trying their best not to appear excited by the appearance of this intense newcomer.

Now he had removed his hoodie Heather and the class could get a good look at him. The lad was tall and wiry for his age, with a mop of jet-black hair and a fringe that could almost completely obscure his eyes when he wanted it too. He had a thin angular face and a row of perfect white teeth that made his occasional nervous smiles light up the room.

'Well Joe', said Miss Boniface, 'would you please introduce yourself to the class.'

Joe stood still, looking at the expectant faces. Without any fear, he seemed to meet the gaze of everyone in the class and then, taking a deep slow breath he started.

'My name is Joe Rosenburg and I have just moved to your cold wet miserable country from New England...that's in America.'

'Well Joe, it doesn't always rain here,' said Miss Boniface in a conciliatory move. To the shock and delight of the class, Joe ignored the olive branch and launched into an angry and articulate rant.

'Well I think it sucks. Everything is small and grey and cold. Even your boats are small. My grandfather's boats were huge and his fleet was the largest in north America. Your boats are too small to catch anything. Our boats were massive, with nets that go on for miles and miles. We even have factory boats where the fish are cleaned, gutted and frozen or tinned ready for the supermarket shelf. We even have our own TV adverts and everything. The president of America once visited our factory and my grandfather has a picture on his wall. I used to live in a huge house in a big city where there was loads to do. I hate this village, there's nothing to do, you don't even know how to play football correctly and you all speak in a weird accent and you sound as if you come from a hundred years ago. Besides, most of you don't even have a TV set. My grandfather says that you all live in the past century and that history is going to pass you by.'

Joe stopped, his arms tightly crossed, his face that looked like a thundercloud. The class had now frozen; Heather could sense the initial goodwill being withdrawn. It was as if the actual temperature of the room had dropped a few degrees. A couple of the older and bigger teenagers at the back of the class were beginning to shift in their chairs. Miss Boniface took a deep breath and prepared to begin operation 'Save the Day' but it was too late. Michael Nesbitt, the tallest boy in the class, already nearly a man with arms that would one day be as thick as Heather's father's, stood up.

'Hello Joe. On behalf of us all, I would like to welcome you to our humble, small, grey, cold, boring backward wee village.'

He sneered with barely concealed venom.

'At the first break myself and my close friends here,' – he gestured to his mates – 'would like you to take the opportunity of showing us poor uneducated Scottish kids some of the rules of your game of American football. As we are too poor to afford all of the protective pads that your players have to wear in case they hurt their poor American bodies perhaps you'd be gentle with us.'

His mates sniggered and Heather saw that Joe had recognised the veiled threat and seemed to be looking rather nervous.

Miss Boniface completely misread the situation.

'Oh, thank you Michael,' she said, grateful for what she thought was an olive branch being extended. 'I am sure that Joe would love to teach you a few rules of his native game, wouldn't you Joe?'

Joe had no time to reply as Miss Boniface, anxious to begin the class, had propelled him towards the only available desk beside Heather. The seat was empty as it was considered too cold by most of the class. Heather always sat beside the open window, never worrying if it was too hot or too cold because she could just about see the sea over the grey slate roofs of the cottages below.

As Joe sat down he let out a strangled yelp. Miss Boniface looked sharply at him.

'We don't allow for noise in this class Joe,' she said before turning to the blackboard.

Joe glanced at Heather; she could see that he was holding back tears. Joe gingerly lifted himself a few inches from his chair and pulled a drawing pin out of his backside. He could hear the sniggers from behind him. Heather tried to smile at Joe but he chose to take it the wrong way.

'Don't you mock me as well, Goddammit, I thought you were different.'

He turned and stared straight ahead at the blackboard and avoided eye contact with her for the rest of the class. Heather turned her attention back to the lesson but she couldn't quite distance herself from the intense young man who sat beside her staring fixedly out of the window. Heather wondered quietly to herself what it must be like to leave your home. She couldn't contemplate ever leaving the familiar beauty of the little fishing village she lived in. Heather stole a few sideways glances at the sullen Joe who broke all the rules by pulling his hoody back up over his head in class. As much as Joe's whole demeanour radiated open hostility Heather could see a vulnerable and unsure version of himself hiding just behind his scowl. She wondered again how she would cope if she had to go to another far away town to live. Heather knew that she would grow anxious if she even had to travel as far as Saltcoat only 20 miles away. When she did go shopping she was always conscious of how the local girls would stare at her and her ripped jeans and comfortable warm home knitted jumpers.

Heather didn't get another chance to speak to Joe until lunchtime. As soon as the bell for the first break sounded Joe was scooped up by Michael Nesbitt and his friends who ushered him outside and down to the patch of grass that was meant to be a football pitch. Truth was it sloped so badly that any miskick meant that somebody would have to race down the hill and catch the ball before it rolled down the lane into the harbour.

Heather watched from a distance. She thought the game the boys were playing looked very violent. One of them would throw the ball and then as Joe ran forwards the rest would leap on him, knocking him to the ground. By the end of the break Joe could barely walk. He had a wonderful bruise on his cheek. His fancy sweatshirt and expensive looking training shoes were battered and covered in mud and grass stains.

As he walked back towards the school Heather could see that he was limping slightly.

'Joe, are you okay?' she called out to him as he passed where she was standing.

Joe got no opportunity to answer before Michael Nesbitt caught up with him and gave him a massive slap on the back, nearly winding him.

'Well, Yankee Doodle Dandy, thanks so much for introducing us plebs to your great national game. Thing is, my good old buddies here feel that we haven't quite mastered some of the finer points so I hope you won't mind meeting us here next break time. Hey, perhaps after school we could come by yours and we could play some more. How about it?'

Heather knew that it wasn't a question, it was an order and as Joe nodded glumly she felt she had to do something.

'Well you can't tonight Michael...'

Heather spoke firmly, standing up tall, every bit of her twelve years of experience of dealing with an older brother coming out.

'The boats are sailing tomorrow and you'll be needed to help; besides I am going to Joe's tonight for tea.' Then, smiling sweetly, she added, 'Dad said that it was good to welcome newcomers even if they don't yet understand our ways.'

At the mention of her father Michael smiled and cordially stepped away. Although Heather's dad was fantastic at keeping the collective spirits of the village up when catches were bad and was easily the most respected skipper and fisherman in the village, he also had a fearful reputation for quickly resolving heated issues in the local glue pot with a swift blow of such force that any offender soon resolved to see things his way.

'Well,' said Michael, 'there's always tomorrow. Oh, and the day after that.'

He walked away to join his mates chuckling out loud to himself.

'Don't worry,' said Heather, 'he's a great lad really, once you get to know him....'.

But Joe had walked past her. Still holding back tears, he was limping defiantly back towards the school building.

'I'll see you tonight then?' Heather called after him.

Joe paused and turned; he appeared to consider his lot for a moment. He shrugged.

'Okay, only you had better let me get home first. Grandfather doesn't like visitors much. I'll tell him it's okay.'

Heather wondered if Joe had accepted just to get out of another beating. It occurred to her that she might actually be very welcome. But still, she had never visited the old lodge high up on the cliff and she wouldn't pass up a chance to check it out. From where she sat in the classroom, she often wondered about the grey stone building standing like a proud old man on the bluff of the cliff. It had stood abandoned for many years after the catches had started to decline and the wealthy factory owner from the nearby town had sold up and moved away.

Heather had always been fascinated by the house and had occasionally sneaked up and climbed over the stone wall that ran around the perimeter of the grounds. She had admired the huge rooms but it was the view of the sea from up there that really excited her. Imagine being able to go about your business and have such a great view of the ocean. Heather thought that she must tell Joe how lucky he was but, as she glanced at Joe, she saw that he was sitting lost in a cloud of distraction and sadness. Heather sighed.

She was determined not to let anyone undermine her good humour, but she felt sorry for Joe. He reminded her of a new fish plopped into her aquarium after it had suffered in the nets of her father's boat. Heather knew that Joe still had to find his place in the pecking order of the village. She could see that his dignity was important to him, even if he was hiding under his long dark fringe to avoid making eye contact with anybody.

4
View from
the Hill

Heather arrived home to find that her parents were out and her tea was on the table. A gentle plume of pipe smoke curling its luxurious way towards the kitchen ceiling meant that her grandfather was home.

'Hi Gramps,' Heather called out, jumping up between the old man and his newspaper.

He pretended to get a shock at Heather's sudden appearance and then wrapped her up in his still powerful arms. Heather became entangled in his newspaper and the strong smells of sea, tobacco and beer that always hung around him. Heather laughed as her hair got entangled in her grandfather's beard. As she freed herself from the tight embrace of affection she cheekily checked to make sure none of his tobacco crumbs had fallen onto her. His beard did seem to have an independent life of its own it and would often sweep up all manner of crumbs, tobacco, wood shavings and even dregs of beer. Heather's mother hated it and would blame it for any illness that befell her family. 'Its that unhygienic beard of your grandfather's' she would half joke if anybody got sick. Heather loved her grandfather and, as her own father was away at sea so often, held a special place in her heart for the old man. It was Heather who always defended his opinionated and often grumpy points of view as just, 'Gramps way of caring 'bout us.'

'Hello my angel. Your tea's on the table. Your parents are off to see the new nets, all the way down the coast. It's a bloody long journey so they'll be a good while. Can't see the point myself. They reckon they'll catch more and save them money, I reckon they needs their heads examining.'

'Oh, OK Gramps, I'm going to go out to see a friend after. That okay?'

'A friend, eh? Hmm, I wonder what sort of pirate you are hanging out with now. Guess that'll be fine as long as you are back by dark and you don't forget to do your chores.'

'Gramps!'

Heather loved her grandpa, not just because he always had sweets in the deep linings of his pockets but because he always had an interesting story or tale to tell. He would usually start a sentence with 'that reminds me of the time...' or, 'now it's interesting you should say that because I heard...' and so on. Suddenly, Heather wanted more than anything else to share her bizarre experiences of the previous day. She wanted a pair of wise ears to listen to her crazy story and assure her that she was not suffering from some life-threatening hallucinations. Heather remembered her vow of silence. The seal had been very firm with her. Heather was desperate to get some advice though. Surely her grandfather would be fine with it; maybe she didn't even have to let the details slip. Besides, she didn't really need to have two suppers in one night and a good conversation would distract the old man from how little she ate.

'Gramps?'

'Hmm.'

'Do you believe that some people can actually understand what animals are saying?'

Her grandfather put his newspaper down and peered over his reading glasses at his granddaughter.

'Now, it's interesting you should say that but your grandmother always swore blind that the birds would tell her whenever there was a storm coming. I reckon it's just because they was all heading inland to get away from it.'

'But really be able to understand what animals are saying Gramps?'

'Well some folks say the Selkie are seal people who have the ability to take on human shape and walk amongst us. They say that seals can talk to humans but that you wouldn't want to hear them.'

'Why not?'

'Well they might capture you and turn you into one of them.'

Heather thought of Ran, and how she had seemed to be so kind and loving. Her grandfather must just be telling tales.

'No, I mean really speak to animals.'

Heather's grandfather leaned closer forward to get a real good look at his granddaughter.

'Hmm, I think someone needs to tell me something. I remember when I first met your grandmother. She would always be walking along the beach, just like you. I would often come up on her and she would be startled and scold me for interrupting her conversation. She wouldn't do anything without asking the ocean. One day she told me that ocean told her she was going to have a baby and that it would be a girl, and she was right. Nine months later your mother was born.'

A soft, sad and faraway look settled on Heather's grandfather's face as he spoke. He turned his gaze back to the face of his granddaughter and he reached out and ruffled her hair affectionally.

'You need her now young 'un, don't you. Maybe you have got the sight. It always goes to the women, often jumps a generation. But hear this, I reckons that it's the listening that's the important bit. Your grandmother would make me sit as quiet as a church mouse when the boats were out. Said she was listening to hear where they were.'

Without realising it, Heather ate all of her tea while hanging on every word her grandfather was saying.

'Grandfather, what does the name Ran mean?' she asked suddenly.

Her grandfather looked surprised.

'Where did you hear that name?' he asked, leaning across the table.

'Oh, er, at school, in a book.' Heather lied badly.

'Now it's interesting that you should say that because she was a terrible one, Ran was,' said her grandfather speaking slowly to add tension to his story. 'She was the goddess of the storm and of whirlpools, a dangerous creature; she would drag sailors down to their deaths in her terrible underwater kingdom. Sailors used to throw gold over the side to appease her. Hey, don't be scared little one, it's just a silly story!

Heather's grandfather had noticed that she had stopped eating and was holding her fork mid-air, frozen, her eyes wide open.

'Wasn't she nice at all?' said Heather chewing slowly.

'Oh no, my child. She was said to be one of the fiercest. Look, it's only stories. You see, people got scared of storms and they wanted to think that they could make them their friends. So, they gave them names and tried all sorts of things to buy their friendship. Storms are real, dangerous and can still drag sailors to the seabed. Goddesses aren't generally nice my lovely. Now then, enough of this daftness. Off you goes to your friend whilst you've got time. If you want me I'll be at the pub.'

Heather snapped herself out of her frozen reverie and gulped down the fear that had suddenly welled up in her. It was as if large clouds had just darkened the sunny place in which she had been all day. She felt the flicker of fear pass through her tummy.

'Ok Gramps,' she said giving the old man a big hug. 'I'll see ya later.'

As Heather walked slowly up the steep hill from the harbour and along the lane towards the lodge her head was full of questions. It must just be a coincidence. Ran, her seal, was lovely, she was no terrible goddess. Gramps' words of comfort hadn't helped her. He clearly thought that it was just a story but Heather remembered every detail about her encounter with the seal and the amazing angelfish. Even so, a little doubt was gnawing away inside her. She was paying it so much attention that she didn't notice the view from the top of the cliff. She just opened a huge squeaky gate and wandered slowly up the gravel pathway to the front door of the lodge.

She hadn't even knocked on the large wooden door when it swung open. Heather jumped backwards in alarm. She needn't have worried; it was Joe who peeped out with a mischievous and delighted grin on his face.

'Ha, got you, didn't I? You know this place gives me the spooks. I mean it's like something out of a horror film. Come on in. Grandfather is out. He's actually gone into the village. Run out of whisky probably. Come on in.'

Heather was delighted that Joe seemed to have lost al of his shy and grumpy demeanour from earlier. She had been secretly fearing that it would be a really difficult and tense visit and she was amazed at how different Joe was in his own environment. Smiling, she decided not to show Joe that he had spooked her, pushed past him in a confident manner and then found herself staring into a front room with huge windows.

'Well, I think it's...wow, look at the view.'

'Oh, yeah, hmm, the view is rather cool, I guess. Hey, you want to have a look through grandfather's telescope?'

'Okay,' said Heather absentmindedly. She thinking just how amazing it must be to live in a place where you could gaze so far out to sea all day.

'Come on then. It's upstairs in Grandfather's study.'

Heather jolted herself out of her reverie and followed Joe up a winding wooden staircase to the next floor. The house had recently been modernised. It was warm and clean and must have had a lot of money spent on it, thought Heather. In fact, she decided, it was much nicer on the inside than the grey roughcast exterior. Joe's grandfather had filled it with wonderful pictures and pieces of art and furniture, the likes of which Heather had never seen before. Halfway up the staircase she paused. A magnificent painting caught her eye. It was so large that it filled most of the staircase wall. In the picture stood a tall Indian chief and his bride. They looked young but exuded an imposing and regal air. It was not their amazing traditional dress which drew Heather's eye; it was something about their faces. Both had the most incredible black hair, dark kind eyes and faces that seemed both sad and happy at the same time. She turned to continue her climb and bumped into Joe who had paused his ascent as well. He had a distant look in his eyes and suddenly she realised who the people in the painting reminded her of.

'Joe, you look just like the people in this painting', she said.

'Uh huh. That was my Ma and Pa when they got hitched. It's one of those fantasy wedding portraits. It's not real. I don't like the picture. I wish Grandpa hadn't hung it.'

'Wow, your mother and father are Native American Indians? Why, I think they're beautiful. Where do they live? I think they look really cool I'd love to wear clothes like that.'

'They usually wore jeans and T-shirts most of the time I think. They just dressed up for the picture. It's so phoney, I hate it. I hate them.'

Heather was shocked at Joe's outburst and took a sharp intake of breath. Joe's good humour had vanished and he instinctively pulled up his hoody and scowled at Heather.

'That's no way to speak about your parents,' protested Heather.

'Well, so what. They're dead aren't they! DEAD, DEAD, DEAD and I hate them.' Joe turned and ran up the stairs.

Heather was stunned. She had no idea. She didn't know how to react to Joe's sudden explosive and angry revelation.

She slowly followed him up the twisting and creaking stairs. Heather glanced back at the painting and sighed. She was annoyed with herself and wished she hadn't scolded Joe. She tried to imagine what it must be like to have lost your parents. She couldn't envisage life without her mother and father and big brother. She guessed that Joe was probably still hurting inside and suddenly she felt a great rush of pity for him. No wonder he acts so tough, she thought. At the same time, she was bursting to ask more questions about such exotic parents but her good manners reined her tongue in. The door to the study was open. Heather slowly entered the room. It was large and had a huge bay window that looked out across the sea. It seemed stuffed with all sorts of sea related objects. Joe was standing with his back to her staring out of the window. His hands were thrust into the pocket of his hoodie. Heather took another deep breath and tried to appease him.

'Joe,' I'm sorry. I didn't know. I had no idea. You never said... at school... so I... I can't imagine what you are going through. I guess it must really upset you to see their faces on that huge picture every day. Look, sometimes when a big storm comes in, I get really scared for my dad and I just can't imagine what I would do if he didn't come back.'

Joe slowly turned to face Heather. He dropped his eyes to the floor and took a deep breath. He seemed to be struggling with his emotions. He took another deep breath and then looked up shyly and made eye contact with Heather.

'Yeah, it must be tough for you – I've seen the size of the waves here, they are larger than your small fishing boats. Look - sorry about that. Look I really am. I've got a bit of a temper. I just let fly sometimes. I think I must take after my grandfather. Erm...look, thanks for today by the way. You saved me from another kicking. I don't mean to be rude. I just speak before I think.' Joe tried a shy smile. His humour lifted slightly. 'Look, I just don't want to talk about it, okay?'

'Okay,' said Heather, and gratefully changed the subject, 'Is that the telescope?'

At the end of the room, past a huge desk stood a large telescope. The writing desk was covered in papers and charts all rolled up and bound with string. A huge brass compass was being used as a paper weight. An antique set of chart drawers supported a model boat, pieces of net and pieces of amazing assorted jetsam. Beyond all this stood the biggest telescope Heather had ever seen. Like the compass it seemed to be made out of brass. 'It looks like a great big brass cigar,' said Heather as she stood beside Joe who was busily fixing a viewing piece to the main body of the telescope.

'Yup, its Grandfather's pride and joy and he's going to give me merry hell if he notices I've been in here.'

'Oh, should we leave it alone then?' said a worried Heather.

'Nah, he always tells me not to use it, I always do. He yells, I yell and then we both forget it. Here, look at the harbour.' Heather carefully put her eye to the viewer.

'Oh, wow,' she said, instantly forgetting her concerns.

She could see her dad's boat, *The Flying Fish,* as clearly as if she were standing beside it. She could see her brother lazily cleaning the decking and Tom, the fastest fish gutter in Scotland, daubing the wheelhouse with white paint. She could even see a crafty old seagull sitting on top of the boat's large aerial, ready to ruin Bob's work.

'It's so clear. Wow, this is so powerful.'

'Here,' said Joe, 'let me line it up on the town. Here you go. What can you see now?'

'I can see the shops and the pub. Oh, and look, there's grandfather. He's standing on the steps. Hey, he seems very excited. He's waving his arms about at somebody. I can't tell who it is. He has his back to me. He seems to be waving his arms about, too. Oh dear, I think grandpa's going to be in trouble again.'

'Let's see,' said Joe. He put his eye to the lens. 'Oh man, your old geezer is shouting at my old geezer. Wow, there will be some sparks flying down there. Grandfather turns the air blue once he gets going. Oh, whoops, he's leaving. Seems they ain't gonna fight after all.'

'Let me see.'

Joe let Heather look again. Sure enough, a tall stern-looking, straight backed old man was striding away from the pub. As he passed out of view, Heather was sure that he glanced up directly at her.

'He's gone,' she said to Joe.

'Shoot, we had better get a move on. He must be his way back.'

'Can I just look at the beach?' said Heather.

'Sure. Hang on, let me see. Okay, now look,' said Joe.

He had readjusted the telescope to its normal position and now Heather could see the beach just as if she were standing on it.

'Wow,' she said, 'it looks even more beautiful from here.'

'Yeah, it's a nice day. Come on, let's go out before Grandfather gets home. If he's in a bad mood he'll probably want to pick a fight.'

'Okay,' said Heather. 'Hang on. What's that on the beach?'

Joe looked. 'I dunno. It sort of looks like a rock. It's not moving. It's just above the high tide mark. Hmm, that's odd. Come on, I'll race you down there to see.'

Laughing, the two children hurtled down the stairs and burst out of the front door of the house almost bowling over the surprised housekeeper.

'Just going out,' called Joe, tell grandfather I'll be back soon.'

Then, without waiting for a reply, he tore after Heather.

Heather was as nimble as a mountain goat and as sure-footed as one as well. Joe had slightly longer legs but Heather's lifetime of practice, running helter-skelter down the steep path to the harbour, soon put her well in front.

Heather jumped and leapt and ran down the windy track that lead to the beach. She was soon scrambling across the sand towards the object and still had a way to go when she realised that it was a huge shell.

'Oh wow', she called out running even faster and coming to a sliding halt.

The shell was almost as large as her head and she had to hold on to it tightly as she lifted it because it was so heavy. Joe skidded to a stop beside her, spraying her with sand, far more breathless than she was.

'Wow,' he said, 'it's a beauty. It must have come from miles away. That's from tropical waters.'

'You're right', said Heather who knew her shells, 'I've never seen one as big as this this before. Here, give me a hand so that I can hold it to my ear.'

Joe helped Heather lift it to her ear. Heather gasped. The sound was amazing. It was as if she could hear the roar of the ocean and the call of the seabirds. And then, from far away, she heard her name being called. It was so softly spoken it sounded like the edge of a wave brushing the surface of the sand. She almost dropped the shell causing Joe to struggle to keep his grip.

'Hey, careful you bumpkin. I almost dropped it then. It's really heavy you know.'

She listened attentively. There it was again. So softly spoken, sounding as if it came from far, far away. The closer and more intently she listened, the louder it seemed to get. 'Heather, Heather, Heather.'

'Here, let me have a go. You've been ages,' said Joe impatiently. They swapped positions. Heather wondered if Joe would hear it too. She giggled. Joe had screwed up his face with the effort of holding the shell and listening at the same time. He was sticking his tongue out with concentration, his eyes open wide with astonishment. He soon put the shell down.

'Man, it's heavy. The sea sounds really loud inside it. It sounds like all the storms and all waves have carried this shell across the world all the way to your little beach.'

'It's not my beach, it's everybody's. Yours as well, I mean. Erm, did you hear the seabirds?' Heather asked.

'Yeah, I know what you mean. It's weird. It's as if you can hear them calling out somewhere in the distance. Wow, cool find, Heather.'

'Hey, look, I had better go now. Grandfather doesn't really like me messing about on the beach. I can't swim, you see,' said Joe. 'Look, do you want a hand back with that shell?'

Heather was shocked that Joe couldn't swim. Almost all the kids in the village had learned to swim at the same time they learned to walk. She felt another pang of sorrow for Joe. She supposed it was because he hadn't had parents to teach him. She wondered just how lonely Joe's childhood had been. Joe was still smiling, carefully holding the shell so as not to drop it and Heather felt a pang of compassion for her new friend. They slowly lowered the huge shell together and Heather marvelled at its iridescent colours all hues of pink and red and orange so smooth so perfectly formed, like a star that twisted in upon itself. She glanced at Joe's face. He was also spellbound by the sheer magnificence of the shell.

Heather felt a short tug in her heart like a distant thread being pulled and to her surprise realised that she wanted the shell for herself. As the two of them stood holding the shell they both became momentarily embarrassed by their physical closeness and intimacy of the moment. Heather gently broke the silence.

'Well, do you want to keep it? I mean we found it together and all that. I wouldn't mind.'

'Nah, it's okay. You saw it first and, besides, you can put it in your famous Oceanic Zoo, which I still haven't seen! So, to make it fair, tomorrow after school I'll come to your house and you can show what all the fuss is about. I can help you put the shell into the tank if you want. Deal?' said Joe.

'Ok, deal. It's not really famous though,' added Heather sheepishly.

'Oh yes, it is,' said Joe. 'That's all anybody talks about when I ask them about you. They say you are a bit weird, keep yourself to yourself but have an amazing fish zoo.'

Heather felt a bit confused and it was her turn to look shy. The fact that Joe had been asking about her was nice but, at the same time didn't know that the other kids thought that she was weird. Joe saw her face and grinned and handed the huge shell to her.

'Don't worry, pal, my grandfather says that it's the normal people that are boring. See ya.'

And with that he was racing up the beach. Heather laughed at his sudden departure and staggered under the weight of the huge shell. Heather watched him go and then glanced up at the lodge. She saw a flash of silver in the upstairs window.

'That's weird,' she thought, as she struggled to make space in her schoolbag for the huge shell. 'I wonder what that was.'

Dragging her treasure behind her in the soft sand, she set off home.

5
The Council of Elders

'My, what on earth have you got in that bag this time young lady? I told you before, I don't want any more crabs or lobsters in the bath.'

Heather's mum was in washing up mode; sleeves rolled up, gloves on and clouded in steam from the sink. Heather grinned at her mum; she knew how much she hated washing up. Her father, who was visibly squirming behind the newspaper, had been promising her a dishwasher since anyone could remember.

'Listen to your mother angel,' he said.

'Don't worry, it's only a shell.'

'A shell? It must be huge. Here, let me.'

In one movement, her father had scooped Heather up onto his knee and placed her bulging, sand-covered school bag on the kitchen table. He lifted her as easily as if she were still a small child, not a nearly full-grown teenager.

'What have you got here this time, then?'

He pulled the shell out of the bag. It sat square on the table in all its glory. In the kitchen light the subtle pinks, reds and golds seemed to shine with an iridescent beauty.

'Bloody hell!'

'Language, Robert,' said her mum. Then seeing the shell, 'Oh sweet Jesus, where on earth did you find that?'

'Language, my love,' said her father winking at Heather.

For a few moments, the whole family just stared at the shell. It was huge and unlike anything anyone had seen before. Its surface glistened and sparkled like polished jewels. It had a huge cavernous mouth and curled ornately like a huge snail. It had loads of softly rounded pink spikes radiating from it and made it look even bigger. Heather's mum dried her hands and came closer to the table.

'Lift it up and listen,' said Heather. 'You can hear the ocean.'

'I bet you can,' said her father, easily lifting it in one of his huge hands so Maria could listen. She placed her ear to the wide opening of the shell.

'Oh, that's amazing, Robert. You can hear the sea as loudly as if you were in it,' she exclaimed, her eyes lighting up in wonder. 'Where did you find it Heather?'

'On the beach mum. Me and Joe found it.'

'You and who?' quizzed her mother.

'Joe. He's the new boy, from the lodge up on the cliff.'

'You are not to mix with their kind!'

Everybody jumped. Heather's Grandpa was standing in the doorway swaying slightly. His pipe was clamped between his teeth and his eyes shone with an anger Heather had never seen before. He was tugging his long beard with one hand while his tightly clasped his walking stick as if it were a weapon.

'Hush, John,' said Robert. 'The little 'un has made a friend at last.'

'I don't care. The boy's Yank father is the most crabbit, arrogant, pig-headed man you'll ever meet and he's bloody dangerous to us all.'

Robert looked surprised and amused at the same time. Heather's mother came to her rescue.

'Language, Father! What on earth are you talking about? If Heather has a new friend that's her business. You can't go judging the child's father John.'

Heather was astonished. Her grandfather was everybody's friend and usually you wouldn't find a more mild-mannered man than him.

'He came into my pub, started slagging off my village, our boats, our craft, even our homes, said we was all idiots and that buying new boats and new nets would be the death of us. What do the Americans know about fishing? We taught them everything they know. We were here, in this village, before they was even discovered.'

Heather recalled the altercation she had seen through the telescope between her and Joe's grandfathers. She suddenly felt cross at her grandpa. Her mother was right. At last she had a friend and she wasn't going to have his family bad-mouthed.

'Well, Joe is great, he's my friend and I shall see him if I want to. He's not his father! His father and mother are dead.

That's his grandfather you were shouting at. He's the one looking after Joe. Besides I saw you picking a fight with him. You were waving your arms all over the place and shouting outside the pub. That's no way to treat a newcomer who is probably feeling all lonely and was probably just hoping to make friends himself.'

Her outburst momentarily silenced everyone.

'Erm, excuse me young lady, what were you doing in the pub?' her mother asked.

'I saw them through Joe's telescope.'

'A telescope, eh,' growled her grandfather, suddenly aware he was losing the argument. 'Well, I bet he has it for spying. He was trying to tell me my job...'

'And your pride got hurt, didn't it John?' said Heather's dad gently. 'Come on, sit down and have a cuppa. Leave the children alone. It's good that they are friends. Besides, I wouldn't be surprised if Joe's grandfather isn't having exactly the same conversation with the boy about us, thanks to you.'

Heather was furious and blazed at her granddad.

'Oh, gramps,' she cried, 'now you have gone and ruined everything'.

She pushed the shell back into her sand covered schoolbag and manhandled it to the stairs.

'I'm going to bed and I hope you are proud of yourself.'

'Are you going to let her speak to me like that?' her grandpa scolded Heather's mum.

'Oh Dad,' she said, 'you really should listen to yourself sometimes. Heather's probably right; I expect Joe's grandfather was just trying to be friendly.'

'That man wouldn't know how to be friendly if his life depended on it. He was cursing us all, and you my son, said that we was all mad, that you was an amateur. An amateur! You have been sailing ever since you was big enough to walk.'

Heather's father got up from the table.

'Well, no man should tell another his business, but we must make allowances for newcomers. They don't know our ways. American you say? Them Americans think they know it all anyway.'

With that, he climbed the stairs to his daughter's room and stood outside the door.

'Hi, my angel. Let me in, will you?'

Heather opened her door and found herself swept up in her dad's big strong arms. She buried her head in his chest and began sobbing violently.

'Hey, my little one, don't let gramps get you down. He's just had a few too many. Don't worry. I will go up and see the old man tomorrow and apologise to him for his behaviour. Okay?'

Heather's sobs subsided. 'Okay,' she sniffed.

'Now then, let me put this shell up here on the table. It really is a beauty, isn't it? It must have come from miles away, an entirely different ocean. Remember to sterilise it before you put it in the aquarium.'

'Of course I will, Dad. Joe is going to come up tomorrow and help me. He hasn't seen the Oceanic Zoo yet. Dad?'

'Yes?'

'Do you think I'm weird?'

'Oh, Lordy,' Heather's father rolled his eyes heavenward. 'No, my sweetheart. I think you are one of the brightest, kindest, most considerate girls I have ever met. You are definitely not weird. It's everybody else. Besides, normal people are boring.'

'That's what Joe's grandfather said to him.'

'Well, there you go. He can't be all bad then, can he? Now you get yourself into bed. It's getting late.'

He lent down and gave his daughter a gentle kiss before turning to leave.

'Dad?'

'Huh?'

'Did you get the new boat?'

Her dad turned back.

'No my sweet. It is just too much money. We are going to get some special winches and some new nets which we will put between two boats. That way we should be able to double our catch as long as we work together. Now, off to bed with you.'

Heather woke up with moonlight bathing the room and with the sound of the sea in her head. She sleepily sat up rubbing her eyes. She thought she must have forgotten to close the curtains again. Then, just as she went to get out of bed, she froze. The curtains were closed. The light seemed to be coming from the shell resting beside the aquarium. Maybe it was just reflecting the moonlight somehow, Heather peered at the shell which was glowing and then moving very slowly, she pulled the curtains back. She sighed with relief; the moon was up and it was huge. It hung in the sky like a huge silver disc. That's where the light must have come from. For a moment Heather feared she might be about to have another hallucination.

'Oh, I am silly.' she said out loud to herself. 'The moonlight must have been coming in through a crack in the curtains.'

'Heather.'

A low soft voice whispered her name; it was coming from the room.

'Huh?!"

'Heather,' came the soft voice again.

Heather froze again and listened intently. She could hear her own heart thumping wildly but the house was as silent as a grave. Nothing stirred, so late was the hour.

Heather moved towards the shell.

'Heather.'

Her name was called again. This time it was louder and there was no mistaking it. She went up to the shell. She put her hands under it and, with a huge push, carefully put it on its side so that she could listen to it. The voices stopped but then the room filled with music. It was at once both beautiful and sad. The sound rose and fell like the waves on the ocean. It seemed to be full of seabird cries and choirs of angels.

Deep down inside the shell a low hum started. It seemed to get louder and louder until the hum filled the whole room. Heather started to hold her head. The sound was so loud she was afraid it would wake her family. The sound was pulsing and throbbing and seemed to go right through Heather. She put her fingers in her ears but it didn't seem to make any difference. She closed her eyes the pain and willed it to stop. Suddenly silence filled the room. The shock of the quiet sounded oddly deafening. Heather slowly counted to ten before she opened her eyes to slow her panicked breathing down but before she had counted to three she bumped her head. It hurt. She gasped with surprise. She opened her eyes and couldn't believe what she was seeing. She had bumped her head on the ceiling of her room. Panicking she looked down. Her feet were floating about two feet above the floor. She was floating in mid-air gently bumping off the bedroom ceiling. Heather felt faint and wondered if she was still asleep or maybe even dying. Before she could process the strange sensations the bedroom window suddenly blew open and she felt herself floating towards it. Frantically, she started to kick her legs, desperately trying to scramble back into the room, trying to swim in the air itself. But it was to no avail. As if drawn by an invisible magnet she drifted out of the window and up and over her small house. Heather could feel the cold air which sobered her up a bit and brought her some clarity. She shook her head and glanced around as she drifted. She could clearly see the rows of the fishing cottages, the occasional wisp of smoke curling up from a chimney. The cobbles of the steep lane glinted in the moonlight. The air was crisp and cold and smelt of the sea; salty and somehow endless. She looked ahead. She was floating towards the moon which seemed to be getting larger and larger. Then, unexpectedly, she found herself floating down towards the beach. She gasped.

Sitting in the moonlight, in a great circle, many rows deep, were hundreds of seals. As if lowered by a silken rope, Heather alighted in the centre of the gathering. She felt the chill of the damp sand on her bare feet but it was still as if she had become detached from all normal sensations of reality. The cold air and the damp sand caused her neither chill nor discomfort.

'Greetings, daughter of the ocean,' said a familiar voice.

She looked straight ahead. There was no mistaking Ran. Her large brown eyes and greying muzzle could not hide the distinguished air that was about her.

'Hello Ran,' said Heather, dazed, 'Am I dreaming this?'

'Perhaps all is a dream my little one. The question is, can you dream well enough to know what is truth?'

Heather sensed a subtle vibration in the air. The large seal began to shimmer. Subtle lights and colours pulsed all over Ran's body. Heather gasped as the seal grew translucent and began to change shape in front of her eyes. Slowly the seal transformed until a beautiful woman with long hair as bright as the moonlight stood in front of Heather. Her garments were of the softest gossamer white and she seemed to light up as if with her own luminosity. Her long hair cascaded down her shoulders and almost touched the sand. The circle of seals drew closer around them, their eyes shining in the moonlight reflecting the luminosity radiating from Ran in all directions.

Heather was aware that her mouth was hanging open and she could hear her heart pounding. She became aware of a slight rustle in the sand and looked around her before gasping out loud.

One by one the circle of seals were all discarding their seal bodies and transforming into beautiful beings of light that glowed like Ran. As Heather slowly spun round the figures moved slightly closer to her, decreasing the size of the circle. Each one retained the deep soft eyes of a seal but had now taken on human form.

'Who are you all?' Heather asked.

'We are the council of elders, the servants of the ocean, and we have asked you here because your time is near and you have much to learn.

Heather couldn't work out who was speaking as the voices chimed inside her head. The elder's voices were an angelic choir that gently rose and fell like the waves on the soft sand of the beach. The sound calmed and soothed Heather.

You rescued an immortal and returned it to us. You passed the test. You are truly a child of the ocean. Your heart is open. You love all our family. Your heart is true but these qualities, little one, may not be enough on their own.'

Heather felt confused.

'I have always loved the sea,' she said, 'ever since I can remember but why me? Why have you brought me here, shown me this? Why me?'

'Come,' said Ran, 'let me show you what it is you must know.'

After a thoughtful pause she continued.

'Little one, the love you have for the sea is the love I have for you. You must not fear me as men do for I mean no harm. It is just that I must do what I must do. Here look.'

Heather glanced down and saw a perfect pool of water had formed in the sand at her feet. The moonlight seemed to shine brighter and brighter. Heather was dimly aware of the other beings slowly circling her, singing the same song she had heard earlier in her room.

Suddenly she could see the ocean in the pool of water. Then she could see a fishing boat. It was *The Flying Fish*, her father's boat. She observed her father and brother working furiously to lower their nets and in the distance from them her uncle was doing the same thing in his boat.

Ran's soft voice continued in her ear.

'Once men worked with the ocean. They listened to her, lived in peace and harmony with her and in return she gave of herself. She shared with man and woman her bounty, her fruits. But man became greedy. He took more and more and soon no life was safe. He even attacked and murdered the ancients with spears, hooks and knives until only a few of the dream-holders remained.'

Heather saw the image change to a small rowing boat laden with men straining at the oars, chasing a huge whale. Suddenly, a man built even larger than her father hurled a spear into the foam. Heather shuddered. It was as if she could feel the great beast's cry of pain. The water became the colour of blood.

Ran's voice continued.

'Man's nets grew larger and larger. They began to fish indiscriminately, deeper and deeper. Wider and wider have their nets grown. Not just the bounty of the sea but all life, young, old, even the inedible perished until even the most sacred depths were damaged, and the palaces of the immortals were threatened.'

Heather saw a huge palace shimmering in the depths. It seemed to be made of glass, or perhaps water held solid to make huge curved rooms and corridors that creatures of rainbow light, just like the angel fish, seemed to glide effortlessly along. The whole palace seemed to sway gently in the ocean. Not solid yet strong and flexible. Shoals of fish darted around its spires and bridges. Dolphins darted and played between the immortals, their ever-cheerful chatter filling the vision with a sense of love and playfulness.

'The dolphins are our messengers, our teachers for humans,' said Ran as if she could sense what Heather was thinking.

Then suddenly the picture changed. A huge net was rushing towards one of the upper parts of the palace. It caught the edge of a spire, paused for a second and then brought it crashing down, scooping up shoals of fish and dolphins, and sending the immortals diving frantically towards the darker depths of the ocean.

The vision changed. Heather saw her father and brother again. They were reeling in the nets as the two boats worked alongside each other. They seemed to be really happy as tons of fish poured onto the decks of the boats. Only now, their innocent harvesting of the ocean seemed like a killing frenzy. Heather could sense the aquatic life struggling for survival before it was beaten and cast into the boat's hold. She found herself weeping. Two dolphins crashed to the deck. She saw her father pause and walk over to them. She could sense that they were dead already.

Ran's voice continued.

'Dolphins, sharks, rays, turtles, small whales; the list is endless. They are all killed. This is happening right across the world's oceans. Many are slaughtered just for their fins for reasons we cannot fathom. Man has grown cruel, indifferent, greedy and too powerful.'

Heather was suddenly shown boats, some small like her father's but others huge with on-board factories. The boats were all around the world. It seemed to her that the whole sea and all the oceans of the world were being drained of life.

'You are right,' said Ran. 'That is what is happening. Soon the food chain will collapse, we will all die, the sea will become like the deserts that are beginning to cover the land.'

Heather found that she was growing angry inside. It seemed to boil up from deep down in her soul. Ran continued.

'For every scallop that is caught the seabed is devastated, seahorses and other sea life is destroyed, and all for what, a small creature that only gives a minute amount of food. Once the seabed is destroyed no fish can breed or spawn there. Humans are creating a desert. Soon stocks of sea life will not be able to recover. Do you see that small shoal of fish swimming round and round? The adult fish have been killed, the young have no one to follow, no one to show them where the feeding and breeding grounds are. They are lost; most of them will die.'

As Ran finished speaking, Heather found herself rising up into the sky until she was flying high above the ocean among a flock of seagulls. Their strange mournful call seemed to grab at her heart and she felt the huge sadness rise up in her again. It was the same feeling she'd experienced when she put the immortal back into the sea. The birds around her were calling out as if in pain. Tears cascaded down Heather's cheeks as she looked down to find her feet once more on the soft sand of the beach.

'Yes,' said Ran, 'you are right. They fly further and further but there are no fish. They are starving to death. Soon they will turn to the land where they will lose their sea knowledge. They will no longer return and eventually they too will be hunted down for food.'

Then Heather saw her father's boat again in the clear pool that formed at her feet again. It looked small and vulnerable. In the vision she saw Ran herslf in another form burst out of the ocean. She glowed with a green light and she looked huge, angry and terrible. Heather watched as Ran held out her arms and summoned a huge wave. Higher and higher the wall of water grew until its roar seemed to deafen her.

'I have no choice anymore,' said Ran, her voice was as loud as the winds and the wave. 'I am tasked to save the oceans, to protect the mother. 'It is, and has always, been so. I have only the elements at my command.'

Then Heather gasped as she saw the huge wave hurtling towards a small group of boats, one of which, she knew, was her father's.

Ran's voice rang loudly in her ears.

'Tell them that the next time their nets touch the ocean I shall act.'

The huge green wave roared towards the boat. Heather's sobs turned into a scream as a million tons of water smashed boats, men and nets like matchsticks. The whole vision started to spin until Heather felt ill. She screamed and screamed and screamed. She felt as if the waves were squeezing her, pulling her deeper down into the darkness. She fought and kicked and screamed some more.

'Heather.' She heard her name called.

'Heather!'

It sounded familiar, comforting. Frantically, she kicked out in the direction of the voice. She felt as if her lungs would explode.

'Heather.' Her name was louder now. With a last desperate lunge she struck out for the surface.

Heather opened her eyes. She was drenched, covered in sweat, in her room, bathed in moonlight with her father's strong arms wrapped around her. She looked around the room in panic. Her mother was standing anxiously behind her father and her grandpa was beside her. All of the adults looked startled and worried.

'It's okay, she's awake now,' Heather heard her father say.

'Oh, Dad', she cried as she flung her arms around him and sobbed.

'You're okay, you're okay!'

'Of course I am, little one. Don't worry. It was just a dream.'

Her father soothed her head while her mother kissed her hand gently. Exhausted by her ordeal, Heather quickly sank into a troubled sleep. As she slept the adults exchanged worried glances.

'That were no dream. Did you see her eyes? That were no dream, that was a vision. She saw something and it affected us all.'

Heather's grandfather was shaking as he said the words.

'She's got the sight and it's terrifying her. Oh, she needs her grandmother's help now. Why did she have to leave us before the little one matured?'

'Quiet,' said Heather's mother sharply. 'I won't be hearing it. It was just a bad dream. You stop filling her head with scary stories or you can get up to calm her down next time. Now, put her under the duvet gently and let's all get back to sleep. We're just feeling jittery, that's all.'

One by one, the adults left Heather's room, each one alone with their thoughts, each one shivering as they remembered her screams of fear.

6

A Return to
the Beach

When Heather woke, the sun was already high in the sky and she knew that she had slept in. Slowly she stretched her toes to the end of the bed. She wiggled them until she started to feel awake.

Somewhere far off in her head she knew that something was worrying her but she couldn't quite place it. She had vague sleepy memories of an intense dream but felt like she was floating on the comfy marshmallow of her thick mattress. She tried to focus on her memory of the dream but it slipped out of her grasp like a slippery eel. Heather relaxed and snuggled under her quilt watching the gentle stream of bubbles rise up from the floor of her aquarium. A seahorse floated past her vision looking serene and graceful. . As she lay there she noticed her red leather-bound journal on the shelf above her. She knew there was something she wanted to write in it. Something she wanted to ask her grandmother about, but what was it? Heather reached up and catching the book with her fingertips lifted it down. Squinting her eyes she flicked over some pages until she saw her drawing of a seahorse.

'Shoot,' called Heather. She leapt out of bed. The seahorse: it was no longer swollen; it must have given birth. That meant that, among the weeds, hundreds of babies would be hiding in fear of being eaten. She had to rescue the young ones and transfer them into a separate hatching and rearing tank. That must be what is troubling me, thought Heather. She shoved on her slippers and headed downstairs, all thoughts of her dream momentarily gone from her mind. It was as if her night adventure had been wiped clean.

When she got to the kitchen she was surprised by all the fuss she received. Her mother immediately put some of her favourite pancakes on to cook; she had the mixture ready and waiting and she didn't comment on the fact that it was almost lunchtime. Her grandfather was already cleaning out the plastic hatching tank for the seahorses and her father, who had already gone down to the harbour to work on the boats, had left her some money to buy some new equipment for the aquarium. Heather was bemused and happy with the sudden flurry of support from her family. She thought that they must have been making up for her granddad's outburst the night before. Having some cash to get supplies was great news as she badly needed new salt tablets and fish food.

Otherwise she would have to go fishing with her net and carry buckets of seawater all the way up from the harbour.

'Thanks mum, you're the best.'

Heather smiled as a huge plate of pancakes arrived on the table.

'Here you go, your highness and protector of the deep.'

Heather's smiling grandfather placed the plastic tank beside her. He had positioned old ships' corks around the rim of it so that it would float easily and had drilled hundreds of holes all around it so that the water would flow through it and keep it fresh.

'There you go young un,' he said, stealing a corner of one of the pancakes. He then leaned closer to her, 'Did you sleep okay?'

Heather was aware that this question seemed to have a hidden meaning but she pretended not to notice.

'Yes.' she said, 'I don't remember anything, I must have slept like a log.'

Her grandfather and mother both smiled and seemed to relax.

Just then, there came a knock at the door. Heather's mother raised her eyebrows and smiled at her.

'Who on earth can that be?'

The door opened slowly and then Joe's face peeped round into the room. His dark eyes flashed with merriment and his shock of black hair was sticking straight up making him look as if he had been dragged through the hedge backwards. Joe saw Heather's mum first. He said in his politest voice.

'Hi there, Heather's mum. Is Heather in? It's just that she invited me up to see her zoo.'

Heather's mum seemed impressed by this lively and polite teenager. She stepped back from the door to reveal the kitchen and Heather beside a pile of pancakes.

'Well, young man, your timing is perfect. Why don't you ask her yourself?'

'Hiya, mate', said Joe, catching site of Heather and then 'Wow,' as he set eyes on the pile of pancakes.

'Hello, young man, and welcome to our humble abode, erm... I hope that my histrionics yesterday haven't put you off our wee family?'

Joe carefully surveyed Heather's grandfather and entered the kitchen as cautiously as a cat.

'Hello sir,' said Joe, 'it's great to meet you.'

Joe extended his hand in friendship. Heather's grandfather shook it warmly and seemed to Heather to be impressed by the confident young man who held his gaze. Heather's mum had an almost uncontrollable grin on her face at the sudden formality of the situation.

'Right then, young man,' she said, 'you better be sitting yourself up and having some pancakes. I imagine if my daughter has anything to do with it you'll be kept busy today, I hear there may be new life needing tended upstairs.'

'Thanks,' said Joe, who sat up beside Heather and gave her a large wink.

'Back home we would have maple syrup, fresh blueberries and cream with our pancakes. Mm, these are good though...'

Joe spoke gleefully, reverting to being an informal hungry young teenager, and stuffed a pancake into his mouth.

'Well, in this house we have my homemade syrup and lemon with today's fresh strawberries.'

Heather's mum placed a bowl with sliced strawberries on the table with a flourish. They both started to munch happily and Heather started to tell Joe of her plans for the day.

'Okay,' she said, 'we have to get more salt water, we have to collect some shells for the hermit crabs to choose from, we have to set up the isolation and breeding tank and we have to sterilise the shell before placing it in the tank. And then we have to make sure that we have captured all of the baby seahorses.'

'Wow,' said Joe, his cheeks bulging with pancakes. 'This zoo stuff is well complicated.'

'Look, we can't keep calling it a zoo. That was what I called it when I was little and couldn't pronounce oceanarium,' said Heather.

'Oh, okay boss,' said Joe looking up suddenly as Heather's grandpa came back into the room. Joe fixed him with his dark black eyes and, after swallowing a huge mouthful of pancake, surprised the old man by speaking to him.

'Erm, please don't be cross 'bout my grandpa. He always comes across like a miserable old cuss but, underneath it all, he has a heart of gold really. He just don't know how to say what he feels in a way that don't upset folks. He's got lots of strong opinions and just wants to save the world really. Besides, even with just one whisky in him, it's all fighting talk, I reckon.'

Joe finished his surprisingly long speech with his very best winning smile.

Heather's grandfather, didn't say anything for a minute, caught off guard by the turn in the conversation, but Joe's huge smile won him over.

'Er, well I guess I was a bit hasty yesterday, you know, he is a newcomer and he doesn't know our ways. Anyway, don't you youngsters worry yourselves about us old 'uns,' he said, mimicking Joe's American accent, we ain't perfect you know.'

****

Operation Seahorse went well. Joe was amazed at Heather's aquarium; he couldn't believe how huge it was. He made her laugh when he said that he was worried that he might fall in and drown. He listened with amazement as Heather told him the story of how her father had had to strengthen her floor and how he had built the low table it stood on out of old railway sleepers so that it would be strong enough to hold the weight of all that water.

'It weighs over a ton,' she said proudly.

Joe was a good assistant and learned quickly. He had soon mastered the 'sea vacuum' which cleaned the sand. He eagerly rushed to and from the bathroom to throw away buckets of sludge. He even made two trips to the harbour to bring up pails of fresh saltwater so that Heather could save her precious salt tablets. He helped her gently lower the breeding tank into the aquarium. He watched her as she gently rounded up the tiny seahorses with her special net and helped her secure plenty of seaweed fronds so that the small creatures could hide and feel secure.

They decided against putting the huge shell in the tank as it needed to be sterilised with a purple iodine solution and something deep inside Heather seemed to advise her against that. So, instead, they placed it right in front of the aquarium to tempt the hermit crabs to grow really big. It was well into the afternoon when they had finished their zoological tasks.

'That was amazing,' said Joe as he and Heather relaxed watching the sea life scurrying around in the tank. 'You are so lucky, but now I really appreciate all the hard work you have to put in to maintain it.'

Heather laughed at his choice of words.

'Well,' she said, 'it's easy really, you just have to think of what the inhabitants need before they know it themselves.

Especially if you have baby sharks or predators in there. If they don't get fed on time then they'll eat everyone else.'

'Wow, man, you're kidding me, you've had sharks in there too?'

'Oh yes,' said Heather with a modest nonchalance, 'Well, really only small dogfish and I have to release them once they start to grow, but at least they get a chance to recover from the ordeal of being caught in the nets.'

'Hey', said Joe, 'this place is a sort of sea hospital as well then isn't it?'

'Yes, I guess you're right. Okay, come on then, you land lubber. You've helped me. Now I am going to help you.'

'What do you mean?' asked Joe.

'Well, you can't swim and you are still scared of the water so I'm going to teach you.'

Joe looked both excited and nervous.

'I ain't got no trunks,' he said.

'No problem. Wait here.'

Heather quickly returned holding up a pair of trunks.

'These were my brother's; I thought mum would know where they were. So come on, let's grab a towel and a sandwich and we'll go down to the beach. The tide should be out by now,' she said, consulting a chart on the wall of her bedroom, 'and it'll be perfect right now.'

The two children made their way out of the house with a bag of supplies and bathing gear. Joe was so excited that he forgot to be nervous. Just as they approached the sand of the small beach, Joe stopped.

'Look,' he said urgently, 'grandpa don't like me near the water. If he catches me he'll go mad but don't worry, I can handle him no danger. We're okay. He's gone into town so he won't know.'

'Oh, sure, okay,' said Heather. 'Come on, I'll show you our bay's worst kept secret.'

Most afternoons the tide went out leaving a huge pool of water halfway up the beach. It was easily as long as a full-sized swimming pool and in the summer was soon delightfully warm and just the right depth to learn to swim in. Other children were already splashing around and playing games. The sunshine had brought everybody down to the usually deserted wee cove.

Joe walked slowly into the water. It was warm and even at the deepest points only came up to his waist. Heather watched him, allowing him time to feel confident. She could tell that he had a fear of the water and she knew better than to try and hurry somebody to face a fear before they were ready.

Heather could swim like a fish. She bobbed and floated, dived and turned underwater handstands, occasionally splashing Joe. She put on her scuba mask as she loved to float underwater watching out for the small fish that darted about and looking for razor fish and crabs. Sometimes she would just float for hours with her snorkel, which allowed her to watch the comings and goings of the sea floor without the challenges of breathing under water. Heather stopped and offered Joe her mask, but he was still too scared to do anything other than dip his face in, so she swam through his legs, popped up behind him and then chased him with a huge piece of seaweed until he was laughing so much his fear of the water seemed to vanish.

Later on they teamed up with some other children from Heather's class, who seemed to have happily forgotten the earlier incidents at school and were only too willing to play a game of sea polo with an old football. Joe stood in the equivalent of a shallow end of the large beach lagoon and laughed with the rest as he tried to keep the ball in the air before batting with his hands to somebody else. Heather, with her ability to swim faster than anybody else could leap out of the water like a dolphin and strike the ball so hard that it sailed over the head of the other team to win them vital points.

Soon the sun started to dip and the sea edged nearer the beach pool. The other children waved and started back to the village for their suppers and soon only Heather and Joe remained.

'Hey, Joe', said Heather, 'shall I show you how I learned to swim?'

'OK,' said Joe keenly.

'Well look,' she said. 'I held my breath, closed my eyes and then kicked my legs. I couldn't believe it, I shot along like a torpedo. Look the water is so shallow that even if you panic, which is cool,' she added quickly so as not to hurt his feelings, 'you can simply stand up.'

Joe put on her scuba mask, placed his hands by his side, took a deep breath and then dropped himself into the water. Heather watched with glee. Joe shot through the water and sped past her like a splashing torpedo. After a few metres he popped up for air, sputtering slightly before shouting for joy.

'I CAN SWIM!'

After that there was no stopping him, he kept on diving and swimming past Heather like a torpedo. He couldn't swim with his head above the water yet, Heather knew that would take a couple more visits, but he had lost his fear and was having the time of his life. The sullen teenager Heather first met on the same beach had been replaced by someone who acted as if he had just rediscovered living.

'Look at me!'

Joe yelled to get Heather's attention and then swam between her legs like a fish.

'Hey that's fantastic,' called Heather. Hurry up and practice though because the tide is coming in.'

The sea had now breached the seaward side of the pool cooling the water and sending ripples across its surface. Heather wasn't alarmed. She knew that it would take a while to fill up, but she made Joe practice closer to the beach side of the fast disappearing lagoon as the water would soon be getting deeper.

Heather turned and looked at the sun, which was just starting to set. It was wonderful. As the waves rolled onto the beach the orange light shone through them, lighting up the foam with a deep red.

Heather could see the silhouettes of small fish darting through the waves and occasionally a gull would dive into the sea to catch one. She saw a cormorant dive for sand eels, disappearing beneath the waves for what seemed an impossibly long time before resurfacing with a sand eel in its beak. Then Heather froze; she saw a dark shape bobbing just a few metres out to sea. She squinted to focus her eyes and watched as the shape was picked up by the waves and propelled closer towards where the sea now met the beach pool. Checking to see that Joe was still okay she turned to swim towards where the waves met the warm tidal pool. Kicking out strongly she swam out to get a closer look. Perhaps it was a giant turtle. Heather had always wanted to see one close up. She took her time enjoying the way her body cut almost effortlessly through the water, letting the rise and fall of the waves lift her up and then propel her backwards until at the last minute she kicked her feet and propelled herself forwards.

She was now near where she had last seen the shape. Heather ducked under water to have a better look. Joe had her mask so she couldn't see as clearly. Then she caught sight of something below her so she swam a little deeper, peering through the salt water. A wave brought her suddenly up close to the shape. Almost at once it transformed itself into a clear object in front of her. Heather gasped and started to choke with panic as the lifeless body of a seal was shoved up hard against her by another wave. Part of an old fishing net was tightly wound around the lifeless seal and, as it rolled over, Heather could see that had tangled around the animal's flippers. Heather could tell that the poor creature had drowned before getting pushed inland by the sea. She could see where a boat's propeller had finished the job, leaving gruesome slashes across the seal's soft fur.

Heather was shocked, but she surfaced, took a deep breath and dived once more just to make sure that the seal was dead. On the sandy bottom it was now bobbing slowly, rolling over and over, weights on the net keeping it under water. Heather felt so sorry for the creature but, as there was nothing that she could do, she turned to strike back to the surface. As Heather reached for the water's surface she was suddenly pulled short. Something was dragging at her foot. Still she kept calm and investigated. A piece of the bright orange net had wound round her foot, and as she pulled it just seemed to get tighter. The weight of the dead seal being pulled by the sea and kept on pulling her foot in a jerky movement . Straining her whole body, Heather managed to just get a mouthful of air before a wave crashed over her head. She set off to the seabed again to free herself.

Suddenly the seal's body fell into the beach pool and started to sink a little deeper. Heather was now starting to feel panicky as she was pulled down with the poor seal's body weighed down by the net and weights. She struggled and tried to prise the net from her foot yet everything she did seemed to wind the net tighter and tighter around her foot. This time Heather couldn't reach the surface to take another breath.

Heather had no fear of the sea and rather than panic she kept calm but she knew that her lungs were fast running out of air. She began to feel light-headed and a slow buzzing began to sound in her ear. In a flash Heather realised that she was in trouble. The dead seal sank even deeper pulling her down with it. She tried with an added determination to free her foot. She tugged and pulled and twisted and fought it with her fingers, her eyes blinded by salt and sand being thrown up from the seabed. Suddenly Heather realised that there was no way it would come free. Every time she pulled the net it bit deeper into her ankle. A small drop of blood coloured the water. Heather began to think of all the people who would miss her if she drowned and felt a twinge of panic and sadness. She had no more air left in her lungs and felt her consciousness starting to slip away; her vision began to cloud. Typical, she thought to herself. 'The best swimmer in the village drowning in a shallow pool.' She felt the strange calm and euphoria of the oxygen starvation drift over her. Just as she prepared to surrender herself to the sea she saw a strange water vision in front of her eyes. In her mind's eye a figure was approaching her in the water swimming fast. As it grew closer Heather could see that it was the native Amercian lady she had seen in the painting at Joe's house. Heather smiled as she fell deeper into unconsciousness. The woman appeared to be shouting something, a name that she didn't understand. Heather smiled at her and the vision smiled back as Heather lost consciousness and swallowing a mouthful of saltwater drifted downwards.

7
Seven Ancestors

'**R**aven!?'
Heather sat bolt upright then immediately wished she hadn't. She was seized by huge wracking coughs that sent saltwater pouring out of her mouth and nose whilst a headache larger than her head seemed to be wanting to thump her unconscious again. She was dimly aware of a weight on her chest and the fact that she was lying on the sand and was no longer in the sea.

Suddenly two strong arms lifted her up. As Heather's eyes cleared from the stinging sea water she found herself staring into a white bearded face with a pair of the most intense blue eyes she had ever seen. The blue eyes stared back at her. They seemed to look straight through her then, for just a second, softened. The face gave a long deep sigh of relief and then barked some orders in a strong American accent.

'Right Joe, grab her clothes, come on, follow me back to the house, let's get this young lady warm as quickly as we can.'

Heather became aware that she was being carried at a tremendous rate. Whoever was carrying her had a huge stride and she felt as if she was on the deck of a ship or on the back of a camel. She was sorry for her rescuer as sea water seemed to keep wanting to flow out of her mouth causing her to cough and retch.

She heard Joe's voice and opened her eyes again. He was scurrying in front of the huge strides of her rescuer. Joe caught Heather's red eyes and his face changed from a picture of alarm and terror to relief as his usual huge smile lit it up.

'Are you OK Heather?'

'How do you feel?'

'I thought you were dead for sure.'

'I think I lost your mask.'

'You scared the bejeezus out of me.'

Joe was blurting out anything he could think of in his relief to get his friend back. Even with her thumpy head Heather found herself burst out with laughter as Joe, trying his best to scamper up the hill backwards so that he could see Heather, fell over a tussock of sea grass and let out a yelp.

A gruff voice called to him to be careful and then softened a touch to tell Heather to relax and not wriggle or lest she get dropped on her head. The thought of that image sent Joe and Heather off into peals of laughter and then suddenly her ride let out a huge growly laugh that was so unexpected both the children started again.

As soon as they all reached Joe's house Heather found herself the centre of a whirlwind of attention. She was rubbed dry with huge fluffy towels, made to wear a massive jumper, wrapped in a real bearskin rug, propped up on the couch and was instructed to drink a huge mug of scolding hot chocolate. As she allowed everybody to fuss over her she realised that the intense blue eyes, white beard, strong arms and growly laugh came from Joe's grandfather.

She could see how people must find him scary as he had a way of staring straight through you with his striking eyes. He had close cropped white hair and a lean angular face with a large noise. His voice was as gravelly as his laugh and he had the air of a military general or something. She could just imagine him shouting orders to soldiers or sailors to make them do what he said. He kept barking instructions at Joe and Isabella the maid but both of them seemed to be impervious to his formidable airs and just carried on what they were doing. The moment Joe's grandfather left the room Joe smiled and shyly sat down beside Heather.

'He's a bit terrifying isn't he? He scares most people and likes even fewer. Seems to like you though. Grandpa just has to feel in charge,' said Joe as he crawled under the bearskin to get closer to Heather. 'He's getting mellower in his old age though. He has had a terrible time. He lost everything, his business, his family and even his country so all he has is me and Isabella now, so I suppose that sort of reminds him to be nicer these days. Isabella told me that he used to be terribly stern and that he used to love it when everybody was afraid of him but now it's just the way he is and inside he's just the same as anybody else.'

Just then Joe's grandpa strode back into the room with a pile of clean towels and, turning a chair around so that he rested his arms on the back of it just like a cowboy might, sat directly in front of Heather and Joe.

Heather felt slightly uncomfortable as the pair of eyes, as blue and terrible as the ocean, seemed to stare right through her for a second. She knew that she was about to get a lecture. Adults were always serious when they wanted to lecture you about something. Usually lectures meant being banned from doing something you liked. Heather began to fear the worst; would Joe's grandpa ban them from hanging out together? She remembered that Joe had told her that he had been forbidden to go into the sea.

Heather challenged the icy gaze; 'Thank you very much for saving my life sir,' she said peeping over the top of her hot chocolate. To her amazement, a tear welled up in the corner of his eye and got bigger and bigger until it made its slow journey down the old man's cheek and into his beard.

'Call me Jim.'

Joe's grandfather growled, breaking the ice, and with a large sniff plucked a bright handkerchief out of his neatly pressed shirt pocket.

'Ok,' said Heather, 'thanks for saving my life, Jim.'

She smiled. Jim smiled too.

'It was nothing,' he said.

'No it wasn't!' Joe suddenly piped up. 'Grandpa had seen us through the telescope and he was on his way down to the beach to tell me off for going near the water when he saw you go under and not come up. Lucky you had your knife eh grandpa? Go on, show Heather.'

The old man stood up, revealing a huge Bowie knife in a leather pouch at his side.

'Grandpa strode into the sea and cut you free from some netting or something, said you was lucky to be alive and that we would be the death of him.'

Joe stopped, his grandpa had put the knife away again and had motioned for him to be quiet.

'Now then young, 'erm, lady.' Jim started in his gruff voice.

'You can call me Heather,' she said.

'Ok, Miss Heather', continued Jim, his face cracking a slight smile, 'can we keep this our secret? Seeing that you are Ok and all, I reckon that there is no need to alarm your parents. I saw what you were doing, helping Joe learn to swim and I reckon that you are alright, so I don't mind you two hanging out as long as you promise me to keep him away from deep water until he can swim like you. Seems like you need to be a bit more careful in the water yourself young miss. It's always when we think we are safe that life can get very dangerous very quickly. Never underestimate the power of the sea. That's how...'

Jim's voice trailed off abruptly and he gave a quick glance at Joe before affixing Heather with his formidable stare again.

'Yes Jim,' said Heather meekly.

'Right then,' said Jim as he stood up, 'I can't stand around here all day rescuing teenagers from the folly of youth.'

Then, just as he was about to leave, he turned and looked straight at Heather once more.

'Young, erm Miss Heather, do you remember what you said when you came round? You called a name, a name I haven't heard in a long time, do you remember what you said?'

Heather thought for a second then, as if from a long way away she seemed to hear a woman's voice calling out the name Raven.

'Oh yes, that's weird, I remember, Raven?' said Heather.

Jim started, he let out a long, slow breath and rocked slightly on the balls of his feet. He seemed to visibly age, his body stooped a little and he looked incredibly sad.

'Where did you hear that name?' he asked, his voice losing its growl and sounding as soft as the bearskin in which Heather and Joe were wrapped in.

'I don't know' said Heather, 'this may sound daft, but I think I heard it whilst I was under the water.

'Why do you ask?'

Heather managed to recall her fleeting, near-death vision of the lady who had called out to her. It all seemed a bit confused in Heather's mind so she decided to not to mention it. She didn't want Jim to think that she was losing her grip on reality. Jim frowned as if he read Heather's mind. He sighed and looked uncomfortable. He went to stand up and leave the room but then he paused and his gaze fell on Joe.

'It was Joe's father's American Indian name, given to him when he became a man.'

Jim turned and strode out of the living room. In the distance the waves crashed on the beach and the seagulls cried their mournful cry, but the two children sat completely still for a moment. Heather was aware that Joe was struggling with something, and she felt it unwise to speak until he had reached his own conclusion.

'Grandpa hasn't mentioned daddy in ages,' said Joe, 'and I'm afraid that he will start blaming himself all over again.'

'What's an Indian name?' asked Heather gently.

'It's the name given to an Indian when he becomes a man. My father was a north American Indian and that was his name. Maybe I told you that already?' said Joe, looking at Heather as if he was slightly unsure whether to cry or laugh.

'It was the weirdest thing. I heard a woman's voice call the name to me. She was swimming towards me when I was drowning. Joe, it was the woman in the picture, your mother, I saw her when I was losing consciousness.'

Joe suddenly jumped up. His brow had darkened. Heather recognised an old hurt rising in Joe as an uncontrollable anger he couldn't deal with.

'What? That's impossible! 'he shouted, 'you're lying! You're mad! I think you should go now!'

Joe leapt up and stormed out of the room, almost knocking over Isabella, who had just come in her arms full. She frowned momentarily, turned to go after Joe then sighed, smiled, and instead hurried over to Heather. Isabella had an armful of assorted clothes in her arms.

'Don't worry miss Heather; oh the men in this house are so caught up in their past they don't notice what's in front of their noses. Come, don't fret, Joe will be fine by the morning and will have remembered that it was you that had the terrible time and that he had no right to be so rude. I'm afraid he stills swings between missing his parents and trying his hardest to not blame them for not being here.

Heather felt hurt and shocked and abandoned by her new friend all at the same time. She cursed herself for sharing such a ridiculous story with Joe. As she tried on dry clothes with Isabella carefully and gently helping her Heather wondered if she was losing her grip on reality. What's more the dream from the previous night had returned and with it a whole whirl of mixed emotions. Heather's knees buckled slightly but Isabella easily steadied her and taking stock of the situation distracted Heather by drawing her attention to the clothes that Heather now wore.

There, that's you, why those clothes really suit you even if they look slightly out of place today.'

Isabella led Heather to a large mirror. Heather smiled, the dress was wonderfully embroidered, and it went right down to the ground. It looked as if it had come out of an old cowboy movie. Isabella finished the effect by tying a pinafore round Heather's waist and they both laughed as Heather did a wee curtsy.

'It must have been in the family for ages, probably Joe's grandmother's or maybe even his mother's Sunday best,' said Isabella. 'The young folk still wore dresses like this at special occasions then you know. These must have been important to Jim to hang on to. Well he won't miss them. I know for a fact that trunk hasn't been opened for ages. '

'If you don't mind me asking, what actually happened to Joe's poor parents?'

Isabella stood quietly for a second and began to absent-mindedly plait Heather's long hair.

'Your hair is as long as hers was. It's not for me to say miss Heather,' said Isabella. 'Joe's mother was his Grandpa's only daughter and I reckon he sees something of her in you. I have never seen him so soft with an outsider. So, I think you should come visit us some more, maybe one day they'll tell you what happened, but I reckon those two have to face up to the past and make their peace with it. Sorry my darling, some things are best left until the time is right. Are you Ok to get home?' asked Isabella quickly changing the subject; 'I can come with you if you want?'

'Oh yes, I'll be OK,'

Apart from a sore nose and throat from coughing and choking on the seawater she actually felt fine. Heathered wondered if her near death experiences had affected her mind. For some unknown reason Heather felt really light almost as if a great fear had been lifted from her forever.

'You had better tell your parents that the wind caught your clothes and flung them into the sea when you were swimming,' said Isabella with a slightly mischievous and conspiratorial wink. 'I'm afraid what with all that splashing about you were doing nobody thought to rescue your clothes from the tide. I think they must be well off to America by now.'

Heather chuckled at the idea of her clothes turning up on a foreign beach.

'Here,' said Isabella, 'take these cakes I've baked back home with you and please keep the dress. You have done me a great service teaching young master Joe to swim. His grandfather wouldn't let him near the water, too terrified that the sea would claim his life as well.'

'As well?' said Heather. 'Was that how Joe's parents died? Did his parents drown?'

Isabella had turned away and Heather realised that that was all she was going to get out of her.

'Thanks for the cakes,' she said and gave the surprised Isabella a kiss on the cheek, 'don't worry, I'll visit again soon.'

Isabella led Heather downstairs. As they passed in front of the large painting of the two proud American Indians Heather noticed that in the scenery behind them was the sea and on the sea were lots of fishing boats, just like her father's. The fishing boats were surrounded by canoes and on the horizon a great storm cloud was gathering. As she looked up at the proud faces of the young couple standing so strong in their traditional clothing Heather felt as if they had been caught just before going on a great adventure. Something in the eyes of Joe's mother reminded Heather of

Ran. It was the same strong, severe but wise look that scared you and comforted at the same time.

Heather waved goodbye to Isabella as she left but the door had already closed. She walked down the path to the gate and spun round, suddenly certain that she was being watched but all she could see as she stared at the windows of the house was the reflection of the sky and clouds.

Poor Joe thought Heather as she began the walk down the hill to her home. No wonder he had been scared of the water. Losing family at sea was something she could identify with. She knew that her village had felt the sad and sudden loss of many sons over the years as their small fishing vessels had foundered in the heavy seas and violent storms that sometimes blew up out of nowhere. As a young child Heather had stood with the scared women on the harbour, looking out to sea, eyes fixed on the horizon, desperately straining their eyes to locate the first glimpses of the returning fishing fleet.

It didn't take Heather long to walk down the twisty path to the harbour. She still felt strangely elated. Pushing open the low door to the cottage she went in. Heather's mother greeted her with a mixture mild curiosity and anger at her daughter carelessly losing her clothes. At least they were her old jeans and jersey Maria thought quietly to herself in exasperation. Ss soon as she had stopped being cross she started to tease Heather regarding her new look.

'Well that will teach you not to forget to put your clothes under a nice heavy stone. I don't know, only you could go for a swim and come back with a new party dress.'

Leaning closer, Heather's mother began to admire the intricate detail on the dress.

'I used to wear a dress like that when I was small, and your grandmother certainly did when she was a child,' she reminisced.

'But this is an American dress,' said Heather.

'Well I guess a lot of us went over there looking for a better life so perhaps our clothes were similar. Anyway, you had better take it off so that it doesn't get damaged. I must thank Isabella for the cakes,' said Heather's mum as she placed them on a plate. 'They smell delicious and it will save me from having to bake today. As long as your grandpa doesn't eat them all first that is!'

Heather took a sandwich and one of Isabella's excellent spiced apple and cinnamon cakes to her room. She felt really tired; it had been a long and exhausting day. Heather's brush with death, although absolutely flooring her, had left her with a weird and slightly comforting sense of peace. It was as if the whole world had just become simple and pure again. Every detail of her bedroom seemed clear. Her aquarium glowed brightly and seemed serene as the filter bubbled away. As Heather fell into a kind of quiet and tired reverie she felt brave enough to think about Ran again. Somehow the day's experience had put the whole world into perspective.

What was it that Ran had told her in that terrible vision? All of Ran's anger had centred on the new fishing nets. Heather shuddered as she recalled the image of the poor seal, its lifeless body wrapped up in the strong twine of fishing net. It was so unfair, the poor defenceless creature drowned by nets just like her father used. Heather felt an edge of anger approaching in her like a far-off thundercloud. She clenched her fists and resolved to marshal her limited resources to come to the aid of all the sea life she could. There must be some way that her family and the small fishing community could make an honest living and not harm precious sea creatures. Heather decided that in the morning she would ask her father about the new nets he was buying and tell him of her fears and worries. Surely he would listen to his only daughter. Heather felt confident that her father would listen to her pleas, surely she could make him see reason. Besides, Heather thought, her anger now growing into a large storm across her brow, if all the fish vanished from the ocean then he would be out of a job, and so would the whole village.

Heather lay down on her bed and gazed at the gentle movement in her aquarium. She listened to the soft bubbling of the filter and watched the reflections of the light on the water's surface dance on her ceiling. With a deep sigh she realised that her eyes felt heavy and in a couple of moments she was sound asleep.

****

Heather was not surprised when she awoke to find that it was the middle of the night and that she was still wearing her dress. Her mother must have looked in because the curtains were pulled shut and she had her duvet laid over her.

She lay still, holding her breath: what had woken her? On the very edge of her consciousness she discerned a faint sound. It sounded like beautiful and far off singing. It was faint but sounded like the tinkling voices of choir of a thousand small angels. As Heather's eyes grew accustomed to the darkness she sat bolt upright and held her breath to try and identify where the sound was coming from. In the dim light of the aquarium she could see the outline of the huge shell that she had found.

Heather carefully got out of bed and tiptoed over to the shell. Gently turning it onto its side she gasped. A deep and beautiful choral sound seemed emanate out of it, just as if the shell was a loudspeaker. Some of the voices sounded like angels, they were so high and pure. The singing grew louder then, deep within the layers of the magical song, Heather heard her name being called over and over. The beautiful voices seemed to be calling Heather outside towards the sea. She could hear the soft sounds of the ocean carried in the song. Heather, now wide awake, knew that she had to get down to the small beach as quickly as possible. There was magic in the air and she felt an electric thrill in her stomach. Heather slipped into her tracksuit and trainers and crept downstairs. Quietly opening the front door, she stepped outside into the moonlight and made for the sea once again.

8

The Spiral Dance

Heather hurried down the sandy path that lay beside the harbour wall. In moments she was standing on the beach, feeling the sand crunch beneath her trainers. She was warm enough in the cool night air but felt slightly worried what her parents would say if they learnt of her nocturnal activities. Heather felt wide awake, the few hours' sleep had somehow completely recharged her batteries and the warm sea breeze and gentle sound of the lapping waves invigorated her senses. As Heather turned her gaze to the beach she felt a flutter of excitement in her stomach. A thrill of anticipation coursed through her young body and she strained her eyes into the dim light out across the waves and towards the sea.

Heather jumped slightly as she heard a sound just beside her and turned to see a huge grey seal shuffling up. Her heart jumped with joy as she recognised her new friend, and a sense of relief flooded through her.

'Oh Ran, it's you, I am so glad, oh my god, I was so worried, I thought, I feared, I was worried that you were dead.'

Heather dropped to her knees and flung her arms around the seal with relief. She pressed her face into the silky softness of the seal's coat and laughed with a mixture of tears and joy.

'Hello daughter of the sea,' said the seal. 'Are you well? I heard your cries yesterday and I was worried. You did not call my name, so I could not help.'

'Oh Ran,' said Heather, almost sobbing, 'I thought it was you in the net.'

'No little one, poor Bruin was old and grey and not fast enough, he followed the fish and was drowned in an old net. Seals cannot always see man's nets.' 'Today a seal is a seal, tomorrow we return to the ocean, all comes from her, all returns to her, Bruin will be remembered by us all.'

The seal looked straight into Heather's eyes and the huge brown orbs were filled with concern.

'I called you here young Heather to help you,' said Ran. 'What you saw in your vision of awakening can be a terrible burden for someone so young. You will need to see further and deeper than any human has done before. You need more help and reassurance though. Your Grandmother was our friend and she wants us to instruct you. She is worried that your young heart is not strong enough for your task.'

Heather thought of the vision she had seen last time she was with Ran and shuddered for a moment. A quick scan of her emotions made Heather realise that something fearful inside her had left. An ancient and unresolved fear of the power and might of the sea had gone. She wondered if she no longer feared death itself anymore. Her near-death experience the day before had brought Heather peace, not anxiety.

'Do you know what Ran, I'm not sure that I'm afraid of anything anymore. I'm just angry and sad at the same time. I'm angry that we humans cause so much suffering and I'm sad that I'm so small and insignificant. What on earth can I do to help?'

Ran chuckled softly at Heather's passionate outburst. It struck Heather that a seal's laugh was the sweetest thing she had ever heard. It sounded like the peals of distant bells yet was as infectious as the chuckle of a baby.

'It is good to be brave little one, it is good to have faced your fears but never underestimate this universe my child. Its many challenges require we use our lives sensibly, carefully and wisely. We never run knowingly into danger unless first we have understood it. We all need the help of each other in times of danger. Our weakness is not calling on each other for help when we need it,' said Ran warmly.

Heather let Ran's words of advice and comfort sink into her mind. It seemed to Heather that the world had changed so very much in such a short time. Loosening her hug on Ran she aired a thought that had been scratching away at the back of her mind like a dormouse in a biscuit jar.

'Did you know my Grandmother?' enquired Heather, 'Did you meet with her like you do with me? Grandpa says that she used to be down here talking to the sea all the time.'

'I knew your Grandmother well and she will always be alive to us, even now,' said Ran.

Heather looked slightly crestfallen.

'I miss her you know' she said, 'grandpa said that I would need her. I wish she had told me about you. I seem to have so much to learn about the world. Nothing is what I thought it was.'

'You dear grandmother didn't speak with me as you do my child,' said Ran. 'Your task is more than hers. The world has spun faster and faster since her passing. The seas have been dredged for life with greater and greater ferocity. Life is vanishing from my world quicker than I can count. Your Grandmother's ocean was not in such an urgent need then, at least not in these waters. It was in Raven's home waters that these troubles began.'

'But who is this Raven?' asked Heather, 'Oh, and Ran, do you know anything about a Native American Indian lady?'

Ran declined to answer. Instead she raised her gleaming nose into the air and gave a soft whistle. The long mournful note echoed out across a sea now kissed by the light of the waxing moon and the note reverberated long after Ran had turned back to face Heather again.

'There are many stories for you to learn little one. Tonight, you will need a guide for you are to travel far.'

Suddenly a smaller seal beached beside Ran and shuffled out of the water until it stood in front of Heather. The seal looked directly at Heather and in Heather's mind she heard the clear voice of another woman speaking to her.

'Hello Heather, my daughter of the ocean, do you recognise me with your human eyes, or are they still clouded by tradition and fear?'

The seal's voice was so familiar to Heather that her mouth hung open and she found herself gasping like a beached fish. The seal's voice brought memories flooding back to her. It couldn't be, there was no way but ... Heather squealed with surprise.

'Grandmother?' she cried. 'You sound just like my grandmother.'

The moon was still strong and cast plenty of light for Heather to see the young seal. As she looked the seal's form seemed to shimmer in her mind. The seal gently placed its head on one side and then smiled – just like her Grandmother used to do when Heather was finding something difficult to understand. Everything in the seal's eyes and manners seemed to confirm Heather's first thought. This was impossible though, wasn't it? She closed her mouth and gulped.

'Trust your first thought, your intuition,' Heather heard Ran say.

The young seal started to nuzzle Heather and then it looked straight into her eyes and spoke clearly in Heather's mind.

'I was once a grandmother to a small dark-haired girl whom I see has now almost grown up into a fine young woman.'

Heather dropped to her knees, gasping with amazement she couldn't speak, and tears started to flow down her cheeks. She was overcome with a sensation of relief and amazement. Powerful emotions of loss and disbelief fought with hope and excitement. Heather hugged the young seal as hard as she could and buried her face in its soft fur. Her tears of joy mingled with the salty dampness of the seal's coat.

'Grandmother, is that really you, can this be possible, am I dreaming again?'

'Is not all a dream' said Ran mysteriously, 'knowing what your part is in the great dream is the question that all beings must find an answer to.'

Heather's grandmother seemed to smile and glow with pleasure and gentle kindness.

'Yes, it's really me my darling young one. I am the same and yet so different. I have returned but a short while ago. I am now younger than you in years yet so much older. I am here to help you this night Heather my darling. I hope I don't scare you. Does this knowledge bring you happiness?'

Heather's mind whirled like a tornado. The ancient stories were true. Humans could really come back as seals. Somehow her Grandmother was now a young seal speaking with an ancient voice.

'Well yes, of course, I mean it's amazing, oh it is really you. Grandpa will be amazed.'

'No my child, you must not share these secrets with the unsighted. They could not deal with these truths and it would only bring them upset and greater pain. Some memories must be left as they were found. They are a balm to soften the passage of life. One day he will know and he will be able to choose a new life for himself.'

'But, but, how come you are now a seal Grandmother?' Asked Heather hugging the animal tightly.

'Still so many questions, even you, even after your visions – you know the truth Heather; you are just starting to remember it again in this lifetime? Most humans have forgotten their ancient link with the sea. Some remember only in dreams. Some only remember in nightmares. I was born knowing and, when I left my last body, I chose to return. That's all little one. It is very simple. I have much work to do here. The great ocean is very angry with the world of men.

I'm afraid that humans need somebody to plead their case. It does not look good.'

Heather let her grandmother's voice wash over her. It was as if with each word an ancient memory and insight unlocked deep within Heather's soul. Her grandmother continued with a sense of urgency.

'Now, enough questions, I am here to help you. The sight is upon you and you are starting to remember. I am afraid that with this power comes a huge responsibility. The burden of it may feel too heavy to carry at times. The gifts will need to be used and used wisely. We all have a place and a time within the great dream. You face a challenging task, but you are to have all the help you need.'

As the seal spoke Heather found herself remembering her grandmother's kind face. It was her grandmother who had taken her for long walks beside the sea to comb the beach for treasures. It was her grandmother who had taught Heather all of the names of the birds, fish and sea life and told her the names for all of the creatures who ended up in Heather's aquarium.

'Yes, you asked many questions even then,' said the seal, as if reading Heather's mind. 'Now listen my darling young one. Soon you will begin to see and know much more than you dreamt of. You will be able to speak with the elements and understand their thoughts. You will have the power of the Word, yet you must remember that these gifts are not to be abused or treated as playthings. Spend as much time as you can beside the sea. Learn her rhythm and her moods and learn as much as you can about what man is doing to the great ocean mother and to her children.'

The seal brought her soft grey face close to Heather's.

'You will be the link between sea and man. You have to make them listen and that will not be easy. Men are deaf to anything other than their own desires and are stubborn. Even the role of the wise woman is no longer respected and celebrated and is now feared and thought of as mere superstition.'

Heather began to stroke the seal's soft fur and marvelled at how her voice tinkled in her head like a thousand small bells or like the song of birds at dawn.

'Listen little one. The ocean wants to share her harvest with humans in remembrance of her own origins. Humans were once creatures of the sea millions of years ago yet now they have forgotten. Early humans lived between land and water. Human mothers would return to the arms of the ocean to give birth and let her protect them from land animals. A child would be birthed into the water, the sea would support and soothe the mother. All babies can swim Heather they just forget once they have been on dry land too long. But now humans dwell only on the land and they only see the ocean as a source of food and somewhere to dump their rubbish and waste. The poisons from the land threaten our young and humans use their technology to empty the oceans. The great mother ocean is in danger, terrible danger, a danger that will speed up and kill all life on this planet.'

'That is what Ran told me grandma,' said Heather suddenly scared again. I saw a terrible vision of father's boat being destroyed, what does it mean?'

The seal seemed to grow sad and lent in and began to nuzzle Heather's long hair.

'It means my child that things have become critical. The whole future of life in the ocean is hanging in the balance.

Mother Ocean needs human beings to listen to her or she will have to try and stop the destruction. The whole cycle of life on the planet comes from the ocean. She is the Great Mother of All and she is angry and hurting. She shows you what might be and what does not need to come to pass. We must work to ensure that the terrible dreams remain as dreams and not become a reality. Man ignores the fact that he creates deserts on the land. Now he ignores that he is creating a desert of the ocean. He has fallen asleep. We must wake him from his sleep of ignorance and indifference before it is too late.'

Heather shivered in the night air and felt a sadness tug at her earlier sense of joy.

'What can Mother Ocean do to us grandma?'

The seal breathed in the night air deeply and then continued.

'The ocean is elemental, she is the life giver of life to all, she is the cradle of all things and she is so much more than just water. She can commune with the other elements to engage their help when she thinks it appropriate. The winds will conspire with her to create huge waves and terrible storms to banish men, but even that may not save her.'

Heather felt a great weight come to rest on her young shoulders.

'But I am only a child. What can I do? Nobody listens to me. No one would believe me. They would think that I had lost my mind. I would be locked up somewhere.'

The seal gently moved away from Heather and lent on Ran. Ran was huge in comparison to the young seal and she turned her large head and great brown eyes onto Heather. Ran spoke, and her voice was strong and calming.

'You are not long to be a woman Heather and people are already listening to you. You show them who you are by your actions, by your love for the sea, by your sight. You will have our support and you have the help of others. The newcomers bring a great curse and a great riddle and a great hope for your community. You must learn the answers and bring everyone together.'

Heather's grandmother shuffled towards Heather again and leaned in to the kneeling girl who hugged her tightly again. Heather's grandmother spoke once more.

'I chose this life as a seal to tell the great Ocean Mother that humans are not all bad. I went to her and begged for help. Now She has replied. She has said that She hears my truth and that She knows humans have fallen asleep, fallen into ignorance. She has said that She loves all life equally. Now Heather, listen to Ran, she wishes to initiate you, and introduce you to the universe. Don't fear her or this journey, I shall swim beside you.'

The huge seal moved closer to Heather and her grandma and towering over the kneeling girl made her stand to meet her gaze.

'Look into my eyes child,' said Ran and her gentle voice echoed like small bells inside Heather's mind.

Heather turned and looked straight into the large warm brown eyes of the seal. Ran's soft gaze washed over her, and she felt her senses open like the fronds of a sea anemone. Deep within her soul Heather felt and heard the ocean. It called to something unfathomable within her being. Suddenly Heather became aware of her young body lifting up into the sky. She felt lighter than air. It was as if a blanket of warm energy surrounded her. Then with great force she felt herself dive into the ocean. The waves parted and Heather was flung forward at a tremendous speed. The water parted in front of her and glowed green as it passed around heather's body. Heather felt calm and exhilarated at the same time. It was as if she was in a dream that was somehow more real than life itself. As she rushed forwards through the depths of the ocean Heather was aware that beside her swam two seals, one small and one as large as Heather herself.

Together they seemed to travel great distances. Heather became aware of tropical seas, Arctic oceans, shoals of fish, pods of whales, schools of dolphins and porpoises and she heard their songs, their sounds. The experience thrilled her. It was as if she could open her mind and see right around the world. She found that she could follow the line of a whale's song. The strange and haunting melody became a language to Heather; she was amazed that the thread of sound continued for thousands of miles. The notes talked of love and family and where the best food could be found and it spanned whole oceans before it was picked up and replied to. She passed by coral reefs, their white palaces bustling with life and shot past sharks circling around a wreck deep on the ocean floor. The three of them went deeper and deeper into water that seemed so dark and so cold that life itself seemed to disappear. Yet a great luminance spread out around them and Heather saw the strangest cloud, a rainbow kaleidoscope of fish glistening like jewels. They passed deep valleys teeming with creatures she had never seen. Many looked like monsters, yet all life seemed to acknowledge her and she felt a great understanding of how perfectly every living creature seemed to live in harmony with every other creature. It was as Heather could understand the great cycle of life and death, not as brief moment, but as a continuing spiral dance continuing onwards through eternity. She realised that life began with the smallest microscopic creatures and then evolved upwards and upwards to the dolphins and mighty whales.

Then suddenly the great rush stopped, and Heather found herself hovering, suspended in front of a radiant being that was floating in a great hall of water and light. Heather thought it was as if the sun had fallen into the depths of the ocean. Huge corals were illuminated by the golden glow and millions of fish and sea creatures sparkled in the light. The being of light shimmered and moved slowly. It was as if She, for Heather sensed that the being was female, was communing with all of the sea at once. Before Heather had time to consider her situation further the being began to move towards her. The light was so bright Heather wondered if she would be blinded. The being of light reached out a long, feathery strand of illumination and touched Heather in the centre of her forehead. Inside Heather's head multiple universes seemed to explode at once. It was as if a vast quantity of fireworks went off in her mind. Then suddenly, just as Heather heard a great peal of laughter, she felt herself shooting up towards the surface of the ocean.

Heather's consciousness seemed to expand, and it felt to Heather that the ocean met the sky and then became one with the sky. Then the three of them swam up and out of the sea into the path of the moon going higher and higher until the earth slowly spun as an emerald jewel far beneath them. Heather could see that the universe was like the oceans, a great endless sea within which amazing planets were suspended. The stars seemed like bright lights illuminating the great depths of a being in whom whole galaxies were made to spiral and swirl before her. It was as if the millions and millions of bright shining galaxies moved in a great slow dance swimming through the blackness of space.

Heather could see the whole universe stretching out before her. Galaxies joined a flickering dance that surrounded her. Great beams of illumination filtered through the blackness and lit up the heavens.

Then, just like colossal translucent whales, huge entities swam slowly across galaxies. Heather was not sure if they were angels or vast swarms of beings but their song was deep and beautiful and seemed to hold together the very fabric of space itself. Their presence was awesome yet reassuring and suddenly Heather felt very, very small indeed and humbled in front of such brilliance.

The amazing dance seemed to speed up and Heather watched galaxies whizzing past her at a tremendous rate. Individual planets appeared as gleaming islands rushing through the midst of an endless ocean all spinning around each other in a never-ending dance. After some time Heather saw a small green and blue shining jewel fly towards her. With a gasp she recognised the planet Earth approaching them at great speed. Heather, Ran and her grandmother flew down through the soft caress of whispering clouds, down towards the great ocean, down and across the surface of the sea until she was standing once more on the wet sand of the little bay clutching the young seal at her side. A great wave of energy passed over Heather and then pulsed back out towards the sea. She rocked slightly on her feet and collapsed to her knees on the damp sand of the beach.

As the vision ended and began to dissolve once more into the dawn sky Heather experienced a great joy rising in her heart. She tingled from the ends of her toes to the end of her nose. As Heather looked down at her body she saw ripples of light pass over and through her. She thought she could see spinning galaxies within her very own being, millions of minute worlds reaching into infinity.

Heather felt a great sense of belonging and wonder at the magic of it all. She felt huge and small at the same time. She felt more alive than she could ever remember. And even the damp sand under her body seemed to sparkle and teem with life as ancient as the stars in the sky.

'You now see that all is connected, that all is One and you have remembered what most humans have forgotten,' said Ran. 'This dream must now grow within you. It will make you strong; it will make you able to speak with the authority of creation. You have passed through the veil, you have entered the great dream and now you can create within Her'

'But now', her grandmother's voice was now firm, 'you must return to your bed and get some sleep.'

The seal's voice was steady and commanding, and Heather found herself quickly hugging both seals and turning to walk back up to the small harbour and her house. She sped along as if gliding just a few inches above the ground. She could hear the joyful laughter of her new friends echoing down in the cove and it lifted her steps and filled her heart with a wonderful feeling of joy. Slipping quietly inside her small house Heather went straight back to her bed just as the first rays of dawn's early light danced at the edges of her curtains. As she lay on her back she felt as if she was still floating on the ocean and inside her felt as if she was made up of an endless sea of stars. As she looked at her aquarium in the dim light of dawn it seemed as if all the sea life had congregated in one place and was staring out at Heather. She dreamily waved a hand at them and then fell into the deepest sleep she had ever experienced.

9
Meeting the Elders

The gentle bubbling of the aquarium awoke Heather from her sleep and as her eyes opened and focussed on the new day she spread herself out in her bed and let the memories of the night return. She felt tingly right down to the tips of her toes. From behind her half-closed eyelids she fancied she could still see whirling galaxies and spiralling universes. The sun filtering through the curtains heralded the new day and even though Heather had only had a few hours sleep she felt alive as never before.

Her reverie was only slightly disturbed when her mother poked her head round the door to call her to breakfast. Heather raised her eyelids slightly and greeted her mother with a smile that would have charmed the sea herself. Heather's mum, encouraged by the smile that greeted her, entered the room, with washing under one arm her other hand resting on the small yet visible bump of her tummy.

'Well somebody has woken up on the right side of bed today,' she smiled, and after a pause added, 'You look different today.'

She sat on the bed beside Heather thinking to herself that her daughter's brown eyes, full of their usual wonder, somehow looked different, even deeper and more 'seal like' today. She stroked Heather's hair and looked around the tidy room, dominated by the books and pictures of sea life and the aquarium. Heather's mother always felt closer to the natural elements that surrounded them when she was pregnant. Her condition also made her feel even closer to her daughter.

'I hope I didn't wake you last night, I was feeling rather sick. It must be morning sickness, I always feel rubbish in the early stages.' After Heather didn't reply she added, 'are you all right my love?'

Heather, who would have usually leapt out of bed chattering nineteen to the dozen, was content to lie and smile like a new-born baby.

'I do feel different today mum,' she said. 'I had an amazing dream last night.'

Heather felt a rush of desperation to share her vision with her mother but was mindful of the warnings the seals had given her.

'Do you ever miss grandmother?' she asked.

A small cloud passed briefly over her mother's face.

'Well yes, I do sometimes my sweetheart,' she said. 'But I just think that she has gone some place good and that makes me feel better. I still talk to her sometimes you know.'

'You do?' said Heather half sitting up.

'Yes, whenever I feel sad or confused or worried. It seems to help.'

'Me to,' said Heather.

'Right lazy bones,' said her mum, 'it's time you were up, its late and the day has long started.'

With a laugh her mother went to pull back the covers. Heather didn't hear her mum gasp. She still felt so dreamy, she could almost imagine herself still swimming in the stars. It felt to Heather as if whole universes were swimming inside her like shoals of small fish in the sea. She was hardly aware of her mother's soft voice as she spoke.

'Oh, my darling little girl you have become a woman. I thought that you looked different this morning. I guess it's earlier than I had hoped for but there you go, it comes to us all.'

Heather half closed her eyes, her mum was right, the vision had made her feel completely different and somehow inside she felt young, old and grown up all at once. She still chuckled like a child though.

'You can stay home today if you want, you might feel a bit weak and fragile for a while,' said her mother.

Heather opened her eyes properly not quite hearing her mother. She had left the room and returned with a damp sponge and a white paper towel that looked not unlike a cuttlefish that sometimes washed up on the shore. Heather looked down at her body to see if her toes were there and gave a gasp of horror. Her thighs were covered in blood.

'Mum,' she called out, 'mum what's happened to me?'

Suddenly she felt a great terror. Was she dying, had her initiation done something terrible to her and now she was paying the price?

'Don't fret my darling; you have started your period. You are a woman now. Hmm, just after a full moon as well, not surprising. I started early too,' said her mother cleaning her up.

Heather sat in wonderment as her mother explained all the details about being a woman. She guessed that somewhere in the back of her mind she had known these things but now it suddenly seemed so real, and just a little bit scary. She learned that women bleed once a month at the end of a cycle. She learned that her body was merely shedding her first small egg of potential life to make way for a fresh new one. She learned that this was a phase that happened every month and that the bleeding and grumbling tummy that accompanied this great mystery simply heralded a brand-new cycle.

'Wow' said Heather, all of her fear vanishing immediately. 'You mean that I could have babies just like my seahorse, just like you now?'

Heather stared at her mother and her swollen tummy. Her mother felt as if she was momentarily caught in the brightness of her daughter's gaze. It seemed to both of them that the world had just shifted and would never be quite the same again. Her mother sniffed for a moment and brushed a small tear from her eye.

'Oh my child,' she said hugging her close, 'you are still so young. Yes, in theory you could have a baby, you are now a woman and we must celebrate this in the correct way, but you should wait a good few years before wanting a child.

You have your whole life ahead of you and just because you can doesn't mean that you should. A baby is a very, very demanding thing and you are still far too young for that responsibility. Too many young girls don't wait and then lose their dreams.'

'Don't worry mum,' said Heather, content to be a child once more as her mother lifted her into her arms and carried her into the bathroom where a steaming bath was running. 'I want to train to be a vet or a marine biologist and see the world, and save the ocean and...'

'Gosh, so many things, well I am here for you whatever. First let's get you clean and then you and I can go into town together. My treat. This is a special day and it's a day every mother and daughter should spend together.'

Heather was thrilled. It was as if she suddenly felt a deeper bond with her mum. The thought of just the two of them going into town was almost as exciting as her experience of the night before. Town was not somewhere they travelled to very often, everybody was always so busy with work and Heather had school.

'Erm, what about school though mum?'

Heather closed her eyes and let her mother gently bath her as if she was a small child. She loved school and loved to learn about the world but today she still felt so floaty and dreamy school seemed a million miles away. In fact she wondered what on earth school could teach her that would compare to what she had seen the night before.

'Don't worry about that my angel, I will call Miss Boniface, I think she will understand.'

'Oh, of course, she is a woman too, she will have to understand.'

Heather felt proud and conspiratorial at the same time.

'Yes, laughed her mum, she is, but I wouldn't try pulling that one too often in class if I was you.'

That morning at breakfast everyone treated her a little differently. It was as if it was her birthday or as if she had just won a prize or something, but she noticed that the men in her family seemed to be sympathetic but suddenly unsure of how to be. Robert stepped around his young sister as if she was made of eggshells and couldn't leave to go to the boats fast enough.

'Don't worry, it will pass.'

Heather's mother smiled knowingly as her father displayed an uncharacteristic awkwardness when he went to hug Heather before leaving to meet the new nets.

'They soon forget our challenges. They don't really want to know. You are still a little girl to your father and you will always be his little princess and that is how it should be and has always been. In the old days', she continued by way of explanation, 'boys would have a party to celebrate them becoming a man. It is called a rite of passage. In some countries they still do it. In one country young men are made to wear birdcages full of songbirds on their heads to tell everyone else that for a short while they should not be expected to be sensible. In some countries the young men are still expected to catch or hunt a dangerous animal.'

'Wow,' said Heather, 'what about women?'

Her mother paused.

'Well she said, in our culture we would have gathered together, sung songs and told stories. You would have been sung into womanhood.'

Heather's mother started to hum a strange and haunting melody, which instantly made Heather feel waves of emotion flood over her. Her mum broke off suddenly, she seemed slightly ashamed.

'Oh dear', she said, 'I'm afraid I can't quite remember how it goes.'

From deep within Heather an ancient memory returned. Then Heather started to hum. Somehow she knew the melody. She began to sing softly in a tongue that made no sense to her. She could hear the words in her head yet they had only a fleeting impression of what they meant. She stopped and smiled at her mum who was looking at her with amazement.

'Wherever did you get to learn that old tune?' she asked as she started brushing her daughter's hair. 'It must have been from your grandmother whilst you were very young. She was always singing to you as you lay sleeping.'

Heather's mother had a faraway look in her eye and momentarily looked sad. She saw her mum's deep sadness as old memories resurfaced and she desperately wanted to share her experiences of the night before. Heather gave a small sigh. Deep down inside she knew that her instructions not to share her insights were right. They would have only upset, frightened and confused her mum. Moments later, like a small cloud passing away from the face of the sun her mother returned to her usual jolly self. She finished brushing Heather's hair and focussed on her daughter, who had become a woman, by clearing Heather her own space in the bathroom cabinet.

As her mother cleared out the clutter of almost finished bottles of shampoo, conditioner and face creams she told Heather that once upon a time the village elder women would have come together to make a new dress for a new woman.

'It would have been for your courting and was always fabulous and had ribbons woven into it...'

She trailed off as she caught sight of the antique dress hanging on the back of the door.

'Hmm, not unlike the one you were given yesterday,' she mused as if suddenly getting a glimpse of something outside her ken. 'I'm afraid that for many women it would have been the time to be married off and they would have been expected to work full time on the nets and rear babies and keep the house.'

'When would you get time to play and go to school and study and train to get a job?' asked Heather innocently.

Her mother smiled knowingly.

'That question, my dearest daughter, tells me that you must take my advice seriously and not get pregnant for many years to come. Your generation has time that my generation would have dreamt of. It's your time to make the best of yourself, to find out who you are, to learn, to travel, to become an independent woman. Then, and only then, should you consider the life of marriage and children.'

Although Heather's mum was concerned about her daughter she knew that Heather was a sensible and level-headed girl and hoped she had no reason to worry, at least on that score. Heather frowned for a moment then asked,

'What happened to Tim then? When he became a man? Not that he really is if you ask me. I've heard how he messes about with his mates down the pub and takes chances on his motorbike and chases all the local girls.'

'I'm afraid that the old traditions have mainly ended now. Tim just got a particularly riotous eighteenth birthday party laid on by your father and me. I seem to remember he got quite drunk. It's all about the party now – a celebration without any real depth or meaning. That's why men don't really understand why it is so important for us women to mark our passage from childhood.'

'American Indians are given a new name,' said Heather.

'Is that so, hmm I believe I once heard that,' said her mother who reflected that she was always learning something new from her daughter.

'Joe's father was a Red Indian and his name was Raven, well I think it was.'

As Heather said that she realised that she might be sharing something with her mother that she shouldn't have. Heather's mother gave a curious small smile at the mention of Joe's name, and then went to get herself ready for the trip into town.

*****

Their old car started first time and soon Heather and her mother were careering along the narrow roads that led out of their village. Past the school where the children were all outside playing before lessons started, past Joe's home and onto the main road towards town.

Saltkirk was about ten long windy miles from Heather's village and she loved to go there. It was an old town with the remains of an ancient castle and a narrow bridge that spanned the top of a loch. Saltkirk was where the fish got taken to market and this was the main reason for Heather's excitement. The old market was full of the sounds of the sea and sea life. Fishermen were always standing, arms folded, swapping stories of catches, freak waves and complaining about quotas, the government, prices and foreign vessels. Then there was the auctioneer whose calling of prices sped along in a language that seemed more ancient than the sea itself and yet it was understood by all.

'Well,' said Heather's mother, 'let's go shopping first eh hen. I mean you see enough smelly old fish at home. Your father reeks of it every time he comes off the boat.'

'Ok,' said Heather sinking into her seat. Today she felt different and she knew that it was somehow important to do what her mother suggested.

To Heather's joy her mother made the whole day all about Heather. She was allowed to buy a new dress which of course ended up being a new pair of jeans, some boots, a long-sleeved top and a breathable waterproof jacket which was reduced in the sales. Now she could stroll along the beach and beachcomb without getting cold or wet. Then she was allowed to choose some silver jewellery and even some make-up, an item usually forbidden in her house.

Heather's mum kept humming the same ancient tune that Heather had sung at breakfast. Heather found herself joining in as they wondered around the shops in a carefree manner. At lunchtime Heather was treated to a Chinese meal. This was all exotic fare for Heather who she was amazed by the flavours and the variety of food on offer, but even more star struck by a huge aquarium full of exotic looking fish that made up one of the walls of the restaurant. Heather rushed over to see the fish as soon as they had ordered. She recognised huge golden coy carp and marvelled at the majestic beauty of the fish. Her mother was relieved when the food arrived promptly because for some reason all of the large fish had congregated right in front of Heather's face, which was pressed up against the thick glass. They swirled around her daughter's reflection as if she was going to feed them. Even the staff seemed to look puzzled and then quietly asked Heather's mother if her daughter had been feeding the fish. When she said no they seemed puzzled but began to keep a close and quizzical eye on Heather. Heather's mum was relieved when her daughter returned to the table and was instantly wowed by all the flavours on her plate. She plagued her poor mother with questions on how to cook prawns like the lovely smiling people in the restaurant did. Heather was amazed by such culinary delights as chicken and sweet corn soup, spring rolls and noodles, which she thought were a bit like spaghetti but somehow nicer.

After lunch they went to the old castle and wandered around whilst their food went down. The ancient building, half covered in moss, seemed timeless. Large notice boards told you about the lives of ordinary folk and the history of a castle that had once tried to stop marauding groups of Vikings intent on their pillaging. In the museum Heather watched a video which, to her great delight, showed a girl just like her mending nets, wearing a dress like the one she had been given the day before.

Then, before the cold mists started to descend, Heather was whisked off to a small café, built in an old and crooked house, where her mother bought her a huge hot chocolate. They chatted about anything and everything. It was as if they had suddenly renewed their friendship. Heather had never seen her mother so animated. It was as if suddenly she felt she could share everything with her daughter. Heather learned loads of family secrets and was brought up to date on all of the village gossip. On just one occasion Heather saw her mother frown as if she was going to ask her daughter a question that troubled her but decided against it. Her mother clearly felt Heather was keeping something from her but decided to put it down to hormones and too much sugar. Heather was having such fun openly chatting to her mum like an adult and she desperately wanted to tell her mother everything, but Ran's stern warning kept echoing in her mind.

Heather's mum had just gone to the toilet leaving Heather to finish her marshmallows when something strange happened. A group of four old ladies who had also been holding an animated conversation at a table opposite started shouting at each other. Each wore a selection of brightly coloured clothes. Jumpers, scarves, coats, skirts, dresses and boots were all either vivid colours or had bright images of animals or butterflies on. Heather shyly noticed their long earrings and hands festooned in rings and bangles. The jingle jangling of their excited gesticulations filled the café with a cacophony of sounds. They were getting so hot up under the collar that Heather wondered if they might start a bun fight. The old women, resplendent with brightly coloured hair which finished off their almost carnivalesque appearances, kept squabbling despite a warning look from the waitress. Heather noticed that each one of the ladies was trying to get the upper hand in the conversation and that they were all speaking at the same time. Then suddenly the one with the loudest voice, a tall, thin and angular lady, stood up and pointed directly at Heather. Heather was alarmed and tried to hide her face behind her mug of chocolate. Then, even more alarmingly, all four ladies got up as one and shuffled over to where Heather was sitting. Suddenly she was hemmed in on all sides. The ladies leaned in towards her, blocking out the café around her with brightly coloured jangling mixing aromas of patchouli and frankincense.

'Erm, can I help you ladies?' enquired Heather nervously.

'She says you have the sight,' said one.

'You are too young,' said another.

'Says she sees it upon you,' said the third.

'So then my dear, please tell us which of these rings is real because we can't agree,' said the fourth.

All of the ladies were staring straight at Heather and all were holding out their ring festooned hands. Each hand was radically different, some were thin and pointy, some were a touch on the plump side but they all had beautifully manicured nails. Heather dug deep into her newfound calm, looked up and met their gazes with serenity. None of the old ladies looked dangerous so, taking a long slow deep breath she decided to humour them. Heather was becoming accustomed to strange events and doubted if the old ladies were stranger than her experience the previous evening. The ladies were suddenly silent. They looked expectantly at Heather. Looking at their hands, covered in jewellery, she wondered how she was going to distinguish one ring from another. She knew nothing of jewellery, but she beckoned to them to come closer; she meant to humour them in a good-natured manner. Better to play along, thought Heather.

The old ladies held out their hands in front of Heather's nose. Each extended their index fingers revealing strikingly similar rings that glimmered in the light of the café. A couple of the fingers were chubby and appeared to be straining to accommodate its ring and most were covered in pale brown liver spots. Each of the rings was huge. Heather thought the stones, the milky colours of an opal and the dark sky blue of lapis lazuli. The rings looked almost identical. The same intricate silver setting and similar woven markings. One ring immediately caught Heather's attention. It was on a long finger of the tall, thin lady. Heather felt she had better say something but didn't want to upset any of them.

'They are all very nice and I've never seen so many wonderful stones.'

The thin lady leaned in a bit closer.

'This stone is for the sea,' she said, pointing to the opal, 'and this is for heaven.'

She said this lightly touching the lapis. The women fell silent and turned their attention to Heather.

'Now then,' asked the first woman. 'You have the sight; which ring is it?'

Heather looked slowly at each of the outstretched fingers and the rings. She tried squinting and bringing her face very close, but it was no good, they all seemed the same to her. They were all just rings. Heather was just about to politely explain with a reddening face to the women that she had no idea which ring was which when a strange feeling came over her. As she looked at the rings now being held right in front of her face she realised that she could hear the ocean far off inside her head. Heather blinked. The ring belonging to the thin lady, the one with the thin hands seemed to have a life of its own. The huge stone started to change colour in front of until it became a deep dark blue that seemed to swirl like the sea. Heather was vaguely aware that the old ladies gasped and then fell silent. As Heather reached out to touch the ring she saw a strange scene play out in front of her. The four women were standing on a small hill beside a loch. Behind them was the Saltkirk castle but it was no longer in ruins. The walls were covered in grass and the main battlements were covered in wooden roofs. She could smell the smoke of wood fires. The women were singing a strange and beautiful song, she recognised it, yet it was alien to her. It reminded Heather of the music she had heard the night before, the song of the angelic elemental space creatures. Then suddenly the scene changed, fires were flickering up all over the castle and the huts around it. Wild-looking men were rushing to and fro, waving swords and axes.

She saw the thin lady rushing towards her as she was being chased. She was screaming. She fell at Heather's feet, her hand outstretched and bleeding. Heather gasped – the amazing ring was on it.

Heather jumped up, almost knocking over the table. The room swam for a moment and she thought she might be sick. The tall thin lady put her hand on Heather's shoulder to steady her. Heather realised that she was breathing heavily, her eyes had filled with tears and she felt quite queasy. She took a deep breath and looked at the expectant faces of the women surrounding her. The same faces that only moments before had been running terrified from marauding Vikings. Heather reached out her trembling hand towards the ring on the thin finger she had just seen coated in blood.

'This one.'

The old ladies stood up sighing with pleasure. With one accord they became gentle and compassionate and smiled at Heather with kind, concerned smiles. One held out a handkerchief, another brushed hair from her eyes, another stroked her hand and began to hum a lullaby.

'Don't worry about visions of the past my dear,' the thin lady said gently. 'They only guide us to our potential in the present. You did well. Very well. Better than I have ever witnessed. You are a rare find indeed. Still without preparation visions can be quite unsettling. Let me introduce you to our small group ...'

Suddenly Heather's mother, returning from the toilet interrupted the gathering, her maternal instincts filling her voice with a concerned and protective edge. 'What's going on?' she said more to the women than to Heather.

'What a wonderfully kind and compassionate daughter you have my dear. She managed to solve a heated debate that we were having. So kind of her to help us. What a very special girl you have. She must be a great blessing to you.'

The thin lady's words seemed calm and bewitchingly reassuring and Heather's mum smiled and to her surprise found herself thanking them for their kindness and apologising for her previously abrupt manner. The women began to move back to their table. Each one smiled conspiratorially at Heather and paused to give Heather's mum a kind word and a blessing. The thin lady lingered a moment longer and then, when Heather's mum had her back turned to gather her coat and the numerous shopping bags that were stacked beside the table, she leaned towards Heather and gave her the huge iridescent stone ring from her finger.

'Here child,' she said, 'this ring is yours, it knows you. Blessings be upon you sister.'

Then she winked at Heather and turned to join her friends. The women shuffled to the door, waved a cheery farewell to the waitress and vanished from the shop.

'Who were they?'

Heather's mother was clutching bags and coats and was frowning with concern at Heather. Her daughter had a slightly wild-eyed look about her and appeared a little disorientated.

'Erm, I don't know mum. They were kind of weird but nice. It felt like I'd met them all before...somewhere...erm, I'm not sure why I just said that.'

Heather let her words trail off and went to stand up and grab her coat to change the subject. As Heather's mum passed her shopping bag Heather realised that she had placed the ring on her finger where it fitted as snugly as if it were specially made for her. She held up her hand for a closer inspection. She hadn't even noticed that she was wearing it.

Looking across the empty cups and saucers Maria noticed that Heather's eyes seemed far away. She wondered what Heather was thinking and why her young daughter's eyes seemed so ancient all of a sudden.

'Well you do seem to attract attention – mind you they wear clothes as brightly coloured as you. I thought you were about to run off and join a circus. What do you think they wanted?'

'I think they wanted to test me and give me a message – oh and this ring.'

Heather shyly held up her hand for her mother to see. The beautifully ornate ring flashed and glittered in the light. The stone seemed to change colour almost at will.

'Do you think I should give it back? They said the ring knew me. That was kind of weird. They were nice though and just a bit scary. They asked me to guess which ring was special. I had some kind of weird vision. I thought I saw them in the old castle, before it was knocked down and...'

Heather stopped as her mother staggered slightly and sat back down in her seat. She motioned for Heather to do the same. Then, with a soft sigh she leant forward so that no one else would hear.

'I thought I recognised them from somewhere long ago. They were erm, special women, they adhere to the old ways, the same as your grandmother. I'm sure they visited mum when she was younger, when I was little.'

Heather's mum took a deep breath as if to steady her nerves and then sighed and looked at her daughter. She leant across the table and gently stroked Heather's long dark curls.

Oh, my darling child they think that you have the sight – that's what they said to you didn't they? I saw them looking at you earlier. I thought it was weird.

Heather nodded and wondered what her mum knew. Maria looked misty eyed and thoughtful and held Heather's hand and looked at the incredible ring.

That would explain your dreams and strange behaviour recently. Now you are a woman it will be growing stronger within you. Those ladies must have seen it. That must be why they gave you that ring. Oh, I wish your grandmother was here. She would understand. While she was alive women from nearby villages often visited us. I'm sure I recognised the thin lady from before, she must be nearly a hundred if she's the same one – maybe she always looked old, my memory fails me these days. In the old days Heather they would come to the village and lead the singing and pray for the men if the storm was upon the waters. Show me the ring.'

Heather held out her hand for her mum to get a closer look. It shone and glistened. It seemed to Heather that a miniature sea swirled around in the stone.

'Well, you are a lucky little lady,' said her mum. 'Though I think that perhaps that is enough excitement for one day. Come on, let's get you home before you have any more excitement. How do you feel by the way? Are you feeling a bit weak, a bit dizzy, any pain?'

Heather was feeling fine, in fact she felt stuffed full of food and her natural good humour and curiosity had returned. She still felt the wondeful gentle calm of earlier, but the vision of the burning castle and the blood had unsettled her a little. Heather decided to unpack it later and enjoy the strange experience of the old women. She reassured her mum by smiling and nodding and moving to leave again. The two of them headed to the counter to pay.

'There is no need,' the waitress said smiling and turning away Heather's mum's money. 'Your bill has been paid,' she said, 'by the ladies who were sitting at the table opposite you.'

When Heather's mum looked confused she explained with a smile.

'They come in here all the time. They are my nice regulars. They must have taken a shine to the pair of you. They are, well, erm...quite idiosyncratic. You know, unusual but quite lovely. The tall thin one even read my palm once, and she was uncannily right. That's why I love my job. You get to meet all sorts.'

'Well I never' said Heather's mum as they headed for the car. 'Never in all my life. We must have had scones, ice cream and hot chocolate. That would have cost quite a bit. Gosh what did you say to them? I mean they even gave you a ring.'

'Nothing mum, they just chatted and wanted to see if I could tell which ring was real - the stone in this ring - like I said earlier. I guess they were just really nice and erm kinda spooky in a friendly way.'

As they packed the car with their shopping and clambered in Heather played the vision of the castle over in her mind. Maria turned on the radio and headed the car homeward and Heather kept her gaze on the darkening landscape rushing by out of the window. She could still recall the images of Viking-like men rushing around brandishing axes and the shock of the tall thin lady losing her life. As she played the images over in her mind, she opened her eyes and looked at the huge ring on her hand. The colour was once more a calm and iridescent blue. Heather considered how different the vision had been from the one she had shared with Ran and her Selkie grandmother. Both had been marvellous and terrifying in equal measure. Heather glanced at her mother who noticed from the corner of her eye and shot her a smile before concentrating on the winding road again. Heather wished that she could share everything with her mum. For the first time ever, she felt a new closeness to her. It was like they had become sisters on some level. Heather desperately wanted to share her whole truth but she heeded Ran's warnings and bit her lip to keep quiet. The most troubling thing for Heather was the realisation that the old women had somehow been able to see what she had seen. They had been able to share the same vision. What a day, Heather thought to herself. Suddenly the world seemed very different; it was a world where adults seemed to be stranger than the kids and Heather wasn't quite sure she was ready to be an adult just yet.

10

The Power
of Words

Heather and her mum kept the chat going all the way home even though the wind had risen up to greet them and was buffeting the small car. As they rounded a corner and prepared for the descent towards the harbour Heather could make out a familiar figure. A small singular outline was leaning into the wind, which was whipping his black hair in all directions. The lad looked frozen and as they made to pass him he waved frantically to the car as it entered the village.

'Mum,' called Heather. 'It's Joe, let's give him a lift, he looks frozen.'

Her mum stopped the car with a smile at the sound of concern and urgency from her daughter and flung open the door.

'Hello young man,' she said. 'Needing a lift?'

Joe clambered into the car. He smelt of wind and the sea, and his dark hair was flung in all directions. He glanced at Heather as he got in. His face was covered in a deep frown and his mood immediately affected Heather and her mother.

'What's the matter Joe?' said Heather.

Joe glanced at Heather and then at her mother.

'Can Heather come to mine for tea please Mrs MacDougall?'

Heather's mum smiled; Joe had a habit of asking a question that sounded like an order. Not unlike his grandfather, thought Heather.

'Is that Ok with your grandfather?'

Heather's mum turned the wheel without waiting for an answer and pointed the car up the steep hill towards Joe's house.

'Erm, yup, well he's not there and he said that Heather could come over anytime.'

'Well just for an hour then,' said Heather's mother, 'Heather has had quite enough excitement for one day I think, and I'd be amazed if she could eat another thing for a week.'

Maria dropped the two of them off and turned the car back down the hill. Joe immediately grabbed Heather's arm and marched her towards the house.

'What's the matter Joe?' said Heather prizing his fingers loose on her arm. 'You look as if you are ready to burst.'

'I was heading down to yours actually. Thought I'd save you from all that's been going on. I didn't realise you'd gone out. Thought you might need rescuing. It's a pity you're not hungry though.'

Joe flung open the door to the cottage and burst out laughing at Heather's face as they stepped inside and flung their coats down. The kitchen table was groaning with cakes of every description. It was piled so high that there were leaning towers of cakes teetering dangerously in all directions. Seeing Heather's eyes open wide Joe laughed out loud again.

'I got Isabella to try out an American cake recipe book. Said I reckoned she couldn't bake them, so she had a go at them all. Just didn't fancy killing myself with cake all on my own. Taste this chocolate brownie. Now, you don't get cakes like that here.'

Joe had picked up the biggest brownie Heather had ever seen and was taking a huge bite out of it. Heather laughed and discovered that she seemed to have some room left for more cake, so she copied Joe and stuffed her mouth full of the most exquisitely moist chocolate cake she had ever tasted. The two of them munched in heavenly silence before Joe poured out a large glass of homemade lemonade for them both.

'What ya think? Good eh? Isabella likes a challenge.'

'And she likes to see you with a smile on your face,' Heather replied, 'even if it's covered in chocolate. Wow, these are great, take them away from me before I explode.'

Heather washed down her cake with some lemonade and fixed her eyes on Joe.

'Now then Joe, rescue me from what exactly?'

Joe wilted visibly under her gaze. He flashed an uneasy glance at Heather. She seemed to have changed since he last saw her. Her eyes seemed to flash with a new-found author-ity, she appeared older and it made him feel nervous. He cleared his throat of cake and looked at Heather sheepishly.

'Erm, well it's kicked off in the village a bit. Grandfather's stirring it all up I think. Some man from the fisheries is here. Oh I don't know. Your family have called a meeting – everyone is shouting at each other. Your lot just don't listen to common sense. Best to stay away. Well that's what grandfather said.'

Heather felt a sudden flash of annoyance and rose to defend her family.

'Why is your Grandfather sticking his nose into other people's business? We have been fishing here for hundreds of years why does he interfere?'

Joe looked crestfallen at the sudden turn of events. He wiped some crumbs off his face nervously. This was not how the afternoon was meant to go.

'Oh, who cares what he said, it's just grown up stuff. Nothing to do with us. It's all boring. Grandfather once owned a fishing fleet the size of a ten of your little villages. One of his boats would have been bigger than all of your little tubs put together. He knows what's best I guess. Just persuading your lot is a little tricky.'

Heather checked herself before responding. She was surprised at her sudden strong feeling of anger and replied to Joe with a softening smile of good humour. She deliber-ately made her accent stronger and spoke in a slow voice as if she was a village simpleton.

'Well, things are different here sir. We have different ways sir. We is all just simple folk here sir. Simple ways for simple folk. Anyway, if your grandfather was so successful how come you lot are hiding out here?'

Heather was dismayed to see that her attempt at humour had made Joe even more uncomfortable as he obviously took what she said seriously.

'We are not hiding,' said Joe defensively, 'grandfather just sold up to retire I guess.'

Heather felt a slight spark of electric run through her. She blinked as the room seemed to momentarily pulse with light. She clutched the edge of a kitchen chair to steady herself. Heather wondered what was happening to her now. Maybe it was the sugar rush from the huge brownie. This was different though. This was like hearing somebody in the next room. Something was grabbing at the fringes of Heather's mind for her attention. Something inside her was pulling her attention towards the village hall. Heather closed her eyes and found she could see people arguing and shouting. Heather felt a strong compulsion to go there and find out what was happening. She opened her eyes and frowned. Joe was grew confused at his friend's behaviour and tried vainly to move things along back towards the carefree playful cake filled afternoon he had planned for them.

'Oh, come on Heather, who cares? Let's go upstairs and look through the telescope.'

'What time is the meeting?' asked Heather ignoring him.

'The meeting? How do you know about that? Oh I dunno, about six I suppose, about now.'

Heather eyed the mountain of cakes.

'Hey, I've got a great plan. These meetings always go on for ages. Everybody has to have their say and some of them just like to listen to their own voices, my dad says. So let's take the cakes down there and sell them. We can raise some money to buy a shark for the aquarium.'

Joe looked relieved at this plan. His eyes lit up at the idea of making some money.

'A shark huh? Yeh their stomachs will be growling by seven. Ok, get that large plastic box to put the cakes in and I'll get a tin for the money. Might have to share some with Isabella though.'

Joe scampered off to get a tin and Heather started to cram cakes into the huge plastic container. She paused and touched her new ring, which seemed to be continuously shifting colour. Somehow, she felt that she had to be at the meeting. She didn't know why, it was just a thought, a sensation, gnawing deep within her. Something felt wrong to Heather, something threatened the wellbeing of her village and she didn't have a clue what. She knew that she wouldn't normally be allowed into a meeting of the elders, but she reckoned that her idea to distribute cakes for a few pence would gain them instant access and might even bring in a bit of goodwill. She was right.

A simple bribe of one of the chocolate brownies to Heather's brother guaranteed them entry. They left him happily hand rolling a cigarette and munching his cake. The small hall was packed and everybody seemed to be talking or shouting at once. Heather and Joe had no problem passing between packed seats distributing cakes and collecting money, which was then stuffed into their tin. As they worked the room Heather listened intensely to what was being said, or rather shouted, on the small stage at the front of the hall. Slowly she started to get a picture of what they were all so worked up about. Joe's grandfather was sitting on the stage with a face like thunder and appeared to be sulking. Just like Joe thought Heather. The small man from the fisheries organisation was trying to conduct a discussion but seemed to be losing out to a group of fishermen, led by her father, who were vocally winning the debate. The man from the government agency held his hands up to Heather's father who had a brow like thunder.

'You can't just buy bigger nets with different sized holes when you want to. It's not allowed Robert MacDougall and you very well know it.'

Heather's dad was playing to a home crowd and whenever he spoke he was cheered on loudly.

'We've spent good money on those nets and you are not going to stop us from using them. This is our livelihood and we need to become competitive. If you had loaned us the money for bigger boats we could meet the rising costs, but you didn't, as usual no support from government, you lot just takes, takes, takes.'

This outburst was met with cheers and Heather's dad flashed a winning smile to the hall. Other's joined in and began to heckle the stage.

'Yeah, what do you ever do for us other than push us around and charge us tax on everything we land? These quotas are ridiculous anyhow.'

Another huge cheer and Heather's dad was nodding vigorously. Joe's grandfather was trying to be the voice of calm and reason but even his voice was spluttering with frustration and annoyance. He was clearly not used to being heckled. He spoke, exasperated,

'Look, bigger boats, bigger nets, it's not going to help you. You need to fish less, not more. Even if some of you do go out of business! You have to change your habits. You won't be allowed to land blackfish you know, it's illegal.'

This brought a huge roar of anger from the crowd and Joe's grandfather and the government man looked alarmed.

One of the older fishermen stood up, he was red faced and very angry. He was waving his sinewy arms and hard fists around as he spoke. He looked ready for a fight.

'Shut up Yankee, what do you know about anything? You're not from here. You don't have to go out in them waters day after day. Sod off back to where you came from you grass!'

The fisherman yelped as Joe 'accidentally' dropped the now very full money tin on his foot. Heather caught Joe's eyes and saw the familiar darkness clouding them. Joe's efforts at silencing the burly man made no difference, his calls of defiance and anger were picked up around the hall.

'Go home, we don't need your kind here!'

'Grass!'

'Traitor!'

'Took you in and this is how you repay us!'

The language started to get very colourful and the debate descended once more into catcalls. Suddenly Heather and Joe found themselves being ushered out of the hall. Her brother had finished his cigarette and, in a moment had taken in the situation. Heather's dad had done the same and a quick nod from him to Heather's brother saw them suddenly evicted outside into the safety of the rising winds of the harbour. Before he closed the door Tim grinned at the pair.

'Best you stay out of this young 'uns. It's all about to kick off. Here give us that last cake, they are bloody marvellous.'

Heather held the huge brownie back a moment from her brother and locked her gaze onto him.

'What was all that about, what's going on, why is everybody so angry? I haven't seen dad like that for ages.'

Her brother wolfed down the brownie and grew unsettled under the intensity of his sister's stare. He looked at Joe and squirmed slightly but nodded towards the lad as he continued, "erm well, it's his grandfather isn't it. Grassed us up to the authorities he did, put us all in a spot of bother. Och Heather you ken how we feel about outsiders messing with stuff that ain't their business!'

'About what? What was he messing with that's got you so riled up?'

Heather's brother was just about to fob his sister off by telling her to mind her own business when he found himself locked in the young woman's gaze. He squinted and took a moment to compose himself. He wasn't used to the strange compelling sense of authority his little sister suddenly seemed to possess.

'None of your...erm .... oh well I guess you can know, it's our new nets we bought. Something about too big nets and too small holes. Lots of hogwash if you ask me. We've got to increase our catches, we've got nae choice. That's the finish of it!'

Then seeing Heather's look of concern, he added.

'And don't you go sulking. Fish is our livelihood, it's what pays the bills. Nice cakes though young 'un.'

Heather let him go and appreciated his attempt to make up with Joe. With a look of relief that he couldn't hide Joe turned and darted back into the hall again. As the door swung open a cacophony of sound momentarily burst out.

'Come on,' said Joe after seeing the dark cloud and look of alarm and worry that had settled above Heather's brow.

'Told you it was all rubbish. Didn't see your mum there. Let's go back to yours.'

'No.'

Heather pushed past Joe, flung open the weathered old door to the small hall and dived into the crowd. Joe sighed and raced in after his friend. It was really noisy and heated in the large room now. Everybody was off their seats and

Joe couldn't see Heather anywhere. He cursed the fact that he wasn't taller and tried not to trip over angry fisher folk. Joe lost sight of Heather until he managed to stand on the upturned and now empty cake container to get a better view. He gulped as he saw a small dark-haired figure clamber up on the stage. At first no one seemed to notice Heather. Tempers were now heated, and the language was even riper than earlier. Without warning Heather gave out a high-pitched scream. She must have put her whole being into it because the sound seemed to roar around the hall cutting right through Joe and everybody else in the room. It was a cry of such power, it lay somewhere between a scream and a foghorn. The sound emanating from the small person on the stage seemed far too loud and powerful for such a diminutive being, thought Joe in shock. In a trice, like a wave receding down a beach, the hall fell into complete and utter silence. The silence appeared to Joe to be almost as deafening as the noise that Heather had made moments before. It was a silence that appeared surprised by that very fact it had suddenly come into existence. Every pair of eyes in the hall turned to stare at Heather. When Heather spoke, her voice was hushed, yet everybody in the small hall could hear her.

'It's no good,' she started simply, 'we mustn't use the new nets. We can't take too much from the sea or there will be nothing left. Then it won't matter if we have boats, nets or bigger boats and bigger nets. The sea cannot give us what it doesn't have. This is the only truth on offer here and the only truth that we must listen too. We may not like what we are hearing but it comes to us from wisdom and a desire to help us all. Can't you all see that I'm right, that the government man is right, that Joe's grandfather is right. If we can't admit that we are wrong and that it's okay to be wrong, then we might ruin our own livelihoods and sink our village for good.'

For just a monument the stunned silence in the hall continued. Joe looked around at the red faces and blinking eyes and wondered if Heather had turned the minds of the locals. She hadn't. The hall literally exploded with sound and fury and Joe saw Heather's father racing across the stage out of the corner of his eye as the catcalls made a sound like thunder.

'A traitor, a traitor in our midst!'

'You don't know what you're saying!'

'The newcomer's have turned her!'

'You're just a child.'

'There's plenty of fish.'

'Scientists just say what the government want them to say.'

'We need to cull the seals.'

'Aye we just need our government to stop the Spanish fishing in our waters'

'Robert tell your girl to go home to the women where she belongs!'

As Heather's dad scooped up his daughter in his arms and turned to leave he became an object of scorn and derision.

'Oh aye Robert, you've bred a turncoat there.'

'Can't you control your women?'

'Ask her what her father will do with no job.'

Robert read the mood of the room and, scowling, marched towards the door, the crowd parting before his huge frame like the Red Sea before Moses. Heather's father was still the tallest man in the room and famed for his ability to knock a man out with one punch even if it had been only the once and a long time ago in his younger days. Joe struggled to get clear of the jeering crowd and nearly dropped the full money tin as he collided with Heather and her father striding through the centre of everything towards the door. Heather's dad scooped up Joe in his other arm as easily as if he had been lifting a tea towel and kicked the front door of the hall open. As they exited he slammed it shut with his boot and put them both firmly down on the ground. The pair looked up at the giant bear of a man who seemed to be battling a storm of inner emotions. Joe felt sure they were in for a beating. Heather looked up at her dad. She had never seen his eyes so cross with her before. He seemed disappointed, angry and incredulous at the same time. He took a deep breath, calmed himself slightly and then roared at them.

'Home with both of you! NOW!'

Then with a withering look of total authority he turned on his heels and burst back into the hall.

'Oh, my giddy aunt Heather ya great big numpty. What did you do that for you? Are you stark raving mad? You could have been lynched. What is it?'

Joe instantly regretted his comment as Heather burst into tears. Still sobbing she turned her back on him and walked up the cobbled street towards her house ignoring his calls. She had never felt her father's anger before. She had always been his princess. He had never been disappointed with her before. She felt hurt and confused and yet at the same time Ran's words were buzzing in her head and she felt a storm of conflicting emotions. Joe caught up with Heather before she reached her front door. Heather span round to him, still sobbing.

'Why are adults so stupid? Why can't they see that if they keep on like this, taking, taking, taking – then there will be no fish left in the sea? Don't they realise that the sea will have to fight back?'

Joe caught her by the shoulders and tried to calm her down.

'Look,' he said gesturing to the horizon of stormy blue waves. 'The sea's huge. There will always be fish. This is just a fight over the rules. Men always fight over rules, it's what they do. I'm sure they'll all be friends by tomorrow. Look. See. Here they all come.'

He pointed back down the hill. People were spewing out of the hall heading for the pub. Some were already singing in loud tones, 'we shall not be moved'. Joe tried humour.

'Nothing brings them together like a good fight. It will all be Ok.'

Seeing that Heather was still distracted and distraught, he changed the subject.

'Nice ring. Was that a present? Where did you get it, did your mum buy it for you today in town?'

Heather caught sight of her brother and father heading towards the pub.

'Huh, pardon, what erm yes, I mean no, I was given it today.'

Heather sniffed and gave a half smile of thanks to Joe as she replied quietly and somewhat dejectedly.

'Och, some really nice old ladies gave it to me in town. They were really lovely and kinda weird too.

'It's amazing, bet that cost a few dollars, I mean pounds. It's as big as a false eye.'

Joe pointed at the huge gemstone. Heather smiled and stroked the ring. A faraway look came into her eye.

'It kinda feels magical. Not sure why but I feel like it has always been mine.'

'Wow, look at it light up,' said Joe. 'What is it?'

'A moonstone I think but I'm not sure I've ever seen a stone like this before.'

'From the moon?' gasped Joe intrigued.

'No silly,' giggled Heather, 'it's just called that.'

Heather sniffed and blew her nose and shyly popped her hand into her pocket to hide her ring.

'Look Joe, do you think your grandfather would mind if I came over tomorrow after school?'

'No, it's always fine, I told you so today.'

Joe struggled to hide his pleasure and relief that things seemed to be approaching normal again.

'I'll get Isabella to bake more cakes.'

'Will he be there? Your grandfather I mean.'

Joe looked crestfallen again and felt annoyed at his grandfather.

'Erm, well he might be. But he'll stay in his study. We'll have the house to ourselves and we can use the telescope now, he said so. He's all right really, honest he is. Besides, I think he likes you.'

Heather look distracted as if her mind was far away. She frowned and then turned to go inside.

'Oh, good. Good. Ok Joe, see you tomorrow. Bye.'

Heather opened the door to her cottage to go in. Joe looked down at the heavy tin he was holding.

'What about the money, our dosh, we need to count our millions?'

'Tomorrow Joe, we'll count it tomorrow.'

Then she was gone, leaving Joe staring at the snug little cottage and feeling the wind on his back. He jumped as a strong hand was laid on his shoulder. He immediately recognised the owner of the hand when his grandfather spoke, his powerful deep voice rumbling like thunder.

'She's a good one, that girl. The only one of them with any sense. Come on young man I think that's quite enough for today.'

Joe looked up at his grandfather. He was staring at the cottage with a distant look and his tone softened. Meeting the lad's gaze, the old man suddenly grinned.

'Look at you, my boy. Almost grown. I wonder, I wonder.'

And without any further explanation his steel grip steered Joe away towards their house

When she got back home Heather's mood worsened again. It seemed to swamp her. She stormed into the kitchen and flopped down at the table. Her mum stopped washing dishes and came over to her daughter, looking concerned.

'It's not my...it's not...its.... Just not right!'

Heather frowned as she tried to speak to her mum who look dismayed that her daughter's earlier good humour had vanished. Heather was tired. She wasn't making sense to herself anymore and felt weird. Marie dried her hands and smiled knowingly.

'I think it's time for you to go to bed my love. You may feel a bit more tired and irritable while you have your period you know. Feelings and emotions seem overwhelming at first. What am I saying, they always are. Who'd be a woman? Come on I'll run you a nice bath.'

Almost carrying Heather upstairs her mother smiled at how young and vulnerable her daughter looked again.

'Ahh, she said half to herself. Not yet a woman, no longer a child. Those men don't have the foggiest.'

11
The Herring Queen

The next morning Heather woke early, the sun was barely up. She knew she'd have to go to school but she yawned and stretched, shoved her feet into her slippers and let herself do a bit of early morning housekeeping in the aquarium. She fed some of her guests and cleared up after other ones and smiled when even the seahorses flocked to wherever she was delicately working with her special water vacuum.

Once she had finished she popped her new ring back on her hand and quietly reflected on her crazy and magical life. Even in the early morning gloom the ring seemed to shimmer and gently pulse with light. It was as if small sunbeams danced across a flat seascape. The stone was huge and Heather wondered if it looked a bit ridiculous on her finger. She decided that the delicate and intricate silver work seemed to balance the whole effect. Heather had never seen anything quite so amazing before. Holding her hand up to the light Heather looked at the ring through a large magnifying glass that she kept beside the aquarium. It had been her grandfather's, but she had long since borrowed it on a permanent basis telling him that it was vital to monitor the health of some of the smaller guests in her sea zoo with it. Heather tried to make out what the design on the ring was meant to be. Then, as she slowly moved her hand she realised that the ring was not carefully wound fronds of some kind of plant but in fact the knotted tentacles of an octopus. Gasping she realised that the stone then became one enormous eye for the octopus. Heather wondered why she had not realised the meaning of the design earlier.

Her concentration was interrupted by Heather's mum calling her to come to breakfast from downstairs. Heather's mind grew even more distracted as she remembered her outburst at the village hall. 'Whoops', she thought, that could spell trouble for her with the family for some time. As she pondered on what she was going to say at breakfast she noticed that her ring had turned slightly darker as if a miniature cloud had passed over its surface.

Heather sensed that there was a change in the mood in her house the moment she poked her nose into the kitchen. Everyone was having heated debates and nobody paid her any real attention, apart from a half scowl from her brother who was devouring his breakfast. As Heather sat quietly at the end of their long wooden dining table she listened in to the adults to gauge whether she was in trouble or not. To her relief she quickly worked out that the tension was all about the 'adult' matters, which meant that her outburst the previous day had been all but forgotten. She was used to being side-lined in adult matters, but Heather didn't feel like she was a child anymore. Soon her relief turned to a low feeling of frustration.

Heather gathered from the terse exchanges between her brother, father and mother that the meeting had gone on very late in the pub and had become very heated. There was talk of legal action, strikes, protests and Joe's grandfather's name seemed to have become a dirty word. As she slowly ate the breakfast that her mother placed in front of her, Heather began to feel more and more alarmed.

Her brother Tim was agreeing with her father about their new nets. Because all their savings had been spent acquiring the nets, they had no choice but to use them. Whatever the man from the fisheries was saying her family seemed to be united in this one fact. Heather heard discussion of 'black fish', and 'other's do it so why shouldn't we'. Her father talked of government spies, scientists who knew nothing and ineffective politicians who just made matters worse.

Heather's emotions were in turmoil. Her stomach felt like a bucket full of eels. It was the first time she had ever felt a strong opposition to what her father said. In fact, she had had never disagreed with him before as far as she could remember. Sensing the atmosphere, she tried to hold her tongue. But when it became obvious that they were all preparing to set sail at high tide later that day she couldn't contain herself any longer.

'Daddy please,' she said suddenly, 'please don't use those nets, I'm scared for you.'

Heather's father paused his rant and observed his daughter closely.

'Ah so that's why you were so vocal yesterday little one; you were scared that we might get into trouble with the law.'

Of course, Heather's father had no inkling why she was really afraid for him and assumed that it had something to do with the government and the police. Heather bit her tongue again, how on earth was she going to explain what she really felt?

'Don't worry about me lass,' he said. 'They can't do anything to us. Besides, even if they try, what are they going to do, confiscate the boats?'

Heather was about to launch another protest when she caught her mother's eyes; her look said clearly, leave it until later. She sighed as her dad continued.

'The flipping authorities can't agree anything anyway. Scientists can't even agree with each other. The Europeans have passed a law, which won't help the fish, and it certainly won't help fishermen so we are going to take matters into our own hands. The cod has moved south, the hake has moved north and we aren't allowed to land a decent catch.'

Her brother chimed in and the debate picked up again.

'Our government should just keep the foreigners out of our waters, it's them that take too much fish. They don't respect our laws.'

The two men then started to hotly debate a matter of European law, using some very colourful language in which a great many people were named and shamed. Heather's mother was trying her best to referee and placate everybody with cups of tea. Heather realised that her mother would watch to make sure that the men didn't get out of hand and decide anything too foolish. As more fishermen joined

Heather's family at the table to pick up the meeting from the night before she realised there was no way that any of them would listen to her. Heather decided to sneak out of home and go and find Joe. She still had plenty of time before school anyway.

Throwing on her new jacket and trainers Heather started up the hill and the narrow path to Joe's house. When she got to the low stone wall she saw him waving out of an upstairs window and taking that as an invite she went up the path and pushed the door open. As soon as she entered she noticed that her ring had turned dark again. If the mood had been stormy in her household, it was far worse here. Joe's grandfather was on the phone in the hall and was bellowing at somebody. He never swore but somehow his use of long words in his precise accent seemed more threatening and more powerful than Heather's father's wild rants.

'Psst,' Joe called her from the stairs and waved for her to come up. She slipped past his grandfather and headed upstairs. As Joe's grandfather was standing and shouting at someone on the phone she noticed just how tall and powerful he looked. Even though he was much older than Heather's father, who was built like a brick outhouse, so everybody said in the village, Joe's grandfather's body was lean and sinewy, and his trimmed grey beard and steely blue eyes somehow gave him an increased air of organised authority.

'What's going on?'

Heather quizzed Joe as the pair hurried into the living room. Heather barely noticed the amazing view as Joe started to babble at her.

'You won't believe it, oh the shame, I mean I can't go to school now, what do you think they will do to me, they all think I am a traitor, that I want them to stop fishing, lose their livelihoods, that I grassed them up, it's just not fair, he doesn't think of anyone else, he's on the phone to a government scientist now, if he doesn't watch it we'll have the press all over us again...I bloody hate him!'

Joe's dark eyes seemed to well up, but he stopped his outburst and wiped them with his sleeve. His brow darkened as if a huge black cloud had passed across the young man's mind. Heather decided she needed to know more. It was as if there was another story raging inside her new friend. It was a story that seemed to rise too often and cause him pain and anger. Heather was not used to disharmony in the village, her family or with her friends. It seemed to her as if suddenly everybody had decided to go to war yet at the same time everybody was missing the vital point about the ocean. As Joe sniffled Heather got a gentle question in.

'Joe, why is your grandfather so against the village?'

Joe looked at her. He seemed to appreciate the distraction from his own potential troubles with the village children.

'It's something to do with his past: you know I told you that he used to have a huge fleet of fishing boats, bigger and better-equipped than yours?'

Heather nodded.

'Well even with all that money and wealth he soon lost everything and was ruined. The fish just disappeared one day, as if by magic, and that was it. Of course, then there was the trouble over mum and dad. Soon everybody hated him. That's why we left. And now,' he said, livid with anger and tears welling up in his eyes, 'now he's gonna do it all over again.'

Joe's eyes darkened again. He clenched his fist tightly and turned away from Heather to stare out of the window down to where the village snugly sat protected by its harbour walls and lit up with early morning sunshine. The fishing boats were beginning to bob gently as the tide lifted them higher and higher up the stone walls. Heather took a moment to marvel at the view she never tired of and then tried to pull the thorn of worry out of Joe's paw.

'But he doesn't fish anymore. Why is he so concerned?'

Joe scowled and growled at the darkening skies outside the window.

'He's what they call an eco-activist. He's always going on about the ocean, fishing and sustainability and things like that. I don't mind that, it's just the fact that he's going to get us hated by everyone again.'

Heather sighed, realising that for Joe, a newcomer to the village, fitting in was the highest priority. She looked out of the window. Clouds were scudding in across the turbulent seas. Heather wondered if that's what she was becoming, an activist. She wasn't too sure what an activist was but she knew she was worried by the vision that she had shared with Ran and her grandmother, and she was terrified for the fishing fleet that was beginning to head out to sea. She held her hand up and looked at the ring. Its colours swirled, and Heather felt a sudden jolt inside her. It was as if a small electrical charge had zapped her. A flurry of half-images and sounds spun through her mind. She saw huge fishing boats surrounded by canoes and dark-skinned people waving and shouting. People on the boats were laughing and spraying water onto the small vessels. The vision was filled with shouting and screaming. Suddenly a massive storm blew up and Heather saw a monstrous wave bear down on the dwarfed fishing boats and the flotilla of vulnerable canoes. Then, as unexpectedly as it had started, the vision vanished, leaving Heather breathing heavily and clutching the arms of the chair so tightly her knuckles had turned white. She glanced at Joe to see if he had noticed but he was still looking out to sea and sniffing loudly. Heather steadied her breathing. One image remained burned into her mind. One of the shouting and screaming faces in the canoe had been the tall, dark and beautiful Native American lady from the large painting downstairs that she had seen in her earlier vision. It was the face of Joe's mother. Heather wasn't sure if she had just witnessed a prophecy, or a vision of what had actually happened. She realised that this wasn't the moment to ask Joe; it was time for them to run the short distance to school. Outside, the sky darkened and rain began to fall. Heather steadied her hand and then reached out to touch Joe on the shoulder.

'Come on Joe, it will all be okay. We love a bit of a barny here. It will all be forgotten by tomorrow. Come on, let's get to school and you and me will say that we think your Grandfather is completely stark raving mad and that...'

She stopped abruptly as Joe's grandfather suddenly entered the room. His whole body seemed to crackle with energy and his face was grim and set hard.

'Stark raving mad eh mistress Heather?'

Joe's grandfather spoke in a low and dangerous voice. Heather swallowed and put on her best and most innocent face. Joe spun round and stuffed his hand in his mouth to stop him from sputtering with shock and laughter.

'Of course, we don't believe that,' Heather said, recognising that he's not the type you can lie to, 'but it's just so that Joe will be alright at school.' Besides,' she added quickly as Joe's grandfather's brow darkened, 'we know that what you say is right.'

She ended with her most sincere and earnest look. Joe's grandfather softened just a fraction and gave a quick warm smile of such kindness that Heather's heart melted. He really did care very deeply about things. Then he returned to his 'man of action' persona and frowned.

'Well your father and the rest of the village don't agree, and they must,' he added firmly 'or you will all suffer. Now come on, off to school the pair of you.' Then, as they were leaving, he added, 'don't worry Joe, if I need to stand alone I will.' Then he slammed the door behind them.

'Oh, sorry Joe,' said Heather, 'I didn't mean to get you into more trouble.'

Joe seemed to brighten, and then burst out laughing.

'I bet that's not the first time Gramps has been called mad. Don't worry,' he said. 'It wasn't your fault. I know you were just looking out for me...erm, thanks.'

Heather found herself blushing ever so slightly at that and was immediately cross with herself for having helter-skelter feelings. As they approached the school, Joe asked,

'If it were your dad you wouldn't deny him would you? You would support his views whatever? You wouldn't make him stand alone?'

There was a group of boys milling outside the school and they both noticed them.

'No, I wouldn't deny him usually,' Heather whispered and felt for Joe's hand. She gave it a quick squeeze and added, 'not unless I was absolutely certain that he was wrong, and I think your grandfather may have a point. He might be the only one talking sense at the moment.'

In the back of her mind Heather began to recall the terrible prophesy of Ran. She saw the image of little boats being swamped by a huge wave. This time they seemed to be the little colourful boats from the village. Sensing Joe's fear as they approached the school she realised that she had a knot of fear deep within her as well, but it was not fear of the local children. As they got near the group of boys hanging about outside the gates she stood up straight and tall and prepared for battle. To her those boys were nothing compared to the threats of an ancient sea deity like Ran. The whole small playground turned round as the pair entered through the school gates. A cacophony of noise turned into a deadly silence. Heather saw inquisitive looks on her girlfriends' faces, eager to get all of the juicy gossip out of her. However their silence was broken with small gasps as they all noticed that Heather was still gripping Joe's hand tightly. She met the girls' faces with a subtle smile. She then quickly turned to face the approaching group of boys whose faces all said the same thing: Fight!

Heather and Joe were saved by the sudden appearance of Miss Boniface, the head teacher and Heather's class teacher. Miss Boniface could be the kindest and most inclusive person in the school, but she commanded the rare gift of being able to control young people without the need to shout. Other teachers would render themselves hoarse some weeks but Miss Boniface seemed un-phased by rebellious behaviour. Nobody ever wanted to get on the wrong side of her, teachers included. There were rumours that she could reduce even the biggest lads into blubbering wrecks with just a single word and a glance. Miss Boniface marched straight towards the gathered schoolchildren and firmly requested the boys to go inside. She held them in her steely gaze and pointed inside. Fearing Miss Boniface's legendary wrath, they meekly complied and turned away, only making the secret signs that all school children know meant 'see you later' and 'this is not over'.

As they all turned to go inside Miss Boniface approached Heather and Joe. If she was surprised to find them holding hands not a flicker of emotion showed on her face. Shooshing the other girls away with a wave of her hand the teacher fixed Heather and Joe with a formidable stare her eyes flicking over the two of them. She cocked her head on one side for a moment like a bird before smiling slightly, she beckoned them to follow her back into the school.

'I need you two help me with some things before lessons begin,' she said mysteriously.

Heather and Joe suddenly felt self-conscious and quietly let go of each other's hand without saying a word. Standing tall they matched their steps and moved through the remaining group of children who were all dragging their feet as the school headed back inside. The boys circled them like a pack of young wolves as if looking for any weakness or division. Heather and Joe looked straight ahead and followed Miss Boniface into the temporary safety of the schoolhouse. Miss Boniface didn't look back but they knew to follow her without question. Once inside Joe gently took Heather's hand again. Heather smiled to herself and accepted it. She wasn't sure what she felt about Joe other than he was becoming her unpredictable friend, but his touch made her smile. They quietly marched down the corridor perfectly in step until they reached their classroom. They followed Miss Boniface inside and smiled as the familiar sight of desks and vibrant artwork welcomed them. Miss Boniface looked around the classroom to ensure that no one was in the room, closed the door and then turned and fixed her gaze on them both. Heather felt her heart rate increase and her mind sharpen. A crystal clear clarity came over Heather. She felt calm yet knew something was happening. She hoped that it wasn't going to become a potentially embarrassing moment for her. The feelings reminded of the day before in the teashop when she had met the old ladies. Heather noticed that Miss Boniface was staring almost unblinkingly at Heather and Joe's clasped hands. Heather quickly released her grip on Joe who easily acquiesced realising that the show of affection was suddenly inappropriate behaviour for a school room. Miss Boniface's gaze lingered just a moment too long on Heather's hand and ring. Heather was aware that she hadn't realised that Heather had been gripping Joe's hand. Then Heather noticed the ring on Miss Boniface's hand for the first time; it was a huge moonstone in a familiar intricate silver setting. Heather was amazed she hadn't seen it before. Then in a flash her memory replayed hundreds of moments when Miss Boniface had worn the ring. She could even suddenly remember Miss Boniface cleaning it after helping Heather wash out the classroom's small aquarium. With a glance of heightened perception Heather took everything in at once. The ring wasn't as large or as ornate as Heather's and it didn't seem to pulse with colours like hers but there was no mistaking the design. Time seemed to move ever so slightly slower and Heather couldn't believe how clearly her senses seemed to be picking up a host of subtle sounds, sights and smells in the classroom. Heather glanced up at Mrs Boniface and her surprise must have shown on her face. Miss Boniface looked directly into her eyes and smiled. It seemed as if for a split second the world stopped, and a very secret sign was exchanged between them. Heather froze, and felt a rush and a glow as if she had just been privy to something extraordinary.

'So, children,' began Miss Boniface, 'I think it best that the two of you help me with the festival preparations today.

We should probably keep Joe out of the playground until tempers are calmed somewhat. And,' she added, turning to Heather in an almost conspiratorial way, 'young Heather's outburst yesterday at the village meeting might not have made her the flavour of the month either, however popular her father is.'

Both children showed a visible sign of relief and entered into the preparations with a sense of enthusiasm and gratitude to their teacher. The Herring Queen festival parade didn't usually interest Heather. She was not a girl who worried about how she looked and never gave much attention to the squabbling of the other girls who vied to be chosen to lead the procession. Heather had always gone to see the procession with the rest of the village and carried one of the torches to light the way. It was a welcomed and ancient holiday for all the fisher folk and their families. Sometimes July even brought good weather. Miss Boniface was a young and progressive teacher and she sat them both in front of a computer.

'Right,' she said, 'start here, you can do the research for the class project. Afterall,' she added knowingly, 'you are our resident fish expert, Heather.'

Heather felt herself relax, the world seemed back to normal. The colours dimmed again, everything grew quieter and normality returned.

'Oh good' said Heather to Joe as Miss Boniface left the classroom to call in the other children, 'I'm not much good at art, this is much more fun.'

She thought how jealous the others would be of the fact that she was allowed to use the school computer.

'Erm...the thing is Joe,' she whispered shyly, 'I don't actually know how to use it. I mean, I can turn it on but....'

Joe looked at her and grinned, suddenly pleased to be of use.

'Hey, no danger, I've had one of these for years,' he said, 'in fact, my one is way better than this, we have a satellite link to the rest of the world at the house. Grandpa is on it all the time. That's how I watch movies and everything. Now let me see... let's break free from the school and check out what's really happening out there...'

To Heather's amazement in under two minutes Joe had bypassed the school's online security system and was exploring the internet freely.

'Look,' said Joe excitedly, 'this Herring Queen thing is an ancient fire festival. Torches are carried to the sea. Its pagan. It existed before the Christian church, possibly before the Vikings. It's a kinda ritual to ensure the fishing was successful for the year. The villagers welcome the herring as they shoal past their shores. It says here that the Herring Queen is a fertility symbol and she was the sister of the Seal Queen, whoever she is. I bet we can even get some video of it, mind you the connection is a bit slow, and of course it's only going to be from recent times.'

Heather looked up from the notes she was making and tried to maintain her composure. She spoke as casually as she could.

'A seal queen?'

'Yup. Weird eh? Tell you what though, there isn't much here. I think we are going to have to be creative with facts. That's what grandfather says the newspapers always do.'

He turned to look at Heather and realised that his friend was miles away staring into space. Joe watched her carefully. He was becoming used to the almost trance like state Heather would seem to go into. He remembered how she had looked when his grandfather had brought her back to his house, wet and still semi-unconscious from sea. She had been staring straight ahead and babbling in a strange language before suddenly calling out, over and over again, for someone called Raven.

Heather was looking out of the window. A gannet, one of the largest gulls, with the wingspan of a small car was staring straight back at her. He had perched on a bin outside the window and had fixed them with a cold blue-eyed stare. The bird tapped on the window in front of Heather. Joe noticed that it seemed to be staring straight at her. Heather smiled at the bird and then to Joe's surprise murmured, 'Okay I will.' Suddenly the spell was broken as the other children burst into the room. The huge gull flew off and Heather quickly turned back to the screen. Joe felt slightly freaked out and quietly quizzed Heather who had returned to busily scrawling notes on her pad.

'Okay Heather, that was weird. I wonder what that bird wanted? Do you feed it as well as all the other local animals?'

Without thinking or looking up Heather replied.

'I have to go to the beach after school, promise me that you won't follow.'

Joe's mouth was hanging open and he was just about to laugh when Heather's look became fierce and she stared straight at him with a glance that gave him no choice but to respect her wishes. Joe blinked at Heather's expression. It occurred to him that Heather's moods switched quicker than the local weather.

'Erm yes of course,' he replied, 'I have to erm, catch up on my homework anyway.'

Yet as they turned back to work Joe wondered what was up with his new friend. Sometimes she was just like him, a young person, carefree and joyful at the possibility of everything, other times her eyes looked incredibly old and she seemed to have the weight of the world on her shoulders.

The rest of the day passed quickly. Avoiding the playground at lunch and break time Heather and Joe compiled a large folder full of information. They almost ran the school printer dry of ink with all their printing. Once the other children had left to go home Miss Boniface beckoned the children over.

'So, what did you two secret squirrels find out then?'

Miss Boniface glanced at the bulging folder and smiled at Heather and Joe's eyes which were tired and red from staring at the computer screen all day. They pair hadn't even stopped for a proper break and Miss Boniface had allowed them to eat their packed lunches in the classroom. Thus, she had maintained peace in her small school. Heather and Joe told Miss Boniface all about the festival. They showed her some of their research that revealed the festival's ancient roots. They told her that it had been resurrected fifty years before as the church had once banned it. They told Miss Boniface that it was linked to the ending of the last world war and had been called a Peace Picnic to celebrate eventual peace. Heather babbled about hundreds of details about the herring fish and showed her dozens of pictures of traditional dresses she had printed off, something that Heather had little interest in. Miss Boniface seemed impressed – then she smiled and bid them hush.

'Well done, you two. We can share all of this with the class tomorrow and make a really great project. Now,' she said, turning to Joe, 'I think it will be safe for you to go home. The boats are sailing tonight so everyone will have forgotten about you.'

The children got up from the desk and, stretching their limbs, got ready to go home. Then, just as they reached the door Miss Boniface called Heather back. Joe begrudgingly left Heather.

'Oh, erm I'll see you tomorrow then?'

Heather smiled back at him and felt a warm glow.

'Ok, don't worry, you will be fine now.'

The moment Joe left Miss Boniface turned to Heather. The classroom seemed to dissolve around them. The air grew thick and Miss Boniface drew herself up to her full height, her eyes flashing with power. Her face grew stern, strict and scary in a way Heather had never seen before. It was as if the kind, schoolteacher had been replaced by an all-powerful woman whose eyes now flashed with fire. Miss Boniface fixed her gaze on Heather and began to fire questions at her. Heather was taken aback and she found that she was powerless to resist Miss Boniface's questioning. She heard her own voice answer from a far-off place.

'Tell me what you know about that boy?' Where does he come from?' What is he doing here? What is his story? What have you learned about his parents and his grandfather?'

With every question Miss Boniface asked Heather found herself answering truthfully, telling Miss Boniface everything. When she got to the part about Joe's parents and the painting Miss Boniface seemed to relax, a smile returned to her face and Heather felt her own body calm down and she knew she was once more in control of what she said.

'So, it has come to pass. These are troubled times indeed young Heather.'

Then she looked away, her interrogation complete, and added,

'But he is a good lad, good heart and a great destiny, but it is our destiny which has the most importance right now. Our paths are woven together. You can go now Heather. Well done. I will see you tonight.'

Miss Boniface stared at Heather's ring hand again and her gazed lingered. For a second her face looked hungry, as if she wanted to devour it. Then the moment passed, and Heather felt herself gradually relax as Miss Boniface's magnetic attention was turned to closing the classroom windows ready to leave for home. Heather realised that she was meant to leave so she gathered up her bag and exited the classroom. Heather just put the experience into the same box as all of her other recent ones, something to process later on.

If Heather was puzzled by how Miss Boniface had transformed into an all-powerful goddess earlier she was even more puzzled by what she saw a short while later. As she climbed the slope away from the school before it dropped down to the village she looked back and saw Miss Boniface standing in the playground feeding scraps of food to a huge white gannet. Heather paused to look back. It looked like the same bird that had somehow spoken to Heather earlier in the day. Heather was amazed at how Miss Boniface was lovingly petting the huge bird. She knew how sharp gannets' beaks were and how dangerous they could be. It appeared that Miss Boniface was talking to the bird. Heather was reminded of her conversations with the seals and just how unbelievable it seemed in the cold light of day. She frowned. Suddenly the world seemed very strange, it was as if nobody was who she had thought they were.

But, although Heather was confused by what she was seeing, she knew in her heart that she could trust Miss

Boniface. She had always been kind to Heather and seemed concerned about Joe. Miss Boniface reminded Heather of the ladies she had met in the teashop. Heather wondered if Miss Boniface had some deep insight into the strange new world she was experiencing.

Heather remembered how her new ring had transfixed Miss Boniface and how she had felt a momentary flash of unease at the covetous gaze of her teacher. Heather needed someone to share her recent experiences with. Somebody nearer her own age who might be able understand and make sense of it all. She needed some human advice and wondered if Ran wouldn't mind her speaking to Miss Boniface. but she had to be sure. Then Heather remembered the message of the gull that she had hidden from Joe. The strange, sharp language echoed again in her head.

'You must come to the sea tonight. All will be revealed.'

She turned for home. The gannet had to be Ran summoning her. That felt good. Maybe Ran would help her make sense of it all and give her some advice. Heather felt like she needed to get grounded. As she lengthened her stride down towards her house and the harbour, she smiled at how close she now felt to Joe. She did worry that it now felt like it was the two of them against the village though. Heather loved her village and all the folk who inhabited it. Everybody knew everybody else and everybody else's business, but it was always meant with a kindness. Heather realised she was worried that everybody seemed to be picking sides. She picked up her stride and prepared for more confrontation but once Heather arrived back home she realised that everybody was down at the harbour readying the fishing boats. Normally she would have headed down to soak up the bustle but she couldn't face another argument. She tried not to worry about her father and after quickly eating her supper she put on some warm clothes and then headed for the cove. She never doubted that the gannet had spoken to her or that she was meant to go. As Heather left the road and joined the sandy path towards the small beach she realised that very little would surprise her now. At the same time she felt excited. What on earth was going to get revealed to her? Heather felt excited and anxious at the same time. She glanced at her ring and then shoved her hand back into her pocket. She didn't want the fact that it had turned ominously dark to upset her light hearted mood.

12
An Interrogation

'**B**ut herring feed on plankton and plankton numbers vary according to the salinity of the water and fluctuations.'

Joe's grandfather was on the phone to somebody and was speaking very slowly, as if to a child, trying to get somebody to understand what he was saying.

'No,' he corrected, 'numbers do fluctuate according to weather, climate and plankton; they do not begin to nosedive off the chart.'

Joe could hear his grandfather becoming more and more exasperated.

'Of course they bloody well returned in the pacific, they stopped all fishing for four years.'

Joe smiled to himself. He had found the very same information out that day on the computer. As his grandfather slammed the phone down with only the smallest hint of politeness he noticed Joe.

'What are you grinning at me for boy? You spying on me? You laughing at me?'

Joe's grandfather growled in his usual gruff tones but both of them knew that this was just an act. The old man doted on his only grandchild yet was obviously conflicted between how to teach character strength and how to be kind and loving. Both he and Joe knew this fact yet were unable to articulate their feelings to each other. His grandfather was from another generation of men who were okay doing things but not so good sharing how they felt about what was important to them. The two of them had worked out a kind of emotional shorthand. Joe knew when his Grandfather really meant business but also saw his job as chilling out his aged protector. Joe knew that even though his grandfather was not able to be emotionally demonstrative or able to handle intimacy that he would protect those he loved like a lion protecting his pride. Joe's grandfather was still a fit, powerful and intellectually astute man who had unfortunately never taken the time to learn any real social skills. The trouble was, the older he got the more driven he was to put the world to rights. Joe realised that his new friend Heather had some of those inherent qualities. Joe wondered if he also had inherited an inability to speak what he felt without upsetting other people. Joe knew in his heart that he really cared about what other people thought of him but sometimes he felt totally overwhelmed by his feelings and was unable to think clearly. For a brief moment Joe realised that he got as angry as his grandfather when he was unable to get other people to see his point of view. He wondered what other character traits he shared with his grandfather and which ones he had inherited from his mother and father. Joe quickly brushed away those thoughts for he knew that whenever they arrived like a dull storm in his mind, he would soon feel depressed and withdraw from those around him. Joe knew that he cared just as passionately as his grandfather and Heather about the natural world but unlike them he didn't feel confident in just standing up and speaking his truth. Joe already regretted that he had alienated the other young people in the village on his first day. Looking at his grandfather he realised that both of them went on the attack when they felt vulnerable or unsure of what other people thought. He did wish that other people could see just how caring and concerned the old man was though. He went over to his grandfather and gave him a hug. Jim frowned and then smiled.

'I thought you might be mad at me again,' his grandfather sighed. 'Its' just that...'

'I learnt all about the herring today. Heather and I worked on the computer at school. It's not as good as ours but I still found out lots, for instance that the Herring Queen procession is done to celebrate the return of the herring. So that's good isn't it? It means the herring will come back again!'

Joe's grandfather smiled and cocked his head to one side tugging thoughtfully on his white beard as he looked at Joe.

'It might need more than a festival to encourage the herring to return, and cod, and haddock and...'

He stopped unexpectedly. Joe looked up at him.

'Worked on the computer you say? At that new school of yours? Proper research not just regurgitating things out of old books?'

'Yup!'

'Excellent. Splendid, sometimes small schools can encourage great learning and intelligence. When I was a boy that's all there was. No computers though. You've got a good teacher there my boy. Right, come on then, let's go and see which page of the recipe book Isabella has recreated for us tonight.'

As he spoke Jim led the way into the dining room where Isabella had prepared them fish pie and soft golden mashed potato. The food was amazing. Joe ate the delicious meal slowly, silently appreciating every mouthful that the devoted Isabella had created for them. Then a thought slowly made its way into Joe's mind.

'You called Miss Boniface didn't you? You asked her to keep us safe? It was your idea that we work on the computer wasn't it?'

Joe's grandfather spent an age enjoying a mouthful of food.

'Great fish pie Isabella,' he said momentarily ignoring Joe, 'local recipe?'

Isabella looked at the two of them across the table, smiled and nodded.

'So that's why Miss Boniface had met us at the gates! You called Miss Boniface didn't you grandfather?'

Joe was smiling at his grandfather. He knew he was right. Joe's grandfather stopped chewing and looked embarrassed; he seemed to find it hard to speak. Joe smiled – he knew when his grandfather was having difficulty expressing his emotions. But he pushed on.

'You had to meddle though didn't you?'

Joe's grandfather ignored the hint of criticism from his grandson and slowly met his gaze.

'Well young Heather seemed very concerned for your safety this morning and I thought I would just...well...'

'Interfere?'

Joe grinned, they both knew that he was teasing but the older man could see that Joe was also serious.

'Look, I'm sorry, I didn't mean to embarrass you. Sure, you could have dealt with it on your own and all that...but well, I just thought, I mean after all you've been through...'

He paused unsure of what to say. Joe reached across the table to his grandfather and, to the old man's surprise, squeezed his hand.

'Thank you,' he said. 'I will stand up to anybody, you know that grandfather,' he said suddenly, looking fierce 'but I can't take them all on. Besides, Heather was there and she's a girl, erm a woman, oh you know what I mean...'

His grandfather grew serious.

'I know Joe, I know. There are times to take them all on and there are times to retreat. We may lose the battle, but we can't afford to lose the war. That's when the innocent get harmed.'

Joe was alarmed and frowned at Jim withdrawing his hand.

'War? Who are we at war with grandfather, this is our new home, we should be making peace.'

His grandfather looked thoughtful for a moment and then sighed deeply.

'Perhaps you are right Joe,' he said. 'I tell you what, let's go for a stroll after supper. Like we used to back home with your ...'

His voice trailed off and he got up to help Isabella clear the dishes. They both knew why. One of Joe's earliest memories, reinforced by a picture in his album book under his bed was of his mother, father, grandfather and himself walking the cliff path high up over the town back home. Suddenly Joe realised why the walks had stopped. They reminded his grandfather of his loss which filled him with worry over how Joe would react. Joe smiled at the old man. He wasn't as tough as he made out.

'Come on then grandfather, I'd love to. You know the names of all the birds, you can teach them to me. That will impress Heather tomorrow. You should have seen the huge one she was chatting to today.'

****

Heather reached the cove and set out across the beach until she clambered over some rocks and rounded the point to where a second, smaller hidden bay sat nestled into the cliffs. The sea was getting rough and, although the tide was out, the waves were crashing onto the pebbles, raking them backwards and forwards so that they hissed like a great serpent. As the sun began to slowly get lower in the horizon it illuminated each wave before it broke, lighting it up from behind so that they turned an amazing golden colour.

Heather looked all around her; she could see no sign of life, no familiar wet nose peeping out of the sea. She felt the wind chill her and suddenly she sensed that things were not quite as they ought to be. The sea was breathlessly beautiful, but there seemed to be no birds or animals anywhere around. She was puzzled. Where was Ran? She was sure that the bird had said this spot. Heather wondered if it was because it was still light. The sun had not yet set, but it was weird that there were no sea birds. Then she laughed as a rather large gannet thumped down a few feet from Heather, making her jump. She chuckled and scolded the bird, which simply stared back at her, saying nothing. In fact, it just fixed her with its amazing eyes and started to move towards her in a rather menacing fashion.

Heather grew more puzzled and just a little scared; she knew how sharp the beaks of these birds were. It seemed to have lost all of its earlier friendliness. Startled, Heather tripped over a rock and fell backwards onto the sand. Immediately the bird had hopped up onto her chest with its beak inches from her face. The weight of the bird made it hard to breathe. Heather lay motionless not wishing to alarm it in case it attacked her. Her heart raced as the huge yellow beak came closer and closer to her face – she could lose an eye in an instant.

'What do you want? What is it? What's wrong? Tell me. I'm your friend you silly creature.'

The bird gave no sign that it understood or even cared. It just stared straight into Heather's face. She could smell its fishy breath. Slowly, Heather's hand felt around for anything that could help her, just in case. Her fingers scrabbled through the sand like a small crab but were unable to find anything larger than a pebble. Then suddenly the bird leapt off her, the weight of its take-off almost winding her. Heather sat up. It had hopped a few feet away. Heather coughed and spluttered for a moment and rubbed her chest where the big bird had been standing. As she checked herself for any signs of damage she kept her gaze fixed on the gannet just in case it wanted to attack her again. The bird turned its head and in that instant, to Heather's relief, she saw Miss Boniface clamber over some rocks at the entrance of the little cove. Phew, thought Heather and gave her teacher a wave. Miss Boniface waved back. In her hand she was carrying a basket and in the other a shawl. Rescued again by Miss Boniface thought

Heather gratefully. She brushed the sand from her clothes and stood up smiling to greet her teacher. Funny, thought Heather as Miss Boniface walked towards her, it was almost as if she knew Heather would be there. Heather wondered if they were connected on some strange level in the same way that she had experienced with the old women from Saltkirk.

'Hello Heather,' said Miss Boniface, 'thought you might be a bit peckish.' She glanced at the gannet, smiling, 'I've brought some cookies I made myself.'

Miss Boniface threw down the blanket and invited Heather to sit beside her.

'I hope that Iki-Ryo didn't upset you too much, he can be a wee bit excitable sometimes.'

'Oh, he's... I mean you speak to him...I mean you have given him a name?'

Heather felt suddenly foolish and not sure what she should say to Miss Boniface, who was smiling at her with some amusement. As Heather sat down she glanced at Iki-Ryo and frowned. He definitely seemed more than just excited, she thought. He looked down right mean. She looked back to Miss Boniface, who smiled sweetly at Heather and passed her a cookie. Then she took out a flask and started to pour some hot chocolate into two mugs. Just then the sun started to dip and a shadow fell across her teacher's face. Heather realised that it was odd that she had never noticed how much her nose resembled a beak from the side. Miss Boniface passed the hot drink to Heather.

'Well that was quite a show you put on yesterday. We were all amazed at your passion. You certainly made the men listen even if just for a moment. What on earth did you hope to achieve?'

Heather was surprised that Miss Boniface had wanted to talk to her about the event in the town hall. She was still not sure what she really felt it was a kind of mixture of anger frustration and hope. Heather was touched that her teacher was so concerned for her well-being that she had taken time out to console her pupil. She began to imagine that the two of them might share a special connection that was somehow linked to all the strange experiences of the past few days. Heather hated feeling angry and was concerned at how strong her emotions had been when she had stood and confronted the whole town. In fact, the strength of all her recent emotions concerned her but at last she had someone she could confide in, someone who would listen, someone like herself.

'I know, it was so frustrating. It's as if they just don't want to listen to common sense. They all seem to be blinkered and unwilling to see the bigger picture. I mean the sea is our livelihood but it's also the source of everything. Why can't they see that they are all in great danger.'

It felt good to Heather to finally have somebody that she could express her emotions to. She smiled with relief as she turned her head to look at Miss Boniface but her teacher's expression confused her. Miss Boniface looked alarmed. This was obviously not the answer Miss Boniface had expected to hear and turning her full attention to Heather she spoke sharply.

'What?' she asked severely, 'danger you say? Why would you say that then?'

Just as Heather was about to open her mouth and tell Miss Boniface she felt a tremor in her tummy, an uneasy sort of feeling and, declining another biscuit, she said nothing. Maybe she had read the situation wrong. Maybe Miss Boniface didn't share the same vision that Heather had. Miss Boniface changed tack and her smile became sweet again though Heather noticed that Iki-Ryo was moving closer. Miss Boniface reached out her hand and lifted Heather's finger gently up towards her face. She smiled conspiratorially at Heather as she took a closer look at the huge ring on the girl's finger.

'I see you have a beautiful ring. It's amazing to see another one and in such great condition. Has it been in your family for long?' Gosh, isn't it like mine? So strange, I thought these rings were quite rare.'

Miss Boniface held her ring hand up for Heather to examine. It was almost the same as hers, yet the large gem was a beautiful and quite normal moonstone. It didn't seem to have the same sparkling and iridescent qualities as Heather's ring. Heather noticed that her ring was turning quite a dark shade of blue and she wondered if Miss Boniface had noticed. As Heather's hands touched her teacher's she felt a strange but all too familiar sensation sweep over her. Without warning a vision exploded into her mind's eye. Heather could see a heavily shrouded figure moving across the cliff top. It was carrying an old-fashioned lamp on a tall pole which swung around in the strong winds. As the vision grew stronger Heather could see that it was a foul night and the person carrying the torch was fighting against the weather. She couldn't make out if the person was male or female but she could see that they appeared to be signalling to somebody. She wondered if the signal was meant to guide fishing boats safely home through the storm. In a flash of lightning the vision changed and Heather saw and heard the rending timbers of a tall-ship foundering on rocks. This was no small fishing boat. As the huge wooden vessel began to splinter and break up the figure on the clifftop stood still. The vision shifted and suddenly in a flash of lightning

Heather could see the rain drenched and exposed hand of the signaller holding the lamp. She could clearly make out a large ornate ring and long neatly manicured fingernails. Heathers stomach churned as she became aware of screams of terror emanating from the doomed ship. She felt confused alarmed and wondered at what she was witnessing. There was something wrong in this version something which didn't quite add up and something which made Heather feel very small and very vulnerable. Heather shook her head to clear the vision from her mind and withdrew her hand from her teachers to steady her nerves.

'What are you seeing? What do you see? You just saw something didn't you. Of course, you did. You have the Sight don't you?'

Miss Boniface shuffled closer to Heather; her eyes had taken on the same beady quality as the sea bird and she was leaning towards Heather as if trying to see inside her head. Heather started.

'Umm, er, nothing, I saw nothing I'm feeling very faint and queasy today. I'm not sure why.' Heather didn't want to share any more.

'Oh, erm, maybe it could be that I guess. It's just that I thought we had an understanding.'

Heather tried to cover her deceit by spilling her chocolate on Miss Boniface's blanket.

'Oh sorry I'm so clumsy as well. Yes, I've felt like it for the last few days keep on thinking that I see things I'm sure it's nothing. My mum says it will pass.'

Heather took a deep breath to steady herself and looked her teacher in the eyes. To her dismay she could see that Miss Boniface was not deceived and in fact looked even more intent on discovering the truth of the situation.

Heather covered her ring with her other hand and met her teacher's inquisitive gaze. Heather realised just how powerful her teacher was at making you do what she wanted. Her eyes were blazing, and she could see that Miss Boniface did not expect to be disobeyed. Heather wondered briefly if her teacher was a hypnotist. Deep inside she felt her anger burn and realised that she had had enough of being interrogated.

'I know that you are hiding the truth from me Heather. Tell me everything you saw and everything you know about this ring of yours.'

This time, Heather was ready for her. She felt a rush of energy pulse through the very fabric of her being and allowed her eyes meet her teacher's square on. She no longer felt intimidated by her teacher and had had enough of how weirdly she was behaving. Glancing at her ring she noticed that it was pulsing a dark red colour in time with her heartbeat. For the first time in her life she found that she could easily resist her teacher's coercion. Miss Boniface, her face hardened, kept grilling Heather but this time about her ring. She seemed to have dismissed all thoughts of what Heather may or may not have seen in her vision.

'Where did you get the ring?

'A friend gave it to me.'

'Your ring is very rare, friends don't just give them to little girls. Who was it that gave it to you?'

'I don't know, just someone I met in town. It was a present.'

A present from whom? Tell me who gave it to you. Did they tell you about its true value, about what it stands for?

Like I said, it was an old friend of my mum's and she gave it to me that's all. Why do you keep asking all these questions?

Frowning, Miss Boniface began to rub her ring. She sensed that something wasn't right and kept on firing questions at Heather over and over again. Heather found herself struggling to keep the truth shaded from Miss Boniface as her teacher's eyes locked powerfully and darkly onto hers. For Heather it felt as if the words kept rising in her mind and wanted to escape into the air to tell Miss Boniface everything, but still she resisted with all of her strength. Then Miss Boniface raised her ring to Heather's face and muttered a couple of strange words under her breath. Her ring lit up and the intensity of its light took Heather by surprise. A dark red light from her teacher's ring broke through Heather's defences and crumbled her resolve. She felt powerless. To her dismay the details of her strange meeting with the old ladies came pouring out of her lips. She experienced the weird sensation of hearing her own words but as if somebody else was speaking them. It was if she had moved to a spot somewhere just beyond where she was sitting and that her body was answering for her. As she spoke Miss Boniface grew more and more angry.

'You are too young and weak to be able to resist me Heather. You are much too young for that ring. No one had the right to give it to you! No one asked me for permission to pass it to you! This is my village! Hang on... where were you when it was given to you?'

'Saltkirk. In the café, beside the old castle.'

For some reason this made Miss Boniface jump. She drew her breath.

'Did you pass a test to get this ring?'

She asked this with an almost trembling voice. Heather tried to resist but it was in vain.

'Yes.'

Miss Boniface slowly held out her hand and extended her ring finger. The sun had just set, and it was fast becoming dark yet Heather's ring still glowed with it's ominous warning light. Heather found herself raising her hand towards Miss Boniface's. She watched as she extended her finger towards her teacher, powerless to do anything to stop it. Miss Boniface brought her ring alongside Heather's. Slowly the two rings began to glow brighter and brighter. As Heather looked down transfixed her own ring suddenly blazed with a blindingly bright blue light. It outshone Miss Boniface's ring. Like the flash of a camera going off it nearly blinded both of them.

Miss Boniface withdrew her hand quickly gasping with pain. Heather found she had power over her limbs again. She jumped up, furious and livid with a sudden rage. Heather hated being bossed around or bullied. She wanted to scream with anger at Miss Boniface but controlled herself when she noticed that her teacher seemed to have withdrawn inside herself and was visibly shaking.

'The ring knows you,' she said dully. 'It should have been mine. This just cannot be. You are too young, you are just a child.'

Heather spoke cautiously but her anger still bubbled under the surface.

'It's just a ring! Why were you asking me all of these questions? Why couldn't I refuse you? Who are you?'

But Miss Boniface wasn't listening. Her face grew dark and she stood up. She held out her arm and the huge gannet landed on it with it's web feet, balancing effortlessly. Then Miss Boniface turned to Heather, holding out her ring hand again.

'You don't mind if we swap do you? As you said, it's just a ring and I am sure mine will fit you much better.'

As Miss Boniface locked her in her stare Heather began to feel all of her strength drain again. But this time she was ready. From deep within her she called to Ran and the ocean. In her mind she heard Ran's cry ring out as loud as a bell. Immediately Heather felt as if a huge wave of unmeasurable power arose within her. Summoning all of its energy she spoke her simple word of command;

'*No!*'

Heather was surprised at the sound of her own voice – it sounded deep and powerful and ancient. Heather's answer knocked Miss Boniface backwards. Her hypnotic abilities evaporated, instantly releasing Heather from her teacher's control. Miss Boniface's pretty young face exploded with anger and rage.

'You dare to challenge me! You, a mere child! Get the ring Iki-Ryo and take her eyes as well.'

Heather leapt sideways and screamed as the huge bird lunged for her. She fell backwards, her ankle twisted and she felt a stab of pain. The bird was upon her almost immediately. Heather felt a stab of pain as its beak slashed at the arm Heather was covering her face with. The pain made Heather lose her focus and she felt her power ebb away again. 'No,' she called weakly this time as the bird wheeled around, leapt into the air and then started to dive straight at her as if it was aiming to spear a fish in the water. Heather screamed;. the bird squawked and was thrown off course. It plummeted to the ground and lay there stunned. She gasped and spun round in time to see Miss Boniface collapsing into the sand at the same time. Heather couldn't believe that she had so easily averted the attack of the huge bird. Then she found herself lifted off the ground by a strong pair of arms and she realised that Joe was standing beside her.

'Quick, check the teacher,' said a familiar gruff voice.

Joe obediently went to help up an ashen-faced Miss Boniface, who staggered slowly to her feet. Heather looked round. The gannet had mustered itself and had leapt into the air and was weaving away from the beach in a drunken fashion. They all watched it fly away.

'Wow,' said Joe, with pride in his voice. 'You must have winded it Grandfather. What a shot. I never knew you could throw a stone that well.'

'It's a trick I learnt from your father,' said his grandfather, causing Joe to open his eyes as wide as possible.

The moment of sharing was broken with a distraught Miss Boniface suddenly babbling.

'Thank god you came, that dreadful bird…it was attacking us, I was terrified … oh thank you.'

She held out her hand to Joe's grandfather who took it like the gentleman he was and helped her to her feet.

'Oh please help me back up the cliff path, the shock has made me weak.'

'Hey Heather, are you alright?'

Joe pointed to Heather's arm. A long thin cut was bleeding freely. It was clean and would heal quickly but Heather shuddered as she realised how lucky she was the bird's beak hadn't touched her eyes. She looked at Miss Boniface. She had completely changed her demeanour. She was acting all weak and feminine. Her voice was soft and pleading. She was allowing Joe's grandfather to help her up the cliff path as the tide had now cut them off from the beach trail. She didn't even glance back at Heather.

'That bird it was terrible, I'm so glad you came when you did, it must have sensed I had food… my, how strong you are, can I lean on you?'

Joe's grandfather helped Miss Boniface up the path.

'Never seen a gannet do that before, must have been crazed, possibly poisoned or something. Here let me help you.'

Joe gave Heather his handkerchief for her bleeding arm.

'You wuz lucky,' he said. 'We only just got here in time. That bird was huge. Did it attack the teacher as well?'

'No Joe,' said Heather, 'she made it attack me!'

'What?!' gasped Joe, goggled-eyed.

Heather kept her voice low as they followed the adults up the path to safety.

'She's not as nice as she makes out, it's all an act. Look, she's got your grandfather eating out of her hand. He didn't even see my cut arm. She's dangerous Joe.'

Joe was silent and found himself agreeing with Heather. His grandfather never usually missed anything with his laser eyes. But why would their nice, kind and supportive teacher want to harm Heather? Joe frowned; he wouldn't have believed anyone else but Heather. He put a protective arm around his friend's shoulder and helped her to steady herself on the steep path. He decided that they should take a slightly different route.

'Come on Heather, I'll walk you home.'

13
The Storm Approaches

Just as they got to the top of the cliff Heather let out a gasp and half groan. In the distance, in the last rays of a setting sun, she could easily see a flotilla of small boats leaving the harbour. Already specks of white, sea birds were wheeling around them, and they were headed for the wide expanse of the sea.

'What's the matter?' said Joe. 'Look, they're leaving, now, today, tonight, I forgot, I didn't wave goodbye to dad. I always do that. He says I bring him good luck.'

Heather felt a knot twist tightly in her stomach. She

was confused how could she have missed the boats leaving. It was true she had been distracted today but she had never forgotten to say bon voyage to her father before. She looked ahead. Where the path forked to allow Heather and Joe to head back to the harbour and her house Miss Boniface stopped. Joe's grandfather was stooping to look at a flower growing on an outcrop of rock. Miss Boniface, her red hair billowing in the breeze, was looking back at Heather; she had a triumphant and threatening smile on her face. Heather squeezed Joe's arm so hard that he almost yelped in pain, but he looked up and caught sight of Miss Boniface's lingering grin. Miss Boniface flung her attention back round to Joe's grandfather, and suddenly seemed to remember her act of feigned feminine weakness. She staggered a bit on the rocky path and gave out a little cry of fake shock. Joe's grandfather, politely and with great concern, took her arm again and then handed her a single stem of a small purple flower. Joe growled in a low voice.

'Ok I saw that. She's a tricky one for sure. Look at her playing grandfather like a fiddle. I have never seen anything like it in my life. Grandfather always keeps a distance from folk.'

'I just don't believe it. She's always been so nice to me. Joe, she tried to steal my ring!'

Miss Boniface looked around quickly and fixed them both with another winning smile which lingered just too long in Joe's direction. As she stared at Joe she touched her ring. Heather glanced at Joe and saw him blush. His eyes changed for a moment and he blinked as if confused. Suddenly Joe pulled away from Heather.

'She tried to steal your ring? She set a sea bird on you? Heather are you sure that you have got your facts right? I mean, I'm on your side but...'

'Yes Joe, and I'm sure she prevented me from watching the boats leave as well. What don't you believe me now. I'm not making this up I think she kept me from the boats on purpose...'

Heather snapped at Joe with far more anger than she had meant to use.

'Oh come on Heather, why would she do that?' said Joe looking with some alarm and confusion at Heather.

Heather's frown matched Joe's as they slowed down. She absentmindedly took his arm – just like the older couple now some way ahead. Joe grew resentful of just how familiar Miss Boniface ws being with his grandfather. He forgot what Heather had said and suddenly his anger flared up.

'He said he was going for a walk with me.' said Joe fiercely – his anger seemed to clear his head and he turned back towards Heather.

Heather let her anger at Joe pass. She could see that he was confused and feared that her teacher was messing with his head. She felt a wave of sympathy and realised that Joe was probably the only person that was there for her. She also realised just how protective of his grandfather Joe was.

'It's Ok Joe, it's her, it's not him, she could charm anyone. She just wants to divide us. I'm sure she has a reason for everything she's doing, I just don't understand what she thinks she's up to. I really don't understand adults at all sometimes. Come on let's get down to the harbour, I can't make it out from here, perhaps Dad's boat hasn't gone yet. Maybe we're not too late'

Heather's mind was spinning as the pair took the path in the cliff park that lead back down to the harbour. Joe's grandfather and Miss Boniface didn't notice them slip away. Heather heard the hope in her own voice, but she felt the despair in her heart. She tried to lift her spirits and, despite her sore ankle, keep up with Joe who was laughing as he tried to run down the steep slope without slipping up. Heather felt cross with herself and confused by her teacher's terrifying behaviour. The world seemed to have got weirder and weirder over the last few days. Heather tried to comfort herself with the fact that she hadn't told Miss Boniface about Ran. Her promise was safe. Joe paused for a second to catch his breath and Heather slid to a stop almost crashing into her friend.

'What's the matter?' she cried, anxiety raising in her voice.

'Look,' said Joe. There was no mistaking the huge white gull that was flying slowly back up the cliff. The children could see from where they were that it seemed to be labouring in its flight.

'I think your grandfather must have bruised it,' said Heather and allowed herself a small smile.

'Good,' said Joe fiercely. 'I saw that bird attacking you, it was nowhere near her at all, she was just standing watching, I swear she was laughing now I come to think about it. Mind you, it was a flipping good shot with that stone. Never knew Grandfather had it in him.' Joe chuckled, 'must have hurt.'

'Wish he'd killed it.'

Heather shocked herself with the thought. She felt instantly ashamed. That was so unlike her. She had never wished harm to anybody or anything before. She felt her thoughts darken towards Miss Boniface again – it was her fault that she felt this way. Heather checked her emotions. They all seemed so strong at the moment. Heather ws struggling with perspective. She wanted her usual clarity to return. She promised herself that whatever happened hate was not an emotion she would allow back into her heart again. She allowed her concentration on the steep path to clear and quieten her mind. Bit by bit she felt a deep calm and clarity return. With every breath her emotions quietened down. As she steadied her breathing she noticed that the pain in her ankle disappeared. She glanced at the cut on her arm, it had already begun to scab and heal over. She felt her energy rise in her again as her heart once more lifted with the memories of all of the amazing things that had happened to her of the last couple of days. She noticed that her ring was once more a gentle blue colour. With a sudden howl of delight she easily passed Joe who lost his footing, surprised by Heather's sudden unexpected turn of speed.

Heather felt as if she hadn't time to stop and really consider the rapid chain of recent events and bizarre experiences. Heather worried about her extreme emotions though; she had never wished any bird or animal harm before. The earlier thought had scared and shocked her. As they approached the cobbles of the harbour and the sun finally sank below the horizon Heather shivered. As the air grew colder it seemed to her that there was a darkness around her village that she had never noticed before. They had to slow their pace as they nearly collided with a procession of villagers, good humouredly filing back up the hill away from the harbour. Some were veering towards the pub and others towards the warmth of their cottages. Heather called to Joe as she slowed to a walk on the cobbles.

'It looks as if the whole village came out.'

Breathing heavily, Joe slowed to a walk. The run had taken more out of him than Heather. He had little experience of the steep pathways of the Scottish coast and he was secretly wondering if Heather had been a goat in a past life and whether his legs would ever recover. Some of the villagers passed Heather and gave the young folk tolerant smiles. Heather found herself warmed by their inclusive kindness. She had always been popular amongst the local community and was proud at how quickly town folk forgave each other. It was as if there existed an unwritten understanding that life moved on as quickly as the tides in the harbour. When life was precious it put things like disagreements into perspective. Anyhow, Heather's cheerful and upbeat manner and her infectious laughter and genuine kindness towards her neighbours had earned enough credibility for them to easily forgive her outburst at the meeting the night before. Heather almost bumped headlong into her mother.

'Oh it's my wee bonny princess and...'

She left the sentence unsaid. Her mother could see the concern on her daughters face but it was not that which stopped her, she could see the fiercely loyal expression in Joe's eyes. She smiled to herself. This intense young man with the black eyes and wild look had definitely made an impact on her daughter. Still, at least she had a friend now, and even better than that, one that wasn't a fish.

'Has Dad...?'

'Yup you've not long missed them – he said to me to give you a great big kiss from him.'

Heather was anxious.

'Have all the boats gone out? I don't want to jinx them, I always wave goodbye.'

'Don't be silly Heather, don't you get all superstitious on me. I thought you were the scientist in the family.'

Heather's mum could see that her gentle teasing hadn't worked so she decided that honesty might be a better tack with her hyper-sensitive daughter.

'Yes, they have all gone after the herring... your Dad knows that you are busy with your life and the best thing you can do for him is not worry lest you get all nervy like the other women of this village. I'll make a cup of tea and warm the place up. Bring Joe if you want.'

Her mother called out the last few words after the two children as they darted towards to harbour walls.

As they approached the edge of the harbour walls the night was not quite upon them. The sky was still light, and the water reflected back a greenish hue.

'That's odd,' said Heather

'What's odd?' asked Joe.

'Look, they've left their nets.'

Heather pointed to several piles of orange nets neatly folded and weighted down.

'Perhaps they have spares.'

Joe dropped a pebble into the deep harbour water so that it made a satisfying plopping sound. Heather's heart raced. She felt pure panic rise inside her again. She held her hand to her mouth and turned pale.

'Oh no, they must have taken the new ones, the large nets, the ones that all of the fuss is about.'

'What's the difference?'

Joe observed her mounting concern. Heather looked as if she had seen a ghost.

'Oh, they are larger and have smaller holes. Fishing for herring means fish for food and fertiliser, they don't care what they catch.'

Heather strained her eyes out towards sea and the rapidly disappearing vessels.

'So, what's the problem?' asked Joe, 'they'll just catch more, they'll come back sooner and all will be well...won't it?'

His voice trailed off as Heather slumped heavily on a couple of lobster pots.

'I'm just worried what will happen if the try to use those new nets,' said Heather.

'That's funny, so was grandfather,' said Joe, suddenly remembering overhearing his Grandfather on the phone. 'He said that using those new nets would be like vacuuming the seabed. That's why he grassed your dad up to the authorities. I just thought he was being an interfering old bugger as always. But why are you so worried? I'm sure the authorities will slam a ban on them?'

'Yes, but they will start landing black fish, fish that's sold on the black market. We've never done that before in this village. They just don't know how dangerous this is for them. Maybe we can stop them.'

Joe fell silent. He felt as if he half understood Heather's fears but as if a huge piece of the jigsaw was missing. Heather was standing and looking at the small tin shack that housed the radio for the fleet. She ran over to it, so Joe followed.

'What ya doing?'

Heather was desperately trying to open the door. It was tightly locked as usual. It was probably the only door that was ever locked in the village. The radio was the fleet's only hope of being contacted directly, unless the coastguard, positioned miles away needed to speak with the boats. Joe grabbed Heather's arm alarmed that they might get into serious trouble.

'And what would you say exactly?' he asked. 'Look, I know you're concerned about your dad but why are you so worried? You can still try to persuade them, tell them to change their fishing techniques when they get back. We could research on the school computer, get all our facts straight and...'

Heather had turned away, she wasn't listening, and she gave the lock one last impotent rattle. She wished she could tell Joe everything, but she knew that her secret must be kept safe just as she had promised. And what could she say to stop the fleet? They wouldn't listen to scientists and politicians so what could she, a twelve-year-old girl say or do to change their habits?

'Come on,' said Heather suddenly, trying to change the mood, 'let's grab some tea and cake, it's starting to get late. My mum usually makes a chocolate one when the boats go out. Dad says it is the best in the whole of Scotland.'

'Ok,' said Joe agreeably. He was starving again, so much for the fish pie filling him up. It had been an active day and his tummy was making noises that he could hear above the waves crashing into the side of the harbour walls.

When they reached Heather's house Maria scolded them both for letting a sea bird attack them. She was concerned about Heather's arm but on closer expectation she realised the cut was healing well and only needed cleaning and a large plaster.

'You were lucky there Heather. That's strange; a gannet, you say? A herring gull protecting its nest; or after your chips, but a gannet! Bloody huge those birds are. You were lucky love. Not like you though...'

She finished with Heather's wound and placed a steaming mug of tea and a huge slice of cake in front of them. Joe ate the cake slowly savouring every mouthful. Heather's dad was right. It was the nicest, creamiest, chocolaty cake he had ever tasted.

'Mm, this is just amazing Mrs MacDougall' he said with his mouth half full.

'High praise indeed. I hear that Isabella's cakes are world beaters.'

Heather's mum winked at Heather and put another generous slice onto Joe's nearly empty plate.

'Come on Heather, eat up, you've hardly touched yours.'

'Mum why have they taken the new nets?'

'I don't know my love, it's because of a combination of reasons I guess. The yield of fish has gone down these past four seasons. It does this sometimes. Trouble is, with all the payments on the boats and the new nets, well, we have no choice. Not that I agree with it totally Heather.'

Heather's mum had notice the cloud settling over Heather's head. Joe looked from one to another and begrudgingly paused eating his second slice of cake.

'My grandfather says that you have to let the fish stocks return.'

Both women turned to look at him.

'Look, I know none of you like him, I know he's a crotchety old bugger, whoops sorry Mrs MacDougall, but he knows what he's about.'

'And why, all of a sudden, is your grandfather an authority over the likes of us who have fished this coast since before he was born?'

Heather's mum was still smiling as she quizzed Joe, teasing him. Joe seemed embarrassed by his outburst. His voice lowered, and his eyes welled up. He looked at Heather and her mum and quietly began to speak.

'Grandfather, he, he once had a huge fleet of boats. He was really successful. He had a factory and a cannery. Pretty much ran everything. Then it all went wrong. Everybody wanted him to stop fishing but he didn't. The fish stocks just dwindled into nothing – just like what's happening here, and then, one season, there were no more – they vanished. Must have ruined him 'cause we had a huge house over there and now look where we live.'

Heather punched him gently on the arm.

'You only live in the best house in the whole village, why, I would kill for that view.'

Heather's mum looked anxious for Joe and wanted to make him comfortable again.

'Now Heather, in America the houses are much bigger than our wee fishing cottages, am I not right?'

'I didn't mean to be ungrateful Mrs MacDougall, and I love living here...' he glanced at Heather and back, 'it's just that my grandfather knows what he's about. He's just rubbish about how he says it to folks. He always seems to make everybody around him angry. I just don't want to have to move again.'

Joe hid his eyes in his tea and cake and filled his mouth quickly so that he didn't have to speak any more. He wasn't comfortable giving speeches. Finishing his plate he stood up to go.

'That was delicious Mrs MacDougall, he said, 'See you tomorrow Heather.' In a trice he was out of the door.

Heather and her mother burst out laughing.

'Did you see how red he got, bless him Heather I think he's got the hots for you.'

'Oh shut up Mum,' said Heather, grateful for the chance to laugh. 'We're just friends. He seems to understand me, he needs a bit of a helping hand getting used to the village and our ways.'

Suddenly the small radio in the corner of the room stopped playing an upbeat summer song. The local station crackled into life.

'Just interrupting this show to bring an early storm warning to the west coast. It's brewing quickly out in the Atlantic. Seems to have come out of nowhere. Might miss us completely. Might not. Might reach storm force before dawn so lock up and stay inside safe tonight. Now back to the swinging sixties...'

Heather and her Mum froze.

'Mum what is it?' asked Heather. 'That's good news, the boats will turn back wont' they?'

'I don't know child. They weren't travelling all the way out to the fishing area today. They were going to trial the nets first. It's just that I worry for the men. The sea was strange today. There was no storm forecast earlier. The Met Office predicted calm seas. I heard the report on the radio myself.' She glanced out of their small kitchen window. The sky seemed to be turning darker. 'Now look at it, there is a storm in the air, I swear.'

'Don't worry mum', said Heather, forcing herself to be calm and reassuring for her mum. She suddenly felt very tired. It had been a long day. Her nerves needed a rest. She wanted to try and forget her worries. Even with the weather forecast her concerns seemed small when she was at home. Heather knew that her dad wouldn't risk the fleet in a storm. They would turn back soon. Then it would all be ok again. Sleepily she said to her mum,

'It's always stormy somewhere and they have the best little boats in Scotland.'

Then she gave her mum a kiss and headed for bed.

*****

Heather awoke suddenly from a very deep sleep that had been full of images of huge waves. She sat up, her heart racing. She was covered in sweat though the night had turned cool. A strong wind was tossing her curtains backwards and forwards. Heather could hear the moan of the wind as it gathered up strength across the roof of the house. Heather was wide-awake – she felt refreshed yet anxious.

She leapt out of bed and ran to the window. The stars were still bright and there weren't any clouds, a good sign. Heather could see across the grey-slated rooftops of the village to where an almost full moon was reflected in the sea. The wind was throwing waves up into the air which crashed into the harbour wall. As Heather scanned the horizon she could see that a huge swell was forming.

Heather quickly threw on a t-shirt, her trainers, a pair of warm tracksuit bottoms and a jumper, and crept downstairs. She paused to remember which stair would creak and, allowing herself a small smile carefully stepped over it and made her way downstairs. The TV was on and blaring away at the back of the cottage. That meant that her grandfather was back from the pub as he always turned the volume up due to his deafness. Heather snuck past him. He was snoring, the remote control still in his hand. She darted into the kitchen, closed the back door behind her and headed down towards the small cove.

Heather's dream was fresh in her mind and was nagging her. It was the same one as she had started to have since she had met Ran. It had been the same image of a huge wave crashing down on her father's vessel, replaying over and over again. Heather felt a flood of anger and frustration with Ran. It had been Ran who had scared Heather with the vision. It just wasn't fair. Heather suddenly felt very small and weak. How could she, still almost a child of twelve, change the minds of grown-ups? It just wasn't fair of Ran to expect her to be able to help.

Arriving on the damp sand she slipped off her red trainers and shivered as her toes made contact with the beach. Heather walked along the bay until she came to the headland and then went around and into the small cove she had been to earlier that day. She was could feel the energy of the waves as they crashed against the cliffs. She sensed the changes in the air and knew that a storm was marshalling somewhere far off. She saw surprised sea birds flung in all directions and then the large bright eyes of a seal bobbing in the waves just offshore.

'Ran,' Heather cried, all of her anger gone and raced down to where the sea foam made patterns on the sand. The large seal swam slowly up and onto the beach. It indulged Heather's need for contact and rolled and laughed as she hugged it.

'Oh Ran, I'm so glad to see you, I have had the strangest few days.'

As Heather said the words she knew them to be true. It seemed strange that the most reassuring presence in her life at the moment, apart from Joe, was a large magical seal. Ran sat upright and then looked directly at Heather. Heather felt the seal's gentle mind bidding her quiet.

'I am sorry that we could not protect you from the witch, but she used cunning and hid her intent. We were in deep council and were making many preparations.'

Heather gasped, amazed at Ran's words.

'Witch? The witch? You mean Miss Boniface?'

'Yes child. She is not like the old ones; she knows little and has only a desire for power. She thinks the legend is only about conquest, not survival.'

'Legend?' quizzed Heather putting her arms around Ran's soft warm neck.

'You have a powerful destiny young Heather and there are few who can truly help you. Beware of the witch. She has been blinded by the ways of man. She is not an elder, she has stolen what she knows. She is being used by darkness to divert the attention of the old man.'

Heather instinctively knew that Ran meant Joe's grand-father. As Ran spoke it was if Heather saw images inside her own head. She saw Joe's grandfather lifting her out of the water, she saw him throwing the stone that struck the gannet, she saw him shouting at the villagers in the hall.

'Yes, my dear child' continued Ran, 'he is your ally, your friend, he has a debt to the ocean. We are allowing him to repay it as he has repented of his old ways. He may even hold the future of your village in his hands. You will soon need to call a gathering; you must gain power over the witch. She has not the true sight. Call what you need to help you but remember to send it back. The ring is true, it is good, it will help but your best ally will be your open-hearted intention to help save us all.'

Heather looked confused; she had caught a glimpse of herself surrounded by a dark swirling cloud.

'Don't worry child,' continued Ran, 'your dreams will help you. Your grandmother has gone to the fleet. She failed to intercede. She knows her task.'

Heather felt the old dread grip her again. Her mouth went dry. Her tummy knotted up tighter than a tangled fishing line. Heather remembered why she had sought Ran out.

'Oh Ran, the dream, the vision, it mustn't happen, I beg you. Look we humans may be stupid but we do care. My father would never hurt the ocean if he really understood.'

'His eyes are clouded by the darkness,' said Ran. 'He sees through fear of loss, fear that there is not enough for all. He cannot release himself from his chosen path. He will not see another way. He is unable to change himself. All he can see is what he will lose if he ceases to fish.'

'But the wave?' stammered Heather.

'What do you smell little sister?'

Heather stopped and sniffed the air. It was obvious to her nose and her senses. She had lived all her life beside the sea and didn't need any magical powers to know the signs of the weather. Her voice shook.

'A storm is coming.'

'Then it has begun,' said Ran.

Ran raised herself up and gently nuzzled the terrified girl's cheek.

'You are now a woman and you must take up your position. Remember, you saw only what might come to pass. Nothing is yet written. See deep into your dreaming, make your dreams one with the universe, She will hear you and if She is pleased by your dreaming She will agree to your terms.'

Heather felt confused. Ran wasn't making sense. Heather shivered; a sudden strong gust of wind battered her young body and a larger wave caught her ankles and washed around Ran.

'You have many sisters who are coming to help you my child. You have their ring; they are sighted ones and not interested in power. Their memories go back to before the times of the church of man, before the time when he became scared and stopped listening to Her.'

Heather felt panic rise in her again. She turned to Ran, who had started to move back towards the sea.

'What do I do? What must I do with the ring? Who are my sisters? What gathering?'

But Ran had reached the sea and was plunging into the waves. Her head bobbed to the surface and Heather heard her voice in her head again.

'The ring will defend you,' Ran called back, 'I must not be seen'.

'Ran, don't go!'

Heather called after the seal but she was gone. Only a ripple remained, fast erased by ever-bigger waves that were starting to rise up out of the dark green sea. Heather looked up as a large cloud, boiling and twisting in the wind, hid the moon. Heather pulled her jumper tighter around herself and turned to make her way back along the beach. In the distance the small church bell rang the first of the twelve bells of midnight. Heather didn't notice a dark shape moving silently from behind the rocks towards her. Like a self-propelled shadow or a swirl of sea mist it scudded along the ground towards Heather. Heather's ring flashed red and she spun around suddenly, her senses heightened by the thought of impending danger. She gasped at what she saw and turned to run back towards the pathway where her trainers waited patiently for her. The dark shape seemed to predict her route and cut her off. Heather dug her toes into the sand and darted left and right but the dark mist simply expanded and with incredible speed it overtook her and then completely enveloped her. It was icy cold and took Heather's breath away making Heather's teeth chatter. It was so dark Heather couldn't see anything at all. It was pitch black. Not even the wind seemed to be able to penetrate. The mist had a strange aroma, it was sweet and sickly but before Heather had a moment to work out what was going on, she felt her knees buckle. It was as if all of her energy was just sucked out of her. She tried to resist by but she couldn't even find her thoughts anymore. She felt like she was dissolving, losing any idea who she was or why she was on the beach. She was dimly aware that she was falling forward in a kind of slow motion collapse. Heather was unconscious before her body crumpled onto the soft damp sand.

14

Dark Magic

Heather's eyes flickered open. She felt groggy, her mouth was dry and she was very cold. At first she couldn't even raise her head, and when she did it felt as if a herd of elephants were stampeding around inside. Heather shivered and slowly raised her thumping head to look around. She was on the floor of a small room. It was fairly dark, and at the far end a fire was flickering. The room appeared to be empty. Heather looked up and, seeing the humble ceiling, realised she was in a bothy, a simple herder's cottage. She tried to move her arms but found that they were tightly bound. Her head span as she tried to force herself free from the bindings. She sagged to the floor again. Just then a door to her right crashed open and a tall figure, covered in a black shawl, swept in. The wind came in with the figure and pushed the shawl from her head. Heather recognised Miss Boniface the moment her red hair spilled out from under her shawl. Realising that Heather was awake Miss Boniface displayed a brief flicker of relief, which was quickly replaced by a look of cold indifference.

'Good you've come round! Now sit up, I don't want you to be missed.'

Heather tried to and failed.

'I can't, my hands are tied.'

'Of course they are. I can't have you waving them around. Who knows what you can do. Did you really think that our conversation was over? The old man was easy to distract, though not unlovely. Hmm, I might take him for a lover,' she mused out loud as if Heather wasn't there. 'Now listen young lady, this is what is going to happen.'

Miss Boniface threw another chunk of peat on the fire where it crackled and cast an eerie orange glow face. Heather saw how mean her teacher's eyes looked and shuddered.

'You are going to give me that ring,' Miss Boniface declared, 'Then you are going to take this drink, which will make you forget everything. Then you are going to walk home and go to bed. When you wake up in the morning you'll think that you have had a bad dream.'

Heather's mouth was too dry to answer. Her tongue felt like a duvet and her jaw ached a little from where she must have fallen earlier. Also, other parts of her body ached. Heather realised that she must have been half dragged to the hiding place.

'Need a drink,' she croaked.

Miss Boniface drew closer and splashed a few drops of water onto her mouth from a flask. Heather licked her lips greedily. At the taste of water, she began to feel better, a shift that Miss Boniface must have noticed as she suddenly drew away.

'Now don't try anything fancy – you are still just a girl and I grow more powerful with every moon.'

'I trusted you. I thought you were my friend. What do you want from me?'

Heather's voice almost cracked as she tried to sit up and get a bearing on her new surroundings.

'I told you. Your ring; the Moon Ring,'

Miss Boniface snapped at Heather and began to stir something in a large tin mug.

'Why?'

Heather roused herself onto one elbow and, blinking into the smoky room, began stalling for time and straining at her bonds. Miss Boniface looked at her closely. Her lips curled into a snarl of resentment and anger.

'Didn't they tell you anything when they gave you the ring? Well, how short sighted of them, pun intended! Stupid old women. They never learn, lifetime after lifetime. Ridiculous. To trust it to a child. Madness!'

Miss Boniface leaned in closer to Heather. Heather flinched as she lifted up a small silver knife to her throat.

'Now then child, I am going to cut your hands free and you are going to give the ring to me and you are not going to try anything, understood? This is a ceremonial knife. It is so sharp it can slice a hair in two. Much sharper than the beak of Iki-Ryo.'

Heather nodded slowly. Miss Boniface kept her gaze firmly on Heather and bent low to grab her arms. Heather winced with pain as the ropes bit deep into her arms. Miss Boniface cut her arms free and then stepped back. Heather could hardly have raised them if she had wanted to. They were numb and the feeling of blood rushing back into them made her cry out. Quick as a flash Miss Boniface had tied her left hand behind her again and had grabbed Heather's ring finger firmly. Heather winced with pain as Miss Boniface tried to pull the ring off. She could see that her finger was already bruised as if someone had tried to wrench her ring off already. Miss Boniface saw Heather notice the bruising on her hand.

'Well I had to try. If you hadn't woken up, if that wraith had sucked you dry then I would have simply cut your finger off. Now take it off and give it to me.'

'I can't,' croaked Heather. I only have one arm free.'

Miss Boniface looked confused.

'Oh,' she said, 'I see, not just a word then, I thought it would be released with a word. I should have known,' continued Miss Boniface as she started to cut Heather's other arm free again, 'that this ring would be difficult to get. Any tricks and it's all over for you my pretty.'

Heather was feeling stronger by the second. Her head was clearing and she felt a slight surge of energy and adrenaline flood her body. She glanced at the sharp little blade and felt it wise to hide this fact from Miss Boniface. Heather was amazed. It had never occurred to her that the ring could not be removed by anyone else. She wondered what else the old women had failed to tell her. Heather was still unsure of why the ring was so important. She realised that it provided some kind of warning to the wearer. It was still glowing red, which Heather now knew was a warning of danger.

'Why do you want the ring so badly?'

Heather played for time as Miss Boniface resigned herself to massaging feeling back into Heather's fingers, trying to reduce the swelling so that the girl could remove the ring easily.

'The Moon Ring? The Ring of the Seer? Because it should be mine of course. Besides, I am the only one who has any idea of its power.'

Heather remembered what Ran had said about Miss Boniface's lust for power.

'What sort of power? I wasn't told anything. The old ladies never told me anything.'

Heather kept up her dazed and confused persona, hoping that the swelling on her fingers remains a bit longer while her strength returned.

'More power than you can imagine, in the right hands, hah, pun intended - again!'

Miss Boniface looked pleased with herself as she pulled Heather upright. She noticed that her legs were still tightly bound, and the pins and needles were beginning to hurt.

'Now' she said, holding out her small silver knife, 'take it off slowly and give it to me and you can keep your finger.'

Heather looked down at the ring. She tried to raise her arms and faked how heavy they felt. Her mind raced.

'NOW!' commanded Miss Boniface, rotating the silver knife between her fingers.

Heather lifted her hands and clasped the ring trying to move it. It wouldn't budge.

'What's the problem?'

Miss Boniface shouted with annoyance as she tried to grab Heather's hands to help her.

'Ow!' yelped Heather, 'My finger is bruised, if you hadn't tried to steal it my finger wouldn't be so swollen. Give me a moment. This really hurts.'

Miss Boniface stood stone-still and then swore out loud. She could see that Heather was right; in the light of the fire they could both see that her finger was half as big as the others.

'I'll get some oil out of the lamp, and if that doesn't work then my knife will help us.'

Miss Boniface turned to blow out the small oil lamp. The bothy was plunged into a darkness softened only by the spluttering fire. Inside Heather's mind she suddenly heard Ran's voice call 'NOW! Heather raised her ring hand and fought to clear her head. The moment she did she felt her mind race along her arm to the ring. Like a torrent of flood water her consciousness connected with the magical stone. She focussed all her attention on it. The ring began to glow and she felt its presence like the sun breaking out through the clouds. Then, as if her mind reached out across the bay, across the land and high into the atmosphere Heather silently called out one word, 'HELP!' Miss Boniface span round from the guttered lamp and noticed Heather's movements a fraction of a second too late. She grabbed Heather and slapped her face causing her to fall to the ground.

'Oh no you don't, young lady. That ring won't work for you anyway – you are still a child. What a shame you won't ever get the chance to know it's true power.'

Heather held her gaze and through her tears of pain managed a knowing smile. Miss Boniface suddenly grew pale.

'No, you can't have, no, you are too young. Not yet. You are still a child. Oh my god, what did you summon?'

Suddenly the fire went out. The door burst open, showering splinters of broken wood in all directions, and a dark swirling storm rushed into the small building. The bothy was filled with a darkness that rumbled and roared like a ravenous animal cornering it's pray. The sudden impact of the explosion and the all-engulfing dark was terrifying. Like the breath of an angry dragon the hot black sulphurous smoke made it hard to breath. Heather was horrified and rolled against the wall curling up like a baby. She shielded her face with her ring hand and cowered down onto the damp floor. A sudden white light of calm and ancient wisdom exploded into her mind like fireworks going off. Heather felt a surge of amazing pure energy pulse through her. A rush of strange words tumbled out of her mouth and a circle of light expanded out from Heather and wrapped itself around her like a cocoon. Within the swirling chaos she could hear Miss Boniface screaming and cursing and thrashing around blindly .

'Heather, what did you summon?! What did you call up?! You stupid girl, it will be the death of both of us!'

The darkness seemed to boil around Heather's cocoon of light and she shrank further against the wall. Miss Boniface screamed. This time her teacher's scream was the most terrifying sound that Heather had ever heard. Yet as soon as it started it cut short and a terrible silence filled the room. The silence seemed to growl and move as if searching for something. The air grew so thick Heather found herself gasping for breath. It felt like the very darkness was beginning to press down on her like a large dog pushing against the boundaries of her diminishing bubble of light. Suddenly Heather remembered Ran's words. Quickly, she marshalled her senses, found a fraction of calm from somewhere deep within herself and focussed her mind on the ring. She sensed it respond and, in a flash, with her last strength she shouted out: 'I command you to return to where you came from!'

Heather lost consciousness momentarily. Seconds later her adrenaline kicked in and woke her with a start, her senses alert and breathing regular once more. Heather could hear her pounding heart beginning to slow and she felt a reassuring wave of calm flow into her mind. The glowing peat in the fire crackled back to life and a warm glow spread into the room. Heather sat up and quickly nursed her fingers into action. Keeping her eye firmly on the black heap on the floor that was Miss Boniface she hurried to untie the rope that bound her legs together. Heather winced with pain as she willed her bruised fingers into action. It seemed to Heather that it took longer than she could possibly imagine freeing herself. The moment that the last knot came free, still keeping her gaze on Miss Boniface, Heather leapt up and made for the open doorway avoiding the splinters of wood that lay all around. Leaping outside, she found herself on a familiar track. The wind was now howling around her. Her own long dark locks of hair whipped Heather mercilessly as she tried to see where she was going. In the sporadic moonlight that kept breaking out from behind the clouds scudding across the sky she recognised that she was not far from the cliffs that she knew so well; she would be home in a few minutes if she walked fast.

Heather tried to run down the rutted path but stumbled and fell almost immediately. The feeling had hardly returned to her legs yet and as she lay on the ground getting her breath back she felt the odd sensation of blood starting to flow through her veins again. Heather counted to five in her mind and pulled herself upright. She felt ready to begin her run again but instead she froze. Directly in front of her were the dim outlines of four shadowy figures. As her heart thumped and her senses prepared for flight, the figures all began to speak at once, fighting each other for attention. Heather sighed as she immediately recognised the warm and kindly tones of the old women who had given her the ring back in Saltkirk.

'Hello again little sister.'

'Are you all right?'

'What happened to you to cause you to call us so loudly?'

'We're sorry we took so long.'

'The way was not so easy.'

'We're getting old.'

'A violent storm blocked our path.'

'Oh hush sisters, the child is exhausted.'

One of the figures stepped forward and swept Heather into her arms, just as her numbed legs gave way. Heather instantly recognised the tall, thin old lady who had given her the ring. Heather tried to answer her questions but her voice came out as a babble, as if she had lost the power of speech.

'Hush little sister, shh, no need to speak. Come on sisters help me carry her back to the bothy, we can't take her home like this.'

'Here,' said another and made Heather take a drop of fiery liquid from a small silver flask. It tasted like a sweet concoction of fruits but with an alcoholic zing that travelled all the way to Heather's toes, making them tingle with warmth. At once Heather felt a great calm come over her. With the help of the willing hands of the old ladies she was now able to half walk and half stagger back to the bothy. The short and stout lady motioned to the group to pause and went into the bothy on her own. She quickly remerged and beckoned the rest in. Whatever she had done in those few seconds was amazing. The fire was roaring, the lamp was lit, and Miss

Boniface was neatly tied up and still unconscious on the ground. The four old ladies appeared tremendously excited.

'Who have we here?'

'It's that teacher from the village school.'

'Oh yes wasn't she a...?'

'Yes, that's right...'

'She was always a devious one.'

'As arrogant as a man.'

'No sight, no memories.'

'She deserves the title of witch.'

'If she is a witch then who are you lot?'

Heather suddenly found the power of speech again. She felt warm and safe in the cramped conditions of the bothy surrounded by her rescuers. The old ladies were clearly her friends. They all bustled around, tidying up the mess in the bothy, trimming lamps. One checked the very pale Miss Boniface, who was hardly breathing. Heather's question made them all stop what they were doing and they all turned to look at her.

'Well,' said the thin lady, 'come sisters, the tea is ready, let us sit and talk. We can slow time for a few minutes. The child, our sister,' she corrected herself, 'deserves an explanation.'

The four old ladies sat down on the floor beside heather. A huge tin mug of piping hot, sweet, black tea was passed almost ritually between them.

'My name is Muriel, this is Gladys, Jean and Susan.'

The thin one tilted the mug to each woman as she introduced them. Heather told them her name, they all smiled, and she realised that they already knew. They nodded smiling at Heather and she thought that the women resembled a classic bunch of sweet old grannies. She almost chuckled at the absurdity of this small group of old ladies being her powerful rescuers. Muriel continued:

'We are not witches, yet you shouldn't fear us even if we went under that title.'

'One bad witch does not all witches make bad.'

Muriel glanced with a frown at Miss Boniface.

'Besides, there is no such thing as witches, it was a name given to us Wise Women by ignorant and scared men. They wanted our knowledge for themselves. They wanted to ....'

'Hush Muriel,' interrupted Gladys, 'No, my youngest sister, we are simply Wise Women, seers, healers, midwives; we are the keepers of the knowledge that preserves us all. Jean,' she said to the plumpest of the four, 'you are the historian, you explain to Heather.'

'Oh Heather, my dear sister,' Jean said, 'It was the Christian church that gave us that title and created the myth, changing us into symbols of fear. The church wanted control, over everybody and everything. The old ways were sometimes brutally repressed and so the idea of a witch was born to create an enemy for the church to protect you all from. You see, the church is still run by men and men saw our knowledge as power, as a challenge to their authority. Now of course times are changing and we can all pretty much be who we want but some women still choose to take up the old title and practice the ways of knowledge and magic for themselves. We never had to do that up here as the church never really got control in some places here in the Highlands, we were so much a part of everyday life. Our communities never forgot that we were mothers, daughters, wives, sisters first and then healers, wise women, seers and the like second. They loved us, protected our knowledge and cherished us. We chose to bear the burden of this world for the good of all. We live and die, love and lose, celebrate and mourn with our families.'

Jean paused to sip the tea and winked at Heather. She seemed pleased to be able to share her vast knowledge. Heather found herself warming to the old women and felt excited to be in their company. As she started to feel normal Heather glanced around the bothy. Her rescuers all seemed eminently sensible, grounded and kind, and they all emanated a deep sense of deep wisdom and insight.

Gladys spoke, unwinding an overly long scarf from around her blue rinsed curls.

'When we gave you your ring it was to fulfil a prophecy. See, we Sisters have had that ring since the beginning of time. That is the oldest one known to us and the prophecy says that you should have it as a symbol and sign of respect to the tradition that birthed you. Your grandmother, bless her immortal soul, bore it faithfully for nearly a century, through famine and feast, heartache and pain, and never abused the power or vested in her.'

The tin mug was passed to Susan, the quietest of the bunch, who stared warmly at Heather through thick glasses. Her voice was quiet yet strong with kindness and love.

'We knew that your sacred mother would come if we called to her in her dreams. We recognised you immediately, you have your grandmother's eyes. You see my dear, your path does not lie as ours, you have access to all the mysteries of the world for it is She that is speaking to you. You are one of the chosen ones. Born at this time to wake up humanity and help it save itself from itself. You must intercede for all humanity. You see child, the great mother, our dear blue planet, she is going to choose a new way soon, a new beginning for all life. She has been thinking long and deep, she feels the pain of our ways and once she has reached her decision there will be no turning back. Catastrophic events will start to happen as she gives humans final warnings. Humans are hurting her too badly. She weeps at the loss of life, her life, yet she knows her strength. Her time is not like ours. For the great mother, we come and go like butterflies, like mayflies, like flowers; living for mere moments, and then are gone, back to her. But although she has spent thousands of years gently rearing us to be her helpmates, she can wait a millennium if needed for a new race to evolve. That is if we don't persuade her otherwise.'

Susan paused; she seemed embarrassed at her long speech but the others all gave here approving looks. Heather was touched by the love and mutual support shown by the women to each other.

'But why did Miss Boniface attack me and try to steal my ring?'

'Oh she is caught up in her own petty games of power. She has chosen to think like a man and desires power over knowledge and death over life,' answered Muriel. 'But I think...' she chuckled, looking over to the still form of Miss Boniface, 'that her days as a witch are over.'

Suddenly Heather was concerned.

'Will she be alright, she won't die will she, I mean she is my teacher?'

'Yes,' said Gladys sternly. 'She'll regain consciousness in her own bed, we will see to that. She will feel terrible and remember nothing.'

Gladys spoke a word in an ancient tongue and the sound of it momentarily transported Heather to an ancient time. Somehow she knew that it meant 'release'. Gladys then quietly slipped Miss Boniface's ring off her finger.

'She will have no power and no memory of it.'

'What did that terrible smoke-devil thing do to her? It terrified me. It was as if the smoke came alive. I didn't mean to summon anything bad. I just called out for help. I'm not a bad person. I wouldn't harm anyone.'

Heather remembered her anger at the gannet the day before. She wondered if she was as nice as she thought. Gladys lent over and rubbed some scented oils into Heather's bruises.

'You are not bad little sister. We know your heart is good. Never doubt yourself. You just called out with your power when you were scared that's all. Fear calls out to fear. That's why we have to practice our art carefully. Mind you, who knows,' said Gladys, rubbing some cream gently into Heather's fingers, 'your terror conjured something terrible – it is the same on all levels. Perhaps if you had found your incarceration an amusing incident, rather than a terrifying one, you might have conjured up a huge pink rabbit.'

The women laughed out loud at the thought of a large pink rabbit terrorising Miss Boniface. Heather laughed too and suddenly felt herself growing very sleepy.

'Come sisters,' said Muriel, 'let's restore our little world to order, at least we have the power to do that.'

She bent towards Heather who was snug in a shawl.

'Sleep now child and when you awake remember this; simply use the ring, say our names and we will hear your thoughts. In two nights the moon will be full.'

Heather felt herself lifted as if she were as light as a feather, and sensed that she was leaving the bothy. She was half aware of a dreamy flight home across the path of the moon.

15
The Storm Awakens

When Heather awoke the next morning it was to the roaring of the wind. She could hear it booming and moaning as it wooshed its way around the roofs and chimney pots of the village, rattling tiles, torturing aerials and making windows chatter like teeth on a cold night. Heather paused for a second, wondering how she had got back home to bed. The horrors of the night replayed in her mind. She shuddered as she remembered Miss Boniface and her murderous intent. Heather moved slowly, her body seemed to ache all over. Stepping carefully out of bed she glanced down at her legs and then her arms. Although the Wise Women's healing potion had reduced the swelling on her fingers there was no hiding the fact that she had been in the wars. Heather glanced into her mirror as she put some food into the fish tank. The bruises and rope marks on her legs and wrists were turning all the colours of the rainbow though the cut on her arm was scabbing nicely. She hurried to put on some clothes; she didn't want to alarm her mother. Heather was only just in time as her mum suddenly popped her head round the bedroom door.

'How are you feeling today my little one?'

'Fine mum, thanks, I'll be ready for school in a mo.'

'It's Saturday dafty,' said her mother.

Heather pushed her dirty and torn clothes under her bed with the end of her foot.

'Oh yeh I forgot.'

Then, noticing that her mum was lingering she asked,

'What is it mum?'

'Have you seen the weather darling?'

'Yep it looks really windy.'

'I still think there is a huge storm on the way, the radio is crackling away and none of the so-called experts seem to have an idea of what's going on. Apparently, the seas are raging all around the coast of Britain. It's not too bad here yet but the boats should have come back in. I can't imagine what's keeping them. Your father never puts the boats into jeopardy.'

Heather realised that her mother was worried, scared even. She looked as if she hadn't slept very well and Heather surmised that she had been anxiously waiting for her daughter to wake up so she would have somebody to chat to.

Heather realised that her mum wanted her to take the lead. She spoke what was on both their minds.

'Should we give the fleet a call and ask them back in to shore?'

Heather gingerly followed her mother down the stairs into the kitchen where the smell of pancakes filled the air.

'Your grandfather has gone down to the wireless centre to do just that. Bless his cotton socks, at least he has a use for something. Mind you, the wind could blow a man off his feet and your grandad don't weigh that much.'

Heather's mum tried to laugh and did her best to sound positive.

'Don't worry mum, they would have seen the seas and I bet they are already heading back. They would have heard the shipping report, heard the coast guard's warning. They'll be fine.'

Both women paused, thinking the same thing. They knew that once the boats had made it to the shoals of fish miles out to sea then they would hang on as long as possible before making any decisions to turn back.

'Nobody seems to know which way the wind is blowing or how bad it might get. I've heard conflicting reports all morning. The radio has reported everything from squalls to hurricane winds.'

Heather's mother made herself busy and began to serve Heather delicious pancakes. Cooking was a great way to take your mind off worry. Some of Heather's mum's greatest creations had happened when storms came. Suddenly the kitchen door was flung open and Heather's grandfather walked into the room, or that's what he tried to do, in reality he was bounced into the small kitchen by the wind.

'Heavens to Betsy, it nearly had my hat completely off out there.'

He roared and slumped down in a chair. Grabbing a pancake he mopped his brow with his other hand.

'Never seen winds like it. Doesn't seem to know which direction it's coming from. Seen the clouds racing past? Got through to the boys on the radio though, they are going to try for a catch a bit later and then hightail it back here. There's no wind where they are. Said they were keeping a close eye on the conditions. They are not too far out. Mmm, these pancakes are perfect love. We're going all American now with pancakes for breakfast?'

He turned to give Heather a large wink, which made her blush. Heather got down from the table and went to the window to look out. She could see the clouds racing past the rooftops, heading inland. She was troubled by the news that the fleet was still going to try to catch some fish with their new nets.

'The wind seems to have settled to an on-shore north westerly, no hang on a south westerly no hang on...oh I see what you mean grandpa.'

Heather mimicked the radio announcers for fun, trying to change her mood.

'Yup,' murmured her Grandpa through a mouthful of pancake, 'see what I mean. It's doing just what it wants to. Squalling in every direction at once. Pure madness. This is going some even for this coastline.'

Heather looked across at her mother. The fact that her grandpa had got through to the boats had relaxed her slightly. Maria had many years of experience of storms and waiting back at home. Heather knew that her mother would begin to clean the house from top to bottom and polish anything that wasn't nailed down. Heather knew that it was best to leave her alone whilst conditions remained the same.

Turning to ask her mother's permission to go and visit Joe she could see that most of the worry had lifted from her face at the news from the boats.

'Wrap up warm and take a raincoat,' said her mother, 'who knows what the weather will do next?'

Heather played games all the way up the hill. There were moments when the wind was so strong that she could completely lean against it if she spread her arms out. Then she would almost fall as the wind switched direction. The only thing that seemed to be constant was the fact that the wind was blowing onto shore. She pulled her coat tight as the heavens suddenly opened and the heaviest rain she had ever seen thundered down. By the time she had crossed the short distance to Joe's house she and her coat were soaking.

'Goodness,' said Joe, 'I watched you coming up the hill, and you looked like a rag doll being blown this way and that. I thought you were going to fly. Looked great fun though.'

'I know,' said Heather, taking off her dripping coat, 'look, the rain has stopped and now it's snowing.'

Both of them looked out of the window. Snow was flurrying around yet it wasn't settling. 'You wait till you hear my news,' said Heather as Joe led her into the kitchen and started to make dangerously sweet and chocolaty hot drinks.

'Snow in July, maybe we'll get sun at Thanksgiving for a change.'

Joe frowned, his young face aging as he stirred the hot drinks. Heather looked puzzled as she accepted a huge mug of hot chocolate.

'What's thanksgiving?'

'It's when we celebrate the harvest; we give thanks for the survival of the Pilgrim Fathers, some of the first white settlers in America. An American Indian called Samoset helped them. It's a great story and I used to love it back home. We don't usually celebrate it until the fourth Thursday in November.'

'Wow!' both children jumped as the wind made huge banging sounds outside. 'What was that?'

'I think that was our dustbins getting airborne,' laughed Joe. 'Come on, let's go upstairs and see what we can see happening through the telescope, it's bound to be hilarious.'

For a short while Heather was content to play kids' games and laugh at people they saw being blown this way and that by the wind. Even the birds seemed to be having fun, swooping along the air currents, trying to see how much they could defy gravity and the power of the wind. Often a black headed gull would appear to be hurtling to his death against the side of a chimney or roof when suddenly, at the last moment, he would slightly adjust his wings and swerve at an incredible angle to regain his trajectory and compo-sure. They marvelled at the huge waves that crashed into the harbour wall, sending exploding mountains of white spray so high into the air the small radio shack was covered with sea water cascading down its corrugated roof. So far the rain seemed to be coming from the direction of the ocean. They could see huge boiling dark clouds racing across the sky as if chased by angry sky dogs. The clouds were going so fast and were so large and black that they looked like solid living beings. Heather thought that it looked as if they were running to a battle somewhere.

Heather squashed her eye into the sight of the telescope and turned her attention to the village. The telescope was so powerful it brought everything so close and in so much detail it made Heather think it was probably the best bit of equipment she had ever seen, after her aquarium anyway. She saw, in close detail, Mrs Dawson, who ran the local post office, fight with the wind, struggle to control her umbrella and then lose spectacularly as she was bowled over and her brolly took off high into the air. The children watched as it raced up the cliffs, startling daredevil gulls before literally disappearing into the clouds. Joe remarked that it was daft to put up a brolly in such winds but later when they saw Mrs Dawson get drenched by a big wave they realised why she had attempted to raise it. Heather had never seen such waves; she saw one huge roaring wave crash over the harbour wall and actually beat on the door and windows of the pub. The unusually powerful wave made Heather start to feel uneasy as she remembered what Ran had said. She felt cross and anxious that her father hadn't yet turned his ship for the shore.

When their eyes needed a rest from the telescope and Joe had made a couple more of his amazing hot chocolates with marshmallows and squirty cream, Heather made him sit down and listen to her story. From the word go he sat with his jaw hanging open in surprise and disbelief. Heather was so glad to share her adventure the words literally tumbled out of her. She felt a whole range of emotions pass through her as she shared the night's events. Joe could see how shaken his friend was by the revelation that her beloved teacher could be so evil. Joe quaked as Heather graphically shared her near death experience and the terrifying smoke creature that she had somehow summoned. Heather shared everything she had learned about her new Sisters, though all the time avoiding mentioning Ran and the seal folk. She showed Joe the wheals on her arms and legs. Joe sat transfixed and when she had finished his mouth gaped open and his hot chocolate remained unfinished. Heather gave him a nudge to jolt him back into the room. Joe reacted with his familiar anger. He was furious that Heather had been put in such danger. His eyes flashed angrily, and he jumped up spilling his now cold drink. Heather was touched that Joe felt that way but was alarmed at how quickly her friend could get so angry and so totally judgemental.

'That evil woman. How dare she. She's poison. I thought she was odd. Maybe she's dead, maybe you killed her I wouldn't care. Maybe the witches threw her lifeless body into the sea maybe her body will wash up somewhere.'

'Don't say that Joe, no she was just lost to the madness of her ring, I guess it made her lose perspective, lose a grip on what was real, what was right and wrong. Besides, the Wise Women will see her alright, they promised. Calm down Joe, that's not the kind of people we are. We don't wish harm on anybody – do we?!'

Joe copied Heather and took a deep breath. He seemed embarrassed by the severity of his outburst. He looked anxiously at Heather slightly unsure of himself for a moment. He just couldn't control how intensely he felt his anger burn but the kind and smiling face of his friend calmed him down. He blushed and changed the subject.

'Can I see your ring close up?' he asked shyly.

Heather held her hand out. The ring was beautiful, and was behaving itself simply reflected the light back at them.

'Looks nice, really intricate design but pretty ordinary. Any Californian hippie has a ring like that. But wow, what a story, what can you do with it?'

Joe was slightly disappointed in the ring. He had hoped for more.

'I don't know really, I think I can call the Wise Women with it though.'

'And they said that you had special powers?' quizzed Joe.

'Well I guess so but I don't really know what they are. Look, all I know is that this crazy weather is somehow connected to what we are doing to the sea and I know that we have to try and get the village to change the way it fishes.'

'Oh, not again,' groaned Joe. 'They didn't seem to want to hear last time. Tell me about the monster again.'

'It wasn't a monster, actually I have no idea what it was, but it sure knocked out Miss Boniface,' said Heather, rubbing her wrists.

'She's gonna be furious when we go back to school.'

Joe burst out laughing and tried to imagine what would happen on Monday morning.

'Well the Wise Women said that she wouldn't remember anything, so fingers crossed,' laughed Heather.

'You hope,' grinned Joe.

'Look Joe, reason I'm telling you because I know that you are somehow involved at some level in all this and I might just need some help,' said Heather suddenly serious.

'What, like rescuing you from witches, from drowning and from being lynched at village meetings?'

Joe laughed, refusing to take the moment seriously. He couldn't imagine what part of this crazy story he might be part of. Heather laughed as well. Poor Joe. Ever since they had met he had seemed to have to be pulling her out of some sort of dangerous situation. Or else it was Heather getting him into trouble. It was Heather who was meant to be looking out for him, she confessed sheepishly to Joe.

'No, well yes, maybe, but if I don't have someone who believes me I might start thinking that I have gone quite mad.'

Joe laughed and then looked serious.

'Were those other women, the ones who gave you the ring and rescued you, were they witches too?'

'No, well I don't think so. They said that they were Wise Women. I think my grandma was one, I think she was once the Wise Woman of the village and I think that Miss Boniface stepped in and tried to fill the gap when she died. I guess she didn't have the ring though, or the Sight.'

'But Miss Boniface is a witch,' said Joe, getting confused.

'Erm, I'm not sure that witches exist, just people who choose to do what's good and those that don't. She was no good to the village, she wasn't wise, or a healer, I guess. She was just interested in her own power and that sort of thing and so couldn't help the village.'

'Or didn't want to, more like.'

Joe winced, remembering the episode with the gannet on the beach. He sipped his drink and pressed on with his questions.

'So what does a 'Wise Woman' do then?'

'I really don't know,' said Heather, slowly screwing up her eyes as she thought. 'I 'spose that she listens to nature and gives advice to people when they need it.'

'Why don't you use your ring and call one, right now, and ask her?'

Joe leapt up grinning, daring Heather to act. Heather stopped, she was doubtful if that was the right sort of thing to do with her ring. She tried to remember what the Wise Women had said. After a few minutes she felt her mind go quiet and peaceful and she knew the answer.

'If I choose to call them then it will be Ok,' she said, 'I don't know how I know but I do. Thing is, I don't know whether they will want to meet you or not.'

'I could hide in the cupboard and...'

'I think they would know.'

'Look, let me try and if they come then we could ask, if not, you would have to go downstairs. What about your grandfather?'

'He's not here, he's gone to Glasgow, won't be back till late tonight. In fact with the weather he might not come back 'til tomorrow. Isabella will be here at supper time and will stay over.'

'Ok,' said Heather, 'be quiet then.'

She sat down onto the huge leather sofa and held onto her ring. She let her mind go quiet and imagined Muriel's face, her long slim fingers and her kind eyes. Then she let her mind call out her name: Muriel. Then Heather imagined Joe's house and saw Muriel park a small red car and start to walk up the path to his front door.

'There you go Joe, I called out to her I ...woa!'

The two children jumped, as quite clearly there came a loud knock on the door from downstairs.

'Wow,' said Joe, 'that was fast.'

He leapt up to answer it. Heather jumped up too. Surely that couldn't be Muriel, she had only just called. Surely even Wise Women couldn't make their cars fly.

Joe flung open the front door, making the unmistakable figure of Muriel, all wrapped up in a long coat, scarf and hat jump slightly with surprise.

'You gave me a fright young Joe.'

Muriel stepped straight into the house with a purposeful air.

'I expected Heather to answer, not a young man.'

Muriel lent over and stared straight at Joe unblinking for a moment and then stood upright.

'So, there is more to this than I first thought,' she said smiling at the two children. 'Well then,' she said, 'Heather tells me that you make the best hot chocolate this side of America.'

Joe closed his mouth and jumped into action. Heather led Muriel upstairs, looking puzzled. She had no memory of telling Muriel anything about Joe and his hot chocolate. The moment that Muriel entered the living room she turned her head, took it all in with a glance and quickly turned to Heather.

'What I have come to say I must say to you, not that young man. He has a powerful destiny, yet his mysteries will not be revealed to him here, at this time, this is not his moment.'

She sat, or rather alighted like a large bird on the leather couch and gratefully took a steaming cup of chocolate from Joe as he burst into the room. She smiled at him and explained her position.

'Oh, I see, well Heather said you might need to speak to her on your own,' said Joe glumly. 'Couldn't you do some magic of something first though, Heather said you could?'

Muriel looked between the two of them.

'Hmm, did she? I wonder what else my young sister divulged. Magic is all around you all the time, young man. It's just some who take the time to notice it, that's all.'

Joe looked crestfallen. Muriel took pity on him and beckoned him closer.

'Joe,' she said suddenly 'what do you know of your parents, of your mother?'

'Not a lot, I was very young, I remember a few things but...'

'She was a Native American wasn't she?'

'Yes, a Native American, a first Nation princess Grandfather said.'

'She was a Wise Woman too,' stated Muriel

'She was?' stammered Joe, intrigued and alarmed.

'Yes, I see it in you. Something terrible happened and she wants to speak to you.'

Muriel stood up and then perched, birdlike on the arm of the chair. It seemed that speaking like this was the most natural thing a person could do. As if she had just asked for a biscuit. Joe looked stunned and worried at the same time. Heather saw him try manfully to hide the tears as he thought about his mother. Muriel continued and softened her voice.

'Her destiny is tied up in all this too. You have a great task to complete but this is not yet your time. She wants you to assist Heather and she...' Muriel paused, her eyes half closed as if she was looking deep inside, 'and she wants you to know your Indian name, the name you were given, should have been given at manhood. Come here my child,' beckoned Muriel.

Out of a bag she took a small velvet pouch from which she produced a single black feather and smiled.

'I wondered why I was told to bring this. Here, a raven's feather for Raven – that is your name given to you – Raven. Take this feather and keep it until the time of your initiation...your vision quest. Your ways will be similar to ours but different. Your grandfather knows all this but now is the time for you to help him. Now go and watch the door for Isabella, she mustn't see me. I think she will be arriving soon.'

Heather was stunned – so that was why she had kept on hearing the name Raven. Of course, now it made sense. She looked again at the strong features of her friend, his jet-black hair and his dark eyes. It occurred to Heather that Raven was a perfect name for him. Joe started as if from a trance, he was stunned. Everything this old lady had said to him somehow rang true yet he couldn't believe it. Heather saw a myriad of conflicting emotions flicker across his face. She wondered if he would get angry but something seemed to soften his manner and he gave out a long slow sigh. Heather wondered what had just happened in Joe's mind or even heart. It looked like something he had been carrying for a long time had just been lifted from his shoulders. Joe looked at the two of them and then lit up the room with his smile.

'What is it?' Muriel asked Joe as he dragged his heals, trying to delay going downstairs.

'How come you got here so fast? I saw your car, you didn't fly?'

Muriel chuckled.

'I didn't drive very fast, in fact it took me nearly an hour from Saltkirk to get here.'

'But,' said Heather warming to the theme, 'I only called you just now, just a couple of minutes ago. How come you...'

'Ah,' said Muriel, 'did you call or did you see, and are calling and seeing the same thing?'

The young people both looked confused.

'Let's just say that calling for something gives you a clear vision of what is occurring but, and this is important my dear, the knowledge might just be a vision that is instructing you to act. We have to be open to either possibility. Are we seeing something that is happening, will happen or will only happen if we act with the right intent? There, do you understand now? Sometimes we think we are sending out a call to the universe and the universe shows us that She has already acted. She has already anticipated our need and acted upon it. That's what we call Grace. She gives us what we need before we know we need it, even if we haven't asked for it or maybe even when we don't deserve it. If you have the Sight, She will reveal this to you so that you can join her in the great Cause, so that you can join the Spiral Dance and become a co-creator in this great mystery we call life.

Heather was struggling to keep up so Muriel waited while the penny dropped for her. She smiled and carried on.

'This time Heather I believe that the moment you called for me the Goddess showed you that She had already acted on your behalf. The universe was showing you that she works with you and for you even without you knowing it. Heather, I just knew, first thing this morning that I had to come back here to find you. I heard the call and never doubted that it was the right thing to do. As we learn to trust Her we stop questioning and begin to act with increasing speed and accuracy. It's all quite fabulous and, in an ideal world you should have years to learn all of these mysteries.'

Heather scratched her head as Muriel's teachings took root deep within her. Heather realised that the moment she had called Muriel was the same moment she had seen the Wise Woman get out of her car. So, her vision was really just seeing what was happening and not what would happen. Still it did make her headache. She glanced at Joe, he had glazed over. Muriel had either lost him with her explanation or had made sure that he couldn't understand. Muriel glanced at the pair of them and smiled.

'Anyway, I shall give Heather my phone number just in case. It might prove easier next time. Now run along master Raven and help Isabella with the washing up. I believe she has just joined us downstairs.'

'I heard that name when I nearly drowned,' said Heather. 'Someone also mentioned it to me as well.'

Muriel looked at her and smiled.

'Someone mentioned his name? Then you must know a great deal more that you have let on. I imagine that you have contact with a very special person indeed. It's so amazing that the Sisters are now connecting across such vast distances. The world is getting smaller. We are being called to join up and,' Muriel paused looking sadly after Joe, 'assist in healing the men of this world.'

Heather sighed, for an instant she could see deeply into Muriel's eyes and she saw only goodness, pure love, strength, power and wisdom. At last she had somebody she could confide in. Muriel smiled and just as Heather was about to open her mouth and tell her everything about Ran, her dreams and her fears, Muriel put her finger to Heather's lips.

'Hush, keep your pearls to yourself. I'm afraid they are for you alone. I am here for you in every way but there are some secrets that must be kept, even between sisters. Young Raven has a very difficult journey ahead of him but so have you my young one and it's you I have been told to help this day. Now let us begin your schooling for I fear that you will need to make good use of it very soon.'

16

Deeper Lessons

Muriel waited until Joe could be heard clattering around downstairs in the kitchen. His laughter echoed up to the living room and Isabella's laughter soon joined in. Heather smiled, knowing that he was probably engaging his poor housekeeper in a water fight. She turned to Muriel, who had moved to the huge window seat that offered an amazing panoramic view of the harbour. Her thin and birdlike features looked thoughtful as she motioned to Heather to join her. Heather clambered up and the pair of them stared out to sea for a moment. The clouds were dark and threatening and were scudding across the sky like jet planes. Huge white horses pranced high into the air all the way out to the horizon and sea birds were being flung in all directions. The pair watched as a distant cloud scudded towards them, dropping a dark grey sheet of rain beneath it. The rain was upon them in moments, rattling on the window and obscuring the whole view. Heather glanced down at her ring. It was glowing like a rainbow. She touched the stone thoughtfully, wondering who had made it. Muriel broke the gentle silence and turned to speak to Heather.

'Normally you would experience years of careful training before you would have to face any real challenges my young sister. There is so much deep teaching about the plants, the trees, the special energy places and the sea. So many things to learn and remember, so many healing arts to master. Yet here we are, facing a terrible challenge, caught up in a drama that is as big as this precious planet.'

Muriel looked slightly sad and she gently took hold of Heather's hand and gave her a squeeze.

'I sense there is little I can teach you of the sea and truly this is where your calling lies but you need help as a woman and maybe this I can help you with. You have a great responsibility, a great challenge facing you and I fear there is not much time for joy and the experiencing of the wonder of all things. Maybe once this is all over...'

Muriel gently stroked Heather's cheek and, taking a deep breath, rubbed the centre of her forehead before continuing. Heather felt a buzz of energy flood through her and suddenly it was as if only Heather and Muriel existed. Muriel's voice echoed inside her head and she realised that the old woman's lips were no longer moving.

'Yours is an ancient heritage and you already sense much. Your grandmother gave her whole life to your village and at the moment of her death she would have willed her knowledge onto you. I fear that you were too young to receive this wisdom with knowledge, this is not unusual when the knowledge skips a generation. Your grandmother would have known that we would have heard her instructions once you came of age and your identity would have been revealed to us. The one thing your poor grandmother would not have known was the severity of situation that was to come. I feel that the Great Mother has kept much from us, probably hoping that we would change our ways, respect the Earth.'

Muriel smiled at Heather and glanced towards the door.

'Yours is a difficult way, a different way, a way that is not always understood or appreciated, even in these times. You are lucky to have found such a good friend so early. Many of us find it difficult with men as they feel threatened by us and do not still their minds to hear what we are really saying. Even women often spurn us, so we remain hidden. Yet even that luxury will be denied to you. These are end times, decisive times and all that is hidden will be made visible. All will be made to account and all will stand naked before Her.'

Heather remembered the being of light that she had seen with Ran. In a moment her vision flickered through her memory and she recalled her journey to the stars and back. Muriel gasped and for a brief moment their connection was broken. Heather looked at Muriel's face and realised that her new friend had been able to see everything that she had just recalled. Heather reached out with her mind and found that she could easily reconnect with the startled Muriel.

'But who is She?' asked Heather nervously.

'Oh my child, you are so gifted. You have already met an aspect of Her. She has shown you much. She wants you to understand Her nature, Her very Being. Even I have not shared this experience with Her.'

Muriel wiped a small tear from the corner of her eye and smiled warmly into Heather's.

'No wonder you are full to bursting with questions. Well, some call Her the Goddess, others the planet herself, some say nature and for me that covers everything that I know to be. Even with the mysteries of life revealed it is a wise woman who can admit she knows nothing.'

Heather heard the words that Muriel was thinking and even if she didn't fully understand their meaning she sensed that somewhere deep inside her a greater awareness and understanding was beginning to form. Heather felt a strong sense of connectedness. She felt as if there was a soft presence all around the pair of them and as she gave it her attention she sensed that this presence went everywhere and was part of everything. That felt good. Muriel smiled again at Heather.

'Now my child, your abilities, your heritage, let me try to explain the things that I do know; you will be able to see what others cannot. Sometimes you will do it of your own volition, at other times it will simply occur.'

'Will I be able to see in the dark?'

Heather imagined herself able to see through walls, yet Muriel's look cautioned her flight of fancy and she focussed again

'Well not quite seeing like that, it's more with your inner eye. Your inner eye lies just behind your forehead. The ancient skill requires focus, attention and intention - the right kind of intention. You have to approach the Sight with your heart, with an attitude of open-hearted service. Not like your teacher with a lust for power or knowledge.

That is the only way you can be sure that you see clearly and with discernment. Normally you would undergo years of schooling, of training, there is so much herb lore, so many techniques yet you have no time.'

'No time?'

Heather grew slightly nervous. Muriel kept mentioning Heather's limited time. The girl was beginning to fear for her life. Muriel smiled and looked reassuringly at her and gave her hand another gentle squeeze.

'Not like that,' she said. 'I believe your power has come to you all at once for a powerful reason. It has arrived at exactly the time that you need it. This way you will not be distracted by the gift of power itself. You won't be tempted like your teacher, you won't have time to make the mistakes that we all make on the path. It can be so confusing in the beginning. Sometimes our own personalities, our own imaginings, our own desires and illusions can muddy our vision and prevent clarity and truth. You have had no time for such bad habits to grow like ivy around the young shoots of your flowering. You will have a clear eye and clear vision. You are not jaded by the world of men. You have no deep pain or suffering to bewitch you into the darkness. You have an open heart and that is all anyone needs.'

Muriel smiled as she watched Heather screw up her eyes trying to understand all that was being said to her.

'Look Heather, don't feel overwhelmed by these words, your soul knows their meaning and will translate to your mind as you need. Now then, let's have a fleeting moment of practice. Clasp you ring hand with your other hand and place your attention onto the ring.'

Heather smiled at Muriel and was grateful for a moment of practical guidance. Her mind was swimming with the strange words and language. She raised the large ring up and looked at its iridescent surface.

'Now Heather, let you mind, and your intention guide you. Allow a question to form in your mind and then follow the golden thread all the way to the ring so that it can amplify your vision.'

Heather did as she was told. She squinted her eyes at the ring and with a long slow outbreath she allowed her mind to quiet and got ready to ask a question. Before she had a chance, a question arose seemed to take control and she felt her attention shooting into the ring. All at once Heather found herself standing on the cliff top, it was dark, the wind was howling, and she knew that she was back outside the bothy from the night before. She realised that her curiosity about what she had managed to summon to defend her from Miss Boniface had nagged her all morning. Heather only had a moment to wonder if that was a good thing to use her Sight for when a blast of wind almost knocked her off her feet. An almighty roar made Heather call out in fright. It came from directly above Heather. She looked up as the most frightening creature she had ever dared to imagine burst through the dark clouds. It pulsed with fire and smoke and had two large fiery pits for eyes that scanned the cliff top like a cat seeking its prey. It moved like a snake or huge eel and as it wove its path downwards it made the clouds glow red all around it. Heather couldn't discern a mouth, but the eyes were terrible, ancient and hungry. Heather crouched down as the creature darted over her head and crashed headlong into the closed door of the bothy. The old timber door exploded, and Heather heard the chilling scream of Miss Boniface ring out. Heather willed herself to move towards the entrance and immediately regretted it. In a flash she was in the doorway up close and personal with a writhing fire dragon that had wrapped its fiery tail around Miss Boniface. The ethereal creature crackled and burned and brought its head closer to the ashen face of Miss Boniface. Then its eyes glowed and a huge mouth opened to bite her teacher. Heather gasped helplessly. But instead of biting it inhaled and a white light began to leave Miss Boniface. It poured out of her eyes and mouth and into the fire dragon's open mouth. Heather realised that it was draining her teacher. Miss Boniface was growing visibly limper and her face seemed to be aging rapidly in front of Heather. Her teacher seemed to be withering into nothing and Heather panicked realising that the creature was going to suck the life out of her teacher.

'Heather! Heather return now. Now!!!'

Heather heard Muriel's voice ring though her head. She focussed her attention on the ring and ignoring her overwhelming desire to save her teacher she followed the thread of gold back until – Pow! She was back in the calm quiet of Joe's grandfather's study. She realised that she was panting hard and was shaking.

'Sorry my darling I had to call you back then just in case the incredible blast wave you summoned to send the creature back affected you. You can never be too careful. Whatever you did lit up the whole sky for a moment. That's why we were able to find the bothy so easily. You have so much raw power and so many angelic helpers I just hope you don't damage yourself or anybody else. Erm...are you feeling ok?'

Heather had gone quite pale and she reached for her mug and took a huge sip of nearly cold chocolate. The sugar revitalised her and she felt the world steady around her.

Everything looked a bit see-through for a moment or two and then returned to normality, so did Heather's tummy. Muriel just smiled at her young friend and didn't seem at all phased by what had just happened.

'Few, that was intense. I mean it was like I was there. Oo er... I'm feeling queasy still.'

'You were there. Well most of you was. I don't usually eat for a day or two if I'm going to use the Sight like that.'

Huh. What actually happened? How could I be in two places at one time? I mean that's' impossible.'

'It's a bit too complicated to explain and I'm not sure even I understand. Susan is the expert on the whole time and space entanglement thing. Anyhow – well done. So now you know. Be careful though Heather. You have such energy flowing through you. Be careful what you wish for and maybe ask the Sight for a more subtle approach. Try discernment if you are doubtful of someone in the future. If I was a younger woman I would have been quite jealous or your raw power. But maybe don't summon any more elementals unless we are all with you and even then...be careful.'

'An elemental?'

'Hmm, quite beautiful wasn't she. I always wanted to see one but we Wise Women don't usually engage in such practices. As I said before, be careful Heather.'

Heather glanced at her ring and marvelled again at how it seemed to resemble the sea with its swirling colours.

'Maybe I should take it off until I know what to do. safely I mean?'

'Well you don't actually need it. In fact, I'm not sure that you need any help but Spirit has commanded that you do so, here I am. Now then, on to business. I must prepare you as you will need to call a gathering for tomorrow night's full moon.'

'A gathering?'

'Yes, my child, by then you will know why. It will be a gathering as of old. You will call all of the sisters of the village, the sighted and unsighted will come together in the spirit of sharing that is at the truth of our gifts. The truth of Her is that we are all one and without each other we are nothing.'

Heather felt anxious as she replayed her last experience with a crowd of people. She remembered how their eyes had looked straight through her; she shuddered as she recalled how her words had fallen on deaf ears, just like tears falling into the sea, dissolving unnoticed never to be seen again. It had been a shock to Heather. She had thought that her words, spoken from the heart, full of truth and insight would have changed things. She had been stunned when not one heart or mind had absorbed what she said. It had been as if she had spoken another language. Heather gulped and spoke out loud to Muriel.

'Why do I need to call a gathering? Nobody listens to me.'

'The reasons will be clear by tomorrow night, perhaps earlier. My child, it is not the gathering which is the most important thing for you. It is not even what I can teach you today. It is what choices are made far out at sea that will affect us all. Now let me tell you this Heather, my child, you are not responsible for other people and their actions. Whatever they might or might not do is not for you to worry about. Your way will be as it always has been – to hear clearly and speak truly, with as much compassion and clarity you can muster. If you let your emotions run away from you then you will put yourself in danger. You have to let go of other people's decisions. What other people think about us is not our concern. We may just feel sad for them that they have not yet had their eyes opened, but we must never make the fatal mistake that we can change anybody. Free will is our gift. We are free to will good into the world, or bad. This is how we learn. Life is a lesson of consequences. That is why we Wise Women share our memories, so that we do not make the mistakes of our past lives.'

Heather felt Muriel's words spill over her like a soft summer rain. She felt refreshed and invigorated at the same time. With each word she felt as if her soul gasped with pleasure and recognition. As Muriel talked she seemed to weave pictures and stories inside Heather's mind. Sometimes Heather felt she understood everything and at other times she realised she understood nothing. Heather knew deep inside herself that at some point in the future the teachings would make sense.

Muriel smiled at Heather and looked proudly at her young friend.

'I have never met anyone quite like you Heather MacDougal. Now sit in that comfy old chair and let me finish my transmission.'

Muriel bade Heather close her eyes and relax. Heather sat back in the huge old leather armchair and felt the world drift away from her. Muriel began to instruct her, leaning in towards her ear even though she spoke no audible words.

Joe had crept back up the stairs and was spying through the crack left by the open door. From where he could see it appeared as if Heather was asleep and that Muriel was staring into her ear. Joe had hoped to have seen some magic taking place. He wondered if Muriel was hypnotising Heather and felt momentarily alarmed. Yet as he squinted through the crack in the door he could see that Muriel's face was one of pure love and kindness. Joe didn't know much about people, but he could tell good from bad and he knew that Muriel was a good one. He wondered to himself what Muriel had meant when she spoke to him of his mother. He felt a flood of conflicting emotions. His grandfather hardly spoke about his parents. His grandfather was a man of few words when it came to emotional issues. Joe glanced up at the painting on the wall. He had seen the painting for the first time when he moved with his grandfather to Scotland. He had not been able to look at it for a long time as it made powerful and confusing emotions rise up in him. They were not all good emotions and Joe always felt a sense of panic and fear mixed with love and pride.

Joe sat quietly on the stairs and contemplated his new name. He wondered if Muriel was right, or mad, or maybe just making stuff up. Yet when she spoke the words had rung true in his young mind even if he doubted them now. To be called Raven, the name that his parents had given him, his American Indian name, was a dream come true. Joe whispered the name Raven out loud and smiled, it gave Joe a great sense of belonging for the first time in his life. Sure, he was growing to like his new home and of course his new friend Heather but he never really felt as if he belonged, apart from when he was with Heather. Her presence seemed to make everything okay.

Joe looked back up at the painting that hung on the wall above him. It seemed so lifelike today. A proud and beautiful pair of American Indians, standing on an upturned canoe with the sea behind them, their black hair blowing in the wind. Joe felt confused by his sense of pride and loss. He sat and stared and wondered if this really was a picture of his mum and dad. He didn't recognise them but at the same time they looked familiar. He had been so young when they died. Joe felt a tear well up in his eye, which he angrily wiped away. Even though he knew it was wrong, he felt cross that they had left him. He knew that these two life-loving people hadn't meant to die and leave him without parents, yet he couldn't help his feelings. Joe twisted his head and peeked back into the living room. Muriel must have sensed him as she gently glanced up and met his eye. She smiled directly at him and touched her forehead and then her lips as if to beg him to stay quiet. Then, as Joe turned back to the painting the whole room began to shimmer. He gasped, as the painting seemed to rush towards him. The faces of the young couple changed and altered, they became real and were no longer an artist's interpretation. Joe experienced a powerful rush of recognition and a huge surge of tears welled up from deep within him. Through his tears he felt an unexpected rush of love. It was as if in his mind he could feel his parents putting their arms around him and comforting him and then suddenly the blurry vision became real.

Joe opened his eyes and wiped away the tears. He was standing on brush grass on the dunes back in America. He looked down and saw a long canoe pull into the shore. Joe felt himself run down the dune to greet the two people who climbed deftly out of the canoe. He knew at once who they were and flung himself into their arms. He was dimly aware that he was very, very small and was still unsteady on his legs. He felt tears rushing down his cheeks and hugged his parents as tightly as they hugged him. Then he found himself sitting with them, around a small fire. He knew they were discussing some great adventure and then they turned to Joe and his father laid his hand on his head and called him by the name Raven. The Joe felt his whole being rise up into the air. He sensed he had wings, which carried him up into the air until he was looking down on the shining expanse of water fringed by cliffs and great forests. Then he was swooping down to a small flotilla of canoes. He pulled up before the water and felt himself glide ahead in the direction the canoes were heading. He could see a much bigger flotilla of fishing vessels coming towards the canoes. Each boat was three times as large as the small Scottish ones. He whirled with delight as he sensed the cold air and the excitement of the dolphins racing before the largest craft. Then he saw a familiar sight of his grandfather standing in the bow of the lead boat, his arms folded and his great jaw set as strong as stone. How magnificent he looked, thought Joe. Suddenly the feeling changed and Joe saw a massive dark cloud directly in front. He entered it, unable to alter his flight in time and found himself enveloped in a dark and powerful storm. The storm was so strong it was as if he could actually feel it inside him and it made him feel uneasy and worried, worried for his parents down below in their flimsy canoes. A sense of great fear, panic and overwhelming concern for his parents rose up inside Joe, he tried to scream but only a deep cawing sound came out.

'Raven, come back to us – now!'

Muriel's crisp, clear powerful command cut through Joe's vision and in a trice, he was back in his house. He blinked through his tears in shock. He realised that he was still sitting on the stairs in front of the picture of his parents. He became aware that his cheeks were wet and he felt upset, elated, anxious and somehow stronger all in one breath. He felt Muriel's kindly hand on his cheek brush away his tears. Muriel had crouched down beside Joe and she had her arms around him. She glanced up at the painting and then back at Joe.

'Don't analyse it Joe,' she said. 'Just let its meaning flow through you. Eventually the vision will reveal its purpose.

The purpose of any vision is to help you learn about your-self. You needed to know about your parents and now you have met them. Now you know your beginnings. Everyone needs that deep knowledge if they are to write their own story of life. We all need a beginning, even if our beginnings are a mixture of joy and pain.'

Heather, who had been standing quietly beside Muriel, sat down beside Joe. She put her arm around him and hugged him gently. Somehow, she instinctively knew what he was feeling and what he had experienced even though she had no idea of the detail of his vision.

'Well,' said Muriel, preparing to leave. 'What a pair you two are. Heavens to Betsy, a right odd couple and there's no mistaking it.'

She quickly kissed them both on their heads.

'Why not go out for a walk. Let the wind blow through you. Just watch out for any flying debris.'

As Muriel spoke she went to leave and the wind almost snatched the door from her. Laughing, the old woman flung herself out into the storm. Once Muriel had left Heather turned to Joe and smiled.

'Well, hello Raven. It's a pleasure to make your acquaintance.'

Heather smiled cheekily at Joe. Joe was grateful for his friend's company as he still felt jangly inside and unsure of himself. Hearing his American Indian name gave Joe a sense of himself and he found his mind quickly clearing. He stood up and spoke shyly to Heather.

'Call me Joe, for now at least. I don't really understand all that dreaming stuff yet.'

Glancing up at the painting of his parents he smiled.

'Wow, that was an intense dream though.'

Heather smiled, knowing better than to press him for any more information. She now knew how important it was to process new things before speaking about them.

'That was no dream, that was a vision. Yes, they are amazing aren't they? They always make everything seem more real afterwards. When I wake up from sleep I sometimes feel groggy for ages, but after a vision I always feel as if electricity has been running through me.'

Joe wrapped his arms around himself.

'Yeh, I know what you mean. I reckon I need a good long chat with grandfather. I reckon there is more to the story of how my parents died than he told me. There was something about the sea, boats, canoes and a huge storm. Speaking of which, come on, let's go outside. It's not raining at the moment, mind you in Scotland that doesn't mean that it won't be in two minutes.'

As they both started to put their warm coats on Heather snuck a quick glance at her friend. She noticed that Joe could now mention his parents without the violent reaction she had seen few days earlier. In fact, she thought, as she watched him place a hat on his head, it seemed as if he had somehow grown older and wiser in the last few hours. But then, Heather had just been shown so many things by Muriel that she knew she was still seeing with her second sight.

Together Heather and Joe walked unhurriedly up the cliff path making their way slowly towards the ancient viewing point. Leaning on the wind Heather let her mind think over what Muriel had shown her.

She had learnt that in most of the Scottish villages and towns there was still a Wise Woman maintaining the tradition and knowledge that spanned thousands of years. Muriel had told her that now many of her younger sisters, were now legitimate in the eyes of the world and worked as healers, herbalists, botanist, artists, environmentalists because they excelled in areas that are linked to the environment. Heather had learnt that her gifts were something that everybody could have if they worked and practiced hard as she still had to if she was going to truly become a wise woman.

As Heather and Joe leant into the wind, they gave up trying to talk as their words were snatched away. Both of them allowed themselves to reflect on their morning.

Heather and Muriel had got on very well and in their vision sharing state they had swapped many stories. Somehow, they were able to share deep truths in moments. Muriel had been impressed. She was amazed at how much Heather already knew about the ocean and its life. Heather told Muriel how she had read every book in the library and then how she had read books that the fishermen had lent her. Muriel was unable to keep up with the huge flood of information that Heather had tried to share.

Before they had heard Joe cry out from within his vision of his parents the two women shared their love of the sea.

'And you should see the internet,' Heather told Muriel enthusiastically. 'Joe showed me how to work it properly and you can find out tons and tons of stuff there, all proper scientific stuff too.'

Muriel told Heather that she was a marine biologist and that she went diving in the cold clear waters off Scotland. Heather listened, fascinated. She had expected to be told strange esoteric things about visions and magic, yet Muriel had told her fact after amazing fact about nature.

Muriel told Heather of her diving expeditions to all of the oceans of the world. She talked of seeing whales slipping in between the narrow entrances of the fiords. She spoke of dolphins gambolling in the Arabian Sea. She spoke of small Coral Islands in the Maldives that were complete miniature ecosystems perfect in every way and told Heather of how she had swum through shoals of brightly coloured fish.

As they chatted Muriel lifted up her handbag and began to take out objects to amaze Heather with. Her handbag seemed to defy all the laws of physics. It appeared to be bottomless. Muriel pulled out old photographs, a piece of carved narwhale horn, which she explained was really a tooth, amazing shells and even a small fossil which looked remarkably like the sacred angelfish that Heather had returned to the sea before. As she told Heather about the plight of the British waters she pulled a stuffed Puffin out of her bottomless bag, which Heather cradled on her lap. Heather listened in amazement. So much of what Muriel was saying reminded her of what Ran had told her and what she had seen and experienced in her vision. How she wished she could share that story with Muriel.

'Look,' said Muriel, obviously enjoying her new friend and the fact that they had so much in common, 'it's not just the gifts, it's what you do with them that counts. It's gaining the skills and then being able to offer them to the planet. It's asking what She wants and then listening for Her answer. She soon replies and brings you loads of fascinating tasks to do, if you choose to serve.'

Muriel grew serious and started to tell Heather about how the sea was being affected by man's pollution. She told Heather how a phenomenon called global warming was starting to heat up the world's oceans. Muriel grew sad when she told Heather how all of the pollution from fossil fuels was slowly making the sea acidic and that the first worlds to die would be the beautiful and intricate corals. Everything Muriel said confirmed what Ran had told Heather. Muriel plucked a huge piece of coral out of her bag and gave to Heather for her aquarium, saying that it would remind Heather of her purpose.

Muriel then made Heather stand in front of Jim's modern chart of the world that was on the wall of the living room. She showed Heather how currents of warm water were becoming affected as the polar ice caps began to melt. With her finger Muriel traced the path of these huge currents of warm water as they moved all the way from the equator, keeping the British Isles warm. Heather loved the science and knowledge of how stuff worked, especially anything that had to do with the sea and Muriel smiled as her young friend kept up a rapid fire of intelligent and discerning questions. Muriel paused, momentarily saddened, and told Heather of her concern that the mighty ancient currents might fail, plunging the world into another ice age. Heather grew silent, picturing the seas frozen and her little village covered beneath hundreds of feet of snow. Muriel said that the scientific name for the pulses of life that circled the oceans was the thermohaline circulation current. It was a long name, which Heather played over and over in her mind trying to learn it. Muriel smiled, noticing Heather silently trying to say the word. When Heather shared the details of her aquarium with Muriel, Muriel said that it was due to the warming of the water that Heather had a seahorse in her tank, that they only occasionally made their way to the south coast of England, never this far north.

So, it was at the end of their long conversation that Heather and Muriel had found Joe crouched on the stairs. A strange sound, not unlike the sound a bird in distress makes, had made the two of them jolt out of their reverie and dash to the door. When they found Joe crouching at the top of the stairs his eyes wet and spinning, Heather knew immediately that he too had had a vision. Glancing up at the huge painting above them she quickly surmised what it might have been about.

A call of a gull as it was blown past them brought Heather back to their walk on the cliff path. It was funny, Heather thought as she clutched onto Joe so as not to be blown over, but she couldn't imagine life without her new friend.

Heather prayed that the powerful and unpredictable weather would prevent her father from using the new nets. She now understood the seriousness of what his actions might bring. Ran's warning and vision of the huge waves were almost too terrible to contemplate. Heather found herself shaking as she thought of her father and brother and all of the fishermen of the village at sea. As Heather and Joe stood staring out to sea, unable to speak over the roar of the wind, Heather wondered how many generations of women had stood on that very spot anxiously searching the horizon as she now did for the safe return of the boats. As yet more clouds started to close in the first drops of heavy rain lashed their bare faces.

'Wow,' shouted Joe, 'that really stings. This storm is starting to get teeth.'

Laughing as they tried to dodge the stinging pellets of water the pair turned back down the path towards Joe's house. Heather said goodbye to her friend as the path forked and headed down towards the village trying to avoid the stinging rain. She could see the smoke from her chimney forcefully drawn out by the wind. Heather had just dodged a flying plastic bag, failing miserably to catch it to put it in a bin, when she almost crashed right into a figure wrapped tightly in a black shawl that kept threatening to escape. Heather found herself staring straight into the slightly puffy and red eyes of Miss Boniface. Heather halted in her path, stunned. She had completely forgotten about her experience and she wasn't sure what to do.

'Oh er, sorry Miss Boniface, I didn't see you there, it was the wind, my hair, erm, I couldn't see anything.'

Heather was aware that as her eyes met those of Miss Boniface her teacher looked confused, even slightly lost. Heather saw that Miss Boniface was struggling to remember something yet couldn't. She saw her teacher blink with tiredness before letting the irksome memory vanish.

'Are you Ok Miss Boniface?'

Heather shouted over the roar of the wind and waves, her confidence growing, replacing the initial shock she had felt.

'Yes, quite well, thank you Heather,' shouted Miss Boniface over the wind. Maybe I've got some kind of head cold though.' I can't seem to wake up today. Must be the low pressure, feels like a fog in my head is slowly clearing. I thought a walk might do me good. Sometimes walking nowhere in particular is just the best remedy for finding yourself. Don't come too close my darling in case I'm infectious. I feel rather weak. In fact I'll head back in a moment. '

Miss Boniface was clutching a shawl over her head and Heather could see that there was no ring on her hand. Miss Boniface noticed Heather's gaze and glanced at her hand but there was not a flicker of recognition of loss. Instead the young woman gave Heather a beaming smile.

'Don't let me keep you. You had better get in before this really gets bad. '

She gave Heather a wonderful smile and then, wrapping her coat around her, waved goodbye and headed up the path. Heather was glad to have seen her teacher. She seemed to have returned to being the kind and gentle person she had known before the terrifying events of the night before. Heather noticed that as Miss Boniface turned to go she absentmindedly rubbed her finger where once her ring had once been. A quick glance around at the stormy skies reassured Heather that there was no giant sea bird about to attack.

It came as a huge relief to Heather that Miss Boniface seemed to have completely recovered and with no memories of the night before. Heather sighed with relief.

Heather was blown the last few steps home and crashed into the front door. As she burst through the kitchen door, she was smiling with relief.

'Heather, watch out!'

Her grandpa bellowed as Heather flung off her coat, sending rivulets of ice cold water cascading over him.

'She's worse than the storm.'

Heather's mother rushed to shut the door and mop around her daughter. As she caught site of her wild, bedraggled image in the small mirror on the wall they all burst out laughing.

'Now, off to your room and get dry and warm and then come down for your tea. It's chicken pie tonight,' she called.

Heather ran upstairs to her bedroom to grab some dry clothes. She was just pulling a big jumper over her head when she noticed the aquarium appeared different. Moving closer, she turned its light on and jumped back in astonishment. As sure as eggs were eggs the water in the tank was moving. As she drew her face closer she realised that there were miniature waves crashing into the side of the tank. They were small yet big enough to make a splashing sound. Puzzled, Heather went into the bathroom. She filled up the sink to wash her face and noticed that the water was behaving exactly the same. Barely perceptible movements on the surface made small seascapes that splashed around the basin. Even though this strange phenomenon intrigued Heather she felt the cold edge of panic grab her tummy. If this was happening in her basin, what was it like far out at sea?

17
The Gathering

Heather had just got downstairs to the kitchen when the door burst open and Mrs Weaver came in. She had a wild look about her and she was drenched from head to foot.

'Oh Maria, have you heard anything, have you George? It's getting really wild out there.'

Mrs Weaver looked around the kitchen expectantly, Heather's grandpa had frozen with a forkful of pie halfway to his mouth in surprise. Heather's mum nudged him and leapt into action.

'Come in Brenda. Sit down; here, let me take your wet

coat. Now then, whatever's the matter? We don't want to start panicking do we.'

Heather noticed her mother's mood had changed yet she was fighting hard to hide it from her friend. Mrs Weaver took off her coat and started to shake. Heather's mum had shoved a scalding cup of tea in her hand and was fussing over her. Heather's senses heightened, and she felt a great wave of worry and concern shift the atmosphere in the room. Something wasn't right.

'Oh, they say that the coastguard's been hit, that all the radios are down, that there is a hurricane on the way, that they don't stand a chance. Oh, Maria what should we do?'

Mrs Weaver and grandpa George looked at Heather's mum who froze, her washing up cloth suddenly clutched tightly to her breast. To Heather it felt as if the large kitchen had suddenly entered its own universe, one where time moved slowly. She had known many long winter nights when everybody crowded into her house to ride out the storm, and their combined fears, some silent and some loudly expressed. It had been many years since a storm of this magnitude had risen up to strike fear into the heart of the small village. When the last great storm happened Heather's grandmother had been alive. Then too Mrs Weaver had rushed to Heather's house to seek the common-sense advice and deep insight of Heather's grandmother. Mrs Weaver, who was breathing heavily and wringing her hair out, was looking to Heather's mum to fill the gap left by Heather's grandmother.

Maria looked uncomfortable and embarrassed. Heather saw her mum try to control her obvious sense of panic and think clearly but she just froze, unsure of what to say or do. Heather's mum was a good sort, sensible, intelligent and the wife of the un-elected leader of the fleet and therefore the village but this was not a situation that she enjoyed. Maria took a deep breath and rallied herself.

'Come now Brenda, there's no point panicking. We have seen storms like this. Why I bet the men have turned the boats towards the harbour hours ago.'

Mrs Weaver was so desperate that she clutched to Maria's reassuring words like a drowning woman to a life-raft. She nodded furiously and took a sip of tea. The kitchen was just beginning to calm down when the door burst open again and Mrs Coulter, another wife of a fisherman, stumbled in.

'Don't nobody knock no more?'

Heather's grandpa shouted out in alarm as he was sprayed with rain water again. Everyone ignored him, which was just how he liked it and he returned to eating. Mrs Coulter saw Mrs Weaver and sat down beside her waving to Maria for a cup of tea.

'Oh Brenda, thank god you're here already. The others are coming up. We need to sing together tonight. This storm is a bad one.'

It wasn't long before the little kitchen was jammed full of the wives, daughters and sisters of the men at sea. Heather crammed herself in the farthest corner on the top of a huge pile of coats half scared and half excited, she was caught up in the drama unfolding. The women had brought an old net and, as they crammed round the large kitchen table some standing and some sitting, they all started repairing it as if their lives depended on it. Soon one of the ladies, Mrs White, started an old waulking song and soon the ancient song began to fill the room. Everyone seemed to know the words, or at least the choruses, and Heather found herself singing along with them. The song seemed to draw the women together until they became calmed by the very act of singing. Eventually, after a couple of hours and constant supply of sweet tea, a sense of unity permeated the crowded kitchen and a palpable relief began to descend. Heather thought how different it was from the gathering in the local hall a couple of days before. Women assembled in a different way to men, Heather thought. The noisy debate in the hall a few days ago had only seemed to divide brother against brother, man against reason.

As they sang they swayed and sometimes would break off to say a prayer for the men at sea. The old radio crackled and fizzed in the background, turned to the frequency of the boats just in case someone was trying to contact the shore. Heather realised that their cottage easily had the biggest kitchen in the village and she wasn't surprised when the door opened and four more figures entered the room.

The four Wise Women calmly entered the room and handed out bags of welcomed provisions. Strangely, they didn't seem to be very wet nor were the cakes, and home-made biscuits, buns and jam that soon piled up on the table. Heather was delighted to see that her new friends had decided to join in the vigil. Heather's mum vaguely recognised the women from the cafe in Saltkirk and absent-mindedly invited them in. Maria had long given over her private space to whoever needed to come into and be part of the vigil. Some of the women stood up to greet the four ladies and offered them their chairs. The village women seemed pleased to see their elders and the room relaxed a bit further. Muriel carefully positioned her thin frame on a small rocking chair at the head of the table and searched the packed room with her piercing blue eyes.

Her eyes quickly found Heather who was now pressed into a corner. She flashed Heather a fierce wink as she sat down and drew a flask of steaming soup out of her incredible carry bag.

'Heard the storm. We were on the way past here so we called in like in the old days. Besides, your mother will need some help now that she is with child.'

Maria looked shocked and glanced questioningly at Heather. She was yet to make any private confession or public announcement that she was pregnant. She looked stunned, confused and relieved all at once at Muriel's revelation. Heather gulped with shock and pleasure – she wanted to fight her way across the packed kitchen to give her mum a supportive hug, but Muriel was already busying herself with tea making. Muriel's voice rang with an air of authority that seemed to galvanise the women. Heather looked back to Muriel who was studying an old black and white photograph of Heather's grandmother that always rested above the stove. Soon other women were following Muriel's commanding and powerful gaze. They all looked at the faded picture and some of them sighed as if they still felt a sense of loss. Heather realised just how important her maternal grandmother must have been for the village in times of storms. If she squinted her eyes she could imagine her darling grandmother sitting in the rocking chair which was currently occupied by Muriel.

Jean had sat beside Muriel and was removing a long scarf that seemed to go on forever. Seeing Heather stuffed in the corner she motioned for her to come sit beside them. Heather began to squeeze past the fisher wives as they chatted and busied themselves with the net and soon reached Jean. Even though Heather was taller than the old wise woman she lifted Heather up and sat her on her plump knee in one swift move whilst accepting a cup of tea and dunking her biscuit at the same time.

'There's loads enough room for the two of us.'

Heather was glad; she sensed that now the wise women had arrived an atmosphere of hope had lifted the mood of the room. Heather's mum had recognised the women as old friends of Heather's grandmother. She was covering her embarrassment for not making the connection earlier and was chatting to Jean over Heather's head. Heather looked at her mum; she also seemed to find solace in their presence. It was as if a great responsibility has somehow been shared and made lighter and easier to manage. Muriel began to sing. Her voice was soft and tuneful yet still strong. It was an ancient sounding song and was sung in a language that Heather didn't recognise but yet felt familiar to her. With the four Wise Women picking up harmonies some of the village women began to join in and soon a glorious, sad, stirring and powerful melody filled the room. The song seemed to be unending as it soared, lifted higher and higher, weaving an ancient poem in the steamy atmosphere of the kitchen. Before long everybody was joining in and those standing began to sway in time. As the verses were repeated over and over Heather felt her own voice lift to find its harmony within the song. The words started to unravel their meaning in her mind. They spoke of a time before the history of man had been written down. The words called out to a great spirit for support and nourishment, to an ancient goddess who was both the creator of the world and the universe and was also the world herself. As some of the women called out for help others created a chorus that answered with words of love and compassion. If Heather stopped singing for a moment the words lost their meaning – yet as she sang them the stories of ancient times appeared clearly in her mind. The song went on for a long time but the moment it concluded, and a delicate silence filled the kitchen, a loud crackle came from the radio.

'Ship to shore ...hiss crackle hiss... ship to shore...do you read me ship to shore....'

'It's Robert, it's Tim it's...'

'Quiet everybody!'

Muriel's voice rang out with authority and everyone listened. They were straining to hear the reply from the coastguard. The radio crackled and then they clearly heard Heather's dad cursing loudly. Heather found the ripe language hilarious and the expletive momentarily broke the ice, and everybody burst out laughing, grateful for the sudden relief it brought. Even just hearing a voice meant that the boats must be alright.

Then suddenly the radio went quiet as the coastguard's voice could be heard calling the ship to identify itself. The radio fizzed and popped but only static remained until suddenly they all heard a voice speak quite clearly.

'Hello shore we can't read you please send help, in trouble, engine failure in one vessel, can't tow, need help, repeat need....'

Then the radio went quiet or rather burst into a wall of white static.

The room erupted with the terrified sound of women's voices. Everybody was speaking at once. Everybody had a different take on what the message might have meant. Nobody seemed to find any positive angles and many of the voices were fearful. Heather's grandfather was commanded to phone the coastguard for confirmation. He got up, grumbling, and went to go into the small spare room to make the phone call. The women were beside themselves.

'What if they can't get back?'

'Motor's down, didn't you hear, they will start taking on water...'

'Won't be able to keep the pumps going'

'It's too wild to send up a helicopter...'

'They'll put out a boat though won't they?'

Heather's pulse went up as she tried not to panic. Her father and brother, her two cousins and most of the men of the village were in mortal danger and everybody knew it. Her grandpa came back into the room to confirm the worst.

'They reckon it was one of ours but they didn't get a fix so I told them the last co-ordinates that I had from earlier and if there's a break in the weather they'll send up the whirlybird.'

His news hardly made the panicked conversation quieter, in fact it seemed to raise the noise level. No one heard grandpa as he said that he was going back into the living room to plot the maps. Heather knew that her grandpa would have the best idea of where the boats were and would be the one to give tips to the coastguard. Mrs Weaver seemed beside herself. Always a highly-strung woman she was nearing pure panic and beginning to unsettle some of the other women even though Heather's mum kept calling for calm. Mrs Weaver kept calling out the name Katrina. Heather realised that she was yelling for her grandmother.

'Katrina, Katrina, oh if your mother was here Maria, she would know what to do. She would make a peace with the sea. She would guide them home.'

'Well she's not here so she can't!'

Muriel spoke suddenly, and her voice cut through the din like a knife. The room fell silent and an expectant hush took over. Heather was impressed – Muriel could be quite commanding when she wanted to.

'And, I would remind you Brenda to think of poor Maria as you sit and call out for her departed mother.'

Brenda looked momentarily sheepish.

'Besides, aren't you all forgetting the fact that your village does have a Wise Woman. So why don't you ask her what to do?'

A hush fell over the room and most of the women looked straight at Heather's mum expectantly.

'No. No,' said Heather's mum in a quiet voice, 'her gift didn't pass on to me.'

Then she gasped at Muriel.

'No, you can't mean...she's too young for God's sake Muriel, she's only a child.'

Suddenly, all the eyes in the room stared at Heather with a mixture of shock, surprise and eager expectancy. The sudden unwelcome attention unnerved Heather and, if it hadn't been for the kindly Jean gently calming Heather by stroking her hair she would have jumped up and raced out of the kitchen.

Muriel took command again.

'It's quite alright Maria. The child is no more and the young woman that Heather is has the Sight. If we give her the love and support we are capable of she might be able to see where the boats are and what condition they are in.'

Heather looked around the expectant faces and the sudden hushed desperation she saw made her begin to panic. Heather's rising alarm meant that she was completely unable to think of anything let alone quiet her mind. How could she possibly help? Her heart was pounding and she felt as if she might be sick.

It was Heather's grandfather who, having poked his head round the door to see what the fuss was about, suddenly commanded everybody's attention.

'You lot stop scaring poor Heather, right now! You all know me, I'm the oldest one in this room, and as the village elder I have a right to preside. Now I may have not been the best of husbands to my dear Katrina, her ways frightened me, but I remember as much as you all do when she guided the boats back in, and I'll tell you all something, that dear child has got her eyes and her looks and I swear that she has got the gift even stronger within her. Yet,' suddenly he scolded, 'not one of you were respectful at the meeting in the town hall and not one of you heeded her warning so don't you go pressurising her now.'

Heather smiled at her grandfather, who winked at her before heading back into the relative quiet of their small sitting room to listen to the radio. His outburst had taken the room aback. Suddenly a great dawning of realisation seemed to settle over everyone. Women lent forward with apology after apology to Heather, some could barely hold back their tears until Muriel reprimanded them

'Leave the poor girl alone. What was her warning to you all?'

'Not to use the nets.'

A short burst of debate crackled around the room as the daughters, wives and mothers of the village began to grasp at the thin straw of hope that was being offered to them.

'Just superstition.'

'We can't go back to those days.'

'It's science and technology that drives those boats now, not prayers and mumbo jumbo'.

'Well what have we got to lose?'

'It's an ancient tradition.'

'Well it will either work or it won't!'

'Isn't it time we listened to our sisters rather than shouting them down?'

Heather's mother spoke, and her voice was clear as a bell and brought all of the women to silence again.

'Heather warned us all not to use the nets. She spoke of the consequences for us all. She spoke of us challenging the delicate balance of the ocean.'

Heather's mum looked at her daughter fondly with a sudden flash of fierce pride that made Heather blush.

'Yes, it's true, my little girl got up there, in front of you all, and not even her father, who knows her and loves her more than anything on this earth, took heed. Maybe we should listen for once. What do you suggest Muriel?'

Muriel smiled gently at Maria. She could see that Heather's mother was caught in between a sense of duty as mother to protect her daughter and a desire to do anything to save the menfolk. Muriel spoke to reassure her.

'Well,' said Muriel, 'we are probably in for a long night, I suggest that Heather just tries to see if she can locate the boats. She is young and will need the power of the full moon which will not be full until past midnight before she could even consider guiding them in. Besides, with their computerised equipment they may not even need it. If we all give her our complete attention, love and support then she might be able to see far enough to bring us some precious news.'

Muriel made everyone clear a space and suddenly Heather found herself encircled by all the women of the village. She sat on a chair and was passed a glass of water. Her mother sat almost opposite and told Heather that she would stop the process if Heather became distressed. Heather could see that her mother's words were for the doubters in the room as much as to reassure her daughter. Muriel then bade the women to quietly sing an old slow song and then she, Jean, Gladys and Susan gently laid their hands on Heather's shoulders. She softly whispered into Heather's ear.

'Just clear you mind and relax like I taught you.'

To Heather's surprise, her mind quickly became as still as a mill pond and all of her early anxieties vanished like a sea mist before the rising sun. A great calm came across Heather and she felt as if her life suddenly made sense, as if she had been waiting for this moment since she was born. A great peace and sense of wellbeing flooded up inside her, quieting her beating heart and dispelling all of her fears, worries and doubts. The women sang. This time it was a sweet low song not unlike a lullaby. The singing lulled Heather and, as she closed her eyes, she felt as if she was floating in mid-air. The song seemed to lift her higher and higher. Heather felt herself smiling as she imagined herself floating above the heads of the surprised women. Heather could see as clearly as if she had her eyes open. Heather let out a small gasp, but she wasn't surprised to find herself looking down over the village. The colours seemed diffuse, yet the world was sparkling as if a million small points of life had joined up to connect everything with everything else.

'Follow your guide.'

Muriel whispered the instruction into Heather's ear. Then Heather felt a profound rush of joy as her astral body shot forwards and out to sea. She darted down to the foaming seas and dived under. A beautiful seal turned to her and then sped off into the waters and Heather immediately knew who it was she was following. Speeding through the water at a superhuman speed Heather was dimly aware of surprised fish darting out of her way as they breached waves and dived beneath the surface again. Suddenly Heather sensed them stopping. She looked at the seal and smiled with familiarity.

'What now grandma?'

The seal seemed to smile and Heather knew at once. She leapt to the water's surface and the moment she broke surface she soared into the sky, knowing that now she was a bird. Copying the gulls she had seen earlier she was able to hold her position as the winds threatened throw her about. Heather looked down; far below, in the churning grey of the storm seas, she could clearly make out four of the six fishing boats. They were foundering badly as the huge waves battered them, but she could see that they were still alright, their sturdy construction resisting the pounding of the waves. Heather could see their lights shining into the blackness of the storm. As the waves parted Heather recognised the familiar sight of her father's vessel. As she drew closer, struggling against the strong winds to get a better view she saw her father fighting with the wheel to steer the boat and her brother bent over the radio in the wheelhouse. She could see him shouting into the microphone of the radio whilst clutching onto the table for dear life. As Heather watched the stormy scene she felt a sense of relief and reassurance. Her father was struggling but the conditions were well under control and no one seemed in danger. The boats were slowly but steadily making their way home. Heather soared out and up, higher and higher, but could not see the other two boats anywhere. Then a momentary break in the cloud let the moonlight through and she saw two vessels labouring over a huge wave. One was towing the other and they were making quite good progress. The fleet must have drawn together for some reason so were well placed to help each other. Often they would have been spread over a large distance at the fishing grounds. Heather realised their progress would be slow but at least they weren't marooned. She was just about to turn and leave when something caught her eye. She flew down towards the deck of her father's boat and saw something that made her almost lose her senses and crash into the sea. Ran's prophecy and warning about the new nets rang in Heather's ears. The back of the boat showed signs of damage and she could see where the net winding mechanism had sheared away. The nets had been deployed and used.

Heather felt herself cry out in blind panic and, in an instant, she was back in the kitchen, her eyes wide open. Heather stifled her scream as the familiar and comforting surroundings of her home made her blink. She knew better than to alarm the already spooked women. Muriel was vigorously rubbing Heathers back and calling for hot tea. Heather fought to regain control of her emotions to hide her shock of discovering that the new nets had been used. With Muriel's help and after taking gulps of hot sweet tea she managed to temper her emotions so as not to scare everyone. As Heather looked around the room she could see the collective fear of the women looking back at her yet, at the same time, she experienced a rush of their unconditional love and warmth and support, which pulled her further back into her body, and suddenly she was able to speak.

'It's Ok, they are all right.'

Heather blurted out and was relieved as everyone in the room breathed out a collective sigh of relief. Muriel held her hand up to stop the flood of questions and made the women let Heather tell her story at her own speed.

Quickly and softly Heather told the gathered circle what she had seen. Although she played down the sense of danger she had felt and didn't mention the fact that the nets had obviously been used, she told the women of how she had seen the boats, of how they were coping with the storm and of how they were slowly towing in the one without the working engine. As the realisation that no life had been lost settled in a great hubbub of cheerful debate and opinion broke free with everybody speaking at once. Women kept leaning over to pat Heather's hand and thank her and then go back to dissecting her story. Heather looked up as her mother sidled up with another cup of steaming tea, her face still filled with concern. Heather could see that her mum had been freaked out about by what had just taken place. She could see an inward struggle going on, a battle between rationality, concern and desperation to hear the good news from the sea. Heather leant in towards her mum to reassure her.

'Don't worry, when I leave my body, Grandma is with me, she guides me and looks after me.'

Heather's mother looked shocked and then relieved. Suddenly it was if there was only the two of them in the room and mother and daughter clung to each other sobbing into each other's arms. Falling into her mother's arms Heather felt as if she was a small girl running to her mother's arms for love and reassurance. She hadn't realised how much energy the vision had used up. As Heather's exhaustion flooded through her she understood what a mixture of emotions her poor mother was going through. Then, with a quiet word from Muriel, almost as one, the other women gathered tightly around Heather and her mother. Heather was vaguely aware of the two of them being hugged and rocked backwards and forwards surrounded by the arms and the love of everybody in the room.

Heather felt her tears flow. She knew that the intense pressure of the last few days was finally being released in her tears. The women held on to each other so that they could all find relief through their tears together. As Heather cried she felt the panic and fear leave the room. She sensed her mum's pain and feelings of inadequacy vaporise. Maria's huge burden of having to hold the village together vanished. She was now free of the burden because the Sight had not been passed on to her. When they finally all untangled themselves and Muriel called for fresh tea Heather looked up and felt the respect of her peers. Each woman took a moment to thank her, and to bless her as a woman. She would have been proud enough to break if it had not been for her terrible secret.

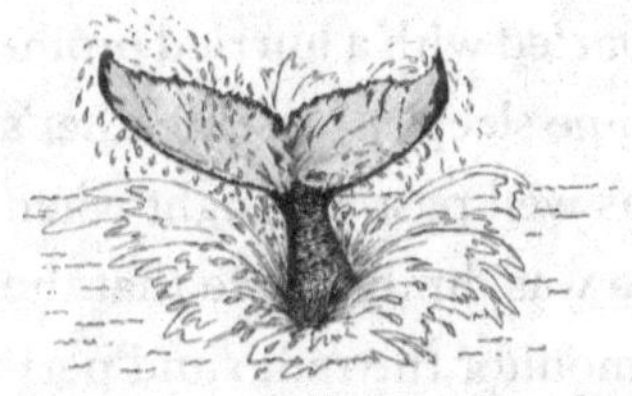

18
A Clash
of Ideals

Heather's grandfather came back into the kitchen with a look of mild amusement on his face when he found all the women huddled together. He waited as they reorganised themselves and began to put on their coats and scarfs. Scratching his head he told everyone the good news that he had been able to plot the position of the ships and that the coastguard would send out a helicopter when the weather subsided a little.

It was Muriel who quickly disbanded the meeting. She and her sisters maintained their quiet composure and sense of calm and soon had everybody cleaning and clearing. The womenfolk began to leave and even Mrs Weaver finally departed with a hurried promise that 'she would try and get some sleep'. At last Heather's house became quiet again. It was well past midnight when Heather was sent to bed and she was dimly aware that the adults were arranging shifts to monitor the radio and periodically check in with the coast guard. Muriel, Jean, Gladys and Susan had come prepared and they soon bedded down. Heather knew that her mum was glad of her surprise houseguests. In the Highlands collective troubles meant collective solutions. It was as if an ancient understanding of mutual support came into being and everyone was a family member at these testing times. Just as Heather was climbing the stairs Muriel caught up with her and spoke with a kindly smile.

'Try to sleep and not dream. I fear the worse for this storm. What was it you that you didn't share with the others?'

Heather paused; of course, Muriel would have noticed the fact that she had kept some information carefully hidden from everybody. She turned to see Muriel's kind, concerned face and met her piercing gaze with a smile. Even though she was half asleep Heather was still surprised at the strength, clarity and power of the woman standing beside her. Again, Heather was reminded of the power of Ran's gaze and how it made you feel that every part of your soul, warts and all was naked and exposed. Muriel smiled and gently reached out her hand and touched Heather's.

'I am here to help you my sweet.' she whispered.

Heather sighed and relaxed. It was so good to be able to share her burden with a friend. She felt a final flood of relief pass through her. Heather realised that she trusted Muriel and no longer had to shoulder the burden of all those terrible secrets on her own. She sat on her bed and spoke quickly and simply to Muriel and told her about the meaning of the nets and the threat of danger their use implied for the men at sea and for the village. She told the story quickly sparing no detail but avoided mentioning Ran or her Grandmother. Then Heather heard her own voice grow powerful and strong and she made Muriel agree to keep it a secret. Muriel dropped her gaze immediately understanding the importance of what she had been told and didn't question Heather any further. Smiling with concern she simply passed Heather a small bottle and made her take a small sip from it.

'The herbs will warm you and guard you.' she said. 'It's not magic, just an expression of support from Mother Nature.'

Then she winked at Heather and sent her to bed. As Heather turned to get undressed she heard Muriel outside in the narrow hallway instructing her mother in the same manner. Heather smiled – what would they do without Muriel and the Wise Women?

*****

The grey morning light snuck in around the edge of the curtains and gently roused Heather. She opened one eye and wondered where she was. She dimly remembered going to bed and then having the best sleep ever. She felt refreshed and full of energy. Heather didn't want to upset the calm of the moment and stayed curled up beneath her duvet and let the roar of the wind outside slowly wake her up. Bit by bit Heather's mind played out the night before. She smiled, it seemed to her like she was watching a mini movie that to her surprise she starred in. One small part of Heather's mind cringed and worried what everybody would be saying about her. The village was a small place and gossip travelled fast. Heather told herself to get a grip and not be childish. She pictured Ran's eyes and replayed some of the amazing visions in her mind. Then she held up her ring to check and see if it was still real. Somehow recent events felt a bit like she was living in a dream. The ring glowed, and small currents and flecks of gold seemed to swirl in its centre. The wind roared like a hungry old dragon outside the house and the sound jolted Heather with a small stab of fear and a slight knot returned to the pit of her stomach. Heather remembered that the boats were not yet safely home in the harbour. The image of the broken landing gear and nets stuck in her mind as much as seeing her father and brother struggling in the severe conditions.

Heather swung her legs out of her bed and let her toes gently work their way into her slippers. As she reached for her dressing gown she could hear the heavy patter of rain on her window. It seemed to be drumming a furious rhythm and was getting heavier by the minute. In the far distance she became aware of the roar of the sea and she was sure she could feel the vibration, caused by huge waves crashing against the harbour wall, ripple through her house. Heather padded over to the aquarium in her slippers and noticed that the strange effect on the water in the tank was still continuing. She looked inside and fed the inhabitants who all seemed to be hiding under a large clump of weed. 'No more babies then my dear' she said smilingly to another pregnant seahorse as it darted out for a second. Heather pulled her dressing gown tightly around her and followed the smell of breakfast downstairs.

Everybody had risen early, and the Sisters were bustling about helping Heather's mother, who was smiling and grateful. A small TV had been found and turned on. A grim-faced newscaster was talking quickly, and Heather saw even more images of huge waves and ships, small and great, making heavy weather in the hurricane conditions. She drew her breath in sharply as she watched image after image of huge waves, damaged sea buildings, ships stranded on rocks and whole parts of the coast falling into the sea. Muriel paused beside Heather holding a stack of clean plates and cups; they both stood motionless, hypnotised by the images of destruction they were witnessing. Muriel spoke softly with concern in her voice.

'It's still continuing. If anything, it seems to be getting stronger. The sea is surging, the tides are so high the water is literally attacking the land. So many ships are in distress, the international coastguards are overwhelmed and everybody is blaming everybody else for not funding them properly. Though one good thing, it seems that the weather here is actually nowhere as bad as the rest of the country. I fear we have much more work to do my young friend.'

Muriel turned to Heather and smiled. Heather's eyes were as wide as saucers and seemed suddenly so young.

'Don't worry my dear, it will all turn out all right in the end I'm sure. You need to rest today, there's no school, I think they have a problem with the roof, apparently a corner of it has blown off.'

Heather giggled half-heartedly and snapped herself out of her TV-induced trance.

'I bet that has made everybody very happy, we were meant to have a test today.'

Muriel smiled and turned to stack plates.

'Here you go young lady.'

Heather's mother presented her with a bowl of porridge. Putting on a posh voice she smiled and said,

'Young master Joseph has called and wonders if you might visit today as school has been cancelled. After you have eaten and got changed though...!'

Maria added her last request quickly as Heather had rushed to put her coat on. All the women turned and smiled knowingly at Heather's enthusiasm to see her friend. Heather found herself blushing again and tried to change the topic of conversation.

'But what about you Mum? Don't you need my help?'

Heather's mum winked at her new helpers who were already getting stuck in to some serious cleaning and cooking.

'Don't worry about me my love. Muriel and the girls are staying on. Part of the road back to Saltkirk seems to have been washed away by a landslide and besides, these ladies are a breath of fresh air to the village. Oh, good news my darling, the coastguard called and there is a navy vessel not far from the fleet and she is going to help them back to harbour. You go and see Joe.'

Heather smiled and breathed a huge sigh of relief. Maybe all of her fears were misplaced. Maybe Ran's warning of the dire consequences of about using the new nets had passed. Maybe it was over at last and now she could go back to her life again, everybody was going to be Ok.

Heather wrapped up warm and put on her waterproof jacket. Even a short trip up the path to Joe's would mean facing the full force of the Atlantic. The sound of the wind still howling like a banshee made her glance out of the window. The little harbour kept disappearing from view as wave after wave of impenetrable walls of rain and hail struck the coast. It seemed as if the sky met sea and then the two ran off together leaving only a great grey nothing in their place. Standing on tiptoe she took one last glance out of the window and then had to stifle a laugh. Through a momentary break in the clouds Heather saw the local pastor battling with the storm. The sight of him made her laugh out loud. The small rotund man was clinging to his bicycle and was being propelled, at some speed, up the cobbled path towards Heather's house. She could see his look of combined terror and exhilaration. His black raincoat kept wrapping itself around him, threatening to obscure his view but she saw that his hands were clenched white from hanging onto his handle bars for dear life. She saw the Pastor brace himself then dismount by throwing his whole body clear of the bicycle which was carried forwards by the wind, past Heather's house, for a few meters before crashing unceremoniously into the wall.

Heather skipped down the stairs to greet their visitor. Pastor Bobby McGowan was simply Bobby to everyone he met and always brought a blast of good cheer and often a handful of huge jaw-breaking toffees whenever he visited anyone. Heather had fond memories of him as he always appeared at celebrations; the blessing of a boat, a marriage and often a birthday. Although Heather wanted to see Joe she felt compelled to see what brought the pastor to the house.

She arrived downstairs just in time to see him literally blown inside their small kitchen, gasping for breath and beaming his good-natured smile. Heather's mum shouted a greeting and the two of them fought to shut the door as his long coat wrestled to have one last break for freedom. Heather grinned and called Bobby's name racing across the kitchen so that the two of them collided in a messy hug.

'Would you merit it, look at the size of you now, what a hug, nearly took my breath away, phew what a day, thought if I let go of my bike I would join the good Lord in the clouds to be sure. Here, want a toffee young lady, might be a touch soggy still that's never put me off, how's about a nice cup of tea Maria and who do we have here?'

The Pastor's flurry of arrival halted dead in its tracks as his gaze met Muriel and the gathered Wise Women for the first time. Heather had never seen Muriel look so stern before. She seemed to have become like stone, flinty and hard and her fierce gaze froze the smile on the pastor's cheery face. It was her Mum who broke the uncomfortable silence.

'Well Pastor, let's be having your coat and let's be giving you a nice cup of tea before you freeze. Come on Muriel, you cut a piece of cake and I'll help Pastor Bobby, our dear family friend,' she added quickly, 'out of his wet things.'

Jean bustled around Pastor Bobby and distracted him from Muriel's hostility with chuckles of good-natured concern and small talk about the weather until the small round man was smiling and glowing holding a huge mug of tea and an even huger slice of cake. Gladys had dried his glasses with a soft cloth, Susan poured some cream over the cake and Jean had found a soft hand towel and was gently drying the small man's hair.

'Well Mary, you seem to have found some royal help these days, who are these wonderful friends of yours? I'm sure I've met, erm, ...'

Pastor Bobby never found talking and eating cake at the same time an issue. He did love a dramatic pause though and he left his sentence hanging in mid-air as he took a sideways glance at Muriel.

'Well actually these wonderful ladies are all good friends of Heather's. They got stranded here in the storm. The ladies have been wonderful and really helped last night when we all gathered to...'

Heather's mum paused, uncertain of what to say next. Jean stepped in to help Maria with her story.

'Make tea, cake and provide some emotional support for the poor wives and daughters of the menfolk.'

'Oh I see, oh wonderful, how great. In fact, that's really why I had come to see you Maria. I knew everybody would gather here, just like in the old days when your sainted mother was alive, God bless her, so I just wanted to offer my help and of course spiritual help...'

'Spiritual help?!'

Muriel snapped at Bobby. Her blue eyes flashing with anger. She seemed to grow larger until she loomed over the stunned vicar.

'Wasn't it you who blessed the nets and brought all this upon the village?'

'Huh, blessings? But of course, I mean I always do, erm its custom...'

Pastor Bobby looked stunned at Muriel's ferocity and his confused face glanced around the room looking for help. It was as if time momentarily stood still; Heather held her breath. A sudden recognition passed across the small man's face and he met Muriel's gaze again. Heather watched a slow realisation dawn on Pastor Bobby. His face darkened and then flushed red.

'Oh I know you, I know where you are from, that women's circle, coven thing. I might have guessed, preying on the vulnerable poor folk of this village as soon as my back is turned. Bringing all your superstitious knowledge here. I hope you haven't been brainwashing a young defenceless girl as well with all your mumbo jumbo.'

The pastor glanced at Heather and tried to smile but he was clearly rattled and caught off-guard. Muriel was looking daggers at Pastor Bobby.

'We are nothing but clear-sighted women who have chosen to keep the old ways alive. Plant-lore, healing and guidance all with a healthy dollop of common sense is all we ladies practice yet not so long ago you and your kind would have had us put to death for such things! Surely you can't be that blinkered Bobby.'

The Pastor spluttered and went bright red. He drew himself up and began to wave his arms around as if he was on the pulpit.

'You are nothing but a bunch of witches, leading good people astray with your superstitious attitudes and your lotions and potions. Maria, send these ungodly women from your house immediately!'

Maria's mouth hung open in surprise and astonishment at the shocking tirade from the normally mild-mannered Pastor. Nobody ever dared speak like that to Maria or welcome guests in her house. Marie always made a point to be sympathetic and kind to everybody. She really didn't have a bad bone in her body. Heather glanced at her Mum and thought that she might cry. Muriel saw the effect of the Pastor's words on Maria and it was as if somebody had poured oil on an already lit flame. Muriel's indignation burst out of her with the ferocity of the outside storm and her voice grew even more powerful.

'Witches! That's what you would like to call us is it? After all these years. You dare to slander a guest in a home of a good and honest god-fearing woman. The home where generations of Wise Women have lived and loved and provided healing, comfort and guidance to each other. You do a disservice to your gender and your so-called faith. Your small-minded attitude is a perpetuation blatant misogyny. If women show any connection with spirituality your kind have to damn us into oblivion, burn us, drown us because you are so scared you might lose your position of power, your nice comfy income and security. You are a throwback to all that is dark, evil and ignorant. It's you that are trapped in childish superstition based on nothing more than dry, empty tradition. If Maria wills it you should leave.'

Pastor Bobby began to protest profusely, alarmed with how things were going. His mouth opened and closed like a beached fish. Colour was draining from his face and they could all see that he was regretting his outburst. He tried to calm things down, but Heather could see that he was terrified of Muriel. Heather wondered briefly if men always got angry and lost control when they were scared.

'No one is going to burn or drown anyone,' he spluttered, going red.

Muriel had turned coldly quiet her voice now low which meant that it carried even more weight. Heather could sense her friend's power rising and with each word and she wondered where this was all headed to. Pastor Bobby turned pale as Muriel spoke in low clipped tones.

'Well your grandfather's father persecuted us, and his father before him and his father before him! Am I not correct Robert McGowan? Are you not from a line of abusers and murderers?!'

Pastor Bobby visibly dragged and held his hand up in front of his face as he tried to defend himself from Muriel's anger which raged around the room with a crackle of electricity.

'My grandfather maybe, my father never... that was such a long time ago... things were different then. A different time altogether.'

'Different!' spat Muriel. 'You just tried to evict us from our shelter here, you called us witches and you tried to damn us with your words! It is your ignorance and stupidity that has conspired with the greed of men to unbalance this world. You support the follies of men and damn the wisdom of women, and now, at this time of great reckoning you are too blind to change. You blessed the nets; you sealed the curse.'

Heather felt a conflict of emotions. She felt loyal to her childhood fondness for the pastor and love for her new friends but protecting her mother's house from this kind of fanaticism won over. Heather felt a great in-balance occurring. She was reminded of what she had summed in the bothy and Heather felt a deeper wisdom flow through her. She saw with a flash the path that anger and the need for revenge would lead to and she didn't like the idea of a huge rebreathing elemental bursting into the small house. A great wave of power surge through her and an ancient connection with an old wisdom seemed to instruct her words. The room started to glow and Heather could see energies swirling around everybody. Her Mum's was golden but kept flashing with a confusion of darker hues as if she was fighting off her fears. Both Muriel and Pastor Bobby's energy swirled around them but was much darker. Susan's was shining brightly and, as their eyes met, she gave Heather a huge wink. That was all Heather needed. Without raising her voice she issued the command that had risen within her.

'Enough! That's enough Muriel, Pastor Bobby, enough. There will be no discord and division in this house. You will both respect my mother's house. Please, everyone calm down and let's all be friends.'

Muriel and Bobby were instantly silent. Heather's words carried a different kind of power. Her dark eyes fixed them both where they stood, like they were much loved but naughty children. Heather didn't need to shout. Her voice grew even more soft and gentle. As she spoke it was as if sunshine filled the room. The Wise Women dropped their heads apart from Susan who just beamed her smile at Heather. Heather was concerned that Muriel might say too much about her vision. She didn't want to scare her mother or betray Ran's confidence. She continued and her voice was calm, strong and utterly compelling; the adults all froze, captivated by Heather's sudden transformation.

'Muriel, you are sworn to say no more. Isn't this the time for men and women to lay down their differences and unite in wisdom and act with a faith that forgives the past. We can't keep on repeating mistakes. We must come together to save the world, not to create more wars.'

A great surge of love flowed through Heather's body and soul. She felt as if the words she spoke came from somewhere just outside herself, an older version of herself. The language she used was not her normal way of speaking, yet she knew the words expressed her deepest truth. Muriel and Pastor Bobby both stood with their mouths hanging open. Heather wondered if anybody had dare check Muriel in full flow before. Heather felt the ancient power compelling her to continue. She could hear her voice ring out and she vaguely wondered how on earth it had grown so authoritative and commanding.

'The past is no more; the future is uncertain and all we have is now. Let us join together and share our ancient wisdom for without it we are all lost. We must come together in love not anger, in peace not in judgement, in forgiveness not in revenge.'

Heather's vision cleared, and the room returned to normal for her. She smiled and looked calmly at the circle of stunned faces. Heather stifled a giggle and then realised that she felt a bit faint. Her head swam, and she had a weird experience of coming back into her body. It was as if her body felt heavy, like an old coat. The lightness of moments before had deserted her as quickly as it had arrived. Her mother and Susan leapt towards her and caught Heather's arms and helped her sit in a chair. Muriel and Pastor Bobby both sat down motionless staring with surprise at Heather. Pastor Bobby was the first to speak.

'Oh my, young Heather, from the mouth of babes...!'

Suddenly he stood and surprised Muriel by taking her hand.

'I am so sorry Muriel, I don't know where that came from. Maria, let me apologise unreservedly to you and your friends, my anger got the better of me. Muriel, you were absolutely right and I'm ashamed I spoke from a place of fear. For the record, I love to immerse myself in nature. I find great solace in walking the cliff path and I find God in all His creations. The ocean and its wellbeing is important to me as a man of God and a man of science .'

Father Bobby looked around the room and pressed on with his apology.

'I actually had a terrible foreboding about trying to increase catches with larger nets. I am an ornithologist; I have seen the seabirds starving as the fish stocks plummet. I'm also concerned with overfishing and the knock on impact it might have on nature and the livelihoods of our wee community. Yet wherever I go and whichever community I serve I try to give them my blessing even if I don't wholeheartedly agree with their reasons. It is,' he turned to Muriel, 'my job, and I am here to offer hope as much as you ladies.'

He turned to Jean, Susan and Gladys and then sat down and reached for his cake as if it was somewhere to hide.

Muriel seemed to have gathered herself realising that the everybody was looking to her to respond to the pastor's apology. She looked past everyone else and directed her words towards Heather. As Muriel spoke she used a much more gentle and kind tone of voice to show that she completely agreed with her younger sister's wisdom.

'I am so sorry my little sister: I betrayed your trust. You spoke words of truth, wisdom, peace and compassion and I spoke from a place of hurt and anger. We women have had to defend ourselves for so long, I've had to fight so many battles in my short lifetime. When I was a child we all hid our abilities from the church because we were so scared. Like Pastor Bobby I spoke from a place of fear. Old hurts are easily triggered and I lost perspective. I can see that maybe a new time is upon us. You are right; we must put our differences aside. I am sorry for bringing discord into your house Heather, and Maria, we all heard your words of wisdom and we will choose to obey them gladly and joyfully. '

Muriel turned towards Father Bobby who was also staring at Heather as he munched his cake, spellbound.

'What do you say Robert?'

'erm...oh, I er, yes of course, as a man, as your dear friend wholeheartedly, but as a man of the church, well, it will be difficult, I fear that we are only at the beginning of this journey. Please let's keep this between ourselves and then we can work together. What happened to Heather? There were angels standing all around her a moment ago. She kind of glowed with the glory of God. Did you see her eyes? Maybe she's turned into an angel and will save us all yet.'

Father Bobby winked at Heather; she felt the tension leave the room and began to giggle. She loved the old Pastor and was relieved to see that he meant no harm. Jean looked across the room to Heather's mother who seemed dazed by the sudden turn of events in her kitchen. Jean spoke gently to the small gathering.

'Heather is like the old ones, but she is different, she has the Sight, she has claimed her power and now she has a light around that I have not seen before. Don't worry Maria, you must remember how it was with your mother when the Holy Spirit was upon her?'

Jean carefully used a term for Spirit that Pastor Bobby wouldn't find upsetting and Heather could see that Jean was also in peacemaker mode with a great concern for Heather's mother. Maria was standing motionless, holding the teapot. When she spoke her voice was timid and Heather felt a great rush of protective feelings towards her mother.

'I was so young, I was very small, mamma was, she was disappointed that I never had...she never...'

Muriel smiled at Bobby and touched Maria gently on the shoulder.

'She loved you and was proud of you and she knew that the sight often jumps a generation. Maria, she cherished and adored you and the wonderful person you grew up to be. To be so kind and loving and wise without the Sight might be a greater achievement than for those who have the Gift. Now then, let's get back to work; we might be in need of plenty of food tonight. Thank all that is holy that we are all great cooks and that we have our chief taster to keep us right.'

She smiled and winked at Pastor Bobby who had demolished his huge slice of cake in seconds. The kitchen returned to its usual buzz of bustling distraction and Heather saw her mother smile, sigh and then start to issue orders for food preparation, confident that this was one thing that she excelled at, looking after everybody. Father Bobby looked relieved and wiped his mouth absentmindedly with the back of his sleeve. He stood and made his way over to Heather. He gently held her hand and his eyes looked kindly into hers.

'My dearest girl that I have known since birth, that I christened and now see before me as a young woman; you have a great gift, the gift of Grace, the gift of the Saints, the blessing of the Spirit of God. I assure you that I am here to help you. I am an old man yet even I can sense the world is changing. You spoke for us all today. Be careful though my dear. You have a great task before you, of that I am certain, and God grants His grace to those who will need it. You have a great blessing so that means you may yet face great challenges. So,' he continued, suddenly smiling, 'it's just as well your mother makes such great cake. Cake will get you through a lot of things in my experience.'

Smiling, he turned to Heather's mother and gave her a hug.

'Keep safe Maria, I'll keep the church hall open if you need more room, look after that wonderful daughter of yours.'

As he turned to go, he was met by Muriel who was holding out his coat and scarf for him with a genuine smile on her face.

'Now then Bobby, you old rogue, you stay safe out there. You are a better man than your father and your family line. I can see that now. Friends?'

As Father Bobby took his coat Muriel held out her hand, which he took and shook warmly. Bobby looked at her and his face lit up with a smile.

'You are quite a woman Muriel. Quite terrifying in fact, you remind me of my mother, God rest her soul. But you do know the church won't change its position even if I choose to disagree with it from time to time...?'

Muriel smiled back and, for a moment, looked younger than her many years. She cocked her head cheekily on one side.

'I hear that you have women priests these days Bobby. And, are you not the church and are you not changing?

Muriel smiled and gently took the old man's hand. For a fleeting moment they shared a look of near fondness. Bobby coughed to cover his embarrassment.

'Erm in some ways I guess so. It's about time really. We were all too quick to forget the important role that women played establishing our good Lord's church in the early days.'

The small man was suddenly engulfed by his hat, scarf and coat. He hardly heard Muriel's parting words as he tackled his clothing.

'So then, if you change, so does the church.'

Bobby smiled at the room and then dived outside into the howling winds of the storm.

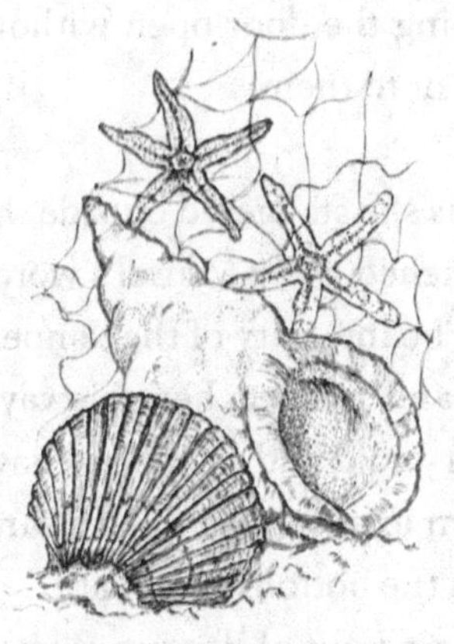

19
Magical Objects

Heather's strength quickly returned once she had finished her breakfast. She had to admit that being a woman certainly required more energy than she had anticipated. It was a strange thing to suddenly find that people listened to what you had to say, even if you weren't sure where the words came from. Remembering her date with Joe she quickly wrapped up and prepared to leave. Muriel gave her a hug and helped her open the kitchen door. The wind was so strong it tried to grab the door out of Muriel's hands and smash it shut again. Heather laughed, as she and Muriel had to put all of their strength into wrangling the door open without any harm or damage to the door or to them.

'Give my love to Joe.'

Muriel shouted after Heather as she staggered outside the small cottage, but the storm snatched away Muriel's words the moment they were uttered. The intensity of the tempest momentarily stunned Heather and pushed her sideways. The rain was now horizontal, very cold and seemed to have the ability to remove feeling from exposed skin like a sand blaster removing barnacles from the bottom of a boat.

Other children were diving in and out of doorways challenging each other to see who could lean into the wind the longest before they fell over. They all waved to Heather and she sensed a new respect and admiration that hadn't been there before. She felt drawn to join them, as they were so happy in their childlike games. Wrapping her scarf tighter around her face she shouted that she was off to visit Joe. To Heather's surprise and slight embarrassment some of the boys even offered to walk Heather all the way up the hill to Joe's house. Heather declined their offer and left them all to the delights of doing wind assisted long jumps that lifted and threw them for what seemed like miles at a time.

Heather took a deep breath and turned to head up the hill path towards Joe's house. The wind was twice as strong as the day before. The short journey was hilarious. Heather's long hair kept escaping and threatening to whip her. Her hat was plucked from her head and preceded to do a dance all the way back down the hill again, leaving Heather laughing and breathless before she caught it.

Heather paused halfway up the hill to get her breath back. She stood with her feet firmly planted on the cobbles, leant into the wind and shielded her eyes as she looked out to sea. It looked like a huge churn of slate-grey madness. Massive waves were rising up to meet the clouds. The harbour walls seemed to diminish in size as vast waves swallowed them up and crashed over into the harbour. The sea was so high it reached right up the harbour wall and was sending huge lumps of foam right up to the front door of some of the cottages. Any higher and the residents would have to get sandbags to prevent the sea joining them in their living rooms.

Heather began to take effortless wind-assisted strides up the path. It wasn't just the wind that made her feel so light. Heather recognised that the events of the morning before had unblocked her inside. Her mind was crystal-clear and she felt invigorated in a way that was new to her. Heather felt so alive it seemed all of her senses were heightened. The sounds, smells and sights intensified. She experienced a deep happiness; it was as if the roof to her head had blown off and let all of the light in. Heather tasted the salt on her lips from the sea spray even though she was now at least a hundred feet above it. She focussed her mind on seeing her friend and sharing her experiences over a warming cup of hot chocolate.

Almost at the top of the hill Heather saw an unmistakable figure approaching her. Miss Boniface opened her black pashmina just enough to let Heather see her face. Heather stood still, awkward, unsure of what to say, wondering if Miss Boniface's memory had returned.

'I hope you are enjoying the day off school Heather.'

Miss Boniface shouted and smiled, her words almost drowned by the roar of the wind and the waves. Then she was gone, hurtling down towards the harbour, her pashmina flapping behind her. Heather's good humour was lifted further. It was as if her lovely teacher was back for good. Even though the storm raged all around, Heather allowed herself the feeling that all seemed well with the world. Heather struggled with the gate and then rushed up the path to Joe's house. She had a sense that she was being watched, maybe through the telescope. She pushed the idea from her head and pounded on the door. It sprung open and a delighted Joe pulled Heather inside.

'No school, fantastic!' Joe laughed has he took Heather's coat, gloves and scarf from her.

'I know,' said Heather, 'I think they are afraid the school might blow away, I mean it always leaked a bit, but I think they are worried that the roof might head off to Saltkirk on its own! Was your grandfather watching me through the telescope just now?'

'Nah, no way.'

Joe moved quickly around the kitchen and prepared huge mugs of hot chocolate. He seemed to have a lighthearted spring in his manner. Heather was pleased to see that he was in a good mood. She hummed to herself as she peered into a steamed-up window, searching for a dim reflection so she could make sense of her hair. Luckily it hadn't knotted but it seemed to have even more bounce than usual. Heather wondered if her hair had a mind of its own and was trying to calm some extra stubborn curls when Joe handing Heather a mug of steaming hot chocolate.

'Here you go pal. I've been helping Isabella because Grandfather has got stuck in Saltkirk. The road has been covered by a landslide and I think the storm is making it hard for the authorities to clear it. Come upstairs. I've got something to show you.'

Heather followed him up to the living room sipping her

drink and letting her toes dig deep into the rug. She glanced out of the large windows to take in the view, but it was obscured by rain lashing the house. The double-glazing kept the sound of the storm to a minimum, but the rain hit the window so hard it made talking difficult at times. On the large wooden coffee table all graphs and maps had been cleared away and a large brightly coloured and cleverly woven bag was lying open. Joe seemed very excited.

'I waited for you. It's been ages since I looked. It's my mother's bag, it's got all of her stuff in it. I wanted to show you.'

Heather looked at Joe curiously as he made her sit down. He seemed at odds with the storm outside. The clouds, which usually settled just over Joe's young brow seemed to have vanished, and Heather realised that he was talking freely about his parents without a pained expression. He chattered excitedly about how long it was since he last went through his mother's possessions and how he was sure that his mother would have wanted him to share them with Heather. The large cloth bag was multicoloured, big and heavy. As Joe unlocked the brass catch it jangled as if full of small bells.

'These were all hers and I think some of them are very old, I never thought anyone would understand 'cause some of the things are a bit strange.'

Joe began to lift out object after object from the bag. Everything had been lovingly wrapped in soft cloth or animal furs or colourful silk and even dried leaves. Joe carefully unwrapped each item and passed it to Heather. The first was an amazing red stone pipe with a long ornate wooden stem that was woven with carved snakes. Joe laughed at Heather's expression.

'It is a medicine pipe, like the ones that Native Americans

smoke in Westerns.'

Next came a selection of carefully painted instruments; a round shaker that sounded like a rattle snake, a rain stick, a small drum with a painting of a star on it, a selection of bells of various sizes and even some metal balls that rang when you moved them.

'I think she travelled a lot before... before she died. Grandfather said that she was very intelligent and spoke a lot of languages.'

He unwrapped a series of small statuettes, some made of stone, some of sweet-smelling sandalwood and some of metal. All were of deities, male, female, animal and some of a mixture of both. One was of a small stone man, which Joe said was from the Inuit of the North. Joe showed Heather a pair of handmade moccasins with designs in red all over them and she wondered if Joe's mother had worn them. Then Heather was distracted by Joe handing her a real, and still very sharp, throwing axe with intricate designs on its blade and handle, followed by an arrow and a spear tip.

'Wow,' said Heather, 'these are still so sharp, I wonder if...?'

Joe laughed as he worked out Heather's unasked question.

'No, I don't think they have ever been used, Grandpa says they were all ornamental or sacred, apart from the arrow, oh and the spearhead. Here look at this, it is a genuine eagle's feather and you are meant to use it to smudge the room with.'

He lifted out a huge feather, which had been carefully wrapped in silk, and a small red bag of leaves.

'These are sage leaves and are used to cleanse a room... erm, or a person,' Joe said, smiling. 'Do you want to smell?'

'Sure, yes please.'

Heather had spied an amazing shell, which she had lifted up and was holding to her ear transfixed, as the clear sounds of waves seemed to echo inside her head.

Joe crumbled some leaf and then placed it in a small red stone bowl. Using one of his grandpa's long fire-lighting matches he lit the leaf and then immediately blew the small flames out leaving only a long plume of blue smoke circling up into the air. Joe then carefully lifted up the bowl and the huge feather and gently started to fan the perfumed smoke up and over Heather. As he did it he began to hum, and Heather thought he looked so peaceful she was almost moved to tears. Joe circled around her, gently fanning the smoke. It smelt divine; it made Heather feel fabulous and as peaceful as her friend. As she watched Joe he seemed to transform in front of her eyes. He grew taller, his hair longer, a single feather in his hair and, just behind him, standing beside the bag was a tall, slender, dark-haired woman, wearing a long brown dress of soft leather. Heather gasped, the woman's presence transfixed her. She could tell that she wasn't 'real' as the light from the window seemed to shine right through her. The woman had huge dark eyes just like Joe and was standing smiling, pointing to the bag. Heather looked to see if Joe had noticed her, but he was lost in his reverie and was now fanning the thin plume of smoke over every object in the room. At one point he seemed to pass right through the woman.

Heather knelt forward towards the bag. She opened it and put her hand inside. The woman kept pointing and smiling. She lifted up a necklace of long sharp teeth or claws, but the woman kept pointing to the bag. Then Heather grasped something long, right at the bottom of the bag. She slowly lifted it out and the woman smiled straight at Heather as she unwrapped an intricately carved short spear. Heather marvelled at it. It had hundreds of sea creatures carefully carved along its length. She could see fishes, turtles, whales, squid, seals, sharks and many she couldn't identify. She looked up at the lady who was now just smiling. Suddenly, a soft clear voice, heavy with accent rang inside Heather's head like soft bells.

'Because you help Raven, I shall help you. When the time comes, cast this wand into the sea. She will accept this gift as many have given their lives already. She will remember their sacrifice and it will appease her. We will meet again when it is his time.'

Heather stared transfixed as the lady turned her head towards Joe who was finishing smudging around the head of the bear rug, lost in his thoughts. Heather followed her gaze and smiled. How happy Joe seemed – she realised that these things brought him the same joy that the aquarium brought Heather.

'But when will I know what to....do?'

Heather's voice stopped as she realised that the presence had left the room. Where the lady had stood a single puff of sage smoke seemed to dance in the air of the large room.

'You what?'

Joe looked up from the bear rug.

'Oh, I see you've found the narwhale horn. That's why I wanted to show you everything, I clean forgot, I woke this morning with the strongest sense to show it to you.'

Heather marvelled at how something as long as her forearm could weigh so little.

'It's breathtakingly beautiful.'

'It's yours,' said Joe, smiling at her and returning to the

table. 'I want you to have it. I never connected with it. It's got the ocean carved into it. Right up your street.'

'I could never...'

Heather began to resist but Joe was having none of it.

'Yes, you could.'

Then suddenly he became serious,

'Look, all of these things were once considered sacred and powerful and were used in all sorts of strange ceremonies. I Googled for ages last night. Anyhow, look at all the stuff you've got to do for the village, and the ocean, and the boats. I reckon a bit more help would come in handy.'

'But Joe...'

Heather began to protest.

'No, it's yours. Besides, Grandpa said that it was used as a talking stick by the Inuit elders and you might need some help next time you try and speak to the village.'

Joe leant forward and carefully wrapped it for Heather.

'Now then, it must be time to get some of Isabella's amazing soup and cakes inside us. I'm starving.'

Joe leapt up and dragged Heather downstairs towards the kitchen before she could protest further. Laughing, they ran down the stairs and then stopped in their tracks. The table was beautifully laid. Isabella was just serving steaming soup into bowls with huge chunks of freshly baked bread. The kitchen smelt delicious. To Heather's great surprise, sitting beside Isabella, chatting in a weird language was Muriel. As the teenagers approached the table Muriel looked up and smiled at them.

'Thanks for inviting me Joe,' she said to the surprised boy, 'Isabella has been telling me so much about you and about your family and how you have helped her over the years. She loves you very much.'

Muriel then returned to her conversation with the smiling

Isabella. Heather and Joe looked at each other, eyebrows raised, and shrugged as they sat down to enjoy the soup.

'Did you ...?'

Joe looked at Heather.

'No, she said you invited her...'

Heather giggled and added, 'and who would have thought that Muriel can speak Spanish?'

'I had the good fortune to spend many summer months in Spain as a child.'

She smiled at Joe and Heather. The old lady's hearing was as sharp as anyone's.

'But the soup was never as good as this. You would be surprised but even this far-flung corner of the world had connections with Spain.'

Muriel turned to the surprised Joe who was happily stuffing his face.

'Well I hope you young people had a great time this morning. Forgive me for interrupting your day Joe but I have to take Heather to meet someone this afternoon. Now what an amazing piece of carving that is.'

Muriel looked at the ancient narwhale horn that Heather had carefully laid on the table in front of her to look at while she ate.

Joe and Heather exchanged looks and Joe shrugged and smiled. He obviously had no idea what was going on but in the short time that he had grown to know Heather he had learnt to expect the unexpected.

'Joe gave it me.'

'Thought it might come in useful,' Joe added quickly.

Muriel smiled at Joe.

'What an intuitive young man you are.'

Finishing her soup Muriel glanced at her ring and then

stood up.

'Now please excuse us but Heather and I have to leave now.'

'Oh, Okay.'

Heather rose with mild surprise and rushed to grab her jacket.

'Thank you for lunch Isabella, that was the best soup I have ever tasted.'

She gave the short plump woman such a fierce hug that she blushed up to her roots.

'Ok Joe, I'll catch you later.'

With her back to Muriel Heather made Joe smile as she raised her eyebrows and mouthed the words, 'no idea where I'm going'. Heather pulled a face of mock annoyance and Joe almost spat out his soup as he laughed. If Muriel saw, she said nothing and ushered Heather outside into the storm towards a small bright red mini.

20
The Lady
of the Loch

The moment Heather jumped into Muriel's small car the weather took a turn for the worse. So much water seemed to fall out of the sky the little windscreen wipers could hardly clear the screen. They got soaked just rushing up the short path to the car and now they were steaming up the windows even with the heater on full blast. Heather didn't care though, she felt great. She turned the beautiful talking stick over and over in her hand, marvelling at the intricate carvings. She felt her mind think back to Joe and his generosity and she felt a new kind of warmth and glow deep down in her tummy. Muriel's voice startled her back into the present.

'Heather I'm afraid that we have just been enjoying the eye of the storm, the relative calm before it all kicks off again. I am afraid that we have only just begun this battle. If what you said is true about the nets, then I think we might need some more help.' Muriel stopped as she was peering through the sheet of water running down the windscreen. 'Now where's that turning?'

'But I thought that Dad and the boats were all right now that they can get back to harbour?'

Heather was alarmed by her friend's serious face and by the way that she was revving the engine of the car, sending it flying along the narrow windy roads at a breakneck speed.

'Your vision was true yet I fear that the storm is telling us that things are about to get a lot worse for the boats. I fear that the Goddess has a point to make and I fear the worse for everyone involved. You did well, to see them and bring a moment of calm to the families of the men but this isn't just about your father's greed. It's about the greed of all human-ity I'm afraid. Your father's nets might have been the last straw in a greater story than we are aware of. If I'm right, and I think that I am, we will need all the help we can get. This is an elemental power and it is ancient and blind to the concerns of us mere mortals.'

Muriel suddenly swerved the car off the tarmac lane and down an even narrower and more bumpy gravel track that sped underneath dark pine trees.

'Dad wasn't greedy,' defended Heather, 'I mean really, he was just trying to make a living, he thought he was doing what's best.'

'We all think that we are doing what's best according to our world view and to the level that we are awake.'

Muriel slammed her foot on the brakes, almost causing Heather to drop the narwhale horn. She turned towards Heather and gave her friend her full attention as the car shuddered to a halt under some trees in a small car park.

'Heather, you are Awake now, you have the Sight, you have to look deeper and farther than other people. Now stop thinking about that boy, as lovely as he is, and focus on the bigger picture. When you think of the storm for instance, what do you feel?'

Heather was alarmed by Muriel's words and there was something steely in the way she stared at Heather. Her words were commanding, firm but not forceful.

'Go on Heather,' she coaxed, this time more gently, 'Look inside. Quickly, we don't have much time, what do you see, what do you feel?'

Heather tried to breathe slowly and deeply. Her heart was still racing as fast as the car had been moments earlier. She relaxed with each gentle exhalation and focused her attention on the storm. She allowed the sounds of the buffeting wind keep her mind in the present moment. Her mind kept on wanting to race off after thoughts about Joe and all the events of the past few days. Heather allowed her breathing to slow and she turned her attention to the terrible weather. By focussing on the storm, how it sounded, how it felt and even the smell of the salty wetness Heather found she was able to hold a single and uninterrupted focus. Soon a restless curiosity came over her and she found her inner vision began to seek out the very heart of the storm. Heather was aware that she could direct her senses where she placed her attention. Heather began to follow her inner eye and looked deep into the centre storm and found...DANGER! She tried to recoil but was unable to. A huge dark swirling presence roared at her. It was deafening and enveloped the village, the boats, and the whole world. It wasn't just a localised storm; it was something more, something massive, and something terrifyingly powerful. It seemed to be alive and angry, angry beyond belief. It was engaged in total warfare with anything it came into contact with. It was the pure personification of war. It appeared to be systematically targeting boats and ships and coastal cities, towns and villages. Then two huge black swirling eyes appeared and, to Heather's horror, turned their attention on her. The black heart of the storm had noticed her. With a massive roaring sound it turned and raced towards Heather. She scrabbled within her mind to escape but couldn't return to her body; she was trapped as the massive swirling black shape hurtled towards her. Heather felt very small and very afraid. The noise was deafening. The roaring sound filled her head until she thought it was going to burst. She felt panic rising and sapping her energy as the huge dark cloud sped across seas and oceans towards her. Heather felt herself begin to black out. It was almost upon her. She felt as if every molecule of her being was about to be ripped apart.

'Return now Heather! You are back! You are in the Light! Come back to me now, open your eyes, breathe child, now – deeply slowly – breathe as I taught you.'

Muriel's words burst into Heather's mind like a crackle of lightning and shattered the vision. With a fizzling sound and a roar of frustration the apparition dissolved and vanished, leaving Heather trembling uncontrollably. She flung her eyes open, searching for anything to focus on and ground her. She realised that she was crying out loud. She was gasping for breath. She looked at her hands and screamed, they were covered with seaweed, barnacles and strands of foam, and her ring had turned black. Muriel's arms were around her as she leant over and murmured words in a strange tongue into Heather's ear. As she stroked Heather's forehead the memory of the vision began to subside until gradually Heather was able to make out what was real again. As Muriel finished her incantation Heather's anxiety and panic subsided and left her as quickly as it had arrived. She blinked and tried to focus on her surroundings. The inside of the small car welcomed her back to earth with its metal and plastic normality. Heather looked at her still trembling hands; there was nothing on them, no storm flotsam, just her good old normal hands with their chipped fingernails. The roaring sound had subsided, but her Heather noticed that her ring was still black in colour. Muriel's voice coaxed Heather back into complete consciousness.

'Calm child, good, keep breathing, remember your training.'

'Oh my god Muriel, what was that, it was massive, terrifying.'

Heather's heart was beating so fast she thought it would break.

'It is why we are here. What you saw is not just one entity, it is the combined power of every storm on the planet. They have joined forces and I am very afraid for us all. Not just your father and brother and dear friends, but for all of us. I needed you to see what we are up against. I needed you to be aware so that if you meet them again you will not be taken by surprise. The storm entities have been sent to attack man and his legacy. They are not the centre of the storm, they are just doing the bidding of the Goddess. Now my love, if you are feeling strong enough – let's get out of this car. We need to find help. You are not ready yet. None of us are.'

The cold stinging rain that beat Heather's face like a sandblaster quickly revived her and snapped her back into the present moment. She took a moment and embraced the rain with her senses. There was nothing like a good old Scottish downpour to slap you back into reality. Heather wiped her face and pulled her hat down over her head. She realised that she had no idea where they were. She could hardly see more than a few metres in front of her feet.

'Muriel, where on earth are we?'

Heather shouted through the wind and rain as Muriel grabbed her by the arm and started to steer her down a narrow track that had been turned into a stream. Heather's bright red wellies seemed susceptible to being swamped and so she focussed all of her attention to avoiding the larger puddles that were expanding into ponds. Muriel ignored Heather's question, she seemed in no hurry spill the beans and kept them hurrying forward, focussing all her energy on following the narrow track.

Bit by bit Heather worked out that the narrow track was perilously close to the edge of a loch. The loch's surface had waves that would have made the sea proud. Heather struggled to keep herself from slipping or falling into the water whilst ducking under low hanging branches of pine trees. It seemed that they slipped and struggled their way for a couple of miles though Heather had completely lost her bearings. She seriously wondered if it would be possible to get any wetter even if she fell into the cold waters of the loch. Deep dark lochs always made Heather feel uneasy, but the challenges of her path kept her mind from dwelling on her fears.

'Ouch.'

Heather suddenly collided with Muriel who had stopped abruptly.

'Shhh.'

Muriel's demand for silence made Heather laugh as the wind and rain was deafening. Muriel held Heather's hand up close to her face under the brim of her hat to expose her ring.

'Watch and learn little sister.'

Muriel brought her ring close to Heather's so that they touched. Then she began to chant in a low voice and a strange language. Heather realised that she could understand the ancient tongue.

'Come Cailleach and calm the waves,

Reveal yourself for your sisters are here

Remember the way, the word and song

We seek refuge and wisdom in our tears'

Heather glanced at the two rings being held so close together they almost touched. The stones on their rings swirled like miniature whirlpools and the flecks of fool's gold glittered like stars. Then Muriel gripped Heather's hand and as her chanting stopped she pointed out towards the grey of the loch. Before Heather could comment Muriel put her finger to her lips and then pointed towards the churning surface of the loch. The dense blanket of rain seemed to part in front of their eyes, creating a pathway into the centre of the loch. The rain appeared to stop, motionless in mid-air. Heather could see the large blimps of huge raindrops all around her like beads on a curtain. She noticed that some small drops of water seemed to be actually floating gently upwards. Then, from the centre of the loch a waterspout rose up and began to twist and turn and spin its way across the surface of the loch towards where

Muriel and Heather stood, both in awe. As the waterspout approached they could see the outline of a figure within the centre. When it got closer the water seemed to drop away from the mini tornado to reveal the most beautiful and terrible looking woman Heather had ever seen. She was literally gliding towards them across the surface of the loch. She glowed with a pale green light. Her long hair reached her feet and her gossamer garments floated around her as if she was still underwater. Heather was transfixed as the woman approached them, her flashing green eyes staring straight at Heather.

Heather sensed that even her tough companion was feeling nervous and she reached out her hand to hold Muriel's. Muriel gave Heather's hand a reassuring squeeze and then led her further back under the trees and into a small clearing. The silence and sudden complete stillness felt as deafening as the howling storm of moments before. The exotic goddess glided up to the edge of the loch. As she took a step onto the ground she instantly transformed in front of their eyes. Heather blinked in amazement. The fierce and beautiful goddess had become a small, nut brown, ancient lady, wearing what seemed to be a pale green nun's robe. Heather stared with surprise as the fierce, shimmering features disappeared, leaving a warm and compassionate face, textured like ancient leather. The lady smiled at them and it was as if the sun came out. Her huge, childlike grin warmed Heather and Muriel's emotions just as if sunbeams were shining on their souls. Her sparkling green eyes now seemed gentle and peaceful as she regarded the two bedraggled women with amusement. Heather realised that she was not much taller than a child and yet glowed with an amazing energy of kindness and compassion. Love just radiated out from her as she looked up into the wide-open eyes of Heather and Muriel.

The small woman gently gestured for them both to sit down. Heather looked around, the rain had started again, it was hissing down on the surface of the loch, yet not a drop fell where they stood in a small glade. She noticed for the first time that the clearing was created by a small circle of moss-covered standing stones. Each stone was low enough to sit on and the moss made a surprisingly dry and soft cushion. The dark pine trees provided a shadowy backdrop to the base of the mountain that began a few feet from the loch. Heather wiped her eyes and absentmindedly wrung some water out of her hair. As she and Muriel sat down the tiny lady sat on an opposite stone, only a few feet away. She then crossed her legs into a lotus position, rested her hands on her lap and closed her eyes with a peaceful smile on her face. Heather noted with some amusement that Muriel seemed to be as stunned and in awe as she was at the lady's transformation and behaviour.

They all sat in stillness for a few minutes. Nothing but the hiss of the rain, the gentle roar of the wind through the trees and the splashing of the waves of the loch caused any sound. Heather stared at the woman, fascinated, wondering who she was and why Muriel thought that they should meet with her. Heather was certain that the old woman was hovering just above the rock in her perfect lotus position. Then she realised that Muriel was motioning to her to close her eyes as the lady of the loch had done. As Heather reluctantly closed her eyes Muriel reached over and lightly touched Heather on her forehead.

At once the world seemed to explode around Heather and a kaleidoscope of greens and blues swirled around her mind's eye. She didn't have time to take it in as she realised there was an animated conversation taking place inside her head. She could hear, like the ringing of small bells, Muriel's voice and the softest and most beautiful voice of the old woman. They seemed to be speaking in Gaelic and the moment that Heather heard the words she found that she also understood them.

'What brings my sisters to my home, for you have travelled far, I sense the salt upon you?'

Muriel quietly responded in the same soft language.

'My lady Cailleach, I have brought this child of the sea to ask advice from you as I fear that the path she is on leads to great danger. If she is to save us all she will need your help.'

'To save us all you say sister. Surely to save the lives of all she must no longer take life?'

Cailleach looked towards Heather and smiled. Heather felt confused. She had no desire to hurt anyone and she was worried by what the goddess was saying. The magical woman's voice continued in Heather's mind.

'She does not yet know of what I speak or why I speak my sister.'

Heather heard the words clearly in her head and with her eyes shut could see the swirling pale green energy that surrounded Cailleach. Heather was relieved when Muriel spoke.

'Her practice is that of the old ones and she does not yet practice as you do Cailleach. She embraces the bounty of the sea as nourishment for her body and soul. She is the same as the creatures of the sea. She takes what she needs and no more. She is sworn to work for the protection of all as is our sacred path.'

As Muriel spoke Heather could see that a luxurious purple energy flowed around her and seemed to dance above her head. Heather wondered if she looked the same. Before she could check to see the conversation continued.

'Her practice is not long begun? The task that you would have her do requires great training and great stillness.'

Cailleach smiled gently at Heather and then turned back to Muriel.

'If my sisters have risen up against the men of the world then it must be a matter of life and death. The question is, whose life and whose death my mortal sister.'

Heather felt a jolt of alarm run through her. Nobody had mentioned anything about death. She had a sneaking suspicion that Muriel had not told her everything she knew. Cailleach seemed to read her thoughts.

'You have not revealed the great plan to her and she is not prepared. Why do you bring her to me?'

Muriel looked concerned and gave Heather's hand a small squeeze. Heather kept her eyes totally shut and focused on the radiant smile of the most peaceful woman she had ever seen. Cailleach seemed to radiate calm and stillness. Just to be in her company seemed to dispel all of Heather's anxieties and worries. The stiller Heather let herself become the more she felt a huge depth of calmness flood through her. She let her breath become gentle and let go of her fears. She decided that she would completely trust this amazing lady. Cailleach turned her attention to Heather as Muriel fell silent.

'You must have learnt well in your past lives for I see that you have great ability and insight. You have seen much and travelled far, there is a great awakening within you, a quickening that I have never seen before and you sit with me as if you had trained for years. Yet to plead for peace and for an end to suffering you must first become the very essence of peace itself.'

Cailleach beckoned Heather to lean forward and as she did Cailleach placed her small cool hands on Heather's head.

'You must renounce all killing my child. You may do this with me for I shall witness your dedication.'

Heather felt a ripple of confusion run through her. Heather loved everything and everyone, as much as she could.

'I don't want to hurt anybody ever.'

Heather realised that she had spoken the thoughts that were in her head out loud. Heather still felt so calm and peaceful she knew that she couldn't conceive of harming anybody at all, for any reason.

'I speak of the wellbeing of all sentient life forms my dear young woman. All life is sacred to us here. My path sees the inter-being of everything. You must cease your urges for the flesh of others. Let me show you my young sister.'

Cailleach had filled her head with images of the food she ate at home. She saw meal after meal of meat and fish and even her mum's amazing fish pie. Suddenly Heather understood. Heather was aware of urges of hunger arising in her. Just the sight of the food was making her hungry. The meals looked so appetizing, she could smell them, the heavenly aroma of her mum's kitchen. Yet she saw what the lady of the loch was asking of her. Heather found that she could see with the eyes of Cailleach, it was not the killing of people she was referring to but animals. The food transformed back into living creatures in front of Heather's closed eyes. She could see cows, chickens, pigs, fish and even crabs and mollusks. As they floated into Heather's field of vision she saw them all as if for the first time. Each living creature glowed with ribbons of light and energy. Each creature had its own consciousness and its own life, which was precious to it. Cailleach gently turned Heather's head so that she was facing Muriel.

'Now open your eyes my daughter and see the truth for yourself and be blind no more.'

Heather did as she was requested and opened her eyes, blinking in the light. Cailleach had removed her hands from Heather's head and was sitting still on the rock opposite her. Heather gasped. Even with her eyes open she could see flickering elements and strands of light that coursed through Muriel and the lady. Heather looked at her hands, they were made up of strands of glowing energy that gently pulsed and shimmered. Muriel's features had vanished and instead Heather could see a radiant being of light and energy with a bright glowing star at Muriel's very center. As she turned to look back at Cailleach she saw a young deer step gently into the clearing. It too pulsed with streams of light and energy, it shimmered and glowed and radiated light around itself. As Heather looked at the deer she felt a deep connection and a sense that they were both linked. As she looked down at her shimmering body Heather could see that strands of energy and light that linked them all, the humans, the deer, the trees and all the plants around them. A huge eagle landed silently on the moss-covered stone near Cailleach. It too glowed brightly and, as it stretched its wings, Heather could see the thousands of filaments of lights that gave the bird its life. Heather felt a great connection with the noble bird. She sensed its thoughts and its impressive life force. Cailleach waved her hand and a pool of water formed at Heather's feet. It was so still it acted as a perfect mirror.

'Use your eyes my daughter, look for yourself,' Cailleach motioned to Heather.

Heather bent forward so that she could see her own reflection. She gasped. She looked just the same as Cailleach, Muriel and the animals. Heather's outer appearance had vanished. She was a swirling dance of light and colour. Her body was made up of thousands of strands of energy that pulsed with colour. All around Heather was a pure golden glow of light that radiated outwards. She gasped, her reflection was amazing, her light was gold where Cailleach's was a crystal green and Muriel's was a swirling purple. Heather lifted her hand and marveled at how the pulses of light sparkled and danced as she flexed her fingers.

'Now you see that we are all connected, we are all part of the same source my child. We are all one in form as we are all formed from the one source. This teaching will free you from the illusion of your eyes and the material world. From now on you will be able to see the truth of life. This gift will be a great healing for the world.'

Cailleach was gesturing towards the floor. Heather looked down and realised that where her feet touched the floor lines of energy radiated out from her and connected with lines of energy from the deer, the eagle, Cailleach and Muriel. Heather could see that even more subtle and softer lines of light radiated out from her in all directions, connecting the forest and the loch. Cailleach spoke again and as she did she floated gently towards Heather.

'Humans have a simple choice to make yet they choose to stay asleep. They forget the interconnectedness of all life. The old urges for blood no longer serve them. They have gone beyond the old ways that protected them. They have forgotten the circle of life. They have lost their sense of sacred that guided them to a deeper awareness. I fear that humans are drifting into darkness and a deeper sleep. All life is threatened by their sleepwalking. They act like blind beasts. They have forgotten the truth. Now that you are awake my child, will you commit to no longer knowingly take life and dedicate your path for the greater good of all sentient beings? Will you help end all suffering?'

Heather looked towards the loch, still fascinated by what she saw. She noticed some fish swimming in the water and saw how they also shone with the same light and energy. Even the trees and moss glowed. A great peace came over Heather and a realisation of the sacred nature of life settled in her mind. However, one doubt rose up and refused to depart.

'My father and my whole family are fisher folk, Cailleach.'

'You have spoken truthfully, but this is an ancient path which can no longer sustain them or you. Do not fear my child. The choice will be for you and you alone. If you choose this path then you will be able to maintain your own special power with greater ease. You will walk closer to enlightenment and a better understanding of the great oneness. You can direct your steps for the spiritual nourishment of all sentient life forms.'

'So it's just my decision then?'

Cailleach smiled a deep and compassionate smile and as she did the whole world readjusted and everything became whole and normal again. The deer scampered off between the trees and the eagle took flight.

'It is a decision that can give you the protection that your sister came looking for. She knows that your great test is coming soon. It is a path that may mean life or death. The ocean is the great mother. She is the beginning and the end for all life. Her ways are not always my ways. She gives life and she can take it away, yet she knows that all life will continue in her.'

'Is that my friend Ran?'

'The entity you speak of is herself a daughter of the great mother and she will bargain on your behalf yet you and only you can go before the great mother. She is moving to protect the continuation of all life. If she grants your request, then I fear her demands may be more than you can bear little one. So, will you pledge your path to ending all suffering?'

Heather felt the great sense of peace envelope her again. She slowly turned to Muriel but she still had her eyes tightly closed and seemed unaware of Heather's conversation.

'The choice is yours. We will just bare witness so that we can speak for you.'

'But what should I say?'

'Find your own words, daughter of man. I was once standing where you are now. I was also not ready, yet I discovered the simple way, the way of peace and of compassion. It has served me well and continues to serve all of those who are awake.'

Heather breathed out gently and slowly. She looked deep within herself and found a great light rising up again. She knew that the light was her own guide and she decided to let it speak for her.

'I shall not knowingly kill and shall dedicate my life for the good of all sentient creatures.'

The old lady smiled and her leathery face wrinkled even more as she spoke.

'I hear you and your words are my words. I have spoken a secret deep into your heart. It will be there for you to use when you most need to call out for help. Call on me whenever you choose. You are my beloved sister.'

Then the old lady stood up and gently leant over and kissed Heather on the head. She turned and rested her head on Muriel's.

'Do not fear for the girl but be encouraged that she has sought refuge in the deeper truth. I shall see you soon and will welcome you home. You have done well this lifetime my sister.'

Then she kissed Muriel on the forehead and turned back to the loch. Heather marveled at how lightly Cailleach walked and how she left no footprint. She watched her new friend glide out across the loch until the rain and clouds drew around her and she was gone.

Heather felt as if she also floated just above the ground. A deep sense of stillness and joy still flooded through every pore of her being. Even though the heavy rain descended once more Heather's spirits were not dampened in the slightest. Heather felt as if she had just met with the secret source of eternal joy so, as she turned to Muriel, she was shocked to see that Muriel was sobbing into her hands. Heather had never seen her like this before. She put her arm around her friend's heaving shoulders.

'What's the matter Muriel? Don't worry, I'm sure everything will be Ok. Cailleach was right. We have the answers that we came for, don't we?'

Muriel looked up at Heather and smiled, yet her tears kept coming.

'Don't mind me little one. My tears are selfish. I cry for myself and for what we have just witnessed.'

'So how come you aren't happy Muriel?'

Muriel took control of herself and went to stand up. She sniffed loudly and blew her nose.

'Don't you worry about me Heather. Now then, what's all this about you forsaking our way and following Cailleach? She only asked you to commit to abstaining eating meat.'

Heather was stunned. Muriel looked cross and hurt.

'I don't know, I just answered truthfully as she requested.'

'Cailleach is wise, in thought and deed.'

Muriel motioned to Heather to gather herself up and follow her back along the path again. Muriel was forcing her way along the narrow track beside the loch at a frenetic pace. She called out above the storm.

'What did she say to you?'

'Didn't you hear?'

'No, my child, Cailleach kept what she was saying to you from me.'

Muriel spun in her tracks and stopped suddenly. Heather almost bumped into her.

'Oh, well I just said that I wouldn't knowingly kill anything and that I dedicate my life to the wellbeing of all sentient creatures – erm humans and animals...did I do wrong?'

Muriel's brow darkened, and she turned to face Heather.

'Was there nothing else, did she just demand your fealty, your loyalty, your commitment for nothing, for no payment, no service? Was all this for nothing?'

Muriel seemed upset. Heather was troubled. She couldn't understand what Muriel was talking about.

'It's not for nothing Muriel, she said it would make me safer, but it's not for nothing, it's for EVERYTHING.' Heather surprised herself with how passionately she spoke.

Muriel sighed.

'I know child. She has got you to commit to the highest path of light. But was there nothing else?'

'Well she said that she had spoken a secret into my heart...'

Heather pulled her coat around her ears.

'A secret, oh great, oh dear, oh well, she is a bodhisattva, an immortal and she was once the same as you and so let's just hope that it was all worth it. She may have taken your powers.'

'My powers?' Heather was stunned. 'What powers?'

She hurried after Muriel along the narrow track. Muriel seemed lost in a conflict of emotions and snapped at Heather that they had to get back to the car. Muriel was shivering in the cold.

'I'm soaking wet. Come on, we must hurry back. I just hope that our journey wasn't wasted.'

Heather turned and followed her friend. She felt confused and a little worried for Muriel yet still had a great sense of calm washing over her. Heather could see that Muriel was anxious and seemed scared. She couldn't understand why Muriel was so upset and unsettled. Heather had felt nothing but endless kindness and wisdom from Cailleach.

Heather absentmindedly waved at some raindrops that were trickling down her face and tried to keep up with Muriel who was walking as if her life depended on it. It occurred to Heather that Muriel had never done this before. Maybe Muriel had never met Cailleach previously and that somehow Heather had crossed onto another spiritual path. It was still too confusing for her to take in. Heather felt sure that such great source of kindness and love would be in harmony with all that Muriel had taught her. To Heather's surprise they arrived back to the car much quicker than she expected. Heather stood still whilst Muriel fumbled in her pocket for the key. She found it and then dropped it directly into a puddle.

'Oh for the love of all things sacred!'

Muriel peered down into the dirty water, trying to see her key. Heather decided to lend a hand. If only she could find the key for Muriel than her friend's mood might lighten. Heather reached down to plunge her hand into the large puddle to feel around for the key. Yet as she did so the puddle literally drew itself back from its center so that all of the water piled up around what was now just a dry hole in the gravel car park. Heather was stunned. Muriel froze and gasped. Then Heather bent down and plucked the key from the hole as the water wobbled around the edge like a large grey jelly. In a flash the water fell back into the hole with a noisy glug. Heather held out the key to Muriel who was staring at her peculiarly. Heather noticed that the water on the key shot off the electronic key fob and fell to the floor. It was dry in a moment.

'Oh she didn't tell you anything special then huh. Well you could have shared your secret with me earlier. I'm drenched.'

Muriel started laughing at Heather's look of surprise.

'You might have kept me dry as well, huh?'

Muriel pointed to just above Heather's head. Gasping, she looked up. The rain seemed to be swerving past her head and avoiding her as if she had somehow reverse-magnetised herself. Not a drop of rain was landing on her. Heather touched her hair. It was dry, not even the slightest bit damp. She looked at her clothes. They were dry too.

'Oh Muriel, I'm sorry, I didn't even realise. I guess I just sort of thought dry thoughts, erm that I didn't want to be wet anymore, and must have made it dry.'

Muriel was still laughing, and Heather was relieved to see her friend looking normal again. Heather reached out and touched her friend lightly on her sleeve. To her amazement the water droplets leapt off her soaked coat. In moments it was dry. Heather went to touch Muriel's hair. Muriel gently stopped her hand.

'Careful child, you might dry me out as well and leave me like a desiccated old prune.'

Muriel gave a huge sigh of relief and chuckled.

'Of course, Cailleach didn't take your powers, she transmitted all of her learning to you. I'm sorry Heather, you were right to not doubt her. Cailleach is a bodhisattva and exists only for the good of all. I was afraid that she had cut the thread that links to you to our ways. Our wisdom is based on the spiral dance of life where all life eventually becomes food for something, and death is nothing to be feared. This path makes us see death as simply returning to the source of all things even our bodies are eventually consumed as food and helped to fertilise the very ground from which we draw our life. Our way demands only kindness and acknowledgement of this universal truth our power is linked to this truth. I'm sorry Heather I was scared that I might have lost you but I see that rather than take something from you she has added to what you already have. She must have seen something pure in you.'

'It's not just in me,' said Heather as they clambered into the car. 'It's in all of us. I can see it now.'

'Well,' said Muriel as she fired up the small car's engine, 'the Sight was already within you. You must have realised it in Cailleach's presence. You have had past lives that I am not privy too.'

'What's a 'body-sat-va' Muriel?'

'She is a special kind of enlightened soul that has chosen to remain in this world so that she can help all living creatures. I had no idea that our cultures had merged like this. Still, I suppose the oceans, the rivers and the rain all meet up at some point.'

Just before Muriel slammed the car into gear to accelerate into the rain she turned one last time to Heather.

'I'm sorry my child but I won't be able to teach you anymore. My way is not hers. I will always be your friend, but you are no longer my pupil. I have nothing more I can teach or show you.'

Then Muriel set her face and stared straight ahead at the road home.

21
The Orders
are Given

The journey back was fairly terrifying. The storm seemed to have grown in strength and power. The small car was pushed this way and that as it sped along. Muriel still drove at a breakneck speed. Heather kept on trying out her new abilities and managed to push the rain away from the windscreen where the small wipers were unable to keep it clear. This must have helped Muriel a little as she sped up some more. Not the reaction that Heather was hoping for because Muriel's driving technique was erratic and aggressive at the best of times. Heather gripped her seat and focused on keeping the windscreen free of the pounding rain. She found that she could create a bubble of dryness around the car but the wall of rain in front still made visibility really difficult. At every bend or sudden breaking point Heather's heart would leap into her mouth. She kept on losing concentration and the rain hit the windscreen again like a wave. This made Muriel swerve even more. Eventually Heather gave up. Making Muriel swerve was more dangerous than the rain obscuring their view.

To Heather's relief they eventually screeched to a halt beside the harbour wall, in front of Heather's house. Heather was just about to leap out when Muriel caught her and dragged her back into the car. A huge wave crashed right over the harbour wall, right over the small cobbled road, right over the car and even over some of the house. For a moment the whole world disappeared and then the small car was dragged all over the place. It bumped and scraped off the stonewalls and the huge torrent of water began to drag the car back down the street towards the harbour as it raced to rejoin the ocean. Heather screamed. The mini was being dragged towards the inner edge of the harbour wall and there would be nothing to prevent it from falling straight in. Through the deluge the harbour wasn't even visible. It was all under water. The surging tide and huge waves came right up to the surrounding road. The car was being thrown backwards and forwards. The surging wave, eager to return to the ocean, picked up speed and began to accelerate them towards the dark churning water below.

'Quick Heather, do something, or we will perish!'

Muriel's face was white and even though she had her foot on the brake and her hand on the steering wheel nothing she could do was stopping the huge tide of water from sucking them into the ocean.

Heather panicked, gazed around and tried to overcome her pounding heart and the overwhelming sensation of terror. She breathed in, focused her mind, settled herself and then shouted out,

'Stop!'

The moment she did so the whole green and grey world of water that surrounded the small car froze. The tidal surge flooding down the street literally stopped as if it were ice. The road river came to a sudden halt and even the surrounding waves in the harbour became motionless. Heather could make out all sorts of bits of net, lobster pots, a child's bike and even roof slates in the sheet of water that covered the car. Heather felt a huge pull within her. It felt like it was going to break her in two. She screamed with shock and pain.

'Don't try to hold all the water in the harbor Heather. Just make the water release us from its hold.'

Muriel reached out to Heather, alarmed at how white Heather's face had become and how loud she was screaming. Deep within her Heather heard the voice of Cailleach.

'Be gentle child. Water flows. Bend your mind with it. Bend with it. Guide it around you. The Way is to transform the energy of the wave into that of a droplet. Now concentrate but let go at the same time or it will break you.'

Heather felt a great calm flood through her and did as she was told. She gave a huge sigh and released the wave whilst holding the idea of the water simply not being able to touch the car. The world shifted again. The huge wall of dark greenish seawater was immediately animated yet swirled past the car without touching it. The wave crashed back into the boiling cauldron that was the sea and the car remained still. Muriel and Heather looked at each other with eyes wide open with fear and relief. The little car was stranded at a jaunty angle across the street only a few feet from the depths of the dark waters.

Heather was stunned. Muriel leapt into action. She grabbed Heather's hand and dragged her out of the car with her, then she bundled Heather across the road and up the steps to her front door. With a single move she opened the door and flung Heather and herself into the kitchen, slamming the door behind them. Just as she did another huge wave crashed off the outside wall. They fell into the arms of a crowd of concerned faces.

Everybody was crammed into the room. Heather's mum, her grandfather, the other three Wise Women, a few of the older men and most of the village's women. Heather's mum flung her arms around her daughter and sobbed with relief.

'Oh my darling, I was so worried, I thought that you might, that the waves, the road, the storm might have...'

'She's fine Maria.'

Muriel immediately acted as though nothing had happened.

'Your daughter is more able to look after herself than you could possibly know. My poor wee car might be a write-off though. Now then, what's the news?'

'Well the worse news is that we are almost out of tea bags.'

Heather's grandfather was doing his best not to look scared and was trying out his much-practiced grumpy face to restore his idea of normality to the world. Heather squeezed herself past her mum and one of her neighbours and gave her grandfather a hug.

Muriel's presence seemed to galvanize everybody into action. A huge pot of tea was made with some tea bags that somebody had brought with them, sandwiches appeared on the table along with all manner of food for the tired and hungry villagers. Heather realized that it had been a long time since she had eaten soup with Joe and, carefully avoiding the meat sandwiches, ate hungrily.

'News?'

Asked Muriel, smiling at the sight of the tightly crammed room full of villagers all pulling together and enjoying each other's company. Everybody began to speak at once until Muriel held up her hand for calm. The lull of excited conversations seemed to amplify the sounds of the storm. The wind roared outside like a jet airplane taking off. The rain and spray from the sea battered the windows and walls of the cottage. Muriel looked at the room of expectant faces. Nobody made eye contact with her. Everybody looked nervously at each other, and it was obvious that no one wanted to break the precious moment of hope. Muriel looked at her friends and it was Gladys who spoke first. Her face grew serious as she did so, and the room's mood dropped a couple of degrees. The roaring of the wind and sea meant that poor Gladys had to almost shout to be heard.

'It's not great, I'm afraid Muriel. The Met office are calling it a superstorm and have no idea when this weather will break. They are predicting that it might get worse. The truth is they have no idea what is going on. They just keep calling it an anomaly. We have had no contact with the ships since this morning and there is no news from the coastguard. We hear that they have sent out a rescue helicopter but they have lost contact with it. The emergency services are stretched to breaking point as it seems the rain and tidal surges are literally drowning towns up and down the country. It's not looking good and I'm afraid we are on our own.'

Gladys paused as she said this and looked straight at Heather. Heather's mum squeezed in around the packed table and put a reassuring hand on her daughter's shoulders. Muriel sighed and looked at her dark-headed, wild-eyed friend who had frozen with her sandwich halfway to her mouth. Truth of what Gladys was saying hit Heather hard. She felt like she was on a roller-coaster of emotion without any time to draw breath or reflect on what was going on inside her. As Heather's eyes began to well up Muriel realised just how young Heather was and how much she had been through over the past hours and days. The somber silence in the room could not be hidden by the roar of the weather outside. Everyone had frozen, all too scared to utter the terrible truth that the fishing fleet must be lost. Muriel sighed as she observed that every pair of eyes was staring at Heather, waiting for her to speak, cry, scream, anything to break the terrible silence.

Heather fought back her tears and took a deep breath. She trembled at just how difficult and challenging it was just to remain calm and sustain the sense of peace she had felt earlier. She brought Cailleach back into the mind and found that the bodhisattva's calming presence easily permeated her own. 'Thank you,' Heather whispered to herself. Looking at the small sea of expectant eyes she sighed, steadied her nerves and gently put her sandwich down. She carefully stood up, not wanting to upset her calm and mindfully put her attention onto her breathing. Heather found a sense of peace flowing up inside her and she knew that fear had left her and in its place her strength returned. She allowed herself to call out for help and someplace far away she heard Ran's voice. She smiled as she instantly recognised the soft magical words. Taking another deep breath, she knew what she had to do. Heather climbed up onto a chair and looked around the crowded room. The heat of so many bodies was stifling, and she felt herself sway. Muriel and her mother held tightly onto a hand each and let Heather know that they were supporting her. Muriel gave Heather's hand an encouraging squeeze, amazed again at how her young friend could suddenly transform a whole room with a single glance.

Heather's eyes flashed green as she spoke. Her voice sounded powerful and far too mature for her age.

'We need to speak with the sea. We need to tell her that we are sorry. We need to tell her that we can change. We need to plead for the lives of our loved ones. We have to act now.'

There was a confused silence in the room. Heather could sense the combination of hope and doubt, of expectation and confusion. Muriel could see an awareness on some of the faces present that Heather was speaking from within her spiritual power. You could have cut the atmosphere with a knife. Muriel noticed with a soft smile that an ancient connection with the sea was being awoken again for the older villagers. She watched as the dormant flashes of understanding and recognition lit up their faces. Muriel realised that this what the remaining villagers now expected to happen, this was why they had gathered again so soon. Word of Heather's abilities must have travelled quickly. There seemed to be twice as many folk in the kitchen as the last time. An overwhelming atmosphere of expectation electrified the room. All the faces looked to Heather to provide them with answers and reassurance. Many of the more worldly neighbours were stuck in a place of incomprehension and wild hope. Smiling, Muriel saw that Pastor Bobby had squeezed himself into the kitchen and was also fixing

Heather with eyes of hope. She gently squeezed Heather's hand to continue. Heather steadied herself and tried her best.

'The sea is alive, this planet is alive, and because of that I believe that she might listen to us. I don't really know or understand what has been happening to me over the past few days but all I know is that we must try. I will need all of your help. I know it sounds mad, daft, crazy even, but I need you all to trust me and help me. It might be our last chance. You need to suspend your disbelief and open your hearts and minds to the possibility of an ancient wisdom because that is the place I must go to. I have to go alone but if you put your faith in me then I won't travel unaided. I will need your energy, your support, your help. If you are all with me then I won't be afraid.'

Pastor Bobby cleared his throat and looked up at Heather.

'I understand what you are saying my child but what can you possibly do, even if God is with you, even if what you are saying is true?'

Miss Boniface, her face a mask of concern and worry, pushed her way towards the table.

'Look Heather, I agree with Pastor Bobby, it's great that you are here and can maybe even tell us what is happening out in that heaving cauldron, but there's nothing that you can actually do. You don't have to take on the collective responsibility of the whole village.'

Many of the more down-to-earth members of the village began to nod their heads. Mrs White, the wife of one of the trawler's skippers, looked kindly at Heather.

'Maybe prayers are all that can help the menfolk now. I'm just glad that we are together, just like the old days, I couldn't bear the wait, the uncertainty if I was alone.'

A sigh of understanding and agreement went around the kitchen at Mrs White's words. It was clear that the small community recognised the strength that they got from each other. Heather carefully climbed down from the chair and stood surrounded by the four Wise Women and her mother. She knew what she had to do but she was concerned that the village wouldn't let her. She closed her eyes and whispered to Muriel in her mind.

'I'm not sure if I really know what to do to help but I have to try. Prayers would be gratefully received but first I need to get back out there, and I need actual physical support as well.'

Muriel gave her friends a knowing look and Jean adjusted her glasses that had steamed up in the hot kitchen. She linked arms with Susan who reached out for Gladys and then started to sing. The song was an ancient song, a song of waiting and of hoping, and as soon as Jean's beautiful voice lifted the refrain everybody else began to join in. In the notes of the song all of the emotions of the small community seemed to be expressed. The Gaelic tongue proved as flexible as the sea in its ability to bring emotions to the surface. As the song went around again some women started to harmonise and the notes built higher and higher. Heather's grandfather and Pastor Bobby began to provide deep, rich bass notes and soon the small kitchen seemed to glow with the sound. Again, the song lifted the mood as smiles and tears poured forth from the mouths of everyone singing. It was as if the singing gave every person the opportunity to finally express their deepest fears and the deep hope they felt in their souls. Mothers hugged children, neighbours held each other's hands, and the whole room seemed to gently sway with the powerful but gentle music.

As the singing built up in volume and in power some folk closed their eyes as if the ancient words were a prayer. Heather carefully pushed between the singers. She moved unseen through the tightly packed room towards the door. She used the cover of the song to wrap herself in her waterproof jacket, tie her hair up, and put her feet into her wellies. The words of the song danced and span strands of light in her heart and mind and somehow Heather understood every word that was being sung. The ancient song also had a deep and terrible truth at its base, a profound sense of loss, Heather understood that the music was a powerful medicine to begin the healing of hearts and minds that would be broken by loss; the impending loss of everyone at sea. Heather's newfound understanding of the world had literally dragged her down from her chair with a calm, deep but powerful sense of urgency. Inside Heather a great hope grew and an even deeper understanding of what she had to do and why she had been so blessed.

Just as she reached the door and was preparing to open it, with both hands so that the wind didn't literally rip her arms off she felt strong hands on her. Susan, Gladys, Jean and Muriel, wrapped in their coats, with eyes flashing with power and certainty stood with her. Their eyes said it all. They were coming with her. Just as the music reached another peak in the volume Muriel spoke into Heather's mind.

'We know what you have to do little sister. My first impulse is for us to stop you. Your actions would appear as madness to the world, certain death in fact. Yet we all see a light in your eyes that tells us to follow you and help. We are terrified for your safety, but we will not abandon or hinder you. You will need our help, our energy, our knowledge, for you are still so young.'

Heather smiled at the supportive eyes of the women. Then she took a long last glance back into the kitchen. The music had transformed the faces of everybody. Where before there had been shadows of fear and dread now every face glowed with hope and the expectation of salvation. Heather went to open the door, but Muriel cautioned her quickly.

'Calm the storm around the cottage or else we will be sucked out into the sea and perish. The mind can imagine the power of the wind and the waves but the reality is a thousand, thousand times stronger.'

'Well here goes then my lovelies,' whispered Heather and turned the handle.

The tightly packed kitchen didn't even notice the sudden opening and closing of the front door. Heather had calmed the wind and waves to such a degree that not even a breeze or a flutter of air disrupted the trance-like musical prayer of the villagers. Only one pair of eyes caught a glimpse of what was occurring. Heather's mum looked shocked and terrified yet also resigned in the terrible knowledge that her daughter was their best hope. She mouthed the words 'Be careful. I love you.' Then she sank into a chair and began to gently cry as her daughter left to brave the elements.

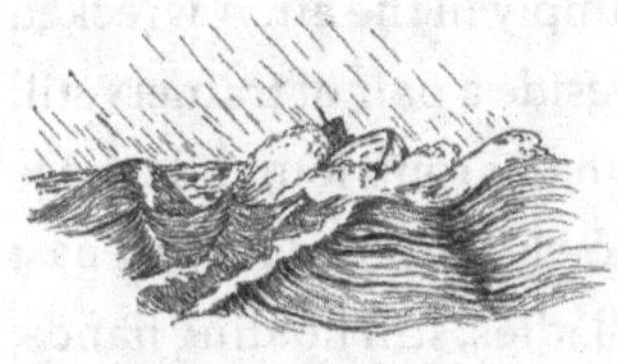

22
A Matter of
Life and Death

As the small group of women bent themselves into the wind they were met by a huge bubble of calm, just as if they were in the eye of a hurricane. The safety limit radiated out about 50 metres in a circle from Heather. The four older women held hands and kept Heather firmly in their midst as they edged past piles of debris. The beach seemed to have moved and was now covering most of the cobbles of the road. Piles of weed, broken lobster pots, rope, nets, branches and even the odd wheelie bin were piled up along the harbour wall. Odd bits and pieces of the villager's lives were momentarily frozen in a kind of suspended animation. Clothes still attached to a washing line hung limply in the air. A wrecked brolly was making a slow dance beside a pair of trainers still attached at the laces. Just as the small group found the edge of the harbour a child's scooter slowly trundled its way past them. Muriel gasped and the four ladies, still holding hands, made a larger circle around Heather. Heather sucked in her breath as she saw what they were looking at. It was eerie. It was scary. It was definitely the weirdest thing Heather had seen for a while.

It was as if the seaward front of the small village was also contained in a magical bubble. Only a few feet from where they all now stood, just over the sea wall, huge waves crashed and fell. High above their heads they seemed to freeze and then slip back down into the sea again. Just beyond this bubble of safety Heather could see that the winds were howling with ferocious strength. Clouds were scurrying across the sky quicker than whippets chasing a hare. Heather could see horizontal rain smashing all around them, huge droplets of water made magical doughnuts in mid-air. Susan looked at Muriel, Gladys and Jean who all slowly came out of their collective shock.

'So, what do we do now? This is amazing, I have never seen anything like it but Heather what do we, err, do?'

Muriel snapped back into alertness, ripped her gaze from the huge waves towering over their heads and turned towards the group.

'Firstly sisters, whatever happens, under no condition, do we break this circle. We hang on as if our lives depended on it. In fact...,' she glanced up at the waves, 'I'm very much afraid that they do.'

'Of course Muriel, but what do we do now?' Asked Jean, her eyes wide open as she looked around them.

'Now we have to help and support Heather with every ounce of our powers and abilities.'

Muriel looked at Heather.

'My dear girl, I can scarcely believe that you are able to maintain this incredible energy field but somehow you are. You are going to need us to do this for you if you are to help the fleet. You are going to need our collective strength and focus. You are going to need every ounce of our life-force if you are to keep this up and also help the ships at sea.' '

Heather looked around at the loving and admiring eyes of the four women encircling her. She marvelled at how they had become such good friends in such a short while. She was amazed at how close she felt to them, how they seemed to almost share a heartbeat. Heather wondered what she had done to deserve such good friends who would risk their lives to help her, her family and the village. She sensed their strength, their goodness, their purpose, yet wondered if this time the strain might be too much for them rather than for her. The women were not in the first flush of youth, their grey hair and lined faces gave away their age, yet their eyes flashed with a strength that was inspiring to Heather.

Since Heather had left her house a deep calm and stillness had enveloped her. The peace and harmony that surrounded the small group began within Heather. It was not separate from her. The tranquillity and serenity within Heather dictated the stillness and calm outside of her. Heather realised that she was unsure what to do next and even how to do it. She knew that if she allowed any fear or anxiety or powerful emotion into her heart and mind she might lose her calm, her deep endless peace, and they would all be swallowed by the waves and drowned in moments. Muriel read Heather's mind and spoke to her thoughts out loud.

'My dearest Heather we must hold this circle of stillness and power for you whilst you travel to help the fleet. You must show us with your mind, how to do this miracle that you are maintaining all on your own. Then we will hold the space, just like the ancient stone circles were designed to do. Then you can connect with the urgency and danger of the moment.'

'Oh my god Muriel, can the four of us do this?'

Jean looked anxious.

'We have to Jean,' said Susan gently, 'we have no choice, this is our combined destiny.'

'We have spent our lives preparing for this moment, whether we knew it or not,' said Gladys.

Muriel smiled and looked with great pride at the anxious pairs of eyes looking back at her.

'Come now ladies, this is our great adventure, this is our moment. Let us calm ourselves and rise to meet this new spiritual revelation.'

Muriel turned her head towards Heather.

'It is time Heather. We four are now ready. Let us share your burden. Come now my young sister, find the knowledge deep within yourself to pass this burden onto us.'

Heather lifted the intricately carved narwhale horn from beneath her coat. As Muriel took it began to glow with light. All the small creatures carved deeply into it seemed to pulse with life. Muriel smiled and held it aloft whilst the others made sure they didn't break their connection with each other. Heather focussed on her newfound powers and became aware that she was beginning to join with the four wise women. Not physically but gently, softy, slowly a hidden energetic aspect of herself united with the energy of her sacred sisters. Heather could see the strands and filaments of light that linked them all up. She could see how the energy pulsed and glowed. In an instant she realised that she could direct the flow and direction of the pulsing light. Heather smiled as she directed a huge flood of energy across the light filaments deep into the four surrounding women. The faces of her four friends lit up and began to softly glow. The Wise Women saw and felt themselves being transformed into beings of pure light. Heather realised that this was the first time for Muriel too and that she hadn't seen what Heather had witnessed and experienced earlier at the loch. Heather has just assumed that her friend had shared the same experience. The four sets of eyes widened in disbelief and joy as they watched and experienced the transformation simultaneously. Before they could indulge in the endless euphoria they all felt Muriel's voice ringing in everybody's minds like the clear call of a bell on a mountain.

'Now focus, with one mind, one heart, one soul and release the sacred vision.'

The ladies closed their eyes and fell into a deep trance. At that moment Heather found herself suddenly alone standing in the middle of a huge circle. Her sisters seemed far away, and their arms seemed to stretch for miles so that they surrounded Heather. They had done it. The four wise women were holding the peace. The churning wind and waves roared around the edge of the circle but all was quiet and still at its centre.

Heather took a deep breath in and prepared herself to try and connect with the boats again. She bent down and plucked a single droplet of glistening sea water from a pool at her feet and then touched the end of her tongue to it. In a flash the salty sting of the sea cascaded into her senses and the ancient magic of before roared through her veins. It was as if a huge bright window opened up right in front of Heather. Through it she could see the kindly face of a large seal. Without a thought Heather delightedly called out 'Ran' and threw herself towards the shimmering opening.

One moment Heather was standing on the grey flagstones of the small harbour as a dark-haired young woman, the next she was hurtling through the wild mountain sized waves of the ocean as a large and powerful seal.

Heather was momentarily overtaken with a burst of sheer childish delight and joy to be once more united with her friend. It was breath-taking to be weaving through the ocean again. This time the vision felt so real to Heather. She could feel her new body shape and powerful muscles propel her through the colossal seas with relative ease. Shoals of fish burst before her and broke like underwater fireworks all around. Dolphins streamed either side of Heather, joining her frantic race through the ocean. She could sense their gentleness and playfulness and could not resist diving through massive green walls of waves with them. To Heather's delight she found she could shapeshift into a dolphin. In a moment she was one of the small pod. Suddenly she was able to attain even greater speeds and have the ability to shift direction at will and even make high jumps into the air. However fast she accelerated, though, Ran sped before her, leading the way through the swirling darkness of the storm. On and on they dashed effortlessly, going faster and faster until their sprint came to a sudden and swirling halt. As they stopped Ran span towards Heather and transformed into a green glowing goddess, her hair extending in all directions. Her eyes burnt like emeralds and she appeared compelling, dangerous and hypnotic.

'We are here my child, where your hopes and fears have led you. You will need to act fast if you wish to help. Take to the air. I will do your bidding, but then we must pay our dues or else face the consequences of our interference. We have only one chance. I can help you only the once.'

Heather became aware that she was transforming again. She broke the surface of the foaming sea and soared up into the air on huge white wings. The feeling was exhilarating, different and yet familiar all at the same time. As Heather beat her huge wings she realised that flying was really just like swimming but in the air. She had to work hard to maintain any kind of balance though. The storm was too strong for Heather to be able to enjoy herself soaring and swooping above the sea. Heather swerved to her left as a roar of thunder seemed to shatter the air around her. Heather beat her wings frantically to avoid a huge helicopter being thrown all over the sky. The machine's engines were screaming with the effort to right itself. It was barely able to keep above the towering tips of massive waves. Heather's eagle-eyed vision could make out the pilots shouting desperate orders to the crew who were hanging on for dear life. The side door was open and a small mechanical arm was suspending a long grey thread of steel, which was whipping backwards and forwards. Heather's eyes zoomed down the lifting cable like a powerful camera lens until she could easily make out the decks of the fishing fleet far below. The boats were being flung in all directions. In an instant she could see that the situation was impossible. The helicopter's lifting mechanism was caught on the bow of her father's boat. As Heather turned and rolled herself out of the way of the thundering rotor blades she could see that the men on board were roped together and trying to cross the deck to free the cable. Each time they tried they were beaten back by huge waves. The towering waves swamped the decks whilst throwing the boat all over the place. The scene was a desperate one. The storm was too strong for the helicopter to rescue the crews. Now that it was caught on the boat it could be flung into the sea at any moment. Heather's vision zoomed even closer until she could make out the terrified faces of her brother, father and the crew. Seeing her father so scared hit Heather in the pit of her stomach. She dived downwards towards the swirling sea and the moment that she plunged beneath the waves she transformed back into a dolphin. Heather faced Ran's terrible grandeur.

'Ran I need you to stop the waves for a moment, I have to free the helicopter so that it can break away.'

Ran's face displayed no emotion and for an instant Heather was worried that she wouldn't get any help. Then Ran smiled.

'Of course, we can free the iron bird, it's roaring and screaming is so sad. But Heather, I cannot interfere again. This is the one time. Is this what you want me to do for you?'

Without a breath Heather nodded and then soared back to the surface again. As her wings returned and she took to the air as a huge calm surrounded the vessels. Ran was holding back the massive waves of the super-storm just as Heather and the four Wise Women were doing in a much smaller way back at the harbour. The helicopter's engines stopped screaming and in a moment it levelled out. Heather could see the men on board the helicopter signalling the men on the boat to make a valiant effort and free the lifting mechanism. Heather flew closer to the fishing vessel just as her brother made a dash across the deck. She saw him reach the bows and then, in an instant, he had freed the steel cable and the helicopter's winching mechanism was free to lift the fishermen to safety.

Yet as she circled the small collection of vessels she realised that something was wrong. Nobody was being lifted. The helicopter was in radio contact with the boat and was beginning to lift itself up into the air heading to where the storm couldn't reach it. Heather realised that the helicopter's lifting mechanism must have been damaged. As it flew higher Heather could see that her brother had made it safely back into the wheelhouse of the fishing boat. She felt panic rise up inside her. That hadn't been the plan. She had thought that once freed the helicopter could rescue the fisherman and fly them to safety. Heather flew in a large soaring circle to regain her composure. She could see the men on the vessels bringing the boats together, putting out towropes to the damaged ones and taking full advantage of the freak lull in the storm to head once more towards harbour.

Yet as Heather circled she could see the massive clouds and violent flashing storm approaching again. Even more worrying was a bank of towering waves that seemed to be rising up ever higher around the boats. She could see that the men on board had spotted the steely blue monsters and were becoming frantic in their activities. Heather dived back towards the bubbling surface of the ocean and, transforming back into a seal, swam up to Ran.

'Ran you have to help again. The helicopter, the iron bird, it was broken by the storm, they can't rescue the men. If you let the storm break free again the boats will be smashed into splinters.'

In Heather's mind she could see the face of her father and brother again and she felt panic rising in her. Ran's face had grown serious.

'I hear your thoughts young changeling but I can do no more. I am only permitted to help you just the once. This storm is not of my making. It is part of a far greater purpose.'

Heather fought to control her panic and fear that she had failed everybody.

'But no, that can't be true. Oh Ran, we are so close, we have been through so much and...'

'My daughter, hold your emotions together or else you will break free of my magic and your human body will return to join you here. The great mother of us all does not will that it be done. It is Her life force, it is Her will, not mine. She has already granted you so much. This is Her great plan. I am but a part of Her and cannot resist Her will. I am sorry Heather, but you must return to your body now. You must re-join your human form. It is too dangerous for you to stay here. I have done all that I can. I can hold the storm back for a few moments longer. You should fly up once more and say goodbye to your kin.'

'No Ran, no, please no.'

Heather felt her fear and desperation arising and as the strong emotions vibrated through her she felt the reality around her begin to fracture and lose form. She knew that to be human out here in the ocean would mean certain, immediate death. Heather took a huge breath and as she exhaled she managed to bring her emotions back under control. Ran was surrounded by adoring seals, dolphins and even turtles and looked every bit a goddess of the ocean. She was gazing at Heather deeply concerned yet still blazing her green light into the depths.

'I know what you are going to say child but it is not my decision. She does not communicate to mortals.'

'Take me to her, please,' begged Heather. 'She will understand, She will help.'

'She is not like me or you Heather. Her way is even more ancient than mine. She was here at the beginning and will be here at the end when all of the land has once more descended beneath her gown and dissolved away from all memory like tears in the rain. To see her would spell the end of your life little one.'

'I don't care,' cried Heather. 'I have to try. You must help me. This is my wish.'

'I will try,' said Ran, suddenly looking fierce. 'But daughter of Eve if you gaze upon her face you will perish.'

'Then let it be so,' Heather pleaded.

Ran frowned and then gave Heather a look of deep kindness and understanding.

'Well, we shall meet again soon then my young one as all creatures pass this way between lives. You have lived well Heather.'

Then Ran reached a long slender hand out towards Heather and touched her forehead with her finger. The sea world exploded around her and Heather was gone in an instant.

Back on the harbour the four Wise Women were flung by the full force of the storm straight back towards the door of Heather's house. The bubble of calm exploded into a vortex of superstorm. Muriel barely managed to fling the door open and pull the others back inside before a huge wave crashed over the house, momentarily cutting the lights. Water poured down the chimney and extinguished the fire. Even with the door open for a second the wave had flooded the surprised and tightly packed kitchen sending teacups bouncing off walls. Muriel leapt to her feet and pulled a crab out of her hair.

'Where's Heather, where's Heather!'

Her screams shocked the room and in a single glance she realised that Heather was gone.

23
The Great Mother

The sea was cold, very cold. It took Heather's breath away. It made her scream with shock. It made her choke on its saltiness. She was blinded by it, pummelled by it, terrified by its power. Things happened so quickly Heather had no time to process what was taking place. In an instant she was back in her body, surrounded by the Wise Women. Next the world around them seemed to explode with a roar as a colossal deluge of water fell from the sky. In the same instant Heather was flung upwards and through the waves and then down and into the dark swirling green and grey of the ocean. This time she could feel the water through her mortal human flesh. Heather had no thick layer of seal blubber or dolphin skin to protect her. Her human senses could not make out which way was up. She had no control over her movement or direction. Her arms were pinned at her side and as she was torpedoed through the water. By some miracle she managed to breath from a halo of salty bubbles than surrounded her head. Water and salt made Heather cough and splutter. Her eyes stung, and the rushing water blurred her vision. She experienced waves of pain in her head and ears and she felt as if her lungs were going to explode. Grey dark blurry creatures seemed to rush past her on the extreme edges of her vision. Strange lights traced past and then the sea grew darker and darker; a great pressure pushed in on Heather for all sides. She couldn't even scream as she felt her very bones start to creak, her eyeballs, her ears, her head sent stabbing pains careering through her body. Just as she felt that she could bear it no more the world seemed to spin and Heather passed out.

Dull sounds began to call her back to consciousness: like the ringing of underwater bells echoing in the distance. Heather didn't want to return to consciousness. It was as if the fringes of her awareness knew that there was something so terrible awaiting her that she should remain unconscious, asleep, maybe forever. Something vast and powerful was calling Heather, tugging at the fringes of her mind. She felt stabbing pains all over her body as she began to awake. Heather fought it, she wanted to return to the deep, still, painless and peaceful darkness.

Suddenly an image of Heather's father flashed across her mind. She was back in the village and rushing to meet the boats. Like a blast of lightning illuminating a stormy sky Heather saw herself running down the harbour path and leaping fearlessly into her father's strong arms like she had done ever since she was a small child. Then the vision altered, and she saw her father on the fishing boat looking up at the helicopter with fear on his face. A flood of memories cascaded into Heather's mind. She saw the storm, the ships, the lives of the crews hanging in balance. With a half sob, half whimper, she allowed herself to slowly return to consciousness and face whatever it was that was terrifying her outside her vision.

It was so deep, so dark, so cold that Heather thought that she would perish. A dim light seemed to illuminate the pitch black up in front of her. Heather realised that she was hardly breathing. Each inhalation and exhalation seemed shallow and lasted for ages. This seemed nothing in comparison to what happened next.

A colossal shape appeared in the gloom in front of Heather. Bit by bit a terrifying form began to emerge from the darkness. It was vast, massive, as large as an aircraft carrier and it stretched as far as the dim fluorescence of the water allowed Heather to see. Slowly, mountains of scales and barbs, of talons and fins rose up in front of Heather. Then with blinding brightness two huge orbs of light blinked open. Heather felt like a rabbit frozen in front of two blazing headlights. The creature was colossal in its size. Heather's dimly working mind wondered if it was the mythical beast the Leviathan.

The creature's eyes lit up more of the surrounding ocean floor, but it was their burning intensity and ferocity that made the young woman physically tremble. It felt to Heather that the eyes burned right through her with a cold and dangerous indifference. It was as if the creature was callously looking into the very depths of her soul. Heather struggled weakly but was unable to move. She managed to tilt her head slightly and saw that she was wrapped up tightly by long thin tendrils that ran from the edges of the biggest mouth Heather had ever seen. Around Heather's whole body was a large bubble of air that wobbled and swayed as she did. The creature was breathing into it, keeping the bubble of air formed. It was keeping Heather alive just enough to consume her. She felt as if she was a tiny sea creature snared by a giant angelfish. The eyes that stared so intently at Heather saw only food. The eyes were examining Heather as dispassionately as a spider would view a fly caught in its web. Heather was very afraid, yet something was distracting her. Something else was wrong. Something was not quite right with the scene. Then she realised, it was simple, she *was* alive.

Heather knew about the huge pressures in the deepest places of the world's oceans and knew that, by rights, she should have been crushed into a pulp. Yet here she was. Alive and with the slowest, hardly perceptible breaths. She was definitely alive. Plus, she surmised, if this huge creature had wanted to eat her it would have been over in a moment.

Heather allowed a long slow breath to pass as she looked deep within her for the calm than Cailleach had taught her. Then with all of her focus and attention she allowed her mind to clearly frame the thought:

'What do you want from me?'

Nothing happened. The huge creature stared unblinking at Heather; the intolerable cold and discomfort continued. The huge pressure was making Heather's head sing and her eyes creak. She tried again.

'Why am I here?'

This time Heather got a reaction, but it was not the one that she had hoped for. The tendrils wrapped around her body began to reel her towards the beast. At the same time the massive cavern of a mouth began to open. The light from the unblinking eyes of the Leviathan revealed rows upon rows of the longest sharpest teeth Heather had ever seen. She reached for her deep inner peace and found, to her surprise, that she wanted to laugh instead of cry. So, this was it then. This was the moment everything had been leading up to. This was to be how it all ended: as the food for an animal that, if Heather had known it existed, would have fought for to protect and preserve. One of the very creatures of the sea that she had devoted her short life to was about to make Heather its supper. The gaping cavern of the creature's mouth grew ever closer yet. Heather's sense of peace expanded and calmed her. She knew in her heart that if she had given her life to only save the lives of the helicopter pilots then it was still worth it. She felt tinges of sadness that she had not been able to do more for her father and brother and the crews of the boats. She felt a sadness that she had not been able to make a difference to the creatures of the ocean and wondered who would look after her aquarium. Then Heather stared straight ahead and prepared herself to face her last moments.

'Tis the last moments of mortal life that reveal the truth.'

Heather heard a distinct voice in her head and was sure that it wasn't hers.

'Tis the last breath that meets with the first and reveals a life well lived.'

The voice echoed in Heather's mind like underwater bells.

'I had to be sure you see, that is enough my darling, put her back.'

This time there was no mistaking it, Heather could hear a voice speaking to her. A procession of lights surrounded Heather and a swirl of colours and shapes rose up and encircled her. She found herself receding from the huge beast. To her amazement Heather's bubble expanded to the size of a house and four huge squid appeared and put their long tendrils over it so that she did not float upwards. Then on a back of a huge blue whale, which was dwarfed by the Leviathan, came riding the most exotic creature Heather had ever seen.

It glowed brightly with a thousand flickering soft lights, which shimmered and pulsed as brightly as the two eyes of the Leviathan. Long lustrous braids swirled around and upwards creating a fan like a peacock's tail. All around the creature a million small illuminated fish swam and danced as if in a strange procession. At the centre glowed a golden sunburst of light that shone a clear beam out before it.

The form kept changing. Swirling, spinning fronds gave way to fabulous coral fringes, which then revealed rows and rows of glistening and gleaming scales which seemed to suggest a long tail. The huge underwater sun that lay at the centre of the creature moved ever closer towards Heather until that was all she could see. The great orb of dazzling light expanded until it seemed to grow bigger than the whale, bigger than the Leviathan. Gratefully Heather could feel warmth radiating towards her; she had begun to shiver from the intense cold. Gradually from the centre of the dazzling underwater star a figure began to emerge. Bit by bit a recognisable and glowing shape began to approach Heather. As it drew ever closer Heather could make out the beautiful form of a smiling woman. She was huge, curved and glowing almost as brightly as the sun of which she was the centre. Two large, green, glowing eyes looked kindly at Heather, giving the poor girl an immediate sense of comfort. Heather realised that she was face to face with the mother of all things. This was the sacred goddess of the oceans that Ran had spoken of and warned her about. Clouds of floating curly hair resembled Heather's and as the goddess drew closer to her she extended out an ample hand and reached through the wall of the bubble and touched Heather's own dark curls. The goddess seemed to smile and a peal of infectious laughter rang out all around.

'Who are you?'

Heather formed the words with surprising clarity in her mind. The huge face of the goddess smiled and Heather felt a surge of affinity for the lady in front of her.

'Ah, child of the land, you have hair like mine – we chose well this day did we not? To meet once more at the edge of all things.'

You have a heart like mine

You have a soul like mine

You have a passion for all that lives

And like me

You care beyond the borders of your own mortality

But no child, I am not woman

I am not creature form

I am not measured in cycles of the sun and moon

I use these shapes only for your pleasure

I am She that was before

I am She that brought breath to the world

I am She who is all Life

I am She who raised up the land

I am She who will remain once the land has sunk back once more unto me

I am deep in the earth, I am under the land,

I am on the land
I am in the skies
I am your mother
I am your sister
I am your beginning and I am your ending
You are the first to see me yet maybe not the last.'

Heather was overcome with emotion as the strange creature spoke to her. The Earth Mother's voice filled Heather's mind like the swirling sound of beautiful choirs of angels all singing at once. Her voice was like the rushing of the winds and the pounding of the waves.

'Are you Ran? Do you have a Name?'
'Whom you call Ran is Me
All who protect the expanses are Me
Their power is mine
Their wishes are mine
Their actions are mine
I am that I am.
I am all that is.
All are me and I am them.'

Heather felt confused yet happy. Deep insider her another ancient truth was coming alive. It was as if Heather's whole soul sang with the sound of the goddess's voice. The glowing lady at the centre of the sun had eyes that smiled with pure love like nothing Heather had ever seen before.

'What is it that you would have of us
What would you ask
For what do you seek
For what do you offer your life?'

Heather spoke out loud and was surprised how gentle and confident her voice sounded. Words that rose in her seemed to come from a much older version of herself. It was as if they originated from many lifetimes ago.

'My kin are in great danger and the storm threatens their lives. I seek you so that you might help me save them as I have sought to save so many of yours once I lived on land.'

The moment Heather finished speaking the vast orb of light flashed angrily. The sun turned the deepest red and orange flames of light flowed all around the lady who grew larger and seemed to pulse with angry flashes of crimson. Her smile vanished and she looked vast and terrifying.

'Their lives are mine
All come from me
All return to me
My children seek to destroy me
They are blinded by forgetfulness
All beings of dust threaten life
The life of all
With poisons
With greed
With ignorance
With cruel indifference
As I warm
As I heat up like the sun
My power grows and must be released
This is their doing
In ways beyond their understanding
I am the sacred balance of life
My power rises to restore
Balance must come
I shall dry up the fields
I shall scorch the earth
I shall blast them all
Back to creation.'

As the being spoke red flames of light burst around her. The water around Heather was warming and the seabed began to shake. The concerns of the goddess rang true with Heather's own deeply held apprehensions and worries. It was the single message that had driven Heather's young life. It was the message that had come time and time to her over the past week. It was the deep worry for the survival of the oceans and for all life. Heather felt tears well up behind her aching eyes yet discovered that she wasn't scared. It occurred to Heather that somehow, she had passed through terrible fears that might have crippled any normal person. Now all she experienced was tranquillity, deep peace and a knowing that she had done all that she could. Heather's voice drew from a wisdom that was deep within her.

'We have not all forgotten our connection with you. So many of us are fighting to save the oceans. So many of us recognise that we need to change our ways. Many of us are fighting to restore your balance. All around the world many of us are trying to save the oceans.'

The huge orb of light began to return to a dazzling gold colour again and the Mother of All's eyes flashed green once more. She still appeared terrible but seemed to have softened once more.

'Truth you speak
Your heart is mine
I see your soul
You share my yearning
You feel the call of all life
You sense the danger
The hour of no return has been passed
Yet I shall grow stronger
My thoughts will rise

My love will destroy
By storm
By wave
By ice
By snow
As I withdraw all will perish.
You fight for survival
Yet at the same time you are the cause
Beings of dust.'

Heather could hardly make out the form of the goddess as she once more glowed brighter and brighter with anger, outrage and hurt. Heather realised that her bubble of air was rapidly diminishing. This time flames began to arise from the seabed around them. Red hot glowing lava seemed to rise out of suddenly erupting vents. The seabed began to shake. Heather felt helpless. She was all out of ideas. The goddess seemed unforgiving and was ready to destroy not just her family and the fishermen but all of humanity as well. As the water swirled around Heather's diminishing bubble of air she breathed gently and relaxed. All creatures, big and small, simply wanted to survive. This ancient and all-powerful goddess was the collective expression of every living thing on the planet. The Mother of All's fear and anger was that of all life that was trying to survive in the oceans.

Heather sensed the gentle wisdom of the Lady of the Loch rise up inside her again. She remembered the knowledge that Cailleach had shared with her at the loch. Gradually an idea for a plea took form in Heather's mind. Heather found that she could identify deeply with the Great Mother and her concerns. She felt the goddess's deep and endless love for life and it resonated within her as well. Heather ignored the swirling danger all around her and found the voice of power once more.

'I am not just dust, Great Mother. I am water too. I am land, but I am also sea. I am rock, but I am also ocean, I am flesh and I am air. Most of my being is made of water. My heart is with you, my body is with you and I give my life freely to you if it means that others may live. That is why I came to offer my life to you, to save life, not to see it taken. Enough death has occurred. Let life help life and let death be a new beginning.'

The Great Mother glowed gold once more and her eyes flashed with green and the shaking of the seabed subsided. She drew closer to Heather and a huge smile began to break out on her beatific face.

'She speaks truth
She speaks from her soul
Her soul is mine
We are one
She sees my secrets
She loves beyond herself
She senses the truth of all creatures
I am one
She is one
We are One...'

The goddess began to glow green and blue and slowly reduced in size until she was not much larger than Heather. Her face appeared gentle and kind again. Heather felt deep waves of love reach out to her.

'Your heart beats in time with mine
You see with your heart
You know the truth of life
You would offer your own life for this purpose

I accept your life
I will use it
You have been true with me
I will be true with you
Your desires are mine
Let me release you'

The goddess reached out her hand just as Heather's bubble of air finally disappeared. Her long fingers gently touched Heather on her forehead. The last thing Heather heard was pure laughter and then there was a sudden rush of cold, of dark and of pressure and Heather's world ended.

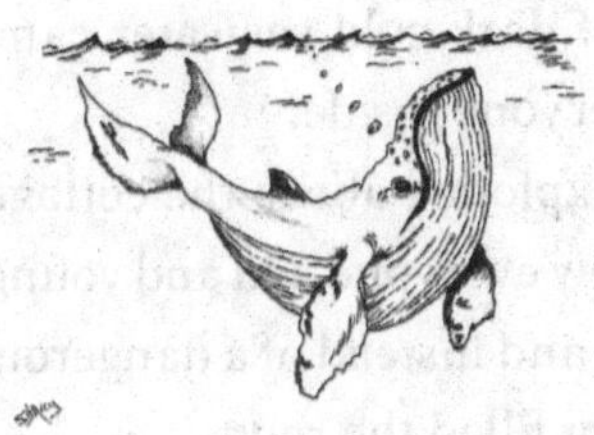

24
The Beginning

As Muriel screamed the whole kitchen burst into life. Everybody turned towards the door. Even as water rushed down the chimney and one of the windows exploded under the pressure of the wave nobody cared for his or her own safety. Somehow without Heather it felt as if all hope was lost. Men and women put their shoulders against the door determined to push back against the onslaught and pressure of the wall of water. Muriel flung herself at the door like a woman possessed. Her fists turn red as she punched and clawed at it. She hurled her whole body at it until the men dragged her off and put their shoulders to the task. Every inch the door opened a flood of dark cold seawater came bursting through, drenching everyone inside.

Then a colossal thunderclap exploded above the cottage. The sheer force of the sound threw everyone, old and young, to the floor. The door burst open and instead of a dangerous wall of water a bright orange light filled the room.

People pulled themselves upright and blinked at the framed picture of perfection that met their eyes. Across the harbour and all the way to the horizon the sea was calm and illuminated in the deep rich colours of the beginnings of a blood red sunset. Across the debris of the harbour sea birds were wheeling upwards, calling out to each other as if for the first time.

Heather's mother, along with Susan and Gladys, pushed past the stunned fisherfolk and burst out into the early evening. Soon everybody was limping, walking and staggering out onto the cobbles of the harbour whilst blinking into the unnatural calm and beauty of a perfect sunset. Like a large family, the thirty or so villagers, young and old alike, gathered around Heather's mum and held onto her as her knees began to buckle. The perfect calm and endless view revealed no sign of Heather. Nothing in the debris surrounding revealed the dark-haired bundle of female energy that had only minutes ago been their only hope. It was as if the ocean had swallowed her whole and left not a trace that she had ever existed.

Muriel staggered out past the group and fell to her knees weeping.

'We failed her, we weren't strong enough, she gave her life for all of us. It was meant to be the other way round.'

Gladys raced to comfort Muriel but was beaten to it by Heather's mum who, with tears streaming down her face, started to stammer words of comfort for Muriel, for herself, for everybody watching.

'She was always headstrong. She wasn't going to listen to anybody. She knew what she was doing, she had that look, she had the sight, she was stronger than all of us. Don't blame yourself Muriel, we are all part of this terrible storm and when all is said and done we must look to ourselves to see what mistakes we have made and how they led to this.'

The group gathered around the women and formed a circle of support. Everybody held up somebody else and as one a great and ancient song of loss was begun. The mourning song lifted upwards and out into the deepening red of the cloudless sky.

Nobody saw a battered Land Rover pull up and an old man and a small dark-haired boy leap out. In a moment Joe flung himself into the centre of the huddled group of villagers calling out for Heather. He pushed through them desperately calling her name until Heather's mum grabbed him and drew him close to her.

'She's gone my love, she's gone.'

Joe's knees failed him and he sank into Maria's arms. He collapsed like a rag doll and Maria clung tightly to him, they began to rock gently together.

Suddenly the voice of Joe's grandfather rang out above the sounds of sobbing and mournful singing. His words rang powerfully above the collective grief.

'Look to the sea, to the horizon, I don't believe it, it's the fleet. Look, it's not just a trick of the light. My god, they have survived. They must have been closer to shore than we thought. It's a miracle.'

People began to gasp and shout and then explode with joy and laughter as they squinted into the crimson sunset and saw the approaching silhouettes of the fishing fleet.

'Oh my god – it's them.'

'It's truly them.'

'They are not lost'

'It's a miracle.'

Heather's grandfather suddenly spoke up and his voice was so loud it silenced the small crowd. It was his turn to find his power.

'This is a miracle, but it has come at a great price. Come, let us greet them in the old way. Our grief and our joy must meet.'

Silently, holding hands, the villagers walked down the cobbles to the harbour. Linking together, they recreated an ancient tradition and formed a human chain that began and ended at the harbour entrance: a circle with an opening to welcome back the ships. Just as in days of old when nobody knew which ships would return and which ships wouldn't, the village united.

Joe, Maria and the two grandfathers stood at the highest point of the entrance to the harbour. Joe looked left and right through his tears and allowed himself a small smile. He realised they were accepted as part of the community, linked forever by grief and celebration. Maria caught Joe's eyes and gave his hand a squeeze. Muriel and the Wise Women linked hands with them as the whole village looked out to sea.

The silence that greeted the ships was appropriate to their condition. Some were towing others, all were severely damaged with windows shattered, radar and equipment ripped out. Some were showing jagged holes above the water line and one was listing dangerously with the men furiously bailing out buckets of water to compensate for a burnt-out pump. As the boats entered the harbour the fishermen stood on their decks to greet the village. As the fleet closely bundled together and began to make port the men's excited waves and whoops of joy dissolved as they were met with the sad and gentle silence of the whole village. All the men knew what that deafening silence was for: somebody had died, and the village was united in grief. The ships were silently and swiftly tied up and the men scrambled up the harbour ladders and into the arms of their loved ones. It was not until Heather's father climbed up the steps and clambered over blasted bits of debris to hug his wife that his great roar of pain and suffering told the other fishermen what must have happened. Shock registered on the men's faces and a great sadness showed in the eyes of the hardy fishermen. None could believe that their respected skipper had lost his beloved daughter. As the husbands, sons and brothers climbed wearily off their boats to be welcomed into the bosom of the village somebody began the ancient mourning song again and the whole village, united and holding hands began the walk back towards the village.

Except for Joe. He had slipped free and had climbed to the topmost part of what had once been the harbour entrance light. He clung on to the splintered relic and wiped tears from his eyes and squinted as the huge crimson sun began to descend towards the horizon. He pulled a small brass telescope from his coat pocket and peered through it.

'Come down young un, there's nothing to see now, come back in and let us all tell our stories.'

Heather's granddad looked up at Joe and smiled for a second.

'We'll all miss her. Come on now, it will be dark shortly, though 'tis a funny kind of sunset...'

His voice trailed off just as Joe gave out an excited shriek.

'It's something, it's something, there's something coming, I can see something... oh my god, can you see it, I think it's a whale, look on the whale, oh my god, it looks like Heather!!!'

Joe's granddad and Heather's family had waited till last to go back to the village and they all turned to see what the noise was. The singing of the village came to a stop as everybody turned around and then the silence was once more replaced by shrieks, gasps and the sound of running feet as everybody turned back to the harbour entrance.

Muriel was beside Joe in an instant and her badly scratched hands clutched his arm. He jumped down and passed his telescope to Heather's father.

Muriel gasped; she didn't need a spyglass to see the huge shape approaching the little harbour. A massive whale was ploughing through the sea, sending sprays of water flying ahead of it. Its speed was matched by a large pod of a hundred or so dolphins hurtling alongside. Above it a thousand seabirds wheeled and turned, their calls making a cacophony of sound. But it was not this that made Joe dance with sheer delight. High on the back of the whale, getting larger by the minute was the unmistakable sight of a young woman, waving excitedly, punching the air, ducking and dodging as the whale breathed huge plumes high into the air.

In a moment the entire village had gathered around the harbour entrance. Whoops of joy and amazement were heard, combined with the delighted screams of Heather's mother and the Wise Women when it became obvious that this truly was Heather returning to them. Her father and many of the fishermen just stood with their mouths hanging open – this was beyond all of their reckoning and even their imaginations. Suddenly the desire to share their tales of survival vanished. The stories of how a giant sea bird had stopped the storm and freed the helicopter and saved the boats, of how the waves had magically calmed and how they had found themselves in striking distance of the harbour was a miracle that now seemed unworthy of mentioning. Nobody had witnessed anything like this before. Nobody had ever imagined that whales could be ridden. But even this spectacle dissolved in the collective sigh of relief that, against all the odds, their very own mascot had just returned from the dead.

The huge whale slowed, extending a bow wave that almost flooded the harbour walls. The small flotilla of boats rocked backwards and forwards as the whale came to a standstill. Rising up out of the sea it allowed Heather to jump with ease onto the end of the harbour wall above the heads of the astonished villagers. Heather shouted with laughter and whooped with joy to see her family, Joe and the Wise Women looking up at her with tears in their eyes. She paused for a moment, wondering why nobody was leaping forward to hug her. Then she glanced down at herself and shrieked with laughter. What a sight she must have been. She was wearing a dress that shimmered and glowed in the last rays of the day. Her wild head of curls had a huge white streak down the centre but that was not it. On her forehead, right in the centre was a large bright green emerald held in place by a woven gold band. Even in the failing light everybody could see that Heather was dripping from head to foot in precious jewels.

Joe shyly held his hand up towards Heather, his face a mixture of tears and disbelief. Heather seemed to glow with power and strength, she was now most certainly a young woman and no longer the girl he had first met. Joe smiled as he saw that Heather's face blazed with her usual joy, sense of fun and self-deprecation. She reached down and pulled Joe up beside her and gave him a hug and, to his delight, kissed him on the cheek. He blushed and hugged her for all he was worth, hiding his embarrassed face behind his hands.

Heather spared him any more discomfort as she turned to face the villagers who had crowded around her, their eyes wide open with delight, shock and surprise. Some of the children were transfixed by Heather, just as excited by her reappearance as by the presence of the huge whale in the harbour. Heather's school friends had their mouths hanging open in amazement at the sight of all the rings, necklaces and jewels that festooned her body.

Heather laughed out loud at their faces of disbelief and then softened as her eyes found those of her mother, father and brother. She was about to leap down to hug her family when she paused. Heather's face cracked into a huge grin and she quickly scanned the faces of the village who were staring at her with complete surprise.

'Hello my darlings, this is nothing, just you wait. Hey Mildred, spill the beans.'

Heather turned and called out to the whale. The vast creature backed slowly out of the harbour and then suddenly it accelerated back in again. Lifting the flotilla of boats with its bow wave it sped up to the back wall of the harbour then, as it breached the surface with a convulsion it opened its cavernous mouth and spat out a massive pile of metal bars that glowed an unmistakeable gold colour. Then, with some difficulty it gently reversed out of the tight harbour entrance and turned and headed back out to sea, followed by the dolphins and sea birds. Heather laughed and caught her father's eyes; she was just about to leap down into his arms when she paused and became serious. Looking out at the villagers she supressed her smile as she noticed shock and awe on their faces.

'These riches have been gifted to us by the Great Mother, by the oceans that give us all life and livelihood. There's enough for us all and more but first you have to hear what I have to say.'

Nobody was going anywhere. Not with a flame-haired bejewelled goddess standing just above their heads.

'These ancient treasures are for us, but only so that we can stop what we have been doing. We have to stop fishing immediately; we have to stop emptying the oceans; we have to put every ounce of our abilities and energy into making a difference. We have to store up the fishing boats and transform the use of others. The fabulous treasure is to fund us all so that we can lead the world and spread the word. We have to return to living in sacred harmony with the oceans.'

The fishermen looked stunned, a few blinked at Heather and some kept glancing at her standing above them resplendent in her glowing dress with their mouths hanging open. A look of utter confusion was slowly being replaced by a deeper look of understanding and hope which turned to disbelief again as they turned to glance at the huge pile of gold bars that glinted like fire in the setting sun. Heather could see that a ripple of awakening was passing through the usually unflappable fishermen. A few were beginning to nod and chat excitably to each other. Heather's voice softened and as the villagers drew closer everybody quietened as they listened transfixed by what she was saying.

'I made a bargain you see. I had to plead for the lives of our menfolk. I had nothing to offer the Great Mother but my own life. So, I promised my life to the sea. I thought that meant I was going to die so that our menfolk might live. I thought that I would never see you all again.'

Heather paused as the memories of the deep flashed across her mind. This was not the time for sharing all of her amazing experiences. She smiled, and continued.

'I was shown that giving your life does not mean accepting death. I was made to see that offering your life to hope and a promise to serve means finding a sense of purpose. It was revealed to me deep under the sea that when you have a sense of purpose you step into your power. Giving a life is not stopping it but rather it's living it, to its fullest, to its glorious end. I have to honour a pledge that I made. A pledge that saved our lives. A promise that brought us this wealth. I will need you all to help me honour it. It means that I must devote my life to working to save our oceans from harm and from further exploitation. To do this I will need all of your support. I will need us all to work together. We will need to be the change. We have been tasked with working to restore the oceans, not deplete, poison and empty them.'

Heather grew serious and her eyes flashed green.

'We have to do this or all of mankind will perish.'

The village was stunned into silence as the meaning of Heather's words sank in. Already many were nodding with understanding and approval. Joe's grandfather was nodding furiously. Heather laughed and continued in a calmer voice.

'These riches will last us for a generation. In that time, we must all work together to bring a great teaching into the planet. Once the world learns of what happened here then it will have to listen. We will convert the boats, make the seas around us a national park and we will tell whoever wants to listen that when we look after the source of all life then She will look after us. Are you with me, or must I throw myself back into the sea?'

A hundred voices clamoured to speak at once, so Heather held out her hand for quiet.

'Then let us sing for our future and for the future of all and never rest until we have brought calm and peace and abundance to the oceans of the world once more.'

At this the whole village cheered as one and, taking Susan's lead, a new song began as the villagers turned to walk back towards the village.

Heather wiped a small tear from her eyes and then shrieked with laughter as she leapt from the wall. Her father caught her easily in his arms and the small family closed together in a powerful embrace. After a couple of moments Heather pulled free and whispered in her mother's ear, who smiled as her daughter turned and walked back towards the harbour wall where a Joe was sitting with his knees pulled firmly up under his chin grinning with happiness.

Heather clambered up, sat beside Joe and put her arms around him. They both sat in perfect silence with their knees drawn up as the sea began to swallow up the sun. A single final plume of seawater threw mist up into the clouds as the huge whale disappeared into the horizon. Soon the only light remaining was the gentle and soft glow from Heather's dress. It's gentle illumination caught Heather's attention. She took a moment to admire how the colours gently pulsed and glowed. The dress was of a material she had never encountered. Its soft diaphanous folds floated around her as if it was made of the sea itself. Heather glanced down at her hand and chuckled at the numerous jewelled rings that were crammed onto her fingers. She wanted to tell Joe all about her amazing experience, about the terrifying goddess of all living things, the huge piles of sunken treasure, her ride on a whale, and the huge Leviathan, but this was not the moment.

The silence between them had found a new depth, a new level of knowing. It was the kind of comfortable place that could never be made but could only arise from a great friendship. Heather gave a large and thankful sigh and pointed to the top of the quay. In the distance they could clearly see the tall and authoritative figure of Joe's granddad instructing the men as they quickly and carefully loaded the piles of gold bars onto pallets and then into one of the ancient stone barns just behind the harbour wall.

'Your granddad is amazing Joe. There's no way this village could all pull together in the same direction if it wasn't for him. He's going to be vital if we really are going to change the world.'

'I never want to feel that again!' Said Joe suddenly, quietly and fiercely.

'Huh?'

Heather was surprised at Joe's sudden outburst but saw the flash in her friend's eyes and let him speak.

'That pain, when we thought you was dead. It was like... NO, NOT AGAIN!!!!'

Joe slumped down for a second. Heather was alarmed. She remembered that he had lost his parents and realised that Joe had really suffered. Then Joe looked at Heather and smiled, his whole face a look of relief that his friend was alive and safe. Joe's anger passed like a ripple on the surface of the sea and he shyly squeezed Heather's hand.

'It really hurt, then it made me feel really angry, then I felt hurt and angry at the same time. It was like losing Mum and Dad all over again. It was so...just promise me you won't do that again.'

'Do what?' Said Heather gently.

'Put yourself in danger like that. You don't think. You just leap before you look and then you get into trouble. You've got to think of others first, how it makes us all feel and... well...anyway...sorry for that. Look, I'm just glad and relieved you're back, that's all.'

Heather waited to see if Joe was going to continue but he fell silent again. She let the silence build up its warmth and familiarity again and snuggled in to Joe.

'I've got a whole life of work to do now Joe. I've learnt so much but I kinda feel like I'm just at the beginning of it all. I was shown a lot of struggles ahead but look, I hear what you're saying, and I don't want to hurt anybody. I guess sometimes there's hard calls to make. But anyway, Raven...'

Heather leapt up, laughing, her glowing dress and glittering jewels sparkling like golden fire. She smiled down on Joe's surprised face.

'...I think it's you we are going to have to watch from now on. I've seen so many things and I think they all point to you. Your great adventure is just beginning.'

Joe stood up and frowned as he stretched his legs. He chewed his lips and looked sideways at Heather.

'What do ya mean?'

'Well, we shall have to see, won't we.'

Heather laughed and with a great shout of joy picked up the hem of her amazing dress and began to run back up the harbour towards her house, sending pulses of fluorescent green in all directions like dancing fireflies.

'Well, come on then,' she called back to the mystified Joe. 'Race ya!'

Joe leapt down and took after Heather. As he ran he began to smile, then laugh and shout with glee. Suddenly all seemed very well with the world and Joe was already wise enough in years to know that these were the moments worth savouring.

*****

Much later that evening when even the adults had all gone to their beds to embrace each other and the warm sense of a new beginning and a new hope, a young woman carried a simple large plastic bucket down to the small sandy cove.

The dark-haired figure gently lowered the bucket into the sea freeing a myriad of small sea creatures. For a moment she stood tall and stared out into the ocean her dark hair gently blowing in the soft breeze a streak of white picked out by the light of a large full moon.

Heather knew that her world would never be the same again. As she cast her gaze out across the moonlit sea, she caught glimpses of life, flashes and pulses of energy as creatures large and small went about their business. The sea was now a living entity for Heather and every life in it precious beyond compare. She smiled as familiar heads began to bob up and down in the waves just out from shore. Heather reflected on the journey she was about to embark on. The mission she had been charged with would alter her life's trajectory for ever. She could see far enough ahead to know that these moments of quiet and solitude might soon vanish. She thought of Joe and looked at her deep feelings for him, yet she wondered if their paths would hold firm. Heather knew that she could never give her life to any one person for she had gifted it to the ocean and all the life contained within. It would be a strong man who could live happily sharing that burden. She switched her attention to her parents. Heather could sense their steady heart beats as they slept, momentarily finding peace and togetherness in each other's arms. Heather wondered if that was something she would ever experience for herself but before the subtle sadness found her and weakened her resolve a huge smile burst across her face. Just in-between the steady rhythm of her parents syncopated heartbeats Heather could make out another much smaller one.' Hello little sister' the young woman thought. 'I might need the strength of another friend in the future.' To Heather's delight a small voice, as clear as a bell echoed in her mind,

'Hello Heather. That's why I'm here.'

Acknowledgements

Thank you so much to Louise Scott at www.louise-scott.co.uk for gifting me use of the beautiful cover artwork and to Sandra D'Arcy who created the gorgeous line drawing illustrations even with failing eyesight and a tatty early manuscript to work from.

A huge thank you to the amazing John Hatfield and Justina Kasponyte' my kind and generous editors' for all your hours of hard work and patience.

A never-ending stream of gratitude to Kim and Sinclair MacLeod at Indie Authors World who so generously and graciously took my labour of love though the creative and technical birthing process. You guys are an inspiration.

Finally, a huge thanks to my long-suffering beloved wife Andrea for her support and to all of my nearest and dearest who have long encouraged me to 'get on with it.'

May you all find a deeper connection with the sea and grow to take delight in, and responsibility for, all the myriad life dwelling within her.

About the Author

Seth Gardner is an award winning film maker and writer who writes vivid, captivating and mystical books that seek to transform our understanding of the world and our place in it.